WARRIORS and MONKS

Pons: Abbot of Cluny

Michael A. Ponzio

Trinacria Publishing Company
BISAC: Fiction / Historical / General

ISBN:978-1-7349723-0-6

ACKNOWLEDGMENTS

Cover created by April Reed,
Design Director Pursue Outfitters

Cover image (1) Knight: Image by permission from Andrea Miniatures, ANDREA EUROPE, S.L.

Cover image (2) Cluny Basilica: Image from Dictionary of French Architecture from 11th to 16th Century (1856) by Eugène Viollet-le-Duc (1814-1879). This work is in the public domain in its country of origin and other countries where the copyright term is the author's life plus 100 years or less.

Cover image (3) Medieval Woman-Shutterstock, Inc.

This novel was enhanced by my wife, Anne Davis Ponzio

Thank you Nancy Soesbee for proofreading.

Ancestry Novels by Michael A. Ponzio

The Ancient Rome Series (Lover of the Sea):
Pontius Aquila: Eagle of the Republic
Pontius Pilatus: Dark Passage to Heaven
Saint Pontianus: Bishop of Rome

Warriors and Monks Series:
Ramon Pons: Count of Toulouse
1066 Sons of Pons: In the Wake of the Conqueror
Warriors and Monks: Pons, Abbot of Cluny

Each novel's story is complete in itself and can be read alone. However, when the novels are read chronologically, connections are revealed among the characters across generations.

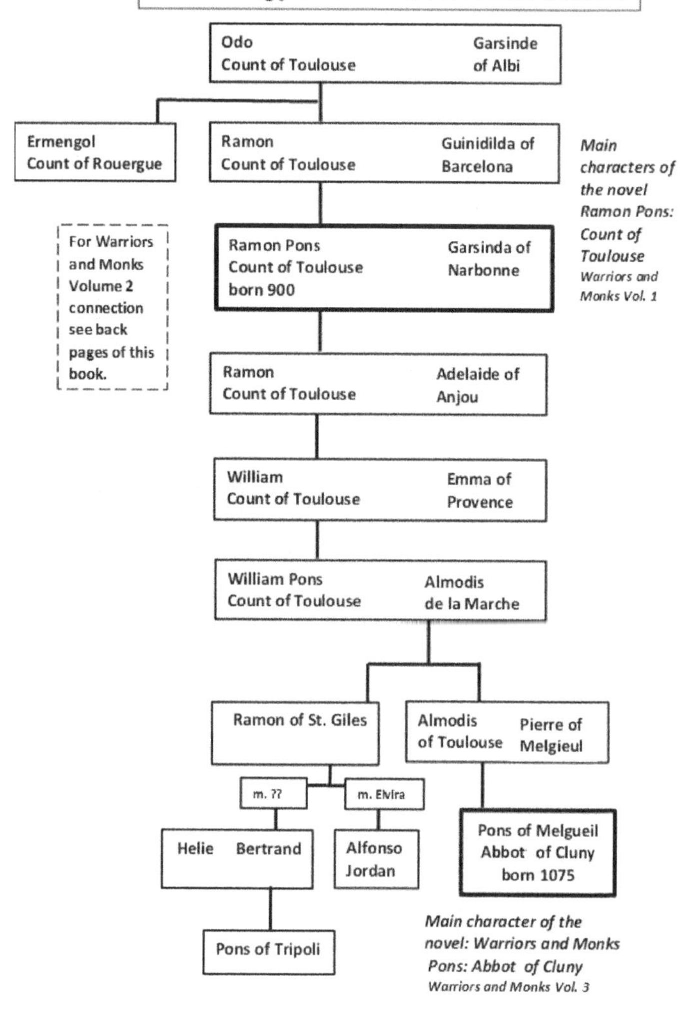
FROM HISTORICAL DOCUMENTS
Genealogy of the Warriors and Monks
Odo
Count of Toulouse
Garsinde
of Albi
Ermengol
Count of Rouergue
Ramon
Count of Toulouse
Guinidilda of
Barcelona
Main
characters of
the novel
Ramon Pons:
Count of
Toulouse
Warriors and
Monks Vol. 1
For Warriors
and Monks
Volume 2
connection
see back
pages of this
book.
Ramon Pons
Count of Toulouse
born 900
Garsinda of
Narbonne
Ramon
Count of Toulouse
Adelaide of
Anjou
William
Count of Toulouse
Emma of
Provence
William Pons
Count of Toulouse
Almodis
de la Marche
Ramon of St. Giles
Almodis
of Toulouse
Pierre of
Melgieul
m. ??
m. Elvira
Helie
Bertrand
Alfonso
Jordan
Pons of Melgueil
Abbot of Cluny
born 1075
Pons of Tripoli
Main character of the
novel: Warriors and Monks
Pons: Abbot of Cluny
Warriors and Monks Vol. 3

Forward

Historical Basis

Pons of Melgueil was the abbot of the powerful and influential Benedictine monastery at Cluny, France, from 1109 to 1124. At the time, Cluny administered hundreds of satellite monasteries in Europe and had influence over a greater number of clergy than the Pope himself.

As abbot, Pons made commendable progress in the construction of the Cluny basilica, which became the world's largest church. He inherited financial difficulties, but he campaigned and successfully procured valuable donations of property for the Benedictine Order and obtained sacred relics to increase the number of pilgrims visiting Cluny. Historical sources also reveal he was an excellent negotiator and his participation in major councils was beneficial to the Church[1]. In contrast, other sources called him secular-minded, contentious, and short tempered[2].

Controversy began when Pons tried to return the lifestyle of the Cluniac monks to the austere ways advocated by Saint Benedict, the founder of their monastic order[3]. The monks of Cluny had become lax and contested a return to a strong work ethic. In retaliation they alleged that Pons was wasting the monastery's resources. This was, in fact, the opposite of his initiatives. The local bishops and nobles were jealous of Cluny's privileges and wealth[4] and joined the conflict.

Did Pons maintain the leadership of Christendom in western Europe achieved by previous abbots of Cluny, or did he drag the monastery further into decline? Read *Warriors and Monks: Pons, Abbot of Cluny* and make your own judgment.

Notes

1. Agnès Gerhards, the Abbey of Cluny, Complexe, Brussels, 1992.

2. "Early Abbots of Cluny" by James E. Kiefer.

3. Adriaan H. Bredero wrote that "The crisis of monasticism at the end of the 11th and the beginning of the 12th century had not left Cluny untouched, many of its monks being defenders of the new way of life." (This "new way" widely ignored the austere Benedictine rules).

   "In the ensuing controversy the abbot of Cluny, Pons, had taken the side of the reformists." Professor Bredero contends "the economic changes and increasing age of Abbot Hugh (who preceded Pons as abbot) created problems at Cluny by the end of his abbacy. Pons de Melgueil introduced reforms which would have meant greater austerity. These reforms, not Pons's defense of Cluny's exemption from episcopal supervision, created opposition at Cluny itself and in its order." *Adriaan Bredero, professor emeritus of medieval history at the Vrije Universiteit in Amsterdam, has, over a distinguished career, published many scholarly articles and two important monographs, Cluny et Cîteaux au douzième siècle (Amsterdam, 1985) and Bernardas van Clairvaux (1091—1153): tussen Cultus en Historie (Kampen, 1993).*

4. Pietro Zerbi argued that "he (Pons) was the victim of opposition from the bishops disadvantaged by the many privileges his order received under his and Hugh's management." (Hugh was the abbot of Cluny preceding Pons). *Pietro Zerbi was a lecturer and rector of the Catholic University of the Sacred Heart where he graduated in philosophy in 1944 with a thesis on Gregory VII and Western Christianity. Ordained priest in 1947, he continued his studies focused on the relations between the Papacy and the Empire from the eleventh through the thirteenth centuries. He wrote 194 works in 455 publications in 4 languages on history, Church history, conference papers, and proceedings.*

Table of Contents

FRANCE in 1095

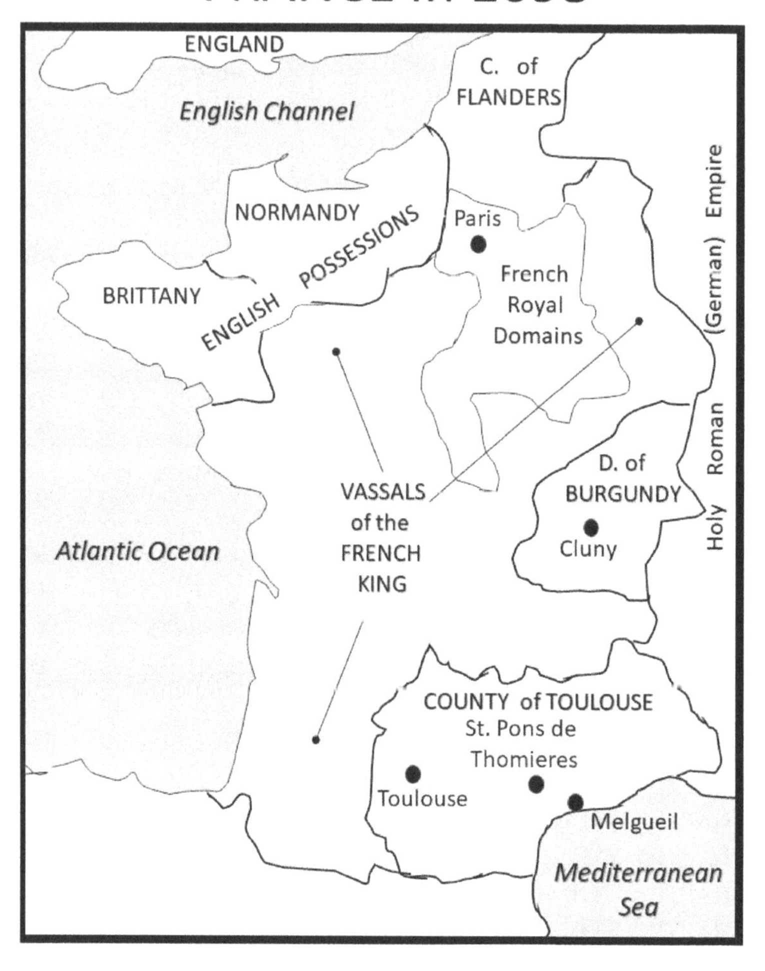

CHAPTER I THE SACRED GEESE

Pons had an almost uncontrollable urge to slap his superior in the face. He wasn't angry, and he wasn't being reprimanded. And it wasn't as if he disliked the abbot—in fact he had great respect for him, the absolute ruler of the monastery. Brother Pons had dealt with this peculiar impulse before. Since the age of four he had lived in the Saint Pons de Thomieres monastery, isolated in the mountains of Provence. Now, in 1095, the twenty year old monk recalled how this odd notion had surfaced over the years when he'd had to control himself, despite wanting to be somewhere else.

He heard only the abbot's last words.

"And since you will work late tonight, consider making a new copy of the 'Book of Hours' for our services." Pons was disappointed. *No, I only want to finish reading the manuscript.* His face reddened, and he felt beads of sweat on his hairless pate, but with self-control he bowed his head in acknowledgment. His crown was shaven leaving a strip of dark hair around his head, the tonsure of an eleventh century Benedictine monk. Pons had begun as an oblate at the monastery, when his father had entrusted him to the Church. His parents had never visited him at Saint Pons Abbey and his only contact with his family was an occasional visit by his godfather. Because of his remarkable aptitude for reading and writing and his organizational abilities, in addition to his faith and integrity, at just seventeen, he had been promoted to sacrist. His responsibilities included the safekeeping of books, vestments, and vessels, and the maintenance of the monastery's buildings. As an officer, an obedientiary, he reported directly to the abbot. Of the forty monks he had but two brothers he could call friends.

The abbot finished his instructions to Pons and joined the monks of Saint Pons monastery as they filed out of the church. Matins, the Liturgy of the Hours service recited two hours after midnight, had concluded with the lector reading Psalms 97 through 108. They crossed the cloister in silence with heads bowed, following one of Saint Benedict's rules: *Look downward when walking, sitting, or standing, so that you think about your own actions and mistakes, rather than looking around for things to criticize.* Each held a candle to light the way back to the dormitory. Between Matins and the next service of Lauds held in three hours, the monks would find a little time to nap, except for Pons. He was going to the scriptorium, elated to continue reading about those whom he imagined were his ancient ancestors.

Pons had only vague memories of his parents. His father was the Count of Melgueil and his mother, Almodis, was the daughter of Guillaume Pons, the Count of Toulouse. Because he was the second oldest son, Pons was not destined to inherit his father's land and title, and his family had given him to the monastery. This provided him a good life and excellent education, but more importantly, in their eyes, increased their influence in the Church. Perhaps if they had stayed in contact with Pons he might have considered himself privileged. But as it was, he felt abandoned and the mere thought of his family brought on his temper.

Pons left the queue of departing monks and glanced back. The brothers wore identical gray habits, their faces hidden in the shadow of their cowls. The monastery's potentate, Abbot Richard, was taller than average height and his stocky body set him apart from the other monks. The abbot was tough but fair and led by example. A formidable leader, he attacked problems head on, solved them, and quickly went to the next issue. He ensured the monks followed the strict Benedictine rules of labor, study, and prayer. Behind him was his second-in-command, the prior, chosen by Richard himself, and firmly in step with his philosophy on overseeing the monastery.

Next followed Guilen, Pons's somewhat mischievous friend. Pons continued to glance behind expecting one of Guilen's roguish theatrics. He was about to turn away, feeling mild disappointment, but Guilen looked up and signaled "Drink wine." The monks used monastic sign language for essential communication during Matins, Lauds, or any of the other six sacred offices, the cycle of daily prayer services. The Benedictine monks strictly followed their vow of silence during the services as well as during the meals. The other brothers continued to walk with faces lowered and did not notice. Pons, with a hand over his mouth, stifled a laugh as he pretended to cough.

He moved quietly toward the copy room. Why did Guilen jest about drinking wine? Now out of hearing, Pons laughed out loud. *Yes! The Lector read Psalms 104, "Wine makes the heart glad."*

His mirth subsided as he neared the scriptorium. *For several years I have been the sacrist of the copy room to oversee the library and the monks copying the old manuscripts and Bibles. No one would question why I work late hours, but dear Lord, forgive me for my curiosity. I am again drawn to a manuscript that may be a prohibited, unholy text!* Parchments were expensive, and documents considered unworthy to copy were commonly scraped bare and reused for new books. So as Pons read, in case someone entered the scriptorium, he held a penknife, as if he was cleaning the unholy parchment. He pushed his sleeves up, which had always been too long. More than once he had thought of cutting them shorter, but then the winter would come, and he was glad of the extra length to warm his hands.

Pons sat at his desk and read the cover of the codex he had been poring over the last few nights after Matins: "The History of Rome" by Titus Livius. *Last night I read how the Roman messenger Pontius Cominius stole pass the enemy lines to reach the besieged Roman Senate on Capitoline Hill. I am fascinated that the messenger's name, Pontius, is identical to mine, as written in Latin.* Pons read, murmuring the words aloud, knowing all his brothers were asleep in the dormitory.

"The Gauls silently ascended the cliff and did not even wake the dogs, animals sensitive to nocturnal sounds. But they did not escape the notice of the geese, which were sacred to Juno. The clamor and the noise of their wings roused Manlius, a distinguished Roman soldier, who ran to call the rest to arms and they repelled the Gauls."

Pons whispered to himself, "Geese sounded the alarm?" *That reminds me. My favorite quill pen is nearly spent. I will need new quills for copying, and the gander's flight wings make the best ones. I wonder if it is time for Cicero to molt?* Pons read on about the sacred geese of Juno, but soon his eyelids became heavy and his head sank onto the Roman manuscript. He slumped against the desktop, having fallen asleep.

Several minutes later, an uproar penetrated his dreams. *Why are the geese honking this late at night? It cannot be a fox again. It's the wrong time of year, there are no goslings, and the flock attacked the last raiding fox, who ran terrified, never to return. No, it's the barbarians from Gaul! They are climbing over the wall! Brothers! Come to my aid, I will vanquish their leader with my sword!*

Pons swung wildly with his penknife and fell, crashing onto the floor. He woke up and spoke to himself. "What? Oh, it was a dream!"

But the loud honking outside continued. *The geese are in danger! Cicero!*

Pons rushed to one of the tall windows that lined the scriptorium, blew out his candle, then cracked open a shutter and peered into the night. Nothing was visible in the pitch dark. He knew the layout of the scriptorium well enough to make it to the door at the stairs, where a tinderbox was stored in a wall niche. In the dark, he found the box which contained the *p*-shaped firesteel and a flint and then remembered, *There is no charcloth! I meant to replace it several days ago.* The ends of his sleeves were frayed, and he used the penknife hanging around his neck to cut off loose threads and rolled them into a small lump. He struck the steel and stone together lighting the threads, then tilted the candlewick into the tiny flames. Hurrying down the stairs his flight almost doused the candle. But he continued as fast as his woolen habit allowed to the bottom of the stairs, across the cloister, and around the back of the dormitory. There between the monks' sleeping lodge and the city wall were vegetable gardens, pens of fowl raised for consumption, and the barn which housed several milk cows and a handful of mules. The flock of geese usually ranged throughout the yard and were kept solely for a supply of quills, not for food.

The honks of frenzied geese echoed amid the stone fortifications and marble-faced building. Pons blew out his candle. There was no moon and as he burst into the court he could hear the geese madly flapping their wings, and he could feel the down flying in all directions.

Then as his eyes became more accustomed to the dark, Pons could barely make out two figures hurrying about the courtyard chasing geese. He shouted, "Thieves! The geese are not yours. You are blazing a path to Hell with your actions." Suddenly he became afraid for his own safety. He pulled up his hood, covering most of his face.

The two figures stopped. Pons stood motionless in his gray habit, almost invisible in the pitch dark. One of the robbers said, "Who said that? I don't see nobody!"

"Nobody said it," said a second voice.

"I mean —do-do you think God said it?"

"Don't be stupid, there is no God. You're makin' me hear things, you cretin. Get the birds!"

Pons stepped toward the thieves and stumbled over the still body of a goose. *I hope it's not Cicero! Where is that gander? My grandfather, the Count of Toulouse, donated this flock to the abbey. The geese are very dear to me.* With these thoughts, his temper began to rise. *The grey Tolosa geese, the best for making the quills, they are sacred; sacred to the abbey, like the geese of Juno in the story of ancient Rome!* Pons stumbled over another dead goose. The discovery fed his anger.

The thieves moved toward their prizes, still unaware of the monk. Pons, now only a few feet away, flung back his hood and exposed his beardless face, capped by a tonsure of dark hair. "Leave now and God will forgive you."

"What?" The thief recovered and laughed. "You dolt! Get over here! See who you thought was God!"

"You do not have to steal!" said Pons. "Both of you may come by the monastery any day and have a meal."

"Yeah, weak porridge. You're no different than them nobles, saving all the good food for yourselves! And your kitchen don't serve juicy goose!"

The monk placed his foot on a carcass. "Leave now!" Torchlight suddenly illuminated the courtyard. Pons saw a flash of metal in the thief's hand, but he dared not look behind. The thief held a bloody knife, bold evidence he had used it to slaughter the geese. He slashed at Pons's face, and the monk instinctively raised his hand, shrouded by the long woolen sleeve. The blade glanced off without harm and the thief escalated his attack, slicing back and forth at Pons's face. The monk responded with a wild flurry of hands. It appeared as if he was swatting a swarm of mosquitoes as his loose sleeves flapped about and parried the knife attacks.

Suddenly the bandit grabbed Pons and spun him around to face a group of monks. In the forefront of the brethren was Abbott Richard. Pons was immobilized as the thief gripped his sleeve and held the knife at his throat. "Stay there or I'll slit his throat like them gooses."

In the light Pons saw before him another butchered goose. *They killed my Cicero!* He grew hot with rage.

Richard's size alone blocked several of the monks, but he spread his arms wide to hold back the brothers. "We have no weapons. Monks will not shed blood! And you! Thou shall not kill a man!" He looked down and saw the dead birds. "Take the geese. You will be forgiven, but do not take a man's life!"

Pons considered the scene. *Richard is remarkably agile for a man his size. He could crush this thief in a blink. Why is he holding back?*

The armed man started to back away and pressed the knife to Pons's throat, forcing him to follow. "Pick up them birds!" he shouted to his partner.

"I'm leavin' with your monk," he yelled to the abbot. "Don't follow! Don't move or he's dead!"

As the pair shuffled backwards, greed overcame the thief. He reached down for a slain goose, and the blade sliced across Pons's neck. The monk threw up his left hand and pushed the blade away. The robber pulled the knife toward his neck again as the men struggled. Pons was strong, having worked long hours in the fields, the thief was tough and frantic with energy, and for a few moments, neither could overcome his foe. Then the monk weakened, and his vital spirit faded. *I am lost! Sweet Jesus!*

A moment later his mind cleared. *But what? I am still alive? My neck was not slashed a second time?* His sleeve of thick wool was wrapped around the knife. Pons realized that his penknife still hung on the cord around his neck. He brandished his small weapon and tried to stab his abductor.

The abbot lurched forward and bellowed, “Stop, do not shed blood!”

Pons ignored his superior. *But that thief killed Cicero!* He stabbed over his shoulder again and again, and then fell to the ground.

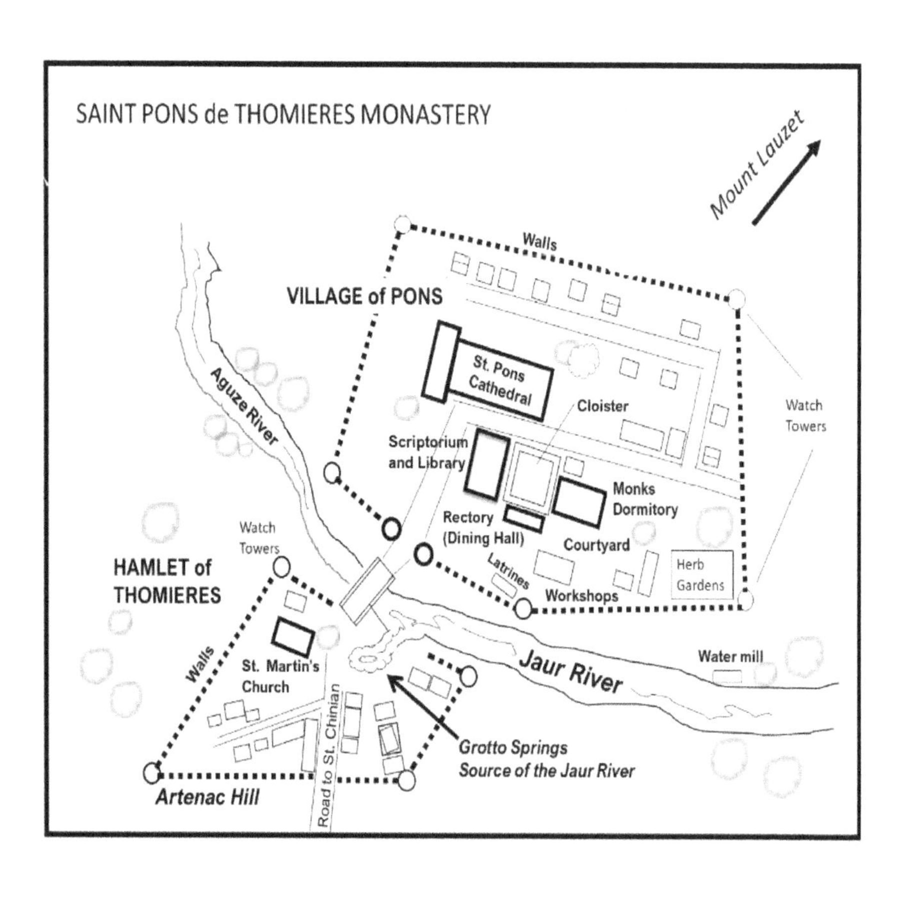
SAINT PONS de THOMIERES MONASTERY
Mount Lauzet
Walls
VILLAGE of PONS
St. Pons Cathedral
Cloister
Watch Towers
Aguze River
Scriptorium and Library
Monks Dormitory
Rectory (Dining Hall)
Courtyard
Watch Towers
Latrines
Herb Gardens
HAMLET of THOMIERES
Workshops
Water mill
Jaur River
Walls
St. Martin's Church
Road to St. Chinian
Grotto Springs
Source of the Jaur River
Artenac Hill

CHAPTER II THE NOVICE MONK

Outside the sun was rising. The candle on the nightstand burned down to the time mark. As the wax melted, the nail imbedded in the candle fell with a clatter on the metal dish, waking the lictor. He blew out the flame of the clock candle and prepared recitals for Prime, including the daily reading of the Rules of Benedict.

After Prime, the lictor handed the literature to Guilen and motioned that he go to the infirmary to read the service to Brother Pons. As he had done for the last three days, Pons lay in bed, his back propped up against the wall. Bandages were wrapped around his neck, a stain of blood showing on the swathing. In the next bed was the thief who had tried to kill him. Guilen arrived to perform his assigned duty. He began to read Benedict's rules and Pons interrupted him. "Why are you reading to *him*?" Pons turned his torso sideways to avoid twisting his neck. He looked at the man who had cut his throat. "Oh, forgive me, uh, what is your name?" *To me his name is the goose killer! I named him that the first day we were both in the infirmary. But each day I am forgiving him a little more. We look like twins, with our necks wrapped in bandages.*

The man grimaced with pain as he said, "B, B . . . Bredo."

"I am sorry about your throat," said Pons. "I again ask for your forgiveness."

"I . . . I . . . di-didn't want to cut you," answered Bredo. "Mistake."

"Uh, yes, so I double forgive you!"

Guilen laughed and continued reading the morning's litany. The infirmarian arrived to change the men's bandages. Guilen paused as the monk removed the wrapping from Pons's neck. He applied an herbal poultice and rebandaged the wound. As he repeated the process for Bredo, he said, "I understand you have asked to join our monastery. As a postulant the abbot must evaluate you for admission, although you should hear the daily readings as well as learn about the Benedictine Order."

He removed the bandage and examined the sutures. "You are blessed that we have a skilled barber. His surgery saved your life, with God's help. Yet another person benefits now from the Benedictines who founded the monastic schools over two hundred years ago, during the reign of Charlemagne. The king ordered that medicine should be taught at all monasteries."

"Char- la mane?" Bredo said in a raspy voice.

"The ancient King of the Franks—Charles the Great!"

"So, so . . . the king saved me!"

"Well, if you will be a monk, here is your first lesson. You would say, 'God guided the king,' that is, God saved you."

The infirmarian left and the men sat in silence for a while. When he returned with a handful of green leaves lined with fine white hairs, the infirmarian said, "I used these leaves to make your poultice. The herb is for treating wounds and to staunch the flow of blood. When you pull weeds in the herb garden, do not disturb this plant. It has small white flowers. And thank God for providing your cure."

"The plant is *herbe militaris*," said Pons.

Bredo had a puzzled look.

"Soldier's herb . . ." added Pons.

"It's also called woundwort," said the infirmarian. "You have learned your first Latin. Knowledge of the ancient language is necessary to be a true monk. And congratulations! When I went to the herbarium to get the leaves to show you, I heard that the abbot has approved your request to study, pray, and work with us. Once you've taken your oath, Bredo, you will be a novice." He looked at Guilen. "Take him to the garden and show him how to weed. Watch his bandage closely and return with him if there is any blood.

"And Brother Pons, I was to inform you that Abbot Richard wants to speak with you right away."

Pons sat in a high-backed chair identical to the abbot's. The chairs were simple in design and had a cross shape cut out of the backrest. They were the only chairs in the monastery with backrests—the other seats were all either stools or benches, much like the simple furniture in hundreds of Benedictine monasteries across western Europe. *Am I called to see the abbot for punishment? Did they find the Roman document I was reading?*

Abbot Richard sat behind his desk. "Brother Pons, how are you feeling after your, uh . . . injury?"

"I am ready to return to my duties as sacrist, Father Abbot."

The abbot poured wine into modest cups. The ceramic containers had no handles and their simple design reflected the austerity of the abbey. After he swallowed, he said, "God provided the south slope of Mount Lauzet for us to grow delicious grapes and to make wine for our communion, but this Saint Chinian vintage made by our nearby Benedictine brothers tastes heavenly."

Pons nodded, relishing a sip.

"I am not surprised you are ready to return to work. What do you think of my approval for a . . . pagan, for Bredo, to become a novice?"

"It is good to bring the unfortunate into the Brotherhood. It seems it is primarily sons of nobles who take up the cloth here at Saint Pons, but . . ."

"But what, Brother?"

"He does not even believe in God!"

"That is why I wanted to talk to you. You disregarded my command to avoid bloodshed in your encounter. What if the man had died? The brothers witnessed the event, so I am assigning you a very challenging penance." Pons raised his eyebrows.

"Although you are not the perfect monk, you will be Bredo's tutor, leading him into the Faith."

Pons could feel the heat rising within. *I'd rather run a gauntlet of the brothers with switches or be put in solitary confinement than have to undertake a task like this! Is the abbot setting me up for failure?*

"Pons, you are upset with this assignment? But the process will help you develop into a great Church leader . . . as I promised."

"Father Abbot, a promise? To whom?— God?"

"Careful, Brother Pons, where you tread. I hope your emotions did not influence that question. We don't trade favors with the Father. Do not mock the Lord." He paused. "No, no, the promise I made was to your godfather, Cardinal Rainerius."

My Godfather Rainerius! The only person I consider as family. My father gave me to the church when I was four and never came back. I have pleasant memories of my godfather. He used to travel from Cluny Abbey to give me personal guidance. His last visit was several years ago when he stopped here on his journey to Rome, where he was promoted to Cardinal-Priest by the Pope.

"I will do my best to make, uh . . . both Cardinal Rainerius and God proud, Father Abbot."

"Yes, I believe you will. By the way, Pope Urban will visit and Cardinal Rainerius will be in the entourage. They will tour monasteries throughout Provence. They are scheduled to come to Saint Pons in a few months, yes . . . it will be the end of November. God has a plan for all of us, Brother Pons, and there is a grand plan for you. Have you ever wondered why your father, uh . . . gave you to the monastery?"

Pons felt the heat rising again as he answered, "My older brother inherited the county per primogeniture."

"From one point of view you could say you are a victim. But on the other . . ." added Richard, "you have been given a very good life—to serve the Lord . . . and to reach great heights."

Pons looked puzzled.

"Your godfather, Cardinal Rainerius, is second only to the Pope. He believes you can make boundless contributions to the Church. Pray, study, work . . . and wait for what God plans for you."

The anger drained away from Pons and was replaced with joyful anticipation of his godfather's visit.

Four hours before sunrise, the clock candle dropped a nail, freed from the molten wax, and with a metal clang the monks across the dormitory rolled out of their beds, except Brother Pons.

He had slept on the floor, giving Bredo his bed. Pons pushed himself up from the floor. Bredo had been issued a linen shirt, hose, and socks to wear to sleep, and his own pillow. The bed he had slept on was made of wooden planks supported by four short wooden legs. A straw filled mattress covered by a rug lay on the platform. As Pons awoke, one of Benedict's rules stirred in his thoughts—*When I was a boy, over ten years ago, I remember we didn't sleep on wooden beds. Benedict himself wrote: "As for bedding, let each brother be content with a sleeping bag, a rug, a sheet, a coverlet of linen or buckram and a pillow." It is easy to forget that we have become soft and have deviated from the austere rules of the founder.*

A memory surfaced that Pons had kept deep within for years. Like Bredo, for his first night at the monastery, he was without his own bed, so a senior monk had let the four year old oblate sleep in his, while he slept on the floor beside him. *I was awakened in the night by the monk's whisper. "Will you be my wife, little one?" I did not understand his request, and remember being confused but more so, I was terrified by the lusty voice. I was afraid to look at him but had the strength to eke out a weak but defiant, "No!" A few nearby monks stirred but returned to sleep. Paralyzed with dread of the unknown, I tried to fight off sleep, but recalled waking later relieved nothing had happened. The monk had already left for the night service. I rolled over and found the back of my night shirt wet. The monks returned to nap before the next service. Although only four, I had exhibited a temper when bickering and contending with my three siblings at home in my hometown of Megueil. Still fresh from the life of a son of a noble, I expressed my displeasure. "You peed on me!" As I sat upon the pallet trying to avoid the wet spot on my backside, the instigator stood silently looking down, under the gaze of his fellows. Shortly, the prior arrived and led the monk away.*

I buried that memory a long time; however, years later when I reached puberty, I realized what the old monk had done. He never threatened sodomy again, but attended his needs covertly at the brothels in the village, like many of the monks, as most agreed that abstinence caused degenerate behavior. The chain of thoughts reminded Pons of a certain maiden he had glimpsed weeks ago in the hamlet across the river, but the soreness from sleeping on the floor brought him back. Pons noted Bredo awoke without a "thank you." *He must learn from my example. Hopefully I have shown him two paragons. To give to others and to accept graciousness with zeal.*

The monks splashed water in their faces. On their way to Matins, the night service, Pons reminded Bredo that he must remain silent in the church. "You may see hand signals, which I will teach you over time, but there is no talking, except for the lictor's reading of the scriptures."

The readings were in Latin, as always. *God's bones! He will not understand the litany. I am going to have to teach Bredo Latin. This is truly a huge undertaking. Was the abbot scheming for me to fail?*

Bredo has lived in the secular world and I have lived my whole life isolated here. But am I not better here? The sinful exertions of the nobles for possessions and power is best avoided. As Saint Benedict wrote: "If it happen that a nobleman offereth his son to God in the monastery and the boy is of tender age, let his parents execute the written promise that they will never give him anything themselves nor through any other person, nor in any way whatever, nor leave a chance for his owning anything." Perhaps when my godfather visits he can enlighten me!

I know today that Bredo will learn the first part of the monks' ideals: work, study, and prayer. But first—we will work and make a bed for him. I don't want to sleep another night on the floor!

The monks returned to their beds for an hour or two nap until Lauds, two hours short of sunrise. Pons lay down on the floor with his blanket. *I used to be heading for the scriptorium at this hour to read, but those forays must end with my new responsibilities. What happened to the ancient Roman?* He fell asleep thinking about Pontius Cominius.

Pons was awoken by the monks jostling to put their habits on for Lauds Service. They filed out of the dormitory toward the church. Intent to teach the novice his first Latin, he explained to Bredo that the title of the service, "Psalms of Praise," became lauds after the Latin *laudare*, to praise.

The lector read from Psalms and the cantor led the monks in hymns of praise. The brothers trailed out of the church to relieve themselves at the remote communal latrine, then proceeded to the lavatorium, outside in the cloister walk. They washed their hands in cold running water. The water was gravity fed through a pipe from the river, then flowed through the latrine. It was nearly time for the Prime service and the monks conversed quietly before entering the church for the sunrise service. After Prime the attendees met at the nearby dining hall, the refectory, for breakfast.

The brothers ate in silence as the lector's assistant read scripture. Bredo made the sign for bread that Pons had taught him: a circle by placing the tips of the two thumbs and index fingers together. Pons passed him a basket of bread. *He had accused us of saving the best food for ourselves! He will see we do not regularly eat meat. The Rule forbids monks to eat the flesh of four-footed animals, but we may eat fish and poultry, as well as eggs, cheese, and of course vegetables and fruit.*

But I savor this fresh bread. And it is from our labors, alone, of course due to the grace of God. We planted the seeds and weeded the fields. We harvested the rye and wheat and threshed the grains, and operated the grist mill to make the flour. Then we baked the delicious bread, of course, all with strength from God. The crust is baked to just the right hardness. With our self-made ale, this is very satisfying!

After breakfast, Pons and Bredo headed toward the carpenter's workshop. As they neared the courtyard, clacking and cracking of wood echoed. Entering the open area, several pairs of monks were sparring with long staves. "Brother Pons, is this part of training to be a monk?"

"Those brothers are getting ready to travel south to found a new monastery. They are sharpening their skills to defend themselves on the road."

They entered the workshop and found the wood needed to fabricate a bedframe. After marking the length on several planks, he left Bredo to saw the wood to make his own bed. Pons crossed the monastery grounds and hurried upstairs to oversee the scribes copying manuscripts.

The second story room had high ceilings and was lined on two sides with large windows. With the shutters opened, the hall was a bright venue for copying and reading. There were nine desks in a three by three arrangement, all occupied by monks sitting on foldable x-stools. The copyists worked with both hands; the penknife was held in the left hand to help smooth and hold the manuscript in place as they wrote with the quill pen in their right hand. The knife was also used to quickly scrape away errors, best done before the ink soaked into the parchment. Two inkhorns were inserted into holes bored into the right side of each desk.

A few copyists looked up when Pons entered the room and nodded; the rest concentrated on their work. The rule of silence was not in place in the scriptorium, but there was typically no idle chatting. The copyists were chosen from those monks that exhibited skill in lettering as well as a keenness for the duty. Pons, his hands clasped behind him, strolled among the desks and glanced at each monk's work to check on their progress. At the first desk the scribe was copying a large Bible complete with illuminated chapter pages. He had three inkhorns, one contained black ink, one red, and one gold, where the ink was infused with the powdered metal. Pons remembered that this Bible had been commissioned by a wealthy noble as a gift for the church in the town of Beziers. The beauty and the cost of such a Bible was astounding. But even this ornate Bible was not the most expensive. The highest quality copies were crafted with gold-leaf, which was burnished to a glossy surface.

As Pons looked over another monk's shoulder, he saw the scribe was making a new copy of the *Saint Pons Abbey Breviary*, the *Book of Hours*. He heard footsteps. Bredo joined him. "Brother Pons, I finished sawing them planks."

"Shhh."

Bredo whispered, "Have to be silent here, too?"

"No, no, just talk softly. These monks are concentrating on writing. They cannot make any mistakes, especially when copying a Bible. And, uh . . .very good, please attach the bed's footers."

"Bed is done," answered Bredo in a hushed tone.

"Fine." They watched the scribe at work. Each time the monk dipped his quill in the inkhorn, he wrote three or four words, then had to retrieve more ink. He paused, held up the pen, studied the dulled tip, and trimmed the nib with his penknife to sharpen the end.

"Bird wings? But no feathers on 'em?" said Bredo.

Pons answered without any hint of belittlement. "The feathers and barbs are removed to make the quill pens; they would just be in the way of the scribe. Then the quills are poked into a bucket of hot sand to harden them, before cutting the nib and point.

"Here, see the book Brother Odo is copying; it is the *Book of Hours* which guides us during each of the Liturgy of the Hours, the prayer services. It consists of eight sections, and each contains prayers, psalms, and hymns. One for each of the eight services we attend per day. So far today, you have attended the first three. Can you remember the names of the services?"

"Um, yeah . . . Matins, uh, Lauds. Then Prime, then we ate."

"Excellent! Let's move your bed to the dormitory, then we will work in the garden. We should have time to weed before Terc, the next service at mid-morning."

At the herb garden, they hoed, then worked on their knees pulling the weeds which were growing close to some root vegetables. They tended those by hand.

"Brother Pons."

"Yes, Bredo?"

"It's good luck. Now I'm gettin' regular meals. Do we get meat?"

"Bredo, a monk doesn't believe in *la chance*, luck, but trusts that everything that happens is according to God's plan. And the Rule of Saint Benedict forbids the eating of the flesh of any animal with four legs, but there are exceptions. We provide meat for monks who are sick, or for the child oblates. Monks can eat the meat of fish or birds."

"Sorry 'bout them geese."

"Bredo, I forgive you. How does that make you feel?"

Bredo's smile revealed a few missing teeth as he said, "Good, Brother Pons."

CHAPTER III THOMIERES

For the next several months, Pons guided Bredo in the traditional life of a monk. He was busy teaching him how to read, and correcting his diction, as well as instructing him in Saint Benedict's rules. They spent long hours working in the fields. The plowing, seeding, and harvesting was exhausting and Pons did not have the energy to continue his late night readings. Pons had stopped thinking about the ancient manuscript written by the Roman historian Livius, until one afternoon making his rounds overseeing the scribes. He studied the document Guilen was copying.

"Where did you get . . .," uttered Pons. "I mean . . . when did you come by that . . ."

Guilen interjected, "You assigned Livius's histories to me last week."

Pons's mouth hung open. Guilen's steady gaze at Pons lacked any hint of deceit. "It is a fascinating account and worth copying!"

That's where it went! Guilen must have found the manuscript on my desk after the night I was injured, and suspected my fondness for it. So it will survive for future generations. "Uh . . . yes, carry on Brother Guilen," said Pons as he recalled an intriguing chapter of the story. *What happened in the forbidden romance between the Vestal Virgin and Pontius Cominius?* The thought of the clandestine relationship warmed his loins, but dissipated as he shrugged away the images and said, "Guilen, your letters are neat and precise despite the shortage of choice quills, due to the loss of our best goose." A feeling of remorse turning to anger over the killing of Cicero burned hot inside the sacrist.

"Are you feeling ill, Brother?" asked Guilen.

"No, no, I just need some fresh air. I will see you at Nones."

Pons's anxiety grew as he descended the stairs. Beads of perspiration covered his bald crown. With each step, in sets of three, he concentrated on the puffs of warm air forced from the neckline of his habit, and whispered, "Father, Son, and Holy Spirit!" Then he deliberated on the motion of the knots at the end of his rope belt as they rebounded, repeating the trinity axiom. He exited the lower floor, beheld the landscape surrounding the town, and relief began.

This beautiful valley was chosen as the location of the monastery by my ancestor Ramon Pons. That was many generations ago, further back than my grandfather's grandfather. No . . . no, it was chosen by his wife Garsinda, the Countess of Toulouse. She selected the location for the monastery. A suitable place for meditation. A very natural setting. The village is small and the inhabitants peaceful, as are the people in the hamlet across the river.

His unease began to subside. He headed toward the west wall and exited the village of Pons through the gate tower named after Count Ramon. Crossing the Jaur River on the stone bridge to the hamlet of Thomieres, he focused on the source of the river: a spring which gushed out of a cave. As he drew nearer the grotto, a cave held sacred by the villagers, his temper abated, not from the coolness of the spring water, but from its meditative quality.

Pons sat on a stone bench at the spring, inhaling the spray, relaxing as he listened to the flowing water. The priest of Saint Martin's Church, the chapel serving the hamlet, approached deliberately, balancing on his cane, his black and white patched cat tracking him as it looped between his legs and staff.

"Brother Pons, it is a beautiful day to meditate on the Lord!"

"Yes, Father," he laughed, "and I see Vincus is your faithful companion."

The cat jumped on Pons's lap, made himself comfortable, and began grooming himself. "Vincus must have missed you. He is quite at home in your lap." The priest sat beside the pair as the feline grunted and snorted with enthusiasm, licking and cleaning his coat. "And you must feel at home here in Saint Pons de

Thomieres. Your ancestors founded the monastery, dedicated to a saint from your ancient family. Your relatives continue to support our abbey, and you have devoted your whole life to serving God."

"I feel gratified, but not . . . not *proud.*"

"No, no, I was not implying you were guilty of the sin of pride."

"It was pride that changed angels into devils," quoted Pons, "it is humility that makes men as angels."

"You are testing me, Brother?" He laughed. "I give up. How can I outwit the director of the scriptorium?"

"Saint Augustine."

"Very good, I will use that in my next homily. And young man, *ça va*, how goes it?"

Pons described his episodes of anger, that they came often, and how he controlled them by praying. The priest had known Pons since he was a boy and was aware of his temper.

"Then you came here as you have many times, because it calms you. That was an excellent idea.

"This grotto has been a place of sanctity and peace since very ancient times. The manhirs were erected by the Celts, then Romans built a temple around the stones, which was then converted into our Christian church. All the cultures recognized the sanctity of the place."

"Maybe I should become a priest like you," said Pons.

"Why? You have shown great leadership as sacrist and your abilities will be valuable to the Church."

Pons added, "You are married and have the love of a woman."

"But marriage for the clergy is disappearing. Decades ago Pope Gregory legislated that anyone to be ordained must first pledge celibacy. Before that the Church never officially forbade the clergy from being married. They had ignored the practice. But that has changed. Have you noticed there are only a few old monks or priests, like me, married?"

Pons said, "Most of Jesus's apostles were married. In Saint Paul's letter to Timothy, he describes the qualities necessary for a bishop: to be a 'kind and peaceable' father, a man with a family. Saint Patrick denounced the heretical Apostolics in their writings and acknowledged the married clergy without criticism."

"Son, I see you have been thinking much about the subject. Yes, many years ago almost all the clergy were married. The late Pope Gregory increased the enforcement of the rule of celibacy against clerical marriage, but there has been much resistance. He even imposed a tax, the *cullagium*, on clergy that kept mistresses. But is that why you said you wanted to be a priest, just so you could copulate? My first reaction would normally be that you have much penance to do, but you are only twenty and, of course, it is harder to abstain. You know there are other ways in the hamlet. Up the hill, Artenac Hill . . .

"I recommend you pay a visit and relieve your physical stress, then concentrate on your library and guiding your copyists. That is your passion. And pray to God for help.

"Did you know that Pope Urban is touring Provence soon?"

Pons nodded.

"It is said that he will bring with him strict enforcement of the reforms that are against clerical marriage as well as disallowing married persons to become clergy. And there are rumors that married priests who ignore the celibacy laws will be imprisoned for the good of their souls."

Pons looked confused.

"Yes, they can remain married, but must be celibate." Pons shook his head. The priest's face softened and he laughed. "So, hurry up that hill before the Pope comes."

A few hours later, as they hiked up the steep hill, Bredo forced out his words between gasps. "Why are we in a hurry? And why aren't we attending Compline? I thought good monks never missed a service."

A quartet of monks rushed up the slope of Mount Lauzet through the monastery's vineyards. They had just finished dinner. Pons raised his voice to answer among the chorus of wooden flails that clacked with the bounce of their strides. "We have only a few hours when the wind will be ideal. Just above the vineyard is the threshing floor where the evening winds will come for our threshing and winnowing." The monks each carried two tools. The flail consisted of a wooden staff, the length which came up to a man's chest, connected by a leather cord to a shorter piece of wood, the swipple or striker, about the length of a man's forearm.

The second tool was a wooden pronged fork, the staff section as tall as a man, with flat forks at one end to scoop grain and chaff and fling them into the air after the threshing. As the sun descended behind the mountains, there were still a couple of hours of light remaining. The cool air from the mountain peak sank into the valley, providing a breeze for separating the chaff from the grain.

They climbed past the furthest extent of the vineyard and arrived at the threshing floor, a flat oval rock area about ten steps in diameter. The barley had been cut several weeks before by other monks using long-handled scythes, then tied into bundles to dry, protected from rain. Pons noted they had left one of their scythes and made a mental note to bring it when they returned to the monastery. The monks untied several bundles and spread the stalks in a low pile across the stone surface. They wielded the long end of the flails with both hands and swung the swipples over their heads, striking the pile of barley stalks. As Bredo joined, Pons instructed, "We are knocking the kernels off. You don't have to hit the kernels with the striker. Direct your blows on the long stems of the grain instead of the heads, so as not to bruise them. The kernels will still fall off."

The monks surrounded the heap of grain stalks. To avoid entangling the cords and the strikers, Pons began a chant so they would hit the pile one at a time. With each word, a monk would hit the pile, followed by the next, repeating in cycles of four. "Matthew!" Pons struck with his flail. "Mark!" Bredo thrashed with his striker. "Luke!" Guilen whipped his swipple down. "John!" One of the copyists named Chard smashed the pile with vigor. They worked up a sweat and Pons pulled off his habit and the others followed his example. They continued working in linen shirts and *braies*, loose drawers that reached to the upper-thigh, held with a drawstring at the waist. *When I was a boy the monks' undergarments were made of wool. Some devout monks even wore hair shirts, but now they are made of smoother linen. As we are becoming softer ourselves.*

Pons repeated his cantillations and the men took out their frustrations on the pile of barley. "Matthew, Mark, Luke, John! Matthew, Mark, Luke, John! . . ." They took a break after Pons noticed all were fatigued and drank some water from the skins they had brought. "We are making good progress. After the next few piles, we will winnow."

On their next round of threshing, Pons invoked the four corners of the cross with: "Father!" S*mash.* "Son!" *Whack.* "Holy!" *Crunch.* "Spirit!" *Crack.* Within an hour they had separated the grain kernels from the husks and stalks. They welcomed the cool breeze from the mountain top for their efforts, but it was even more important for winnowing. "Bredo, now we will use our forks to throw the grain up in the air. The wind provided by our Lord will remove the stalks and chaffs."

They used the pronged wooden forks to throw the mass upward. The wind blew the lighter pieces to the side, while the grain, which was heavier, fell back down on the smooth rock. Over time, the threshing ground was covered with three discrete piles. The kernels of grain fell straight down. The larger pieces of stalk, or straw, had blown off to the side, and the lightest pieces of stalk, the chaff, had blown even further away. As they rested, Chard asked, "Why don't we use the winnowing baskets like the villagers do? It is easier."

"As Saint Benedict wrote," said Pons, "'It is that human labor is not without dignity; it is not a distasteful and burdensome thing, but rather something to be esteemed, an honor and a joy.'"

They swept the seeds into baskets and had eight bushels of kernels which they would take to the water mill on the River Jaur the following day. "We still have a little daylight," said Pons. "This work has given me a knot in my back. Before I heft a couple of baskets back to the monastery, I need to relieve my pain." He placed his flail on the ground and lay on the swipple, rolling it back and forth under his back. "Ahhh! That's it—got it right on my knot!"

"You are a strange one, Pons!" laughed Guilen.

As Pons continued, strangers suddenly burst out of the nearby trees and brush. "Thank you, holy monks! We will gladly relieve you of those full baskets!" Four dirty, slovenly dressed men formed a semi-circle about them. One was armed with a knife that Pons recognized was used by nobility as cutlery. The thieves' leader picked up a pair of winnowing forks and a flail and threw them to his unarmed companions. "Get rid of the rest of their tools." His cronies threw the forks and threshers downhill into the wine trellises.

Pons sensed that Chard and Guilen, his close brothers since childhood, were going to react. They knew him well, and if he was silent, it usually meant action. If he parleyed, it meant he wanted to avoid or delay a fight. He signed to them: *No!* as he composed himself to use the negotiating skills taught to him by the late Abbot Frotard.

Pons sat up. "Good men. You are welcome to come to our breakfast tomorrow after Prime."

The thief laughed.

"Then, we will give you half of the grain. Fair, no?"

The thief was silent, as if pondering the offer. Then shook his head.

"Take seven bushels. We will keep just one," added Pons.

"No, we want everything."

"You shall not steal, commands the Lord."

He ignored Pons's statement and pointed his knife at the monks. "And we might have a little romp. He glanced at the pile of habits. Is that what you monks were about to do with your friend on the ground? Everyone knows monks are sodomists. With each other and with their animals!" His comrades hooted.

Suddenly Pons was startled from the shouting behind him. "It's you! *MON CRETIN*!" screamed Bredo. "You fled with the geese and left me when I was cut!"

The leader of the thieves said, "Bredo! Figured you was dead. You with these pigs?"

Bredo shouted as he brandished the mislaid scythe and pulled it back to swing, "You will be the one cut this time!" One of the thieves fled into the brush as Guilen and Chard bolted toward the vineyards. Pons had retrieved his flail, unseen beneath him, stood, and thrust the long section of the staff backwards into Bredo's sternum as he faced three attacks at his fore. Bredo dropped the scythe and slumped to his knees. Simultaneously, the thief on Pons's right thrust a winnowing fork at him, the leader lunged at him with his knife, and the thief on his left swung a flail at him.

Pons whipped his thresher against the oncoming fork, grabbed the striker as it coiled around, and pulled the forked end blocking the knife thrust. He spun to the back of the knifeman and looped the thresher's cord around his assailant's neck. "Drop the knife!"

The thresher-wielding thief who had tried to enter the fight had banged himself in the head, but had recovered and was whirling the free end to smash Pons. Guilen and Chard rushed in with the castoff forks, parried, then tangled the robber's thresher and disarmed him, as another robber fled. Pons applied pressure to the neck of the leader, who gagged, and who was close to blacking, dropped the knife. The remaining thieves, outnumbered by the armed monks, bolted.

Pons's anger subsided. *What just happened? How did I do that? The Lord must have guided me to avoid another bloodletting event. And failing to keep my protégé out of trouble, I could have been banished from the monastery! Stay in control!* Pons picked up one of the baskets full of grain and handed it to Bredo's former mate in thievery. "I do not want to see you again, unless you are attending Mass! Now go!"

FRANCE in 1095

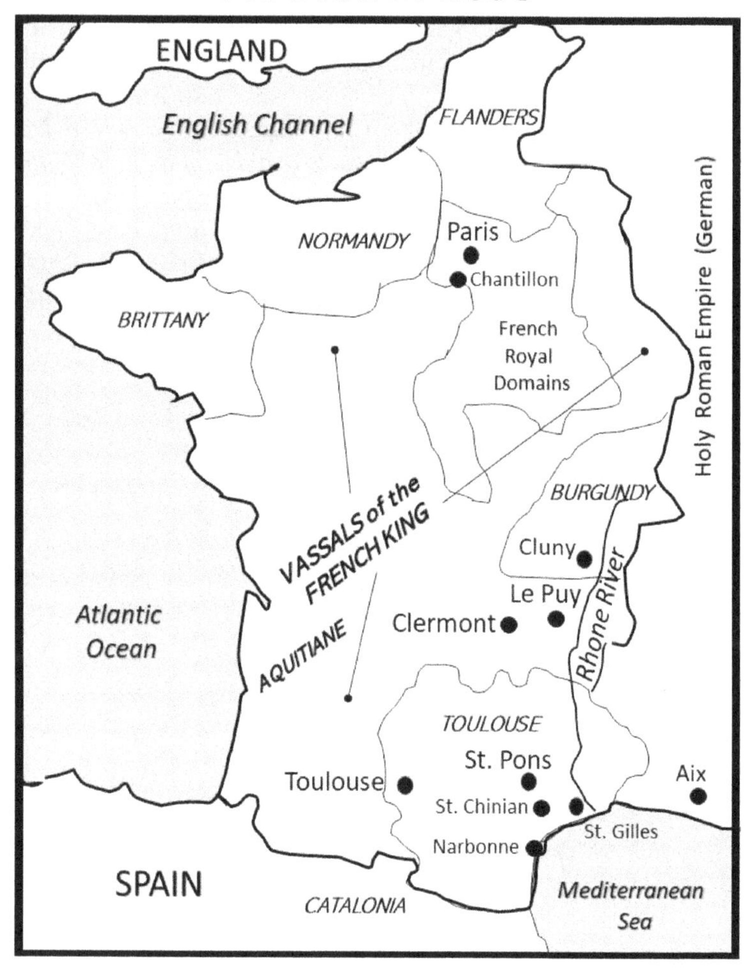

CHAPTER IV THE POPE VISITS SAINT PONS

Abbot Richard had been absent from Saint Pons for over two months, attending the Council of Clermont. He was among hundreds of bishops and abbots who had answered Pope Urban's call to attend the synod.

Although the meeting was 200 miles north of Saint Pons in Clermont, County Auvergne, Abbot Richard was compelled to be present, not only because of the Pope's summon, but Ramon of Saint Gilles, Count of Toulouse, had also personally asked him to attend. The pious count was a generous benefactor to the monastery, as had been his family for over a hundred years. Before he left, Richard had told his obedientiaries, the abbey officers, that he expected reforms would be enacted at the synod. Based on decrees by Pope Urban's predecessor, Gregory, he expected rules would be promulgated against simony, investiture, and clerical marriage.

In Saint Pons, it was a chilly afternoon in mid-December 1095. After washing his hands, Pons strode outdoors across the cloister. His hood was raised against the cold and he once more appreciated his long sleeves which kept his wet hands warm. He continued toward the scriptorium on the second floor above the warming room where monks could chase the chill of winter between prayer, work, and services. He had cleaned his hands solely to avoid damage to his beloved manuscripts, and he was grateful that the scriptorium was built above the warming room to help preserve the valuable books and documents. Just before he entered the bottom floor he looked to the top of the surrounding hills. *It rarely freezes here in the valley but high in the mountains there may be snow and ice.* He was about to enter the building but hesitated when a staccato of clopping echoed from the stone passage through the tower gate. *Is the abbot back?* He hurried to the main road through the village of Saint Pons, a cobblestone street separating the cloister from the abbey church, to intercept the arriving party, expecting to see Abbott Richard and his squad of guards in escort. His entourage was much larger than Pons expected. There were scores of knights and clergy all wearing white crosses sewn onto their outer tunics. Leading the group was a knight sheathed in brilliantly polished armor. One of the leader's eyes was covered by a patch. The monoculist reined his mount to a halt and thoroughly examined the area. His moustache and chin-length hair were an auburn hue, and his sharp nose and beard trimmed to a point were a match. Abbot Richard, riding beside him called out, "Count Ramon, there is Brother Pons, your nephew!" The count's lone piercing eye found Pons.

The squires, knights, and monks dismounted in the square in front of the church. Members of the Saint Pons garrison assisted the squires with the horses to quarter them in the monastery stables.

The count made his way to Brother Pons directly. "I do not need introduction. You are my sister's son—I have no doubt you are my nephew Pons!" The taller man embraced the sacrist.

The abbot relieved his horse of its burden as he jumped to the ground, briefly nodded at Pons as he hurried, and pulled the prior with him across the cloister into the monastery. Ramon continued to hold Pons's shoulders, searching the shorter man. As Richard hurried away his voice trailed off, "The Pope will be here soon! We have only a few days to prepare." Richard stopped abruptly and looked back at the pair. "Sacrist, inspect all the buildings, the guest quarters first. Pope Urban and Bishop Le Puy will be staying there. I want a report after Compline." The abbot hurried on.

"Yes, you look like my sister," said Ramon as he stepped back and let his arms fall to his sides. He observed Pons's gray habit. "You wear an old frayed habit and the keys hanging from your belt show you are the sacrist. By your clothes, I see you follow at least the first of the three Benedictine vows: the vow of poverty—and of course that is noble . . . in your position."

Pons was silent.

"And it appears you take seriously your vow of silence! Then, of course, there is the vow of chastity."

Pons flinched at his last words and finally responded, "Monks must be silent only at the services, Count Ramon. I just am not used to secular conversations. I, I . . . have not left the monastery, except for the hamlet, since I arrived here as a child. I am honored to meet you, and . . . it is . . . heartwarming, to meet a family member. Only Godfather Rainerius has visited."

Ramon hesitated, evaluating Pons, then said, "You must know we are descended from Garsinda and Ramon Pons, who founded this abbey. And I have continued to donate funds and additional properties to the monastery, but this is my first visit here. Please show me around during your inspection for the Pope's visit."

"That will be my pleasure, Count . . ."

"Call me uncle, Brother Pons, here in our intimacy."

"Yes and please address me as Pons or . . . nephew."

"We will head to the guest house first. It only sleeps four visitors. I would think you will be joining Pope Urban and Bishop Le Puy there. Other than the warming room for the monks, where no one sleeps, the guest house, kitchen, and infirmary are the only heated rooms at the monastery."

They moved along an arcade, one of the three which encompassed the central cloister of open ground with fountain and flower garden beds now dormant with the winter. Pons pointed to the sculptured capitals on the columns forming the porticoes. "There is a beautiful set of carvings on that column depicting the story of the Crucifixion—there is Judas's kiss in the garden. And here is the martyrdom of Saint Pontius, er . . . Saint Pons de Cimiez, our family's holy ancestor.

"The building to our left is the monks' dormitory."

"Is there a separate dormitory for the lay brothers?" said Ramon. "I was hoping they could share their quarters with my knights during our brief stay."

"We have only one dormitory," Pons answered. *Lay brothers?*

"Toulouse has several large abbeys, but I see a few differences compared to your monastery," added Ramon.

"Yes?" said Pons.

"Their tunics. Your habit is made from coarse wool like theirs, but they have taken up dying them black, for what reason I do not know. And, they have an extra dormitory for the lay brothers."

"What is a lay brother?"

"Those that have taken the Benedictine vows but do not take part in the full set of rituals and are not ordained monks. They are employed in manual work, so the monks can devote their full time to pray and study."

"Hmm . . . I am ignorant of these ways, Uncle."

Pons stifled his concern about deviation from Benedict's rules in Toulouse. Instead, he focused on his survey of the abbey as he escorted Ramon. He saw Chard and Guilen and they agreed to organize the brothers to gather firewood for the guest house and to clean the quarters.

"Are you familiar with the village fortifications?" asked Ramon. "I must ensure the village is secure before Pope Urban arrives. You never know when King Henry might do his shameful deeds."

Pons looked alarmed but nodded.

Ramon placed his hand on Pons's shoulder with regard. "I will educate you on the political world to the best extent that I can during my short visit. There is much to tell about what happened at the Pope's synod in Clermont. Now, my men should be finished riding the perimeter of Saint Pons fortifications. Walk with me to the west gatehouse where I will review the inspection with them, then I will have them examine the walls in Thomieres. Do you know of sections that might be more vulnerable?"

The two men met with several of Ramon's knights. Pons directed them to a few locations uphill from the north walls of the Saint Pons village, from where a crossbowman's bolt could reach the church entrances. Ramon planned to set up posts and secure those locations before the Pope arrived. Pons and Ramon exited the west gate tower and crossed the stone bridge over the Jaur River, entering Thomieres.

A stone's throw past the grotto springs, they came to Saint Martin's chapel where Pons introduced Ramon to the priest. After a brief visit, the young monk guided the count to the west side of the hamlet to show him a defensive tower that needed repairs. As they passed the last few houses, a faint aroma of chestnut bread was in the air. A woman and two boys were pulling winter radishes in their meager plot. She looked up with recognition and waved to Pons but caught herself. Pons stared ahead as they walked. *This is difficult—she is here, with her aroma of the baking chestnut bread! I wonder if Ramon noticed?*

They arrived at the tower near the top of Artenac Hill. Ramon pointed at the crenellations that were deteriorating. "I see the interior stairs are unusable, but we will use a ladder and post soldiers up there. From here you can look down on both villages as well as monitor the surrounding hills. A perfect observation point." Ramon continued studying the tower. "Nephew, you didn't acknowledge that woman's greeting."

Pons was speechless for a few moments. "But . . . "

"Remember, Pons, I am a man of the world!" he laughed. "And you are a *man*. The bishops in Toulouse have mistresses.

"Don't worry, I will not reveal your secret." He turned to Pons with a serious expression. "She is very poor. Does the priest help her family?"

Finally, here is someone I can talk to besides the priest. Ramon is a family member I can respect. "She is a widow. I bring food to the priest for her and the boys, but . . . they need more. Monks neither own possessions nor keep money."

Ramon reached under his tunic. He removed a leather pouch, the clink of metal suggesting a purse of coins. "Is the priest honest? These deniers will take care of her family's needs for several years, if the priest can manage the coins for her."

Pons accepted the handful of silver deniers. "Thank you and God bless you, Uncle." Stamped on the coins was *RAMVNDS.* "Did you mint these coins in Saint Gilles?"

Ramon chuckled. "No, see on the back. It is stamped *Narbona,* the city where it was minted under the direction of another Ramon, the Bishop of Maguelonne. What is her name?"

"Primavera."

"I learned enough Catalonian when I fought in Spain. Their word for spring is *primavera.*"

I wish I had met Ramon sooner. "Yes, she is a breath of spring to me, Uncle."

As they returned down the hill and crossed back to the village of Pons, Ramon said, "I will talk to the garrison commander and make sure he repairs the old tower in Thomieres. But I am here to protect the Pope in the short term, and the monastery and village fortifications are secure enough."

Abbot Richard sat at the head of a table in the refectory. Most of the monks were working to prepare the monastery for the Pope's arrival. With him were the prior, the sacrist, the cantor who led the holy incantations, the cellarer who supervised the provisioning of the monastery, and the lector entrusted with reading the lessons in church. "Thank you. With God's favor, you have all done a brilliant job preparing for the Holy Father's arrival. During his visit, the Pope will give the Heaven inspired sermon that he delivered in Clermont to archbishops and hundreds of bishops and abbots.

"The Pope's entourage includes Cardinal Rainerius and Bishop Ademar of Le Puy. Some of you may be fortunate to be in the presence of His Holiness."

A few monks squirmed.

"Please pay attention to how to address the senior clergy." Richard stood and demonstrated. "Kneel on your left knee to the Pope or the bishop. Address the Pope by 'Your Holiness' or 'Holy Father.' The cardinal should be addressed as 'Your Eminence.' You have all met bishops before, so you know to address Bishop Ademar as 'Your Excellency.' Any questions?"

"Yes, Father Abbot, I heard that we must kiss the Pope's ring."

"Of course, yes . . . if he offers it. It is called the Ring of the Fisherman."

"And Brother Pons, stay close by; Cardinal Rainerius and Count Ramon will expect you to socialize with the dignitaries. How are their accommodations?"

"All are ready. The guesthouse is warm and clean," said Pons.

"Thank you, Sacrist. But we must be flexible. I had many discussions with other abbots while I was in Clermont. There have been some changes at Cluny, the mother of our Benedictine monasteries—a softening of our austere rules—but do not assume that Pope Urban himself is soft. He had to fight his way into Rome after he was elected as Pope almost a decade ago. He then lived on an island in the Tiber River, almost starving at times. The rightful Pope's residence, the Lateran Palace, was occupied by the anti-pope who was installed by the German Emperor Henry. Pope Urban went to Sicily and stopped the Normans' infighting, gained their support, and finally returned to Rome to take residence in the Lateran, as the true Pope."

Three days later Pope Urban arrived in Saint Pons. The next morning, just after Prime, he held Mass in the abbey church for the monks of Saint Pons, the brothers from the nearby monastery of Saint Chinian, and the high clergy in his entourage. Although a large and grand edifice, the abbey church did not house a bishopric and was not the center of a diocese, so it was not designated by the Church as a cathedral. After Mass, he described how the army of clerics at Clermont had asserted that the secular powers do not have the right of investiture, and therefore must not appoint clergy. He talked of the agreement to ban clerical marriage and to stop the practice of simony, the act of buying or selling of a church office. At the height of his address, he ordered that married priests who ignored the celibacy laws should be imprisoned for the good of their souls. There was no noticeable reaction among the clergy.

Urban then moved outside, followed by his audience in the church, where the people of the village of Pons, the hamlet of Thomieres, the garrison soldiers and knights, and the inhabitants of the surrounding valley awaited. Standing at the top of the steps he broadcast the message he wanted the soldiers and the general populace to hear. "Sons and daughters in Christ, hear me! Last March I received envoys from Alexios Komnenos, the Emperor of the Romans of Constantinople, the Christian empire of the East, asking for help against the Turks who have taken over much of their land. I have just come from a great council attended by bishops in such vast numbers it had to be held in the open air outside the city of Clermont. The Turks are not only preventing Christians from their pilgrimage to Jerusalem but are killing and enslaving them.

"All who die by the way, whether by land or by sea, or in battle against the Muslim pagans, shall have immediate remission of sins. This I grant them through the power of God with which I am invested. Christians, hasten to help your brothers in the East, for they are being attacked. Arm for the rescue of Jerusalem under your captain Christ. Wear his cross as your badge. If you are killed, your sins will be pardoned. And let those who once fought against brothers and relatives now rightfully fight against barbarians."

The crowd was roused and began stirring. Pons watched from his low perch a few steps above the crowd as Urban continued. Pons was very tired, as he and his scribes had stayed up late making copies of Pope Urban's speech in Clermont for distribution. Among the mass of townsfolk, he caught a glimpse of Primavera. Pons recalled the summer morning just after Prime a year earlier. *I was troubled once more that my life as a monk wasn't fulfilling me. There was a void—something was missing. During previous times of stress I had been calmed by meditating at the springs, so again I went to the grotto to clear my mind. As the sun rose above the east side of the valley, the mouth of the cave began to glow. I drew close to the water gushing forth, the opening mostly filled with the outflow, too small for a man to enter without swimming underwater. Then I heard the moans of what sounded like a woman in pain. I removed my heavy woolen habit and underclothes, knowing they would pull me down, and dove into the grotto mouth, the cold water a shock. I could not see well and only by extreme effort and risk, I fought against the current and made it into the cave. I was mesmerized by the bluish light and immensity of the cave roof and I momentarily forgot why I had entered.*

She gazed at me as she lay on the rock ledge, naked, far from voluptuous, her diet poor as most of the villagers, with both hands at her vee, her white skin crowded with bumps of chill, les tetines prominent on her breasts. I climbed on the ledge next to her and stood, the blue glow a color I did not know existed, the water dripping from my limbs sparkling silver. Even in the cold spray and air I was hot. As I tried to hide myself, my seed joined the Jaur and I did not resist when she reached out and pulled my head between her legs, her cries matched the rush of the spring, then subsided. She guided me and once more I spent myself, but this time with intertwining bodies, the cold water could not quench our heat. Pons was startled from his reverie when he became aware of the thousands shouting in unison, "*DIEU LE VEUT*, GOD WILLS IT!"

Pope Urban closed his sermon. "I, or rather the Lord, beseech you as Christ's heralds to publish this everywhere and to pursue all people of whatever rank, foot soldiers and knights, poor and rich, to carry aid promptly and to destroy that vile race from the lands of our friends. I say this to those who are present, it is meant also for those who are absent. Yes! God wills it!"

The large crowd parted as the Pope and his entourage moved to the cloister and monastery. Knots of people gathered and continued talking long after the events. Later in the afternoon, the cantor and lector of Saint Pons Abbey led the clergy at Vespers. After the service the dignitaries met in the refectory to discuss administrative issues, as the vow of silence was only required while dining. The room was not heated, but the warmth coming from the adjacent kitchen made the hall comfortable.

Pope Urban, Cardinal Rainerius, and Ademar, Bishop of Le Puy, stood as they received the other dignitaries. Abbot Richard introduced the clergy. Count Ramon genuflected and kissed the Pope's ring, followed by Bishops Izarn of Toulouse, Petrus Gaufridi from Aix, and finally Geoffroi of Maguelone. Pons studied the clergymen as he waited his turn to pay his respects. Urban was an energetic and robust sixty-year-old, having survived the hardships of constant travel and threat from his archrival, the anti-pope Clement, whom King Henry had appointed. Urban's pate was shaven leaving a strip of hair around his head, the tonsure of a humble Benedictine monk. He also had a small moustache and short beard. Cardinal Rainerius, however, was void of all facial hair and completely shaven bald. Pons recalled that his godfather had told him the ancient Greeks and Romans thought shaving the head was a badge of slavery, and to humble themselves, the custom was adopted by the monks as slaves of Christ.

Although not of coarse wool, the Pope's clothes were modest for his station. He wore the layers of clothes suitable for travel: an inner tunic of linen and leggings covered by an *alb*, an off-white floor length tunic. He had removed his outer cloak, a wool cowl that provided a hood against the wind and cold, revealing his only decoration: a shoulder mantle of three straps, each embroidered with a cross. Next to Urban was the Bishop of Le Puy, also rugged and proof that he could endure hardships, having traveled to Jerusalem on pilgrimage a decade earlier at the age of forty. When Urban appointed the bishop as Pope's Legate, the spiritual leader for the new expedition to the Holy Land, he readily accepted. *My godfather Rainerius is one among these high dignitaries, being the Pope's 'fidus Achates,' like Aeneas's faithful friend in Virgil's Aeneid that I copied a few years ago. But according to Godfather Rainerius there is one powerful official who is not here today, a cleric that has as much spiritual influence as the Pope and administers over 1,000 monasteries in Europe. That man is Hugh, Abbot of Cluny Monastery.*

As Pons waited to be introduced, he noted the Pope was finishing his discussion with the bishops. Pons began to move toward the Pope, then in the corner of his eye he glimpsed Bredo coming out of the kitchen holding a tray full of drinking cups. *No Bredo! The greetings are not over!* He deftly signed for Bredo to turn around. *Good, the dignitaries have not noticed him yet.* The monk spun in a complete circle without spilling the cups on his tray but renewed his mission toward the cluster of men. Then Pons signaled him to wait by patting his hand down toward the floor, so the monk smiled, dropped down, and walked on his knees across the floor with head bowed, skillfully balancing the drinks. *I have failed! Abbot Richard entrusted me to tutor this man!* Pons's temper began its habitual rise. *Who chose him to do this! Why did Richard want me to train this idiot!*

The group around Urban took notice. Richard appeared horrified. The Pope seemed to repress a smile. *Urban fancies this?* Bredo reached the Pope, kissed his ring, and kept his head bowed.

"Please rise, Brother," said Urban, "What is your name?"

"Bredo, Your Holiness."

Pons cooled. *Urban doesn't seem angry.*

"What have you brought?" asked the Pope.

"Holy Father, since you were born in Châtillon, in the north, I poured you an ale. We make the most delicious ale this side of the Rhone River!"

Pons's temperature returned. *What? Shut up, Bredo!*

"But then I remembered you have lived many years in Italy,"

continued Bredo, "so I poured you some red wine. It is the best in the area, grown by the monks of Saint Chinian."

"Thank you, Brother," said Urban as he waved his hand toward his audience for them to serve themselves. A bishop started to extend his arm, but Bredo pulled the tray out of his reach and continued his soliloquy.

"But then the cellarer, who used to live at the monastery in Monte Cassino, told me you were elected Pope in nearby Terracina where the moscato wine is the best."

Through the door to the kitchen Pons saw the cellarer had a look of panic as the man pulled his sparse hair. Pons could feel waves of heat rising from his habit into his face. *Did Richard plan this to destroy me? No! It would be bad for him, too! But I am doomed!*

The dignitaries joined the Pope with signs of polite amusement and smiled. Abbot Richard calmed.

Bredo continued, "We had no way to acquire the white moscato wine of Terracina that celebrated our Lord guiding your election, so we thought we could obtain some of the *muscato nero* grown in the Rhone Valley."

Bredo paused. Again, the bishop from Toulouse reached for a cup, but he pulled back his hand when the monk resumed. The audience was now enthused, interested in what Bredo would say next. "We did not have time to go to Avignon, so the cellarer, who remembers the sweetness of the moscato from Italy, added some honey to our local vintage until it was just right, and here it is!"

"Well said, Brother Bredo!" added the Pope. He laughed and Bredo and the onlookers joined in with a chorus of respectful and well-mannered laughter.

They were entertained! It wasn't a disaster! Pons then approached the Pope and paid his respects, followed by the cantor and lector.

Bredo finally left, tray empty, and Urban lifted his cup, "To Ramon, the Count of Toulouse, Narbonne, and Saint Gilles! He is most pious, supporting the reforms that God has guided us to establish. He has sacrificed for the Faith already in Spain, losing an eye fighting the Muslims. He was the first noble to take the cross to fight in the Holy Land, and as the most powerful count in Aquitaine and Provence, he has much to lose. But he is willing to answer God's call to take back the Christian lands. Sante!"

Ramon returned the salute, "I am but a soldier, a knight, and a servant in this world. Pope Urban, as God's legate, you have channeled the Lord's bidding and inspired all of Europe to answer the call. I vow to carry out your promise to Alexios and aid the Christians of the East. I will not return to our dominions until we recover Jerusalem from the Muslims, or I will die fighting. Sante!"

The men broke into pairs and small groups as Pope Urban, Rainerius, and Richard conversed with Pons. "I have visited scores of cities and monasteries already and plan to continue my journey across Provence," said Urban, "but I cannot go every place, so I will send documents notifying Christians all over Europe to join the crusade. Thank you, Brother Pons and your copyists, for producing so great a quantity of notices in such a short time."

"I am glad I could help spread the Lord's word . . . and your declaration of the crusade, Your Holiness."

Urban changed from French to Latin. "And you are sacrist and barely twenty years old?"

"Yes, Holy Father," Pons answered in Latin, "With the Lord's favor, I have been sacrist for three years."

Returning to the vernacular, the Pope smiled. "Your Latin is very precise." He looked to Rainerius. "Cardinal, tell Pons about your encounters with Abbot Richard as a young monk in Cluny."

Pons sensed the three men were all familiar with what his uncle was about to say. "Centuries ago Irish monks founded monasteries in England and reintroduced Christianity," began Rainerius. "Richard was born in Ireland and educated in one of the English monasteries that carried forth the Irish traditions."

"Ahh! Ireland, the land of saints and scholars," said Urban.

Rainerius smiled and continued, "He wanted to further his studies at the center of the Benedictine order and joined Cluny Abbey. Richard and I were young monks—both working in Cluny's scriptorium many years ago, before you were born, and one day had some, er . . . disagreements about the Latin in the manuscripts we were copying. We agreed on the written language, but when we read the manuscript aloud, our diction was quite different. The sacrist overheard us and intervened, saying we both had dreadful accents."

Pons's head tilted to the side. "Godfather, was it a matter of dialect?"

"Well, yes, in a way, but not that simple. Richard's native languages were Gaelic and English; I was born in northern Italy, near Florence, and the sacrist was from Burgundy . . . three different vernaculars . . . English, Tuscan, and French. We each read aloud a short passage from the Bible in Latin. Then translated and voiced the same passage in our native language."

Rainerius paused, sipping his wine. Pons waited with interest.

"It was no surprise that Richard's English rendition was nothing like his Latin. To me, the sacrist's sounded part Latin and part French. My Tuscan was very close to my own Latin reading, but there were significant differences with Richard's Latin."

Pons's brows knitted. "So Tuscan and Latin are close? Hmm, it is not surprising, the Romans came from Italy. But that means at Cluny and the hundreds of monasteries in France, the lectors are reciting the Bible passages in error?"

"Most *were*, until the Latin of the Irish monks was reintroduced to Europe. The ancient monks of Britain learned proper Latin from the Romans, but fled to Ireland from the barbarian invaders. The next generation of Irish monks, and the next and the next, and so forth, in Ireland and in England, learned from their predecessors and from Latin grammar books, so they preserved Latin better than in Italy and France."

The three older men sipped wine as they observed Pons contemplating his uncle's last statement. Then Pons's face lit up. "Yes! The Tuscan and French vernacular are so close to the original Roman language that our Latin was tainted with native speech and we *thought* we were speaking it properly. Irish is so different from the Latin, that everyone spoke only Irish. Only in the monasteries did they write, read, and recite in Latin, thus preserving a more original form of the ancient language."

Richard placed his hand on Rainerius's shoulder. "Believe me, it was hard for your godfather to accept that his Tuscan was not really Latin!"

Their mild laughter finished and the Pope returned to focus on Pons. "Of course, you come from a noble family that has done much for the Church. Your family's donations to the Church have been considerable over many generations. And your uncle, Count Ramon, has promised the largest contingent of knights to the crusader army." He looked at Rainerius. "Your godfather, Cardinal Rainerius, has informed me of your contributions as a leader, maintaining and improving the edifices of Saint Pons Abbey and the excellent work of the scriptorium, which you just showed by producing the many copies of my letter in so short a time. We are depending on you to maintain your devotion to Saint Benedict's rules and continue your development. The Church will need your leadership in a greater capacity."

The Pope paused. "Abbot Richard, you have the honor to inform Brother Pons."

"Under my predecessor, the late Abbot Frotard, missionaries were sent out to found several monastic houses in Catalonia. And as the importance and influence of Saint Pons Abbey has grown, we are in need of a worthy monk to fill the position of subprior. Brother Pons, you have been promoted to subprior here as my understudy."

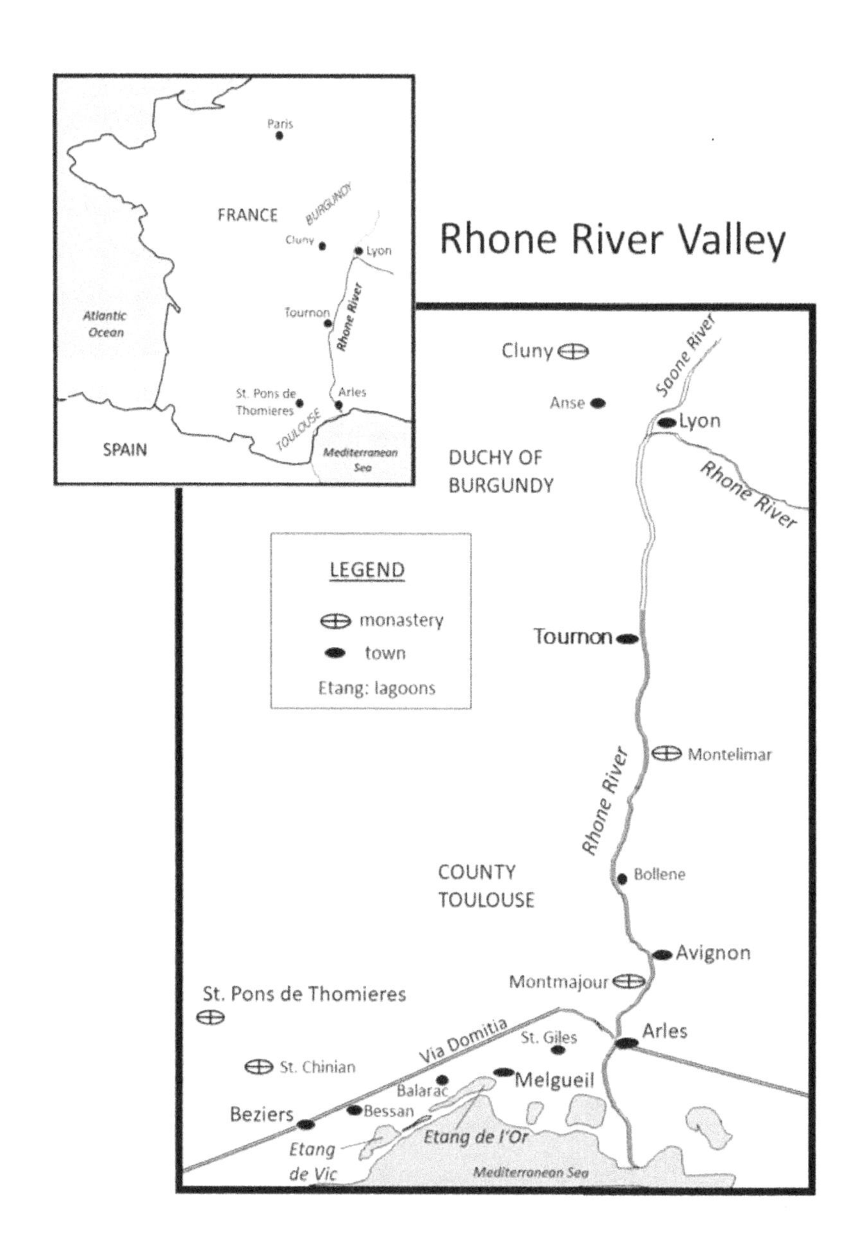
Rhone River Valley
Paris
FRANCE
BURGUNDY
Cluny
Lyon
Tournon
Rhone River
Atlantic Ocean
St. Pons de Thomieres
Arles
TOULOUSE
SPAIN
Mediterranean Sea
Cluny
Saone River
Anse
Lyon
DUCHY OF BURGUNDY
Rhone River
LEGEND
monastery
town
Etang: lagoons
Tournon
Montelimar
Rhone River
COUNTY TOULOUSE
Bollene
Avignon
Montmajour
St. Pons de Thomieres
Via Domitia
St. Giles
Arles
St. Chinian
Balarac
Melgueil
Beziers
Bessan
Etang de l'Or
Etang de Vic
Mediterranean Sea

CHAPTER V A NEW MONASTERY

In 1100, five years after Pope Urban's tour of France to call for a crusade, Christians traveling from Rome on pilgrimage to Santiago Compostela in Spain arrived at the Saint Pons monastery to deliver two letters from the Pope. Abbot Richard and Subprior Pons accommodated the group in the shade under fruit trees in the cloister garden. As they shared wine, a pilgrim removed two packets of leather from his shoulder bag. Both were sealed with bright red wax, impressed with the Pope's signet ring. He gave them to Richard. "Abbot Richard, honor . . . to give this from Papa Pascali . . . um . . . Pope Paschall in Roma. Scusi, Abbot, my French . . . um . . . my Occitan no good, we from Roma."

Richard accepted the offering with a smile. "No, no, your Occitan is very good. Thank God you are here safely. And thank you for going out of your way, leaving the Via Domitia will add several days to your journey to Compostela."

"Good to help la Papa and il Dio, the Lord. After we see Santo Ponzio er . . . Saint Pons Abbey in Cimiez, we come where Santo Ponz . . . where they bury Saint Pons. Scusi. It hard, my language to Occitana." He gazed about the cloister and the surrounding hills. "Il monasterio e grande, big! Bellissimo! Beautiful!"

"Yes, we are blessed. After we finish our wine . . ." he noted a puzzled look, "dopo vino . . . we will go to see . . . vedremo . . . Santo Ponzio's tomb."

Pons thought it was kind the abbot tried to speak some of the pilgrim's language. *Unfortunately, we open his tomb only once per year for viewing, on his saint's day—May 14.*

As Richard lay the packets on the bench, Pons saw that the top one was addressed to him, written in Latin: Frater Pontius. *If Rainerius was here, he would be able to tell the pilgrims the story of Saint Pons, or as they know him, Santo Ponzio, in their own language. Saint Pontius was martyred for proselytizing Christ's word in Cimiez, during the times of the ancient Romans. He was a senator with the surname of Pontius, and his familiar name was Marcellus. Hundreds of years ago when the Saracens destroyed the original monastery at Cimiez, the Christians hid the saint's relics. Ramon Pons, the Count of Toulouse, and his wife Garsinda founded this monastery, recovered his relics, and interred them here to sanctify the abbey.*

Later that evening after Vespers, Pons opened the letter delivered by the pilgrims.

Sorrowful greetings Godson Pons,

Your uncle, Ramon de Saint Gilles, Count of Toulouse, who supported Pope Urban and was the first noble to join the crusade, swearing to regain Jerusalem for the true Faith, has died in the Holy Land. He was the only crusader leader who refused to pledge an oath to Emperor Alexius, for his piety prevented him, but was also the only commander to honor the emperor's entitlements to recover his Christian empire in Anatolia. After months of siege, he led the crusaders to capture the Holy City. They offered Ramon the crown of the new Kingdom of Jerusalem, but he refused, as he felt unworthy to reign where Jesus had been crucified. Just as Pope Urban died before the fruition of his crusade to recover Jerusalem, Ramon was killed during the siege of Tripoli, before achieving his goal to take the city and realize his dream of a kingdom in the Levant. His son Jordan won the city and now rules there.

I have sent a letter to Abbot Richard, entreating your relocation to Cluny Abbey to assume duties as sacrist. I know this will please you, because of your love for books, but your move is simply the first step to spreading your influence and in due course, to become abbot. The last three Popes, as myself, began their advancement at Cluny and with the Lord's guidance, this will also be your journey.

Before his death, Ramon dispatched a relic from the Holy Land, which returning pilgrims entrusted to the priest in Saint Gilles. Your uncle desired to pass it onto you. Your mother Almodis and your older brother, now the Count of Melgueil, have it in their protection. I ask of you a favor, although the task may be unpleasant for you. On your journey to Cluny, stop at the town of your birthplace, Melgueil, and convey the relic to Cluny. Best regards and wishes, God be with you always, your godfather.

Pope Paschal of Rome

Pons felt his stomach churn. *So I am to see my mother.*

Within a month a trio of monks prepared to leave Saint Pons de Thomieres. Richard ensured they were well equipped for their journey. He issued them new strap shoes, full coverage leather shoes in place of sandals which they wore in the monastery. They brought their eating knives and oak walking sticks. Highwaymen were common on the roads and the robust staves could also be used for protection. They also wore new habits. The journey would normally take over a month on foot to cover the 350 miles; Abbot Richard instead provided mules to ride, halving the time it would take them to reach Cluny. Richard said that clergy should ride mules rather than horses as a sign of humility. They carefully planned their trip to reach the safety of a monastery each night. Pons had been shocked when Richard gave each a gold cross as he said his farewells. *What did he mean, "Do not protect the cross, the cross will protect you"?* He tucked the pendant and chain inside his habit after they rode away, ashamed, knowing that Saint Benedict would not approve. But he also knew that a gold cross would be a target for bandits, which they would surely encounter over the long journey.

Pons had entrusted the deniers Ramon had given him to the priest for the welfare of Primavera and her children. His farewell to the small family was brief. She was toughened by a lifetime of hardships and did not show emotion. Pons's tears made up for both. A few miles into his journey, waves of doubt crashed over

Pons. *I was happy in Saint Pons, why am I leaving? No, truthfully, I was angry and irritated most of the time. Will I be like that wherever I go? The priest calmed me and guided me. And Primavera—she gave me confidence.* Without hesitation he told his companions he was going back to Thomieres and would join them the next day in Saint Chinian. Neither Chard nor Guilen seemed fazed. He urged his mule along the narrow earthen road.

I must see her once more. The villagers will notice me and perhaps some of the monks may find out from the guards at the gate. But I don't care. She wouldn't be allowed to come with me. Why couldn't I have lived a hundred years ago when married clergy were accepted and rather commonplace? Saint Augustine lived openly with his mistress and they had a son. The saint himself said, "O Master, make me chaste, but not yet!"

He entered Thomieres and rode the mule up Artenac Hill to her shack. Stone houses were crowded together in the center of the hamlet at the bottom of the hill. He threaded along the narrow streets paved with cobbles and several shutters opened, the residents looking out at Pons. Climbing the hill, the houses were smaller, built of wood, and became more spread apart. Some had small garden plots out front. Her sons were outside and ran into their hut shouting. Primavera came to the open door as he tied up his mule, and the boys ran off looking back, smiling. She called out, "Don't come back until you have fetched a sack full of chestnuts! And only pick them from the ground."

Pons watched them run off. "It's August, the nuts are just starting to fall. There won't be many on the ground."

"I know, but that will keep them busy."

The familiar aroma of baking chestnut bread wafted out the door. Now sans the modest headscarf she wore when in the village, her ink-black hair descended down her back. Pons admired her petite features; a small nose and thin lips were framed by straight glossy hair that matched her dark eyes. "I am not here to stay."

"But you are here now." Primavera flashed a fleeting smile. *She has a hard life and she smiles for others, not herself.* She took his hands in hers, led him into the one-room house, and had him sit on the low sleeping pallet. Pons regarded the way the coarse tunic hung loosely on her body. *She is poor and thin, and I fear she gives her sons most of the food, for they are robust and healthy. Why am I here? Do I truly care for her or is it merely because of carnal desire?*

Primavera crossed her arms in front and in one motion pulled her long tunic over her head. Pons had never seen any other woman naked, but in her he saw pure beauty. *How could it be wrong for men and women to be together?* Her arms, face, and neck were darkened by exposure to the sun but her unblemished skin was white where her tunic had covered. She was slim, almost gaunt, except her shoulders were nicely rounded and her thin arms and legs appeared well-muscled, wiry from the hours in her garden. Pons's gaze returned to Primavera's eyes, their smokiness matching her seductive look. His stare moved to her small round breasts, which were defined and conspicuous because of her slenderness, then his gaze moved lower to her dark triangle below her narrow waist. She reached to remove his habit. Pons held her hands. "We don't have to . . ." But she was insistent and he did not have the willpower to stop her. There was hardly a crease on his muscular and lean body, toughened by long walks up Mount Lauzet and work in the fields and vineyards. He sat on the edge of the pallet and she served him as he had done for her at the grotto. Her mouth was so perfect that he climaxed within moments. He rolled her onto the pallet. He lustily returned the kindness and found her sweet spot as she looked down on his tonsure between her legs. They were not done. *I want to feel her against me.* He was average in height, not much taller than her, and enjoyed the sensation of the match of their bodies. She drew his face to hers, grabbed his hard buttocks, and pulled him inside her. They were oblivious to their moans.

Pons woke. Through the window of the darkened cottage he could see it was twilight. Primavera was asleep beside him. Her sons peeked through the partially opened door. "Come in.," said Pons. "I have brought you some bread." They hesitated. "It's not the chestnut bread you always eat, but made from the monk's dough." They hurried in and dropped handfuls of chestnuts on the table, the commotion waking their mother. The older boy munched on the bread as he gave a hunk to Primavera, "Mother, we have been outside, waiting until you called."

CHAPTER VI VIA DOMITIA

Pons left Thomieres just before sunrise and joined Chard and Guilen in Saint Chinian. They continued south, came to the Via Domitia, and turned east. The pavement of the ancient Roman road was still intact and enabled them to cover over twenty miles a day. Their mules seemed eager to continue the trip each morning. Several days into their journey, as Pons swayed comfortably with his mule's gait, he patted the animal on the neck. *I am going to name this beast yet! Poor Cicero! He provided me with the best quills. When I think of him, a sadness comes over me, yet I did not feel anything when Rainerius wrote me of my father's death.*

Pons grew tired of the long hours in the saddle followed by silent meals at the Benedictine monasteries where they rested each night. *My memories thus far of the trip are hazy. At Saint Chinian it was the delicious wine. When I lay down to sleep at Beziers, I remember my sore rear. This morning in Balarac, the priest served us maslin bread, made from wheat and rye, the same as we ate at Saint Pons. It made me a bit homesick.*

But now my thoughts are of Melgueil, my birth place, only a few hours away. He began to perspire.

"Brother Pons," Chard, riding beside him, raised his voice. "Pons! Are you there?

"Are you as refreshed as I am from our bath this morning? It is amazing that the ancient Roman aqueduct still delivers the mineral waters to Balarac."

Guilen urged his mule to catch up and rode alongside Pons, "Yes, the waters were very stimulating and the church was appropriately named: *Sancta Maria de Aquis, Our Lady of Waters*. And how is your friend doing?" said Guilen, as he patted Pons's mule.

"You mean, how is *Cominius* doing?"

Guilen and Chard traded smiles.

Pons had sensed as they traveled further south that the sweet lavender fragrance borne on the winds was fading. It had been replaced by earthy scents—aromas of salt and vegetation. As he appreciated this long absent aromata, he envisioned an experience from his youth in Melgueil—he was riding a white horse through the marshes. Then the memory was gone.

Forest still dominated the north side of the road, but had thinned out. There were only isolated groves to the south where grasslands and marshes opened the vista toward the sea. The traffic on the road was sparse, but they had occasionally seen farmers bringing their produce into the towns, or nobles and their escorts traveling on horseback. Later that afternoon they saw a trio of monks approaching on foot from the opposite direction. Pons noted the monks wore undyed habits of light gray wool. *I feel blessed that we had the services of a barber this morning.* He made sure his cross was hidden and glanced at his comrades, noting theirs were out of sight as well. The two groups met near a copse of trees and they rested in the shade. Pons offered a small loaf of bread and a monk of the other cluster produced a skin of wine. Together in silence they took communion. Then one stranger asked, "What monastery are you from, brothers?"

"The good Lord has provided us a peaceful valley to work, study, and pray at Saint Pons Abbey. Five days' ride west. And you?"

"Cîteaux." He glanced at his brothers. "Many days . . . by foot, to the north."

"In the north. So your abbey must be attached to Cluny, the mother of all houses? That is where we are going."

"Our abbey is about four days' travel north of Cluny, but we are an independent monastery."

Pons knitted his brows. "I have lived in one monastery my

whole life. It seems I have much to learn about the world. So if you are not with Cluny, then do you follow Saint Benedict's rules?"

"Was that wheat I tasted in the bread, Brother?" Pons nodded. "We follow the saint's canons." He glanced at the mules. "Apparently more strictly than yourselves. Thank you for the communion, brothers." The strangers rose and continued west on the Via Domitia.

As they rode closer to the town of Melgueil, a changed landscape greeted the monks. The terrain became one of marshes and etangs, shallow coastal lagoons. The wetlands and etangs were fertile with life. The rich plant and animal nourishment of these fenlands attracted thousands of birds. The most prominent were wading birds, including pink flamingos, their color due to their diet of shrimp. There was also an abundance of mosquitoes, which were almost intolerable when the breeze from the sea died and the mule's tails were busily swatting at the insects. The water of the etangs was brackish from the high tides running up channels from the sea or spilling across sand bars and islands a few miles south. Fishermen used long poles to navigate their punts across the etangs to set their nets.

When they were a few miles from Melgueil, across the flat landscape, they saw an isolated hill rising above the town's church steeples. The top of the lone prominence was flat and fortified by stone walls. A chateau peeked above the castle walls.

Guilen pointed toward the hill. "That is strange. The land is completely flat for miles around and there are no other hills in sight."

"I think it is a man-made hill, likely raised to build a castle at the top," said Chard.

"I believe you are right," added Pons. "Then it must be my brother's chateau. That's where we will go."

The monks passed through the main gate of the town wall and keeping the castle in view above the town buildings, worked their way through busy cobblestone streets toward the fortification. They soon arrived at a guardhouse at the bottom of the castle mount. When Pons identified himself, a guard ascended the hill while the monks waited.

Within the hour a man with aristocratic bearing arrived,

leading a group of young squires from the castle. He was dark-haired, mustached, and handsome in his bright clothes of expensive linen. "Brother!" He embraced Pons and slapped him on the back. "Brother Pons! Oh, I have made a pun. You are my brother, but you are also a Brother!" He laughed at his own joke as a stunned Pons returned a gentle embrace. "It has been a long time. You were very young—perhaps you don't remember me, your older brother, Raimundus? Over twenty years! You must be almost thirty now, no? The squires will take your mounts to the stables and feed them. Come. I have comfortable rooms for you in the chateau for tonight and you will see Mother in the morning. The chateau is higher than the rest of the town and catches the breeze, which will keep the mosquitoes away."

The three monks sat on a bench in a third floor bedroom of the castle, overlooking Melgueil and fertile vineyards and orchards surrounding the town. But they were not used to seats with backs, let alone the cushions which lined the bench. Tapestries hung on the walls. Pons finished the Vespers reading, which was always Psalms 109 to Psalms 147, and closed the *Book of Hours* they had brought. "Raimundus has asked us to the evening meal."

Chard stood. "Let's go. I am hungry."

Guilen glanced at the other two monks. "What if they are serving beef or mutton? Do we eat it anyway?"

"Don't worry. We are not being tested," said Pons. "We are near the sea, I can smell it, and the fields we passed were full of grains and vegetables. There will be plenty we can eat."

They entered a large high-ceilinged hall on the bottom floor of the chateau. The gray stone floor contrasted with the bright reds, yellows, and golds of the woven tapestries hanging along the walls. Each end of the hall had a fireplace, both currently idle in the summer months. Sunlight diffused through windows of green tinted glass a story above the tapestries. Raimundus stood at the end of a long wooden table made of thick oak planks. "Welcome!" He held out his arm toward a woman, attractive in her colorful layered dress, and a pre-adolescent boy. They both remained sitting. "My wife Maria and son Berant.

"Brothers, please have a seat. We will have a feast to welcome home my brother Pons!"

The monks sat and servants handed them each a cone-shaped

drinking glass, then poured wine into the containers. Others brought plates of steaming seafood, greeneries, and bread, and placed them on the table. Raimundus remained standing as he toasted. "*Sante a la famille*!" He and his wife downed the entire content of their glasses. The monks sipped. "Pons, please bless our food."

After the prayer, the monks ate silently, looking awkward, holding their glasses with one hand and using their personal knives to eat with the other hand. Raimundus noticed. "Do you use cone beakers at the monastery? Of course it is meant to drink in one swallow." He guzzled another beaker of wine. "That's why they make the beakers such that they cannot stand without spilling. And if you use them correctly, you will not be able to stand either." He laughed. "And surely you can talk here while you eat."

Maria placed a hand on her husband's. "Raimundus, perhaps we should honor their customs instead?" She glanced at a servant. "Replace their beakers with the orange vitri. Holy Brothers, do you wish to eat in silence?"

The servants brought flat bottomed goblets that were made of a transparent, orange hued glass. "No, Countess, we want to be pleasant guests, we are simply not used to . . . being outside the monastery."

"What do you think of the fare? The bread is made entirely from wheat, and I see you are enjoying the fish."

"The bread is very good. We monks eat bread made from rye mixed with just a little wheat." Pons held up his knife skewered with a piece of fish. "What kind is this? It has a pinch of sweetness."

"That is eel. Caught in the nearby etangs. And try the asparagus by dipping it in the aioli sauce."

"It is all very delicious, Countess . . . and Count."

"Call me by my name, Brother." He swigged another cone of wine.

It was fleeting, but Pons noticed that Maria gave her husband a disapproving look. "Following this we will have cantaloupe for dessert, gentlemen," she said.

Raimundus had a servant pour him another beaker of wine. "The Camargue cattle supply us with the choicest beef, but I was told monks do not eat that kind of meat."

The count's son spoke for the first time. "Have you seen the pink birds in the etangs? Long legs?"

"Yes, thousands of them—they are large birds with very long legs!" said Chard.

"They are called pink flamingos!" said the boy. He gave a shy smile, "Yes, they are big, but not as large as our mosquitoes!"

The next morning, as he had requested, a servant woke Pons before sunrise. The three monks performed their own service of Prime. They sang a hymn, and Chard read three psalms and chanted a few versicles as Pons and Guilen responded. After a concluding prayer they descended to the eating hall. Raimundus and his family were absent, but a woman in her forties, dignified and with a stoic beauty, sat at the head of the long-planked table. She wore a floor length white tunic, the elegant folds indicating the material was fine linen or perhaps silk. Although it was summer, she had a blue cloak across her shoulders, also of the delicate cloth. Her headrail matched her tunic and was fastened with a headband of golden material, not a metal crown, but conveying a regal look. Long blonde braids reached almost to her lap, accenting the gold chains around her neck. A servant stood by her side and addressed the three monks as they approached the table. "Please, Brother Guilen and Brother Chard, come with me to the kitchen to break fast."

Pons stiffened. *My temper should be rising, this is my mother Almodis! My God, she is also strikingly beautiful!*

"I understand from Raimundus you intended to spend tonight in Saint Gilles, so you must be leaving soon." She waved her hand toward one of the high-backed chairs. "Please sit, Pons."

As he sat he noticed a leather case on the table between them.

"I can see you are nervous. I am used to men reacting to me as you have. Don't feel guilty. You don't know me as your mother." A servant brought a plate of bread and two glasses of wine. "You are my son and a holy man. We will take communion together?"

After their brief ritual, Almodis placed her hand on the leather case. "Inside is a relic acquired by Raymond de Aguilers, who served as vicar for Ramon's army in the crusade—Ramon de Saint Gilles."

Pons's face was blank.

"My brother, your uncle?"

He nodded. "Yes, yes . . . of course."

Almodis continued, "The vicar wrote an account of the capture of Jerusalem."

Pons's eyebrows rose.

"Yes. I have included a copy of the manuscript in the binder. Perhaps you will find the story of your uncle inspiring."

As she untied the flap of the leather case, Pons noticed a light sheen on the folder. *The leather has been oiled to keep the parchment within dry.* She withdrew a clear glass tube about the size of her index finger. It contained a sliver of wood. "The glassmakers in Constantinople are geniuses. They have crafted a vessel worthy to protect this fragment of the Holy Cross." He gasped.

"Your Godfather Rainerius is now the Pope and he has taken the holy name of Paschal. You will follow in his footsteps . . . if you survive the politics and the sensuality of the world. You are still a man and even with your constant meditations and prayers, you are always vulnerable. A good example is my brother, your uncle, Count Ramon de Saint Gilles, a pious nobleman, but he was not perfect. He was the most powerful noble in France, gave up all his worldly possessions to recover the Holy City for the Faith, and refused the crown offered him in Jerusalem. He completed the vow he made to the Pope, but . . . greedily succumbed to claim the power of an earthly kingdom and died trying to conquer Tripoli.

"After Ramon died, his chronicler left the Holy Land and arrived here with the manuscript and this holy relic. Ramon has been a devout supporter of the Saint Pons monastery, continuing the centuries long dedication by our family, and wanted the fragment of the cross to be donated to Saint Pons de Thomieres Monastery. I paid the chronicler to give me the honor to deliver the relic to Saint Pons."

Almodis smiled. "But instead, I give it to you to promote your start at Cluny. Relics entice many pilgrims, and their donations will add to the wealth of Cluny, and thus your advancement."

Pons remained silent. *Now my fire is rising.* Almodis noticed, and there was a displeased look on her face. Then Pons said, "I recommend we do as Count Ramon directed. As you said, it was his wish to donate the relic to the Saint Pons Abbey. After all, the monastery was founded by our ancestor Ramon Pons."

Her stare met his. She sighed. "Your brother and you—both of you—where is his maturity, and where is your worldly sense? You think the Church is kind and fair to everyone, as Jesus taught. And your brother Raimundus still thinks and acts like an adolescent, spending frivolously and not caring about his subjects!"

Raimundus entered, followed by Guilen and Chad from the kitchen. "Pons, I have been at the stables and your mounts are ready."

Pons left in silence and joined his brothers to retrieve their shoulder bags and staves from the guest chambers. They returned through the hall where Almodis had remained seated, the relic case unmoved. Pons nodded to his brothers and Raimundus to go on. He was alone with his mother.

She picked up the case and held it out to him. "Pons, don't reject this because you hate me. Hate me perhaps because I have been an unloving mother, but take the relic." He headed for the door and she cried out, "Do it for your Godfather Rainerius."

Pons looked back. His mother was on her knees, holding out the case. "Forgive me, son!" Pons lifted her up and she hid her tears on his shoulder. "Your father wouldn't let me visit you! And I was weak and didn't fight him. Forgive me!"

He kissed her on the cheek, tasting the salty tears. For the first time he noticed she was tall for a woman, and their eyes were level. "I forgive you, Mother." He accepted the case and hurried out of the chateau to the stables.

Guilen and Chard appeared unsettled as they waited outside the gatehouse at the bottom of the knoll. "Brother Pons, Raimundus insisted . . ."

Raimundus arrived with his squires leading three white horses, each fitted with the monks' saddles. Pons's mouth fell open. The horses had a rugged look but at the same time their bright, wideset eyes were expressive and intelligent. Their shoulders and hindquarters were well-muscled and the manes and tails were full. Pons recovered. "Where are our mules?"

His brother wasn't fazed by his question. "Aren't these magnificent steeds! They still live wild in the wetlands of the Camargue. And even when we catch and tame them, we let them browse freely in the marshes and then round them up again. It keeps them healthy and reinforces their character." He lifted the foreleg of one horse. "Look at their hooves—the soles are large and wide, suited to their marshy habitat."

A servant brought three swords sheathed in leather scabbards. Raimundus offered them to Pons. "The Camargue horses are beautiful, no? And you need more protection than just your walking sticks, Brother."

"Thank you for your generosity, but I cannot accept any of this. As monks, we may not use swords." *I can't leave Cominius. Besides, Abbot Richard gave us these mounts. And what would the monks of Cluny think of us riding into the monastery on those magnificent steeds?*

Raimundus's face reddened, and Pons quickly touched his shoulder. "Brother, thank you for the swords and the beautiful horses, but we must take the mules, and nothing else, to Cluny."

His brother softened. "You can give the horses to Cluny. It would please me if you took it all. "You will be crossing the Rhone River and taking the road to Avignon, no?"

Pons nodded.

"Good, because the road on the east bank is much better. And one more item. You will need fare to cross the river." There was a metallic clinking when he held up a small leather sack. "You will have to pay a denier, a silver coin, for each of you and for each steed to cross the Rhone on the ferry. Don't let the ferryman tell you it is more." Pons embraced Raimundus.

They departed the city and the monks continued east, riding the mules and leading the Camargue steeds. Pons dropped back behind the mules to check on the horses and noted that close up, they looked gray, an illusion produced by their coat of white hair over darker skin. They were smaller than the mules at the shoulder, but very robust. *What will we do with these creatures? And what will we do with the swords? The abbot told me clergymen were typically given free passage on ferries, but the coins may be useful, or given to the Church.*

As they traveled, the monks did not take time to perform every divine service of their order, but when they rested, they did their best to comply with the Benedictine rules. The sun was overhead, and they found a stand of willow trees along the road that provided ample shade. The hanging branches formed a canopy which gave them a sense of intimacy during their ritual. They recited a few passages from scripture for the Sext service. Nearby in the fields, women and men worked the land with sticks and hoes. Pons motioned for the farmers to join them. The monks passed around their wine skin and broke bread, sharing communion with the farmers. They learned that the serfs were from a nearby manor and had consent to work this plot, but their lord was impoverished himself and could not provide tools, oxen, or horses to plow the fields. Their families, even the young children, worked the fields by hand. Guilen whispered to Pons, who smiled and nodded. Guilen asked the group, "We have three valuable swords we will give you. You could sell them to buy a plow."

One stocky fellow answered. "That is very generous, brothers, but no one would believe that you gave us the swords. We would be accused of stealing them. Our lord would beat us if he knew we possessed swords. I have the skills of a *forgeron*. I used to work the metal until our lord could not afford to keep the manor forge going."

Guillen retrieved the swords and placed them on the ground in front of the man. "Receive the Lord's words from the Bible, from the Book of Isaiah: 'They will beat their swords into plowshares and their spears into pruning hooks. Nation will not take up sword against nation, nor will they train for war anymore.'"

The peasants muttered confusion and disbelief, but the smith nodded. "It is a shame to destroy the workmanship of the sword maker, but the metal is more valuable to feed people than to take life. So, yes, I can fire up the furnace and use this metal to make a good plow." Their murmuring turned to immense gratitude. Chard and Pons handed the reins of the Camargue horses to several of the farmers as Guilen added, "Thank the Lord that He has provided these noble creatures to pull your new plow."

The monks journeyed on and bypassed Saint Gilles, although it was their next planned rest station. Pons was not comfortable to be in possession of the relic, falsely obtained by his mother, if he met his Uncle Ramon's chronicler. So they continued on to Arles, where they would turn north on the Via Agrippa.

The sky was clear, though the sliver of moon did not provide much light. They trusted the vision of the mules to guide them.

Pons noted the conspicuous humidity remained as they moved east, but the scent of the air changed, losing its saltiness. It was replaced by a vegetative smell reminiscent of the air after a rain in the forest. The road deteriorated as they approached the river, stone rubble the only remaining evidence of an ancient Roman bridge. A group of people sat around a campfire next to a boat at the waterside. Pons gazed at the reflections of the crescent moon undulating on the river, with the town of Arles noticeable by only a few scattered lights on the far side.

As the three monks dismounted, a man left the fire and approached them. He was average in height, with beefy forearms and muscular chest, the later noticeable through his open shirt. His loose pants ended below the knee above his bare feet. "*Bonjour* or I should say *bonne nuit*, you are traveling into the night!"

"*Bonsoir*. Are you the ferryman?" asked Pons. "We need to cross to Arles, kind sir."

"Yes, brothers. Tomorrow after sunrise I will take you across. See the people at the fire? In the morning, they will be first, then I will take you after them. You can see my boat is not large so it will take some time to get everyone to Arles. I have not seen you before. Is it your first time crossing the river?"

"Yes. And what is the fare, sir?"

"Are you good at ciphering? One denier per two legs."

The monk's brow furrowed.

"Ha! I am only jesting, Brother. The price is one denier for each person and two deniers per mule."

The brothers found a path along the river and followed it until they came to a sward that hadn't been grazed by the pilgrims' horses. When Pons removed Cominius's saddle, the mule nuzzled the monk's shoulder, then eagerly chomped the lush grass. As they bedded down, Pons examined the coins his brother had given him. "We have nine deniers, and although my brother said it would only be six, we have the correct amount. We will need three coins for each of us and our mules. And look," he held the coin up to examine it in the campfire light, "very interesting, this coin was stamped in Melgueil."

Chard lay under his blanket without commenting, and Guilen mumbled from beneath his cover. "We can figure that out tomorrow."

At sunrise the brothers held their own Prime service and ate the rest of the wheat bread brought from Melgueil. Pons swallowed his last piece. *I must go back to eating the simple rye bread. The wheat bread is delicious and I feel guilty craving more of it. But it is very expensive and is the bread of nobles.* He watched as six passengers took their seats on the boat and the ferryman prepared to cross the river. The boat was shaped like the punts the fishermen used on the etangs, flat bottomed and rectangular, but this vessel was larger, with enough space for six seated passengers, or for a horse to stand as two passengers sat.

The ferryman stood at the rear of the boat and pushed the vessel into the river current with a stout pole, three times the length of a walking staff. An oar, the steerboard, was attached to the right side of the stern, but near the shore the river was slow with eddies and backflow, and the boatman used the pole to steer and propel the boat. Partway across the river, when the water became too deep for poling and the river current increased, the ferryman used the steerboard. He pushed and pulled on the oar, propelling the boat as a fish swims with its tail. The current pushed the boat downstream as the ferryman oared toward the shore, but finally, the ferry reached quiet water on the opposite side of the river. From there he poled the boat to the shore and was now downstream a distance about half the width of the river. On the riverbank they disembarked at a beaten towpath. A tow rope was attached to a horse who pulled the ferry upstream, moving the vessel twice the distance it had just floated downstream during the crossing. In this way, only a single horse and towpath on one side of the river were needed.

Several people embarked on the ferry and the process was repeated, this time returning to the starting point on Pons's side of the river. The ferryman carried Guilen and his mule, and then on a second trip, Chard and his mule, to the far side of the Rhone. As they crossed and the ferry returned to pick him up, Pons observed the waterfront of the city. Many boats were lined up on the riverfront, and many more were coming and going in both directions, some being towed upstream by horses, some floating downstream toward the sea.

Pons and Cominius crossed on the ferry and as they

disembarked, the monk handed the boatman the fare. "Sir, here are the coins to ferry us across the river."

"Keep your money, brother, I was jesting. There is no charge for holy men. You are doing God's work, no?"

Pons bowed his head. "You will be in our prayers, sir. I must ask you, please, we want to visit the church of Sanctus Trophimus." He glanced down the crowded street.

"You mean Saint Trophime, the patron of Arles? Go down that street. When you see a tall building lined with arches looming up behind the houses, take the next right. Halfway down the block you will find the church."

At the church they knelt at the altar rail. As they prayed, the priest joined them. Pons introduced the trio and asked, "Father, please tell us of Saint Trophime."

"He is mentioned in the Bible as a companion and disciple of Saint Paul. We were taught that he accompanied Paul on his journey to Spain and returned here to spread the Good News. He later retreated to Montmajour and became a hermit."

"Montmajour—that is the monastery where we are to stay tonight. Can you give us directions?"

"You are welcome to stay here, but I understand you want to be with your Benedictine brothers at the abbey. It is only a few miles north, but it is built high on a massif surrounded by marshes and swampland, and you cannot take your mules there, not for a short visit. There is a place nearby where you can stable them overnight." The priest waved over an acolyte. "He will guide you to the stalls and then to the boat to reach Montmajour. "Before you go, I will show you our most sacred relic!"

The priest led them to one of the church transepts, opened a hidden niche in the wall, from which he retrieved a wooden box. He set upon a table and removed the top. Inside they saw a weathered piece of wood. "It is a fragment of the True Cross!"

Guilen caught his breath. "How did the holy relic come to be here?"

"Pilgrims brought it here after Constantine became the first Christian emperor of Rome. And it is well-known that his mother, Helena, discovered the True Cross in Jerusalem."

Pons searched for the lump in the side of his habit where he had sewn the glass vial containing the sliver of wood. He had not told Chard nor Guilen of the relic his mother had given him. "Father, have you heard of Saint Pons of Cimiez?"

"Certainly, he is revered all over Provence." He smiled. "That is why so many boys are Christened with the name Pons. As have you, Brother Pons. It is a good name."

Pons paused, his thoughts averted for a fleeting moment by the priest's comment, but continued, "I have studied the life of Saint Pons as described in a text from Rome: *Acts of Martyrs.* According to that document, Saint Pons, Pontius, converted the Emperor Phillip to the Faith many years before Constantine was born."

"Hmm . . . yes, that could be, as there were many Christians then . . . and most of the saints have been Romans. We are thankful God guided Helena to find Our Savior's cross."

Pons ran his finger over the lump of the vial but remained silent.

He and his comrades stabled their mules. On the way to the north gate of the city, they came upon the large structure ringed with arches that had dominated the skyline above the houses. They climbed a flight of stairs to its entrance and passed through a portal, soon looking down on the large oval grounds encompassed by tiers of stone seats. Chard called out, "*Estrang*!"

The acolyte laughed. "Yes, it is strange, Brother. You can see the thousands of seats. This was an amphitheater built by the Romans. They staged sword fights—fights to the death, in the arena at the bottom. And before Arles became Christian, martyrs were sacrificed here, too. It has been used as a fortress, but the townspeople have built a market square and shops in the arena. There are two chapels among the buildings. Do you want to visit them?"

Pons was eager to reach the monastery. "No thank you, please guide us to the boat."

The monks from Saint Pons rested two nights and a full day at the Abbey Church of Mary, Mother of the Lord, Montmajour Monastery. From the fortified monastery on a high rocky hill, the landscape was of a lush and green countryside. On lower parts of the island were vineyards, olive groves, and fields of grains.

Among the buildings was a chapel dedicated to Saint Peter and a crypt dedicated to Saint Benedict. They worshipped in the Chapel of the Holy Cross, which had been built to house a piece of the True Cross, where they observed many pilgrims leaving donations. At the extended rest stop at Montmajour, they found peace, comfort, and familiarity in attending the routine cycle of divine services.

Two days later Pons walked on the road to Avignon. Guilen rode Cominius. Chard called to Pons from his perch on the other mule. "Ha! Pons, now you will make use of the walking staff, no? But I am ready to do some walking. Let's stop and rest, then change riders."

They refreshed themselves with olives and maslin they had brought from the monastery. Pons passed the wineskin to Chard. "I am still angry at that stable owner. He took our deniers but said that was what was agreed upon for one night only, so he confiscated a mule in addition."

Chard sipped wine. "He knew we would not be violent."

Guilen added, "Pons came close. Your face was red. But the man knew we were visitors with no friends in the city. Well, yes, the priest, but what could he do? We were in a hurry anyway."

Chard had more wine. "We reported it to the soldiers at the gate, and they said we were not 'citizens of Arles.' They ignored us."

Pons stood, ready to resume their journey. "It must be the evil way of cities. I hope we can find accommodations in the monasteries ahead."

Twenty-six miles later they reached Avignon, the largest city in the region, and stayed for the night. Over the next two days the monks covered another forty miles, stopping at the villages of Bollene and Montelimar. It was forty miles to Tournon, so they would have to sleep the third night outdoors. The monks performed Compline at sunset, left their campfire burning and fell to sleep, exhausted from their journey.

CHAPTER VII THE RIVERMEN

"STOP! Thief!" Guilen's uproar stirred Pons. He pulled down his blanket and was fully awake when the cold drizzle spattered on his face. His blanket was soaked from the rain. The campfire was almost out and in the feeble light stood Guilen pointing his staff toward the dark forest.

Chard's arm was around Cominius's neck. "Just a moment ago, the mules brayed. I jumped up when I saw a man untying Cominius. The thief ran but the other mule is gone!"

Pons added some wood to the fire, and despite the rain, revived the flames by blowing on the coals. "Thank you for saving Cominius. I should have thought to have one of us stay awake. Go to sleep, I will stand watch." For a while, Pons stood next to Cominius, stroked his nose, and draped his arm across the mule's back. After tiring, he sat, but kept hold of the reins.

In the morning, they continued their journey. Their walking sticks were helpful as the condition of the road had worsened. Pons rubbed his mount on the neck. "I am thankful you didn't let them take you, Cominius." He grasped the vial through his habit. *If I am killed or lost, the holy relic will also be lost. I need to tell them about it.*

"Brothers, in Melgueil my mother gave me a splinter of the True Cross to take to Cluny."

"What?" They answered in unison.

Pons waited a few moments, then added, "Do you think it odd that there were pieces of the True Cross at Arles and Montmajour recovered by the Romans, and centuries later our crusaders still find parts of the cross and bring them home?"

Guilen harrumphed. "It seems to me, if Helena had found the True Cross, there wouldn't be any left to find by the crusaders."

"Or one of those isn't the True Cross," added Chard.

"I am also troubled the monks at Montmajour wore habits that were dyed black," said Pons. "There were also laymen working in the orchards. What does it mean?"

"There are changes we have not experienced, being in our secluded monastery," answered Chard. Then he grumbled, "If we had asked why the monks wear dyed habits, and don't work, they would have thought we were questioning the Church."

A few miles south of the river town of Tournon the jumble of holes and broken pavement ended, and the way turned into a wide beaten path. In the distance they heard a spirited crowd. The trio looked at each other with surprise as waves of applauding, hooting, and cheering echoed down the trail. The afternoon sun was still high as they arrived at the riverfront to see a tournament underway across the river. Bargemen stood on punts hefting long poles, their crews rowing the vessels to gain an advantageous position. The bargemen competed using their poles to push their opponents off balance into the river.

The monks watched the fierce matches, entertained as they waited for a ferryman to notice them, but would have to wait for the end of the competition. The men were not brutal, as they refrained from strikes to the face. Instead, they concentrated on prods to a square piece of wood strapped to their opponent's chest. The poles were very long, three times the length of the monks' walking staffs, and the competitors held them near the end to maximize their reach, which required great strength.

It was near sunset when the bargemen ended their jousts, brought out wine and toasted each other. The tournament over, a boatman came over to their side of the river and ferried the monks and their mule across the Rhone in two trips.

They disembarked near the riverfront castle of Saint Just and queried the guards. "We are Benedictine monks on our way to Cluny. May we talk with the count's steward?"

The guard responded, "I will announce your title and name, sir."

"I am sacrist of Cluny Abbey, Pons de Melgueil."

"Did you say Pons?"

"Yes, I did."

One guard left and returned in a short time with two men. A squire took charge of their mule and the steward escorted them into the castle. They spent a pleasant and stimulating evening conversing with the Count of Tournon. Pons's name had aroused the count's interest. The count's brother was also named Pons and was the Abbot of Le Puy 60 miles to the west. After they told the count of the theft of one of their mules the night before, he thanked God their fate was not worse. The count described the bandits that preyed on travelers: some were *footpads*, some on horseback, some river brigands; they came in all forms, sometimes in groups of up to twenty. He recommended they continue their journey by boat, which would be safer, and he gave them the name of a boatman who could take them to Lyon.

The trio arrived at the river front shortly after dawn and searched for the bargeman named Tornier. After passing a few unattended boats, Chard saw three men working on a barge. "We are looking for Tornier. The count said he was an honorable man and would take us upriver to Lyon."

A sinewy bargeman looked up and smiled. "I am Tornier. You may have passage. Wait one moment."

He ducked out of view under a canvas shelter, which served as the quarters of the boat. From the shelter they heard a woman's voice, "No monks again!"

The bargeman returned accompanied by a woman. Her blonde tresses were braided, coiled atop like a halo, and complemented by a blue head band. Pons wondered why she didn't like monks. *She may look like an angel, but didn't sound like one.*

She examined the monks' habits. "Oh . . . *these* monks are welcome."

"My wife, Carlette."

Her eyes closed as she smiled. "We don't have a full cargo, our boat has room. Welcome aboard, um . . . monks and your mule! Sorry, what should I call you?"

Chard jumped aboard first. "You may call us by our names, good woman!" He introduced his companions as they urged the mule across a gangway.

"Good woman?" Carlette laughed. "You may also call me by my name!"

After securing Cominius, the couple and their two-man crew donned straw hats and began to pole the barge upstream. They stayed near the edge of the river where the current was sluggish. Tornier, Carlette, and both crewmen worked together to pole the rectangular barge against the current. Simultaneously, one pair began on the port side of the bow and the other two began at the steerboard side. The bargemen stuck their poles into the muddy river bottom and pushed on the poles, as they treaded along the side of the barge to the stern. Then they returned to the bow and repeated the task. Battens, strips of wood a foot long, a hand's width, and as thick as a thumb, were nailed to the deck, and spaced along the walkway to prevent the crew from slipping while they leaned on the poles. Pons studied their method. "Carlette, we can help punt."

"Ha! I am not surprised you offered! We have had Cistercians like you travel with us before and they worked their passage."

"Cistercians? I am not familiar with the name—is it a religious order?"

"Yes, the monastery at Citeaux. Isn't that where you are going?"

"No, we're going to Cluny." *Citeaux—we met three monks on the Via Domitia that were from that monastery.*

Carlette's face reddened. "Excuse me, Brother. All the Benedictine monks we have seen wore black habits. Your undyed habits made me think you were Cistercians. And the Benedictine monks we have given passage did not help with the poling." She retrieved spare poles for the monks. "And Brother Pons, I am sorry for what I said earlier."

"Good woman—I mean . . . Carlette, do you mind if we work in our shirts and braies?"

"No, of course not, the crew is dressed much the same."

He pulled off his habit, accepted a pole, and smiled. "Benedictines live to work, study, and pray."

"That's what the Cistercians said.

"Oh, and take off your shoes," added Carlette. "You will have better grip with your bare feet."

They tied up to a stout oak tree at dusk. The crew and passengers sat in a circle and shared bread and wine. Carlette produced a large wedge of cheese, and each of them cut off a piece with their knife.

"Tornier, I watched you jousting yesterday," said Pons. "These poles are heavy. It must be difficult to hold the poles near the end when you spar. And I noticed how you parried and deflected the attackers. I believe using those methods with a walking staff could keep an attacker at a distance."

Pons glanced at a crewman under the canvas tarp napping. Tornier noticed. "He will be the night watch and now that you are part of the crew, you will also take your turn, no?"

Pons nodded along with his comrades.

The next sunrise, Pons woke and was only slightly sore. His brothers sat up on the deck and stretched. "Chard, I am not as sore as I expected after all that poling."

"Same with me. It must be our years of hard work at the monastery."

Guilen laughed and added, "Look at our hands! They were already calloused from work with hoes and threshers!"

They ate quickly, put the barge under way, and got back to work poling. After making six miles progress upriver, at the sixth hour, they tied up at the shore and the monks included the crew in their Nones service, praying for them. They took communion together.

Tornier patted Pons on the shoulder as they finished, "After this hard work, do you want to have a little fun?"

Pons nodded.

"You said you were interested in learning to use your staves to fight as we do with the long poles, no?"

Using his foot, he rolled a walking staff lying on the deck toward him, hooked his toes under it, flipped the weapon up and caught it. "The trick with the staff is to hold it with your hands evenly spaced, as most people do. Giving no sign, launch the tip and hit the opponent's hands. All in one motion, with no warning. Like this." He struck with precise control, tapping one of Pons's hands. "You don't need to step, just let the staff bridge the gap."

The monks tried to follow his instructions and Tornier encouraged them. "Act as if you are throwing your staff through the air—like this—and at the last instance squeeze, squeeze the staff to snap the tip onto their hands."

When the monks questioned why they were trying to hit their opponent's hands, Tornier said, "In our jousting, trying to hit the wooden target first is obvious and is usually parried. So as a deception and to loosen your opponent's grip, I snap the end of my staff on their lead hand and then bounce the tip up and hit the target." They practiced with each other, sustaining a few bruises on their knuckles. When Tornier told Pons to try it on him, Tornier matched his stick to the end of Pons's staff, slid his own stick along to hit Pons's hand, and continued his motion to poke the monk gently in the chest. "Most of the sparring includes this initial crossing of the staffs. The man who has the best timing and momentum scores on the opponent." Over the next few days as the crew continued to punt the barge north, the monks practiced in their spare moments.

The morning air was cool but by the end of each day after a hot afternoon of poling, they would plunge into the river to cool off. A few barges passed headed downstream, utilizing the strong current in the middle of the river. The crews of both barges exchanged hoots and friendly taunts. Tornier and Pons walked in a line along the port side leaning on their poles. "Tornier, have you been a waterman all your life?"

"Yes, I was born on this barge. And you?"

"I lived all my life in a monastery. My parents gave me to the abbey when I was four. I never knew them."

"That is sad, Brother. My parents taught me about boating, right here on this barge. When I was a young man they were both killed by river brigands."

"I am sorry, Tornier, God rest their souls. Are these attacks common?"

Pons thought he had offended Tornier when he did not answer. After a long pause the waterman said, "We have to fight off rivermen at least once per year. That is one reason we joust with our fellow watermen."

"Does your wife joust—as with other women?"

"No, hardly any of the bargemen have wives who help them pole, but she has jousted with me. Although she is very strong, she is still at a disadvantage against a bargeman. With a walking staff though, she could duel most men.

"And come to think of it, we have not had to fight for a while. On this trip, since there are seven of us, that may have discouraged the brigands. They are unpredictable, attacking both at night and in the day."

Within a few hours the sun was low and the crew secured the barge on the riverbank. Pons took Cominius ashore to browse. The mule seemed relieved and was frisky now with room to move after a long day tied up on deck. They returned to the barge and the crew and passengers bedded down. One of Tornier's crewmen remained awake as the night watch.

Pons woke to shouting. *It seems like I just fell to sleep but it is already dawn!*

"River brigands! The *Rouge*! The *Rouge* are here!" The watch was shaking the passengers awake. They were barely able to see each other through a shroud of fog.

The monks stood as Tornier and Carlette emerged from under their canvas tent. As the sun rose, moment by moment the blanket of mist lifted revealing a small flotilla of punts bobbing in the water on the river side. Four or five scar-covered, unkempt men, who appeared ready to spring at them, occupied each boat. They wore red kerchiefs which showed only their eyes. On the land side were a dozen more of the brigands also in the same disguise. Tornier and his crew took up their long poles. He looked around as he spoke, seeking the leader. "Let the monks go! They are holy men and have no part in this."

From one of the boats a masked figure responded. "Yes. Put the monks ashore, then follow our punts down river."

Tornier peered at Pons. "You must go. All they want is the cargo."

Pons examined his fellow monks and both showed him the hand sign that they would follow him. He felt all eyes upon him from both the *Rouge* and the barge crew. "Watermen, rivermen, men of the *Rouge*, listen closely. Why you rob and steal does not concern me, but when you commit these sins, you may think God does not see. He sees, but now more than ever, with my brothers and I here, he is watching even closer. Your sins will be observed by Cluniac monks firsthand—a direct link to the Lord!"

Brigands shifted from foot to foot, knocking the punts against one another. Several of the masked bandits eyed each other.

Pons continued, "If all you want is the cargo, I can promise you a prize more valuable, if you take it and depart."

"We are not in the business of taking hostages for ransom, if that's what you mean," said the *Rouge* leader.

"No." He pulled the gold cross from inside his habit and held it out. "This will be the ransom."

Several of the brigands took a step forward. One yelled, "We will take it all, there is no bargaining here!" Pons's hopes sunk. *Dear Lord, what do I do next?* Then he saw the answer to his prayer floating downriver. All hands were watching him, as he proclaimed, "Answer now and take my offer before it will be too late for you, for the Lord has sent us help!"

The Rouge leader looked behind to the middle of the river and a group of three barges had diverted their course, crossed upriver, and tied up on the shore. A waterman on the lead barge hollered, "Tornier, just give us the signal. We will crush these scoundrels. Do you need our help?"

Pons looked at the *Rouge* captain, who nodded. "Give us the gold and we will leave."

Pons detached his cross and threw it to the brigand's leader. His men on the shore disappeared into the woods and the *Rouge* punts left moving with the current downstream.

Tornier shouted, "Let's pole!"

The crew poled the barge up the river the rest of the day, without much conversation, Pons wondering if the *Rouge* would return. To keep the lookouts sharp, that night there were two four-hour watches.

As the sun rose the next morning it was only slightly misty, unlike the blanketing the previous morning. The barge was under way. Tornier and Pons traded stories as they poled. Upstream in the distance, Pons saw a single punt come around a river bend. "Is that a fisherman?"

"Could be, but the timing and location concerns me." Tornier hollered, "Carlette! Wake up and take the steerboard." He raised his voice for the crew. "Keep watch!"

Two more punts appeared from around the bend and the strangers on the three looming boats donned red kerchiefs. Tornier yelled, "*The Rouge*! They are back!

"It doesn't make any sense. Now that they know Cluniac

monks are on board, why would they attack? They know the nobles of Burgundy would hunt them down if they harmed any clergy! Pons, can you and your men swim?" The monk nodded. "Jump off and go ashore now. We are close to the riverbank. They will not bother with you; they must be back for the cargo!"

"Why can't we all jump? And your wife!"

"No, the *Rouge* soaked this barge with my parents' blood! We will not leave."

Three more punts approached to intercept them from the riverbank to their right. Carlette turned the barge toward the center of the river. Tornier shouted, "I fear it's too late for you to flee!"

The three punts were closing fast, running with the current. Chard hefted a long pole as did the two crew members on the shore side of the barge. Tornier, Pons, and Guilen lined the river side. The brigands timed their assault so all six punts would reach the barge at once. Carlette had planned her turn well, and the barge crashed into a punt, swamping the vessel. Tornier drove two brigands into the water with a long pole as their punt banged against the barge hull. Then he thrust the heavy pole downward with all his strength puncturing a punt's deck, and it began to sink. Pons jabbed at another punt full of brigands. Defending next to him, Guilen knocked two of the Rouge to the deck of another punt, blocking others from boarding the barge.

At the shore side attack, the brigands had pulled one of Tornier's crewmen over the side. The punts thumped against the hull of the barge as the *Rouge* boarded. Carlette turned the steerboard so the swifter current in the center of the river caught the front of the barge and swung it around. The stern smashed into the punts throwing several of the brigands into the water. Although the mule remained tied, it was surrounded by chaos and it brayed amid the grunting and shouting of men and clacking of weapons. Carlette hurried across the barge, grabbed the monks' walking staves, threw one to Guilen, and ran to Chard thrusting the other into his hands. "It's close quarters, use this instead."

On the steerboard side of the barge a pair of Rouge, one armed with a club and the other with a knife, had boarded. Guilen kept them at bay, staying out of range as he smashed their hands and jabbed their faces using the full extension of the staff. Tornier had two knives and was spinning, drawing blood as other thieves jumped back. Pons made repeated thrusts with a long pole keeping another boarding party off the barge. He heard Tornier shout, "WATCH OUT." Distracted, he glanced away from his opponents. Tornier swept a long pole at head level across the deck, knocking a pair of brigands overboard. Pons ducked but the men in the punt yanked on his long pole, pulling him headlong into the punt's hull. His forehead struck hard and he disappeared under the surface.

Now I feel free! Free of the world. No sound, no senses, just floating in bliss! The grotto water is warmer than I remember. But she is just as sensuous! I have returned to her. As before, she pulls me to her. Primavera is calling me. PONS! PONS! But she is holding me too tight. I can't breathe!

Chard and Guilen together pulled Pons out of the river by his arms. "His face is pale . . . he's blue!" shouted Guilen. "He's drowned!" As they hauled his limp body up the side of the barge his stomach was squeezed against the edge of the boat and a geyser of water gushed from his mouth.

"Pons!" Chard slapped his face. Pons opened his eyes as they helped him sit up. He coughed out more water. Chard said, "God's blessing is on you! You were lost! We thought the fall had drowned you. It is a miracle you are breathing!"

The *Rouge* withdrew on their punts, running with the current downstream. Tornier, Carlette, and their remaining crewman had tied up on the shore. They retrieved a punt abandoned by the Rouge and searched for hours for their lost mate. After finding no sign of him, they poled the barge another mile upstream before dark and tied up at the shore, hoping the distance as well as the injuries to the *Rouge* would prevent another attack.

One injured Rouge had been abandoned by his mates during the fight and lay unconscious on the deck. Tornier's remaining crewman wanted to toss him over the side, angry about the loss of his crewmate. Pons pleaded that they at least keep him on board until they could turn him over to the authorities when they reached Lyon.

The monks gathered with the couple and crew member and prayed for the lost mate.

Later that night Pons was awakened by grunts and found Tornier striking and interrogating the Rouge prisoner. He intervened. "Good man, that is not the Christian way! Leave him be!"

Tornier stopped and then looked back at Pons. "All he would say was, 'Cluny.'"

The next day, there was not much conversation while they poled toward Lyon, the crew continuing to mourn their loss. In the afternoon, they arrived at the busy river port of Lyon where the River Saone joined the Rhone. As the monks disembarked on the right bank of the Saone, Carlette called out, "Good luck at Cluny. You are hard workers and brave fighters. You've earned my respect."

"Pons, thank you for stopping me from . . . going too far." Tornier stood next to the brigand sitting on the deck with his hands and feet tied.

Pons waved. "God bless you all. And may your crewmate rest in peace."

They were on land again and it would take three days' travel to reach Cluny. The next afternoon they arrived in the walled village of Anse on a small hill overlooking the Saone River. The monks could not find a church, so they headed for the castle of the local lord which overlooked the center of the village. From a side street, a priest intercepted them and welcomed them to Anse. "*Bonjour*, Brothers!"

"*Bonjour,* Father," Pons replied. "We could not find your church. We left Lyon several hours ago and wanted a quiet place to recite our Vespers service."

He held out his arm as they walked, "Welcome to the Chapel of Saint Cyprien, it is a short walk. We will take communion together." They approached a wooden door which appeared to be set in the city wall. The priest ushered them into a small chapel. "They built this sanctuary into the ancient Roman walls of the village, which hid it from casual view. The walls merge so well. That is why you couldn't find the chapel."

After their service and communion, the priest studied them, examining their clothes as if he had just seen them for the first time. He chuckled. "Brothers, did you take the wrong road out of Lyon?"

Pons frowned. "Isn't this the way to Cluny?"

"Yes, but I thought you might be going to Citeaux.

"I receive much news and gossip here. Our hamlet is a stopping place for many pilgrims and clergy, traveling to and from Cluny. And there have been important church councils held here, perhaps because we are in a neutral place between Lyon, Macon, and Cluny. The Archbishop of Lyon and the Bishop of Macon are always at odds with Cluny's abbot. But it is not my position to argue the point of each order."

"Father, we are Benedictine monks relocating from Saint Pons to Cluny. I am Pons and this is Chard and Guilen. Our monastery is isolated and we do not know of these things. Being in the secular world for less than a month, I have had to learn how to live in a new way."

"Yes, son, and the hardest task is to remain true to Christ's teachings. Have you ever heard of Sanctus Pontius? I ask because of your name."

"Yes, of course. The monastery where I grew up is dedicated to him."

"I didn't mean Saint Pons of Cimiez, but Sanctus Pontius de Carthago, Saint Pons of Carthage. I was educated at Cluny, which has an extensive library. There I read of the martyrdom of Sanctus Cyprianus, Saint Cyprien, written by his close friend, Saint Pons of Carthage. This chapel is dedicated to Saint Cyprien."

"I look forward to reading the account, Father." *After all the violence, I can return to reading of ancient ancestors, the routine of living as a monk, and managing the library!*

"God be with you, brothers. I will show our small chapel, fix you something to eat, then it will be time for the Compline, no? And after, you will sleep on comfortable pallets."

The brothers woke before sunrise for Prime, then said farewell to the kind priest and were soon on the well-trodden way, forty miles to Cluny. That day they made it halfway as they stopped at the Priory of Saint Romaine. They learned that according to legend, Saint Romaine had brought food to the eventual founder of their order, Saint Benedict, while the saint had meditated in a cave in Italy for three years.

The monks left the priory after sunrise eager to arrive at Cluny before dark. They had left the banks of the Saone River miles ago and the scent of the rivers they had become used to was left behind, replaced by the fresh air from a bubbling creek. Cominius drank as Pons patted his neck and back. “Brothers, there were a few times I thought our arrival in Cluny was not in the Lord’s plan. I was occupied with all the fear, violence, and sorrow for those who died, good and evil, in the brigands’ attack. But after stopping at the priory in Saint Romaine, I recall what Tornier told me when I found him interrogating the wounded brigand. The man kept saying ‘Cluny.’ And how unusual it was for rivermen to threaten monks, especially from Cluny.

“I recognize that I am naïve, my life formed in seclusion at our monastery. The evil and corruption of the secular world has not surprised me, but I am disappointed by the deviation from Benedictine’s rules at the monasteries we have visited. The closer we get to Cluny, the more inattention there is to the rules of the Benedictine Order. So the laxity must originate from Cluny.”

“And the brigand’s mention of Cluny,” added Guilen, “did the threat from the Rouge also come from Cluny?”

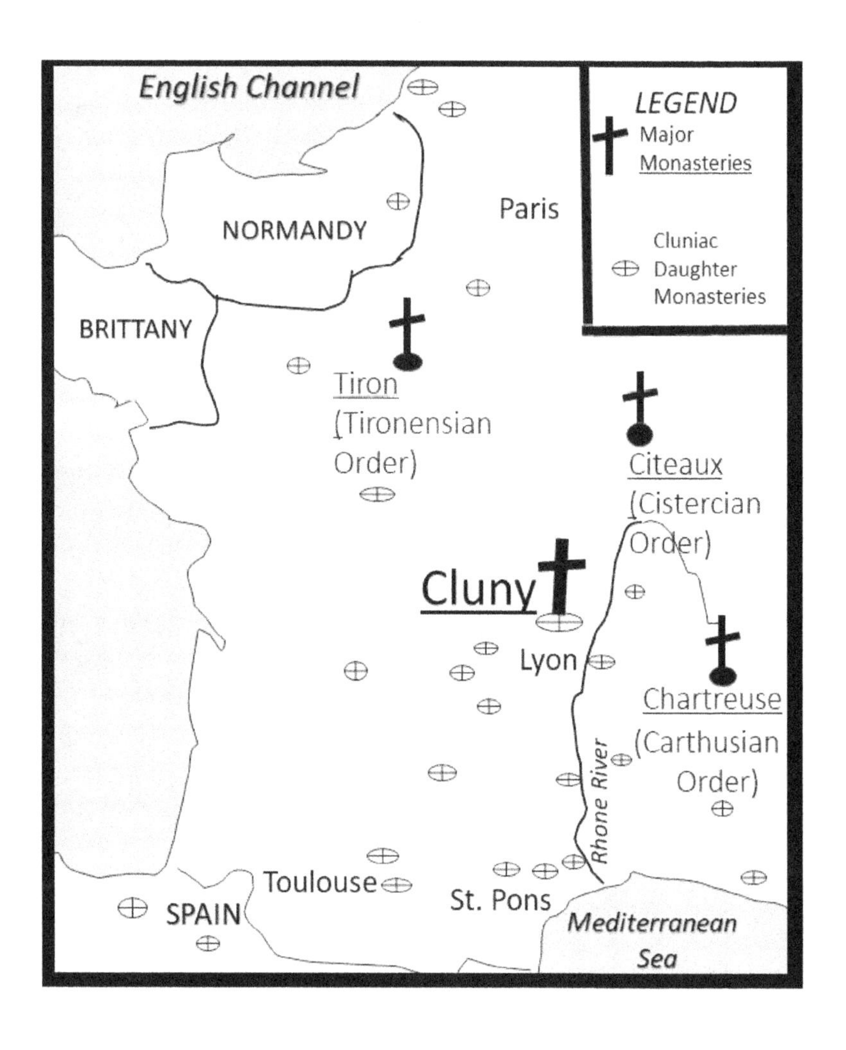
English Channel
LEGEND
Major Monasteries
Cluniac Daughter Monasteries
Paris
NORMANDY
BRITTANY
Tiron (Tironensian Order)
Citeaux (Cistercian Order)
Cluny
Lyon
Chartreuse (Carthusian Order)
Rhone River
Toulouse
St. Pons
SPAIN
Mediterranean Sea

CHAPTER VIII CLUNY ABBEY

The three monks walked without conversation the last miles to Cluny, and Pons thought of all his experiences during his first journey in the world outside the monastery. The trek was easy through the gently rolling hills, leaving his mind free to wander among images from their journey. *The sun is warm, the way is calm. What a contrast to the battle a few days ago on the river! God has truly protected us!*

The road led to Cluny Monastery's main gate, the *Porte d'Honneur*. The monastery was surrounded by walls, higher and more robust than those at Saint Pons. The two towers of the abbey church inside the fortifications soared above the walls. A huge church with its massive bell tower was enclosed by scaffolds and was under construction. Foot and equestrian traffic passed through the open gates and there was no sign of guards. Guilen dismounted Cominius and led the mule through the gate. The entrance was smooth earth, void of grass, trodden by the high volume of traffic in and out the gateway. Beyond the compacted entrance was a meadow bisected by a gravel road several hundred paces long. The road, lined by cypress trees, led to the monastery, an immense collection of large stone buildings which dominated the landscape. As they paused to take in the wonder of their new home, Guilen dropped his reins and their lone mule sauntered to the meadow to graze. "Cominius, you haven't had sweet grass for a while." He joined his brothers, transfixed by the vast monastery. "This abbey is much larger than Saint Pons."

"There are nearly 300 monks living here," said Pons. "When the expansion of the basilica is complete, I imagine decades from now, it will be the largest church in the world. Guilen, do you think I am capable of managing the scriptorium at such a place?"

"Certainly . . ." he glanced at Chard. "With our help!"

From behind them, a gruff voice shouted, "Not only do you spy on the Benedictines, but your mules steal their grass!"

The trio spun toward the gate to see two burly soldiers approaching them. One had drawn his sword. "What?" Pons uttered. He let his staff fall to the ground. His brothers followed his example. Pons held his open palms to his side. "We *are* Benedictines and have come to work, pray, and study at the abbey. I am Pons of Melgueil and will assume the duties as sacrist. Here, I have my summons to Cluny."

He removed the parchment from his shoulder bag and handed it to the guard. Pons noted the soldier didn't even glance at it. *Perhaps he can't read.* "This is a forgery. You want to infiltrate Cluny. Look at your gray habits. Did you think you could fool us?"

"We were told to look for him," added the second guard as he drew his sword.

His words agitated the first guard even more. "Yes . . . um, *them* . . . the Cistercians! The White Monks are not welcome here!"

"At least tell Abbot Hugh that I am here!" implored Pons.

The guards separated and began moving to the flanks of the monks. "Sure, the Abbot. I am going to talk to the Abbot! Leave now! No, better yet, resist. Give me a reason to use my sword."

The guards were being cautious and kept their distance as they continued around the monks to get behind them. Pons's staff lay on the ground in front of him. He placed his foot on top of it, rolled it back, then deftly snapped his foot forward, hooking his toes under the staff. He flicked it up, and in two quick side-to-side strikes, he whipped it left, then right, and smashed the guards' hands. They both dropped their swords and Guilen and Chard promptly retrieved them. One guard held his wrist as he looked behind them. "You had better drop those weapons."

Riding at a gallop across the meadow was a tonsured monk in a black habit. He was escorted by several mounted soldiers, wearing helmets, chain mail, and bearing spears. Cominius calmly looked up as they passed him grazing. The leader jumped to the ground and seized the swords from the monks. “Take them to the *donjon*!”

An hour later, wearing their new black habits, Guilen, Chard, and Pons attended Vespers in the great chapel with hundreds of their brethren. Prior Thomas had welcomed them to Cluny after their frightening affair with the gate watchmen and he had punished the guards with confinement. Pons had thanked the prior for liberating them and when he was issued a new habit, he had removed the vial sewn in his old habit and had given the sliver of the True Cross to Thomas to pass on to the abbot.

As the monks sank on their knees to pray in the spacious basilica, Pons signed to his brothers from Saint Pons: *Good!* He hoped the peaks and valleys of the outside world would now settle to a familiar monastic routine. They were pleased that evening when they were assigned beds, near each other in the monks' dormitory.

After Prime the next morning, Prior Thomas escorted the trio to the scriptorium and promptly left. The hall was set up as at Saint Pons Abbey, with tall windows for daylight, but it was much larger. At his former abbey, nine copyists had worked at the steep sloped desks, sitting on foldable x-stools. Here there were at least four or five times as many scribes and they sat on benches with backrests. Pons did not announce himself as new sacrist nor interrupt the scribes, but simply began his accustomed stroll from desk to desk to view the copyists' work. A few looked up, a couple nodded, but none of them seemed fazed. The monks remained focused on their work. *Good. Whoever was the former sacrist, he led a disciplined group.* Pons turned to Guilen and Chard and whispered, “I will need you both to help me supervise. You know my expectations from working in the scriptorium in Saint Pons. At the conclusion of each session, we will gather and discuss the needs of the copyists.” At that, the trio spread out and moved among the desks.

Several hours later, just before the mid-morning Terce service, Prior Thomas, the deputy to Abbot Hugh of Cluny, entered the scriptorium. “Brother Pons, come with me. I want to show you the library.”

They ascended the stairs to the third floor. The library hall was immense, as large as the floor below filled with copyists’ desks, but instead was wall-to-wall with shelves. There were more books, codices, and scrolls than he could count. Pons’s eyes teared. The prior said, “This must be your calling, Brother Pons.”

At noon the brothers assembled for the Sext service. The architect Hezelon, a Cluniac monk from Liege, had wisely located the new *Maior Ecclesia*, The Great Church, such that it did not interfere with the entrance to the older chapels. He also suspended work during the monks’ Liturgy of the Hours to provide a quiet and meditative atmosphere for the services. After Sext, Pons joined other monks strolling the monastery grounds. Pons visited the stables to check on Cominius and found the mule was comfortable in his new surroundings. He rejoined Chard and Guilen in the meadow between the abbey and the main gate. They enjoyed the sunny but cooler than normal weather of late summer. Every monk wore a habit dyed black. There were no grey or faded habits as Pons had seen in the other Benedictine monasteries they had visited. Guilen spread his arms wide. “I wonder why the monks haven’t planted gardens in this large meadow.”

Chard looked around. “They planted these trees, but they do not bear fruit, and where are their gardens? I didn’t see any yesterday outside the main gate either.”

“I was also surprised that the stable and browsing paddock were large yet with so few horses and mules.” Pons gently clasped Chard on the shoulder. “But we haven’t explored the whole monastery yet, brothers.”

Their attention turned to the pounding of horses entering the main gate, *Porte d'Honneur*. The sound echoed through the portal and off the stone walls of the monastery. The bass staccato suggested the gait of the massive horses ridden by knights. The three monks watched as a troop of mounted soldiers rode through the gate, followed by a black, enclosed carriage. The coat of arms of Cluny Abbey was displayed on the side of the coach: two gold keys crossed over a sword on a red shield. As the column traversed the road through the meadow, a rearguard of twenty more pairs of mounted escorts followed. The monks of Cluny hardly took notice, as if the occurrence was common.

Pons glanced with surprise at his companions. "So many great horses and knights? Is a noble visiting . . . or a king?"

A passing monk had overheard him. "You must be new to Cluny. That is Abbot Hugh and his entourage. He is returning from one of his many travels. The escorts are knights, yes, but they are mercenaries, professional soldiers hired by the abbot from the local nobles. The great horses are destriers, the breed of warhorses ridden by knights."

Speaking above the tumult of hooves and wheels crunching along the gravel road, the monks introduced themselves and traded courtesies. Pons waited for their new acquaintance to leave, then whispered, "The expense! This is hypocrisy!"

After Vespers, as the monks found their way to the large refectory for dinner, Prior Thomas intercepted Pons in the cloister. "You're late! Why didn't you come to Abbot Hugh's residence?" Pons looked confused. "I told the librarian to inform you. The abbot has requested that his obedientiaries have dinner in his suite."

Pons accompanied Thomas to the abbot's residence, a palace-like, two-story stone building. *Why wasn't I told to come to the dinner? It is not a good way to make a first impression with the abbot, being late. Why does he need this large house? It's not for guests. I have seen the large guest residence.* He felt heat rise to his tonsured scalp. *Control yourself and do not be surprised if this dinner is extravagant. God prepare me!*

They entered a hall where a handful of monks sat around a large wooden table. Silence greeted Pons's entrance. Hugh, Cluny's ancient patriarch, was eighty-four years old and tonsured, but wore a beard, in contrast to the clean-shaven monks. He sat at the head of the table. His bright, intelligent eyes belied his stooped posture and the furrows of age lining his face. He locked on Pons. "Who are you?"

Pons bowed. "*Bonjour* Father Abbot. I am Pons of Melgueil, the new sacrist."

"No one told me you had arrived." Then Hugh stood, lost his bewildered look and opened his arms to greet the monk. Pons bowed, and the abbot embraced him. "Come join us, Brother!"

Pons did not dwell on the awkward start and forgot the extravagance of the dinner as the officers of the monastery welcomed him to Cluny. The immense abbey required many more administrators than at Saint Pons. There, he had been third in line behind the abbot and prior. Here he was fourth, as sacrist, below the sub-prior. In addition to the traditional officers, the cellarer, cantor, almoner, and treasurer, there were other specialized positions. The chamberlain, whom he had met when he was issued his black habit, oversaw clothing. The circuitor, in charge of discipline at the monastery, notified Pons that one of the guards he had disarmed had been sent to the infirmary with a broken wrist. Pons also met the guest-master who managed the large residence inn which was needed to accommodate the many dignitaries who visited Cluny. He was introduced to the librarian, who would report to him. Pons thought this would be helpful; with the size of the scriptorium and library there would be much to do. At Saint Pons Abbey as sacrist he had taken care of the vestments, the scriptorium, and the library himself.

Part way through the dinner Abbot Hugh stood and raised his wine goblet. Pons peered at the expensive glass. *Why the extravagance? Use simple cups.* The abbot toasted, "May God guide the work of our new sacrist, Pons of Melgueil! And as Saint Augustine said, 'Pray as though everything depended on God. Work as though everything depended on you.'"

The monks toasted, set down their glasses, and applauded. Pons glanced around at the faces turned his way, smiled, then humbly looked down. Hugh remained standing and produced the glass vial containing the fragment that Pons had carried from Melgueil. *He is going to announce it here. My mother will get her wish and I will be important from the day I arrive.* "The Lord has also sent us a fragment of the True Cross!" There were quiet praises from the gathering, mixed with a few gasps. "Thomas said that he arranged for the fragment to be delivered by crusaders who had returned from the Holy Land. The relic will attract more pilgrims here, which will mean an increase in donations, sorely needed now that King Alfonso has discontinued his annual gift to Cluny."

What? Thomas lied! I gave the fragment to the prior! Droplets of sweat formed on Pons's scalp. The gathering concluded, and preoccupied with the falsehood, he began to follow a few of the officers to the next service, Compline. *And why didn't they tell the abbot I had arrived? That would have been the prior's duty. When we were accosted at the entry one of those guards had said, The prior said to watch out for them—Cistercians." I don't understand—the monastic orders are not at war . . .* Pons's thoughts were interrupted by Thomas as he called across the room, "Pons, Abbot Hugh wants you to stay." Pons composed himself and refused to look Thomas in the eyes, knowing he would lose control.

The table had been cleared and a large parchment was rolled out. Pons recognized it was a map of western Europe and the printed word *Citeaux* caught his attention. Hugh was seated and five monastic obedientiaries stood around the table: the prior, the sub-prior, the treasurer, the circuitor, and Pons. Hugh pointed to a cross on the map. "I just returned from Tiron." He looked at Pons. "A few years ago your godfather, Pope Paschal, made Poitiers Abbey subordinate to Cluny, which Bernard of Poitiers opposed, so he left our order. Bernard has built a monastery at Tiron and preaches without my authorization. His followers consider him the head of the new Tironensian Order. During my visit there, he was respectful, but he refused to place his abbey under Cluny."

The abbot pointed to another cross on the map identified as *Chartreuse.* "Here is where Bruno of Cologne founded his Carthusian Order twenty years ago. The monks also follow the Benedictine rule, but choose to stay isolated in the mountains, out of contact with us.

"I believe here is our greatest threat," he pointed to Citeaux, northeast of Cluny. "Robert Molesme, a former Benedictine abbot, founded a monastery here based on a strict adherence to Saint Benedict's rules. Bruno, whom I just mentioned, visited him at Citeaux for advice, so they think alike. See . . ." he pointed to the map, "they are coordinating, they are surrounding Cluny.

"When you are . . ." the abbot was looking at Pons and halted, "when these rebellious monasteries send out missionaries to establish daughter abbeys, we must dissuade them."

"And, Abbott Hugh," said Pons, "on my journey here to Cluny, I met Cistercian monks on the road near Arles." Pons regretted he'd said that when the abbot's face reddened.

Hugh calmed. "They are that far south? I still believe we can reunite with them. Christian monks all follow the same Rules of Saint Benedict."

Pons did not detect irony in any of their expressions. *They believe they are loyal to the Benedictine order. I see all the leniencies. The soldiers, the horses, laypeople serving feasts, the abbot's huge house, the dyed habits. The extravagance I have seen here. No wonder the Cistercians and other orders are rebelling against Cluny!*

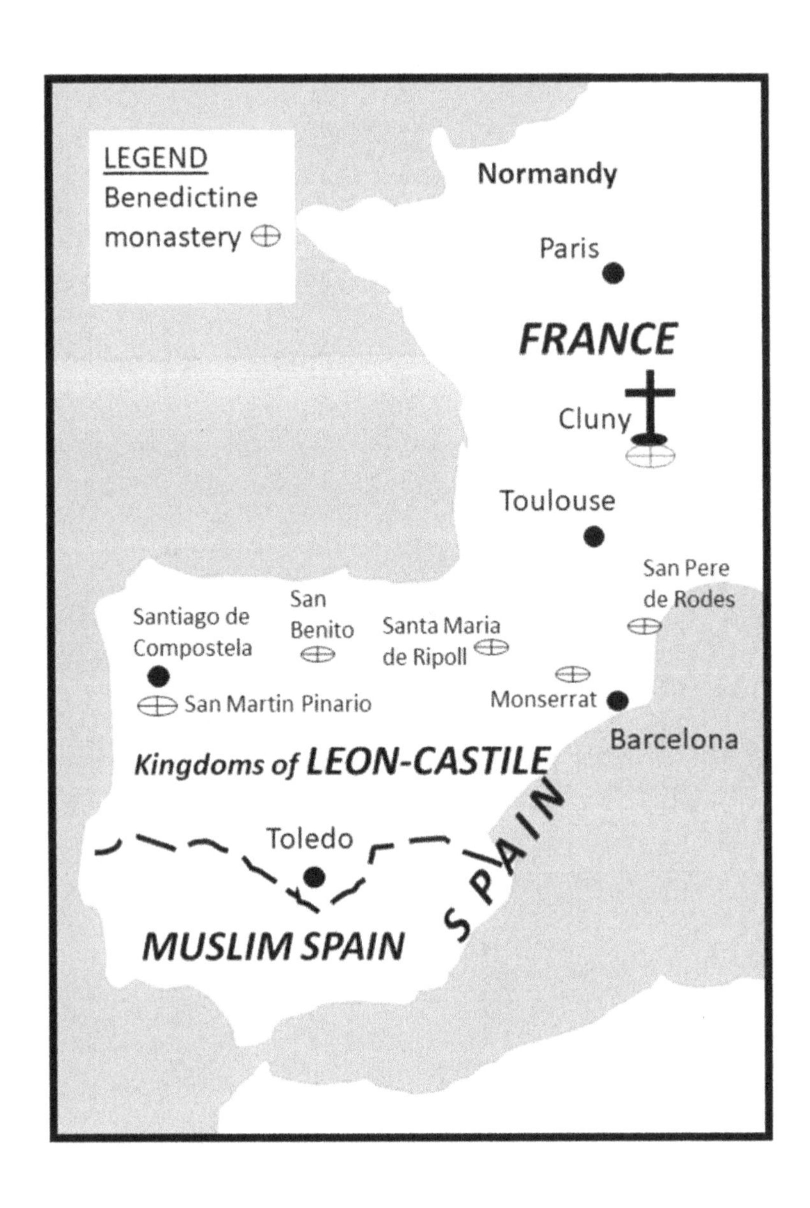
LEGEND
Benedictine monastery
Normandy
Paris
FRANCE
Cluny
Toulouse
San Pere de Rodes
Santiago de Compostela
San Benito
Santa Maria de Ripoll
San Martin Pinario
Monserrat
Barcelona
Kingdoms of LEON-CASTILE
SPAIN
Toledo
MUSLIM SPAIN

CHAPTER IX THE LIBRARY

For several weeks after Pons arrived in Cluny, he explored the monastery and discovered the immensity of the institution. There were four dormitories, the largest for the monks, one for novices, a dormitory for laymen, and the guest residence. The monks spent their time studying and attending the offices of the day, and praying, but not physically working. The laymen managed the stables, farmed the fields and gardens, and performed cooking and housekeeping duties. After one evening meal, he ambled through the cloister with his brothers from Saint Pons. "We have been here several weeks. Are you adjusting? I myself am disappointed with the laxity of the work ethic."

There was a long pause and they continued strolling, then Chard spoke. "I like it here. It is different from Saint Pons, but now we are at the center of the Order! Assigning the labor to the laymen makes sense. Then we can concentrate on prayer and study and become closer to God. And we have been having meat more often, not just for special meals. The monks here sometimes whisper during meals, instead of using signs. That's easier anyway. And I cannot forget the grand entrance of the abbot a few days after we arrived—those magnificent horses!"

Pons absorbed Chard's comment as they strode quietly along the colonnaded walkway surrounding a courtyard. At the center of the cloister, songbirds chirped and darted across the sunny garden, vying for a place to splash in the small fishpond. Guilen cleared his throat. "I am impressed by the generosity of the monastery in supplying for the needs of the poor, and also the acceptance of the public into the infirmary for treatment."

Neither Guilen nor Chard is critical of Cluny. I was going to discuss my suspicions about the prior with them, but can I trust them?

Daily routines helped Pons forget the anxiety he had developed the first few days after their arrival at Cluny. He had to discipline himself to concentrate on managing the copyists, as the huge library beckoned him to spend hours perusing the many tomes and documents.

One night after Matins, the service two hours after midnight, Pons couldn't fall back to sleep, so he lit a candle and made his way through the scriptorium and climbed the stairs to the library. There he found a classical document which caught his attention, another volume of Roman history of the early Republic, by Titus Livius. In 321 B.C., the Romans and the Samnites, a mountain tribe in central Italy, were preparing for war. Pons read: *"The Samnite leaders representing the four Samnite tribes, elected Pontius Gaius as commander-in-chief of the Samnite legions. Gaius was the son of Pontius Herennius, a leading Samnite statesman." Again, I find the surname Pontius, my name written in Latin.*

A stair step creaked as if in pain. Pons paused and turned, expecting to see the glow of candlelight preceding a monk ascending the staircase. There was none. He waited a few moments. "Hello!" There was no answer, and he returned to the document. He read on and shortly the candle flame fluttered as if from a waft of air. He knew the shutters were closed and looked back and forth, then stood and raised the candle but saw nothing. The story drew him back to reading, but after another hour he tired and made his way to the stairs by candlelight. Pons sensed a wisp of air on the back of his neck. As he was turning to look, he was shoved from behind and he plunged down the stairs.

Guilen noticed Pons had missed Lauds service and found him unconscious at the bottom of the library stairs. After reviving Pons, he helped him to the infirmary. Pons spent the next couple of days there, frequently vomiting, bruised, and with headaches from the huge knot on the side of his head. The infirmarian gave him willow bark tea for his migraines. He couldn't remember how he had fallen, but was relieved his candle had gone out when he fell, avoiding a fire in the library.

Months passed. Pons recovered and was busy with the routine of the eight daily services, supervising the scriptorium, and in his free time, reading classical Roman texts. But he was not sleeping well and tired more easily than he remembered when he lived at Saint Pons Abbey. At first he thought the injury might be affecting his energy, but then he noticed that the copyists were also fatigued during their work, especially in the afternoons.

Pons left Guilen and Chard to supervise the copyists one day and joined the laymen in the gardens hoeing and weeding. The next day, he sent Chard to the fields and the next after that, Guilen worked with the farmers. They felt better and energized. Pons had copyists take turns working in the fields or under the direction of the routier, the layman in charge of the stables. Initially there was grumbling among the monks, but after a month the complaints stopped, and some even gave their approval. Pons, however, was called to the abbot's office.

Prior Thomas sat in the other high-backed chair next to Pons as Abbot Hugh sat across from them behind his desk. "Brother Pons, Thomas told me the laymen's stewards have complained that you have sent your copyists to spy on them. The stewards report it makes their workers nervous and interferes with production. The farms are very bountiful, supply all our food, and the abbey derives profits from the surplus."

"Father Abbot," Pons bowed his head. "I believe the Holy Spirit has guided me to defend Saint Benedict's rules: *'Idleness is inimical to the soul; and therefore, the brethren ought to be occupied with manual work. Gathering in the crops with their own hands; for then they are truly monks, when they live by the work of their own hands, as did our fathers and the apostles.'*

"I also am working in the fields as are the copyists, and it invigors us to be more productive. The time they are gardening or working does not reduce the amount of work they accomplish at the scriptorium."

Hugh smiled. "Yes, Brother Pons, you have accurately quoted Saint Benedict's Rule . . . Chapter 48, *Concerning the Daily Manual Work*. However, the prior," he peered at Thomas, "said your monks were *supervising*. You say they were working? Doing manual work?"

"Yes, Father Abbot."

Thomas was agitated. "But the stewards . . ."

"Pons, you may return to the scriptorium."

Thomas began to stand. "Prior Thomas, you will stay."

It was two hours after midnight, Matins had just concluded, and most of the monks went back to sleep for a few hours before the next service. Pons stole away to the library and eagerly continued the story of the Samnite general, Pontius Gaius. *The Roman legions marched south to relieve an allied city besieged by the Samnites. There were two routes they could take: a longer, easier way around the mountains or a shorter route through the narrow Caudine Valley. Gaius sent his scouts posing as shepherds to lure the Romans into the gorge.*

Pons turned the page of the codex and found a loose sheet of parchment tucked between the pages. It was a letter addressed to William Saint Thierry. At the bottom of the page he saw it was from Robert Molesme, the founder of the Cistercian Order. As he read the document, he realized it was an apologia, a defense, of the split of the Cistercians from the Cluniac order. Certain phrases caught his attention: " . . . *the Cluniacs go so far as to count frugality avarice, and sobriety austerity, while silence is reputed gloom. Conversely, slackness is called discretion, extravagance liberality, chattering affability, guffawing cheerfulness, soft clothing and rich caparisons are the requirements of simple decency, luxurious bedding is a matter of hygiene, and lavishing these things on one another goes by the name of charity . . ."*

I agree with the author of this letter! So, should I join the Cistercians, but, no . . I will do more good to advocate strict obeyance of Benedict's rules here at Cluny.

After working in the gardens and fields for several months, the copyists began to experience the benefits of the physical labor and trusted Pons's decision to start the program. But when Pons suggested to Abbot Hugh and his staff that *all* the Cluny monks return to a nominal amount of work in the fields, there were protests from the officers. Hugh did not order the officers to require the monks under their supervision to work, but left it to their own discretion. Although none of the officers followed Pons's example, many monks joined in the work voluntarily.

A few months later, Hugh called Pons to his residence. "Perception is reality, Pons. I know you are doing good work and I believe that God has guided you. But the brothers are used to their ways and gossip cannot be controlled. Rumors abound that you are a Cistercian infiltrator. And the prior has reported that you are authorizing non-Christian, classical documents to be copied. An indispensable part of every monastery is a library. A monastery without a library is like a castle without an armory. And the great defense in the monastic armory should be the Bible. Have you failed to meet any of the orders for the illuminated Bibles?"

Pons could only shake his head as his temper welled up, but he forced out, "No, Father Abbot." *Is my suspicion of the prior unfounded? It has to be the librarian! The librarian was probably frustrated by the copyists spending time gardening, so he used it to incriminate me.* But by the time he left the meeting, Pons was encouraged. The abbot did not reprimand him on duplicating the Latin classics because his copyists were fulfilling the contracts for the Bibles, from which Cluny derived much profit. Pons believed that the copyists were healthier from the gardening and thus had become more productive.

The daily cycle of prayer services was ritual and constant despite the seasons, both in the year and in the temperaments of the monks. New tasks became routines, and Pons was soon a familiar presence. It had been almost a year since he had arrived at Cluny. One day he was making his rounds and glanced over a copyist's shoulder. He saw an entry on the inner cover of the codex being copied.

May the sword of anathema slay.

If anyone steals this book away.

Pons thought it was a creative addition and did not tell the scribe to remove it. The poem inspired Pons to mount a sign engraved with the same words above the entrance to the library. Pons was now keener to the monks adding their own comments. Over the next few weeks, he noticed other inscriptions. In a copy of a *Book of Hours*, read during the services, he saw in the margin:

This is sad! O little book!

A day will come in truth when someone over your page will say, "The hand that wrote it is no more."

Pons saw no reason to remove it. He let the scribes continue to add notes, as long as they were not written in a Bible. But, eventually it got out of hand. He discovered at the end of a book of hymns being copied for a chapel in nearby Anse, on the last page was written:

Now I've written the whole thing: for Christ's sake give me a drink.

Next to the script was a drawing of a cup enclosed by a hand, as if toasting. Pons noted the fingers were well drawn. The sketch gave him an idea, and he forgot about reprimanding the scribe. *We will create a book of illustrations of the hand signals used during the services, when the vow of silence is in effect. Several hand signals I saw at Montmajour and Cluny are different from those at Saint Pons. It can be used to standardize the signs among the monasteries.*

Pons recruited the copyist who so artistically sketched the hand and created a booklet illustrating the hand signals used by the monks. The abbot was pleased and approved making copies for the other Benedictine monasteries.

Wishing to add more Greek and Roman classics to Cluny's archives, Pons consulted the librarian, a senior monk who had held his office for many years. *I am going to have to use my best diplomacy, if it is true he is against me. Perhaps he is being vindictive because after the death of the former sacrist, he thought he should have been promoted instead of me?*

Pons and the librarian sat on stools next to several desks. The seats could be folded flat for portability and storage by closing the x-shape. The desks were the same design as those used by the copyists, with steep slopes, a lip at the bottom to hold books, and weights on strings to keep the pages open. Surrounding them were shelves and racks containing thousands of documents. It was midday, the sixth hour, just after Sext service. Sunbeams highlighted white motes suspended in the air and filled the room with dustlight. "Brother, I am grateful to you and the former sacrist for maintaining such a magnificent library. There are almost 500 books in the library at Saint Pons, but there must be thousands here at Cluny."

"I treasure books, too, Brother Pons. We have nearly two thousand volumes. The abbot encourages the monks to study and read two hours a day. Were the monks at Saint Pons provided daily times to read?"

"No, some read during their free time. What a pleasant distraction to the daily routine. At Saint Pons we did have Bible passages read aloud to assemblies of monks, but we did not have books on law, arithmetic, music, or science, as here in Cluny."

"Those are for private reading," said the librarian, "as are the volumes of Greek and Roman manuscripts. We have manuscripts by the Roman authors, Plinius the Elder and the Younger, Livius, Vitruvius, and Vergilius."

"In these Roman writings," said Pons, "I have seen references to books by Cicero, a great orator and statesman, and they also mention that Caesar wrote commentaries. Where are the nearest libraries that could have copies by these authors?"

The librarian looked down and hesitated. Pons thought he wouldn't be cooperative, but he was simply thinking. "The nearest libraries with large archives are at the Abbey of Saint Germain in Paris and at Montmajour."

Pons gazed into space as his bottom lip curled. "Paris. I have heard of a philosopher in Paris who leads theological discussions and includes logic. It sounds intriguing."

The librarian's face soured. "That is Peter Abelard. He is very popular with the young scholars and is a brilliant dialectician. It is said he has never lost a debate. But he is not popular with the Church leaders. I do not think the abbot wants any copies of his treatises in the Cluny library."

"I am not looking for Abelard's writings. Because he teaches logic, perhaps he has manuscripts by Aristotle, a famous teacher who lived during the times of ancient Greece."

"I have heard of Aristotle, but I have never read any of his discourses. There is an institution in Bologna, Italy, the *Univeritas Magistrotrum et Schlarium.* It is a secular community of masters and scholars and might have copies of Aristotle's writings."

"But it will be difficult to deliver a letter to Bologna. It's not on the *Pilgrims' Way*."

"No, but we can reach the Benedictine Abbey of Saint Germain in Paris. Abbot Hugh sends riders with decrees and messages for the monasteries in Normandy and England through Saint Germain."

Within a few days, Pons sent a letter and a copy of the manual of illustrated hand signals as a gift to Saint Germain Abbey. In the correspondence, he inquired if their library had manuscripts by ancient logicians, specifically by Aristotle. He sent another query letter to Montmajour Abbey, which was carried by Benedictine missionaries traveling south. Months later, Pons had almost forgotten his requests, until he received a letter and package from Paris delivered to Cluny, along with correspondence for the abbot.

Greetings Brother Pons of Cluny,

The Saint Germain librarian passed your inquiry to me. I study and teach in Paris at the cathedral school of Notre-Dame. I am very pleased there are clergymen such as you who are interested in logic. For God gave us intelligence and free choice, so why not contemplate the Lord with all of our mind? I do not have any manuscripts by Aristotle but enclosed with this letter is a treatise by Plotinus, a Roman philosopher. If you find any by Aristotle, I am very interested in acquiring a copy. His writings could be present in the Muslim library in Cordoba, Spain. The archives there have more books, including Greek, Roman, and Christian, than all the libraries in Christendom. I was told that books are more sought out in Cordoba than a beautiful woman or a valuable gem! God Bless you,

Peter Abelard.

Within a month, Cluniac monks returning from the south and Montmajour delivered a book by Cicero to Pons in response to his letter. With these initial successes, Pons wrote to other Benedictine monasteries throughout France, sending copies of the hand signal book as gifts and at times receiving new titles for the

Cluny library. The monks of Cluny had new and refreshing reading material, and Pons stopped hearing gossip that he was secretly a Cistercian.

Pons recalled how helpful the librarian had been in contacting Paris. He remembered the night he fell down the steps and had thought, like everyone else, that he simply fell in the dim candlelight. But now a scene flashed in his mind, the instant before he tumbled down the staircase. *Someone tried to kill me! I was pushed! Now I remember hearing, sensing, that someone was in the library. Who knew I was there? Was it the librarian? He knows the layout of the library so well, he could have easily moved about in the dark. Only Chard and Guilen knew I was there. But Guilen rescued me, so it wasn't him. It can't be Chard!*

Over the next few days, he became preoccupied with the idea that someone wanted him dead. *Chard and Guilen do not have a motive, but the librarian may have one. Does he want my position? His behavior, however, does not show any evil intentions. Wait, I have been so busy, I have forgotten the prior. The day we arrived, although he intervened and punished the guards, one of them said, "The prior said to look for HIM." Then the other guard quickly corrected it to "THEM" and accused us of being Cistercian. Was he covering up a slip of his partner's tongue? And the only word the Rouge prisoner told Tornier was "Cluny." My enemy can't be Guilen or Chard. It must be someone at Cluny who has the power to hire the Rouge and to control the guards. So, could the prior have hired the rivermen? Perhaps the prior knows I am being groomed to take Abbot Hugh's place?* Over the next weeks Pons was obsessed with similar thoughts. But after a month of daily routines and the absence of new threats, Pons wondered if his imagination was out of control, and perhaps, he really had simply fallen that night.

Pons subdued his anxiety as he put his energy into improving the library. He wrote a letter to his first cousin, Count Bertrand of Toulouse, although he had never met him. Bertrand had become the count years before when his father Ramon had gone on the crusade to the Holy Land. Toulouse was home to several monasteries and a major resting stop for pilgrims on their way to Santiago de Compostela in Spain. The treasures of Spain included the great libraries of the Muslims. Pons gave the letter to missionaries going to Tours and requested they pass it to pilgrims traveling on the *Saint James Way*, which went through Toulouse on to Santiago de Compostela. He returned to his daily routine and was pleased five months later when a monk returning to Cluny handed him a letter from Toulouse. Pons read:

Dear Brother Pons,

I received your letter inquiring about Aristotle's books. Unfortunately, there are no manuscripts written by him in Toulouse. Toledo, now governed by Christians, is home to a large Arab library where translators of all religions cooperate in the name of knowledge. Muslim and Jewish scholars translate the Arabic and Hebrew manuscripts into Castilian, then Christian monks translate from Castilian into Latin. I am aware of Cluniac missionaries passing through Toulouse on their way to Benedictine abbeys in Spain, so you should appeal to them to journey to Toledo.

I will soon be moving to the Holy Land, taking my wife and son with me. My father Ramon, your uncle, died during the siege of the city of Tripoli and gave the last years of his life to recover Jerusalem. His dream was to found a Christian state to protect the Holy Land. My devotion to him compels me to carry on his vision, break the siege, and capture Tripoli. Ramon's son Alfonso, my half-brother, and his mother, Elvira of Castile, have returned to Toulouse from the Holy Land.

My ten year old son is also named Pons and as you, inherited the ancient surname of our ancestors.

I am following in the steps of my father, Ramon of Saint Gilles, in that I will not return to Toulouse but live and die in the Holy Land. May God be with you always.

Your cousin,

Bertrand, Count of Toulouse

Pons arrived at the meeting he had arranged with Abbot Hugh. It was three hours after sunrise and he had just left the Terce service. Pons recounted the contents of his cousin's letter. "Father Abbot, we have added many new titles for the Cluny library. May I have your permission to ask the Cluniac missionaries that visit

Spain to search for new documents for our library?"

The abbot smiled. "Did you pray for that last night, Pons?"

"No, Father Abbot, why do you ask?"

"The Lord knows all! I am going to the Spanish Kingdoms of Leon and Castile, then Santiago de Compostela, within a month." He raised his voice and called through the open door, "Please bring me the map that shows the monasteries in Spain."

Estienne, the subprior, came in shortly with a parchment and unrolled it on the abbot's desk. He weighted the ends with smooth river stones so it remained open. "Please close the door," the abbot added as the subprior left. The abbot pointed to the location of several Benedictine monasteries at San Pere de Rodes, Monserrat and Santa Maria de Ripoli, then held his finger on San Benito. "Here at San Benito there is a Benedictine school. Its library contains many books.

"Tell me what volumes you want and if they do not have it, while I am in Compostela I will send a delegation to Toledo to retrieve what you need."

Pons did not try to hide his excitement. "Thank you, Father Abbot! I know you visited the Spanish abbeys years ago to evaluate their progress. Have you also done pilgrimage to Compostela?"

"Yes, and this will probably be my last journey to Spain. But there is another important reason compelling me to go. King Alfonso has made his annual donation of 2,000 gold mithkals to Cluny for decades. I will visit him to show our appreciation so he will continue his support. Without it, I will have to suspend the construction of the new phase of the Cluny basilica. Cluny must delegate funds first to take care of pilgrims and to provide the less fortunate people of Burgundy with food and curative aid."

"Abbot, what is a . . . mithkal?"

"It is the Arabic gold coin used in Spain. Hmm . . . One gold mithkal is equal to over 90 silver pennies, enough to pay for the wages of a laborer for several months."

"I will be crossing the Pyrenees Mountains in a few months to make the long trip to the Kingdoms of Leon and Castile, and I will be absent for at least six months. Please ensure you do not get into conflict with Prior Thomas while I am gone."

Pons nodded, his mood turning from joy to concern as he

thought about the prior. Hugh moved from behind his desk and sat next to Pons. He placed his hand gently on Pons's shoulder, looked at the door, and whispered, "There is no reason for me to be subtle. God has guided Pope Paschal and the House of Toulouse for you to replace me when it is my time. I believe your sense of righteousness is driven by the Holy Spirit. Do not deviate from what you believe is what the Lord wants."

IRELAND
WALES
ENGLAND
NORMANDY

LEGEND
Town:
Monastery:
KINGDOM
Cardonagh
Fahan
Derry
ULAID
Bangor
CONNACHT
LAIGIN
Kells
Saint Brigid
Kildare
Dublin
Kildare Plains
Glendalough
Moone
Whitlow
Mtns.
MUNSTER
Killarney
Tullylease
Innisfallen
Barra
Skellig
Michael
IRELAND

CHAPTER X KILDARE, IRELAND

O'Broin sauntered across the meadow, amusing himself as he tossed his walking staff high above his head. It rotated in the air above him and spun toward the earth. He leaned forward and caught it behind his back. A pair of sheep dogs maneuvered his flock to new pasture. It wasn't difficult to find good grass. The Kildare Plains, The Currach of Ireland, were rich pasturelands. O'Broin gazed across the meadows where a few men tended a herd of racehorses. Beyond the plains of The Currach on the distant hillsides, more sheep were grazing, appearing as white specks on the slopes. He shouted in their direction, "Hill maggots!" The dogs glanced at him but returned to drive the flock. *Instead of tending sheep, why couldn't the monastery breed horses? They could make a good profit selling racehorses to the landed gentry.*

A group of mounted nobles arrived, dismounted, and joined the tenders and groomers. *Oh yes! There will be races today. They hold them every fortnight.* O'Broin whistled for his collies to come. Both dogs quickly obeyed and sat in front of the shepherd, waiting for his next command, but constantly turned their heads toward their flock and back to O'Broin. "Now, I am going over to watch the horse race. Be true to your name, *collies*, useful dogs, and keep the sheep together."

O'Broin wandered among the horses as the *yacheys* mounted, readying for a race across The Currach. A noble, one of the horse owners, said, "Monk, care to wager on the race?"

O'Broin shook his head. "I am a monk as you addressed me, sir. You must know we have no possessions."

"Those sheepdogs are well trained. How about them?"

"They belong to the monastery."

"See those two brown *hobbies* over there?" asked the noble.

The monk nodded.

"Those are the two fastest horses," added the man. "I will bet which horse will win the next race and wage one of the horses against one of your collies.

"I imagine the monastery could use a good horse to pull a wagon or cart?"

"A *race* horse to pull a cart?" said O'Broin.

"Certainly!" added the noble. "Have you heard of Conaire Mór the Great?"

O'Broin's brow wrinkled.

"He was an ancient Irish king who held the first races right here—but they were chariot races and this noble breed of horse, the *hobby,* pulled the war carts."

O'Broin scratched his clean-shaven chin, then rubbed the top of his head, bared from the tonsure cut. "We had a horse . . . once."

"Once? What happened to it?" asked the man.

"The bishop was visiting Kildare Monastery. When he departed he insisted on riding our only horse back to Dublin and would have it returned. He could not get the horse to move, so the abbot told him that the horse had been taught special commands. To make the horse go, you must say, 'Thank God' and to make it stop, strongly declare, 'Amen!' A few days later we received a message that the bishop and the horse were dead."

"What!"

"The bishop had ridden to the Howth cliffs to gaze at the sea, but became terrified when the horse approached the edge too fast, so he yelled, 'Amen!' He was so grateful it stopped in time, he added, 'Thank God!'"

O'Broin departed with the man laughing, returned to his flock, and observed the races from a distance, the ruckus of men yelling and horses galloping dominating the landscape. He didn't trust himself to stay as he might succumb to making a wager. The races ended, The Currach quieted, and O'Broin was again alone with the bleating of sheep and the occasional bark of a collie chasing a stray back to the flock.

I grew up tending sheep for my father and now unfortunately do the same as a monk. A nun founded Kildare Monastery, a double monastery, where I work, pray, and study with monks and nuns, who reside in adjacent buildings. My mother was educated at the abbey and is now a scribe there. She told me that I am fortunate to work, study, and pray at the monastery, renowned for creating illuminated manuscripts. So I am contributing in my way. The wool is used for making monks' habits and eventually the sheep hides will be made into vellum and become the pages of Bibles and codices. It is said that Saint Patrick found God during the six years he was a shepherd in Ireland. Ha! I don't identify with the saint's experience.

But it's not bad here. At least the monks don't eat the sheep. A monk's diet of vegetables, fruit, nuts, and bread is to my liking. And also to my liking, the monastery is a double priory. The last thought reminded O'Broin of his secret rendezvous set with pretty Orlaith after the Matins service, two hours after midnight. *We meet on the night of every right-hand half-moon. It sets by midnight, so it's dark when we are together. It helps that the monks are sleepy after the night service and stumble back to the dormitory to nap before the next service at Lauds, three hours later. At times, I have noticed other monks missing from the dormitory during those hours.*

Fortune was not on the side of the lovers this half-moon. Punishment for infractions usually progressed, starting with a monk's exclusion from common prayer services for the first offense, then lashes for the second or more serious faults, and finally expulsion after a third infraction. However, due to the type of violation, O'Broin was straightaway transferred to Glendalough Monastery in the south. Oddly enough, O'Broin was gratified with the consequences for several reasons. The abbot did not tell his family why their son was leaving Kildare, and O'Broin himself hoped to find a different sort of work besides shepherding. Although he could not discover where Orlaith was being sent, he hoped she was going to another nunnery that she would like. Thomas O'Broin, of clan O'Broin, descendants of Bran, who had been the king of Laigin five decades earlier, would not depart Kildare in disgrace. Only the abbot and a few monks knew about the affair but kept it to themselves. They had their own sins of lust.

CHAPTER XI THE ELECTION

Pons stood among a host of clergy and secular leaders. The two thousand funeral attendees included bishops, abbots, and priests from Paris, Macon, Lyon, and Clermont as well as the 300 monks of Cluny. As the Archbishop of Lyon began the memorial for Abbot Hugh, the flapping of pigeons' wings caused Pons to look upward. A hundred feet above the assembly, the cerulean April sky peeked through the unfinished barrel-vaulted ceiling. Construction had been paused. The workmen had a day off for the abbot's funeral. *The acoustics were magnificent during our sung liturgy and will be even better when the stone roof is finished. It is a shame the Maior Ecclesia was not completed before Hugh's passing. He had started the grand project.*

The foundation, floors, walls, and most of the ceiling were done and when construction was finished, the church would be the largest in Europe. The interior decorations were sparse and other than the high altar, consecrated by Pope Urban in 1095, there were only a few sculptures depicting allegories from the Bible.

Pons's gaze returned to the prior as the archbishop held out his right arm to indicate the large space where the monks were gathered. Their assemblage took less than half of the available standing room. "Construction started on this great church, this fortress of God, two decades ago, under the leadership of Abbot Hugh. He told me at that time the elderly monk Gonzo came to him with plans for this church that were given to him by Saint Peter in a dream. Then Brother Hezelon," heads turned as a few monks glanced at the architect, "transformed Gonzo's dream into reality. Of course, all of them, all the workers, all those involved, were inspired by God. Cluny has greatly expanded since its founding by William of Aquitaine, hundreds of years ago. Hugh the Great, yes, it is fitting to call him *great*. During his tenure, he was legate for the Pope many times and defended the Church against Emperor Henry's attempts to exceed papal authority and steal the right to appoint bishops. Our late abbot established new monasteries throughout Europe. There are now more than a thousand daughter abbeys where thousands of monks work, study, and pray. Abbot Hugh also established the first Cluniac convent at nearby Marcigny as well as the hospital for lepers."

Pons looked upward and his mind drifted as the archbishop continued the memorial. *This great space should inspire me . . . and make me feel closer to God, but I feel His spirit more profoundly when I am outside . . . in nature. In fact, the last few years, my spirituality has faded. The daily rituals have become boring and repetitive. I have been more stimulated by my work managing the copyists and vestments than in the liturgy.*

A pigeon flew noisily off the roof and Pons was again mindful of the sermon. "This *Maior Ecclesia* is the appropriate church for the Abbey of Cluny, for the late Pope Urban named our monastery 'the light of the world' and said 'its community has reached so high a stage of honor and religion that without doubt Cluny surpasses all other monasteries, even the most ancient.'"

The archbishop nodded to the Bishop of Macon, Berard de Chatillon, who then held Mass, reading from the sacramentary. He followed with the Cluny Prayer, joined by hundreds of voices which reverberated in the huge space. "O God, by whose grace your servants the Holy Abbots of Cluny, kindled with the flame of your love, became burning and shining lights in your Church: grant that we also may be aflame with the spirit of love and discipline, and walk before you as children of light; through Jesus Christ our Lord, who lives and reigns with you, in the unity of the Holy Spirit, one God, now and forever."

The funeral guests filed past Hugh's tomb, located in one of the five chapels at the chevet end of the church. The prior directed the officers to the abbot's residence. As the officers entered the meeting room, Prior Thomas remained outside the entrance, speaking with the Bishop of Macon and the Count of Burgundy.

Shortly, the prior and the bishop excused themselves from the count. They joined the officers inside and took seats around a large table. Thomas rose. "The count offered his assistance in organizing the election of our new abbot, but I declined. Cluny has been autonomous from secular control since its founding centuries ago. I also did not accept his request to observe our proceedings. It would be the first crack in the defense of our privileges, many of those protected by the late Hugh the Great over his long tenure."

Thomas paused and smiled at Bishop Berard of Macon. "The last election for an abbot in Cluny, that of Abbot Hugh, was in 1049, sixty years ago. We are all novices as an election committee and we are very pleased that his excellency, Bishop Berard, is here to guide us. And as Cluny is in his Excellency's diocese, he will be confirming the election."

Thomas then read from a codex containing Saint Benedict's Rules:

> "Chapter 64 Part 1: The Election of an Abbot: In choosing an abbot, the guiding principle should always be that the man placed in office be the one selected either by the whole community acting unanimously in the fear of God, or by some part of the community, no matter how small, which possesses sounder judgment."

He examined each monk to see if there would be any comment but detected only a few nods.

Thomas tilted his head toward the bishop. "Although a monk of any rank can be elected, it is likely that one of the obedientiaries in this room will be Abbot Hugh's replacement," said the bishop. "But who is the most qualified? I have known Prior Thomas for decades. He served Father Abbot Hugh with devotion and has proven to be a capable leader. I believe that this group, being pious and sound leaders, as the rules state, 'possess sounder judgment' than the community of monks. I recommend the officers elect Thomas as abbot."

For several tense moments, there were no comments, except for the clearing of throats. Estienne's voice was shaky, "The judgment of Cluniac monks is guided by their devotion to Benedict's Rule and inspired by the Lord." He gained strength as he completed his statement. "I move that we elect Hugh's replacement by a two-thirds majority of the wholly professed monks. The postulants, novices, and laymen are not qualified to vote." The officers all responded at once. It was obvious that they agreed with Estienne. The prior and bishop remained silent.

Thomas frowned and glanced at the bishop. "Does anyone disagree with Estienne's proposal?

"Very well, then the bishop and I will take leave while the subprior reads Rules 64, Parts 2 through 6. Use the Rules to compose a bulletin to guide the monks on the election. We will read it aloud at their meals." He turned over a sand hourglass. "I will return in one hour to review your document."

As he listened to the subprior read the rules, Pons was transfixed with the grains of sand falling in the hourglass. *I still do not know who my antagonist is. Hugh was wise but firm, as an abbot should be, but his kindness to me could have been deception. There were no attacks on me when he was in Spain.*

Pons's attention returned to the Estienne who stood, reading the general rules.

> "When an abbatial vacancy occurs, the right of election is transferred by jurisdiction to the monks themselves, reserving to the bishop the confirmation of the election and the benediction of the new abbot. In abbeys exempt from the bishop's diocesan jurisdiction, the confirmation and benediction are to be conferred by the Pope, the house being taxed with the expenses of the new abbot's journey to Rome. An abbot should be at least 30 years of age, of legitimate birth, a monk of the house for at least three years, unless it furnishes no suitable candidate, when a liberty is allowed of electing from another monastery, well instructed himself, and able to instruct others, one also who has learned how to command by having practiced obedience."

A quarter of the sand had flowed to the bottom of the clock. *I won't be a candidate because my tenure at Cluny does not reach three years until the end of this April. It is somewhat of a relief. But my mother will be disappointed, and what about my godfather, Pope Paschall? He would not interfere with the autonomy of Cluny. What was it Estienne read about confirmation of the election? Thomas said Bishop Berard would approve the result. Yet wouldn't Cluny be exempt from a bishop's confirmation? It is the largest and most influential abbey. If so, the Pope would have to confer.*

The subprior continued reading from Benedict's Rules:

> "Goodness of life and wisdom in teaching must be the criteria for choosing the one to be made abbot, even if he is the last in community rank. May God forbid that a whole community should conspire to elect a man who goes along with its own evil ways. But if it does, and if the bishop of the diocese or the abbots or Christians in the area come to know of these evil ways to any extent, they must block the success of this wicked conspiracy, and set a worthy steward in charge of God's house."

The obedientiaries discussed the rules and as Thomas had bid them, dictated the procedures for the election and request for nominations to the subprior who recorded their directions. Prior Thomas returned just as they finished. Shortly thereafter, the last grain of sand dropped to the bottom of the hourglass. After Estienne read the document aloud, Thomas announced, "Very good. This bulletin will be read to the brothers during the evening meal for one week and nominations may be submitted during that time. The election will be the following week. The subprior and circuitor will be in charge of tabulating the votes."

The officers left, and Pons was the last to exit. Thomas did not hide his sneer. "It's too bad for you that Abbot Hugh could not have survived through April." Pons turned away without looking back. *He has exposed himself, now that I am not a threat to become abbot. It is him.*

A week later the obedientiaries met to review the list of nominations. Estienne sat with a loose pile of tiny scraps of parchment on the table before him. Monks who had submitted nominations had printed their name and nominee on the parchment. A few who were copyists at the library wrote their name in a unique and distinctive scrawl. The subprior selected a scrap of parchment from the top of the pile and read the first name followed with the others. "Prior Thomas, Brother Allain, Guillermo of Turin, Brother Pons ..."

Prior Thomas stood abruptly, "A monk must be of the house for at least three years! Pons is not qualified."

A few nods and weak mutterings of agreement followed his outburst. Estienne glanced at the other monks. "Brother Thomas, please let us finish the nominations and then we will discuss the issue." The others nodded assent. He read a dozen more names and finished with, "Pons, Pons, Pons . . . that's the last one." He counted the hash marks he had made while reading the names and announced, "Brother Pons has the most nominations, Prior Thomas next, then Allain three, and . . ."

Thomas squirmed in his seat. "It doesn't matter how many times a candidate is nominated. And Pons, you know it is not allowed to solicit the brothers to gain nominations."

Several officers gasped at the accusation. An unexpected calmness came over Pons and he realized he had changed over the years. At one time he would have clenched his jaw muscles and sweated in anger in a situation such as this, but not now. Pons spoke, the first time in the meeting. "I forgive you, Brother Thomas. In Chapter 64, Part 16 of Saint Benedict's Election of an Abbot, the saint writes: 'Excitable, anxious, extreme, obstinate, jealous or over suspicious an abbot must not be.'"

Thomas surveyed the assembled officers. Seeing their naked disapproval of his behavior, he slumped in his chair. "I . . . I am sorry, Brother Pons." But then just as quickly as he had softened his tone, he stiffened and countered, "There is still the problem of Pons not meeting the three-year qualifying period."

All eyes turned toward Estienne as he briefly raised his hand and gently placed it on the table. "Prior Thomas, surely Saint Benedict wrote the election rules as guidelines, not as strict rules. Hugh the Great himself was elected to abbot when he was 25 years old, younger than the 30 years stated in the Rules. And Part 1 states that the abbot is 'unanimously elected.' How can that be possible with 300 monks? You are now interim abbot. If Brother Pons is elected, he could assume the abbacy at the end of April."

Estienne added, "I move that Brother Pons be placed on the ballot." The officers approved the recommendation unanimously, with the prior abstaining. Pons, now suddenly eligible, realized he had to find out if the election of the Abbot of Cluny was confirmed by a bishop or by the Pope. *As they proved during the last week, Thomas and Bishop Berard of Macon are allies. If I were elected, would the bishop withhold approval?* The meeting adjourned and as Pons stood he glanced at the scraps of parchment on which the nominations were submitted. Guilen's and Chard's distinctive signatures caught his eye. *They both nominated Prior Thomas. Well, we have indeed grown apart since we have been at Cluny.*

With the election a week away, Pons conferred with the librarian one afternoon in the scriptorium. "Are there any documents that indicate whether a bishop or the Pope is to approve the election of the abbot of Cluny?"

The librarian's face soured. "For Cluny? It is the Pope, of course! Couldn't any of the officers in the election committee tell you that?"

Pons answered, "Bishop Berard of Macon and Prior Thomas have informed us that the bishop would approve the election results."

They went up the stairs. "That Thomas. I am not surprised!" said the librarian. He extracted a parchment from a shelf. "Pope Paschall sent this document several years ago. I am sure Abbot Hugh and Thomas were familiar with it." He pointed as he read, "'Cluny Monastery has the right to coin special money,' and here it is . . . 'its *independence from the diocesan bishop* is reinstated.' So you can see, the bishop does not confirm the election of Cluny's abbot."

The election was held. Pons received most of the votes and Thomas was second, with the remainder of the votes shared by other candidates. A second vote was taken between the two and Pons garnered 220 votes, over two-thirds of the 300 monks. The results made him the next abbot, but he would need to wait two months until May 1 to officially be instated.

Several days after the election, Pons had just left Compline and knelt alone at the altar in the unfinished *Maior Ecclesia*. The hours of services were still held in the older chapel. Construction had ended for the day. He whispered, "Thank you God, not for me, but for the people who believe in me, that I may serve You as Abbot of Cluny. Jesus, Divine Caller of vocations, You invite some to spiritual work! Inspire me to always know within my heart to do Your will at that particular time. Thank You for my heavenly calling and for maintaining the vocation of Your choice!" *It must be God . . . yes, it is God who has sent his angels to carry me over the many barriers that have been thrown up by men to stop me! The thieves, the rivermen, the Cluny guards, the attack in the library, and now . . . now I know . . . Thomas. Dear Lord, I will need all your guidance to deal with him!* Pons's thoughts were interrupted by unhurried steps as someone drew closer behind him. *Brothers come here routinely for prayer and to observe the progress of this magnificent church.* The footsteps stopped, and he waited, expecting another monk to join him on the kneeling rail. Yet in his bones he sensed dread and looked behind him. It was Thomas.

But Thomas was smiling. "Congratulations, Brother Pons."

Thomas invited Pons to the abbot's residence to discuss the future of Cluny. The subprior brought them cups of wine as they sat in the study, a room on the third floor with large windows. The shutters had been opened completely to the warming spring air, leaving nothing to obscure the view of the vast monastery. Two identical bell towers were accompanied by the third larger tower of the new *Maior Ecclesia,* the Major Church. "So I have two months as acting abbot. And with Hugh the Great deceased, I will ignore the issue of the *filles de joie* in Cluny village."

"What?" While he had lived at Saint Pons, he had known other monks visited the village of Thomieres as he had done, to satisfy their lust. *But I assumed that the vow of chastity was strictly followed here, at the leading center of monastic life. How naïve of me. Ahh, Primavera. Yet I have missed her for herself, not her body. I did love her.*

Thomas swigged his wine and guffawed. "You didn't know? The activity must remain discrete, but I will not punish anyone as Hugh would have done. Strict chastity leads to deviant behavior."

Pons calmed and sipped his wine. *I will have to agree with Thomas on this issue.*

Thomas poured more wine for Pons. "That subject was just a vexation of mine. I really asked you here to talk you out of becoming abbot."

Pons's eyebrows raised as the prior continued, "Do you want to inherit an abbey that displays an unfinished skeleton of a church and is on the edge of bankruptcy? You know the primary reason Hugh went to Spain? Not to support the Benedictine monasteries, but to appeal to Alfonso, the King of Leon and Castile, to maintain his annual donation to Cluny. The entire cost to build the new church, the *Maior Ecclesia*, was derived from that Alfonsine donation made each year. Now that huge contribution has been terminated."

"I understand the Christian monarchs of Spain have made the donations for generations," said Pons. "Why have the payments stopped?"

"Alfonso's father spent his life consolidating his kingdom, conquering new lands from the Muslims, and collecting tribute from them. Then in the terms of his will, he divided his kingdom among his three sons. After his death, a civil war among the brothers weakened the Christian kingdoms so that they not only lost territory which had been taken in the Reconquista, but the Muslim states ceased paying the tributes they had been making for decades."

"But what of the profitable enterprises of Cluny?" said Pons. "It possesses vineyards, cornfields, olive groves, mills, fisheries, forests . . ."

"Yes, but those ventures only cover the operating expenses of the monastery, and any profits go first to helping the needy and the pilgrims. And the wages for the church builders are months in arrears. Who will be blamed? Abbot *Pons* will be remembered in history as incapable of managing Cluny."

I don't know if he is telling the truth, but the treasurer will know. "And you, Prior Thomas, you are willing to take the chance of inheriting a disastrous situation?"

His nod and smile warned Pons there was much more to be told.

In the following days Pons intended to research Thomas's alleged lack of funding, but a tragedy occurred that caught the attention of the entire community of monks at Cluny. Several missionaries had returned from the south, leading a donkey cart through the front gate of Cluny. They carried the bodies of two monks, killed by footpads.

Thomas presided over a gathering of the monastery officers. One suggested, "We should send knights to protect the missionaries."

"No, the knights are very expensive, and only hired for the abbot's travels," commented another.

"Could some garrison soldiers go?"

"Then how would we protect Cluny while they are gone?"

Pons recalled his fights with thieves. "Monks should train to protect themselves."

An officer retorted, "But it takes years for soldiers to develop their skills. Monks should work, study, and pray."

Pons looked about the group. "Take some of the time they now work, have them train with the very tools they use gardening, such as hoes and threshers, and the walking staves. The footpads are not armed with swords and spears. Most likely they will have knives or staves."

"Who will lead this training?"

Pons locked his eyes on the prior. *I am sure he was notified of our battle on the Rhone and he knows very well how my abilities have been tested.* "I will, Prior Thomas."

In the preceding years, when Pons had encouraged physical labor for the Cluniac monks, there had been resistance. But the brothers in due course had experienced not only the physical but also the mental benefits of the labor, and had eventually accepted the activity. Now, however, the monks enthusiastically took up training for self-defense using the walking staff. Pons trained them to use long staves, the length reaching a head taller than a man's height. The brothers seemed to have a pent-up inclination for the diversion. After several weeks of training, many monks, even those few who initially had been opposed to the activity, thanked Pons personally for beginning the program. There were also some very skilled monks, including Chard and Guilen, whom he used as assistants to demonstrate techniques. Pons included the extended grip he had learned from the bargemen. Guilen and Chard were skilled in the long pole methods and Pons enjoyed a renewed connection with them. He also taught the monks to use the staff against staff, the staff versus wooden knife, for training purposes, and also training back to back to support each other. After a month of daily practices, training sessions were becoming competitive.

At one of the sessions, an hour after the Terc service, and in the cool of the midmorning hours, a practice outside in the courtyard was interrupted when several of the garrison soldiers arrived. As Pons finished sparring with a fellow monk, he noticed the soldiers removing their helmets, armor, and belted swords. They grabbed staves from several monks. As a few of the monks tried to recover their weapons, a soldier moved toward Pons and bellowed, "Come on, fight me the monks' way!"

Pons shouted to the group battling for the staves. "Everyone! Stop fighting!" Then he pointed to the advancing soldier. "You are not welcome. We are here to improve our self-defense, not for pride! We will not fight you."

"Sure you will!" The soldier gashed a weaponless monk in the head and charged Pons.

Both the antagonist and Pons held their staves in the conventional style. Their right hand gripped the staff shoulder high, the left hand at the opposite hip, the hands dividing the staff into three equal sections. The soldier rushed forward. Both men were still out of range of a conventional strike and Pons extended his staff almost its full length and snapped the tip of his staff against the soldier's temple, as he moved sideways and out of the way. A knot the size of an egg swelled on the aggressor's head.

The soldier was unfazed. He gripped his staff with both hands near one end. "You aren't the only one who can do that." His extended swing was reaching and powerful, but wide and predictable. Pons moved inside the arc, thrust his staff firmly into the turf ground, and blocked the strike. Pons grabbed his opponent's staff with his left hand and slid his own staff along his opponent's weapon breaking the soldier's grip. He jammed the end of the staff into the attacker's foot and thrust the tip of the staff to barely contact the soldier's throat. He now held the soldier's weapon in his other hand. Both men froze in position for an instant, the soldier aware that Pons could have crushed his windpipe. Pons said, "This is how the monks fight. Without bloodshed and without the need to kill."

The soldier's comrades moved to grab their swords, but Guilen and Chard led a group of monks to intercept them and the soldiers were restrained without further injury. Pons made sure they left as the humiliated soldiers retrieved their armor. Guilen slapped him on the back and Chard clamped him on the shoulder. "Reminds me of the fight against the rivermen years ago! Good fight." He laughed as he added, "I think he might be the same soldier who tried to stop us from entering Cluny years ago."

Pons grinned. "Good memory, Chard. I'm glad this happened a month after we started our staff training. I was out of shape and only now just getting my timing back. It's a blessing they didn't attack with their swords. Perhaps they wanted to do me great harm or even kill me, while disguising the incident as a training accident."

Both monks looked puzzled.

"Thomas lost the election. You just spoke of the river battle and effort to keep us out of Cluny. Remember the assault on me at the library? It is all because of Thomas."

Pons waited as they absorbed the idea. Then he laughed, "Did both of you vote for Thomas?"

Chard hesitated and glanced at Guilen. "We love you, Brother Pons, we just don't . . . love your . . . um, policies."

Pons appeared gratified with the answer. "You saved me once before when the footpads attacked us while we were threshing at Saint Pons, and here you prevented the soldiers from escalating the fight. I have another favor to ask of you."

A month later Guilen and Chard returned from a journey as representatives of Cluny to visit the daughter monasteries in the south of France. Before they neared the *Porte d'Honneur* entering the monastery grounds, they diverted and escorted a woman to a stone cottage on the outskirts of Cluny village.

The next evening Pons knocked on the door of the small house. He embraced Primavera and they remained enfolded without speaking for several minutes. She held both of his hands and drew him toward the bed, but Pons halted. "Not now. Not yet. I am in ecstasy just to see you, knowing you are safe! You appear so vibrant and healthy. The priest at Saint Martin took good care of you! Where are your boys, or should I say, young men?"

The candlelight made Primavera's eyes sparkle and her dark hair shine in seductive ways. But Pons was determined to wait. "They are both novices at Saint Pons Abbey," said Primavera. "They wanted to follow your example."

Pons frowned. "No. I mean, yes, they will get an education, at least."

Her look softened. "They have embraced a surname.

"It is Pons."

"I am not their father . . . no . . . I am honored. We will have a new life." Then he noticed Primavera's clothes. They were the garb of a common woman, a woolen tunic, ankle-length and belted at the waist, and dyed a pleasing woad. Quite a contrast with the tattered garments he remembered her wearing in Thomieres, anything so that her sons were better off. "You look very nice. Did the father at Saint Martin buy clothes for you?"

"No, your mother, um . . . the Countess gave them to me. We stopped in Melgueil on the way to Cluny."

"What! Why did Chard and Guilen take you there?" Pons was looking at the ceiling as he continued. "What were they thinking?"

Primavera pulled him close and ensured his eyes met hers. "My love, they could not help it. While they were at Saint Pons Abbey, Almodis and your brother were visiting as dignitaries. The abbot was showing her the monastery when she recognized Chard and Guilen passing through the cloister. She insisted they travel as a group as far as Melgueil and that they stay as her guests before continuing to Cluny."

Pons's eyes rolled.

"They couldn't refuse or make up a lie, especially in front of the abbot, so they agreed. Several days later when they collected me for the journey, I met your mother."

Pons swallowed. "And does Mother know . . . of . . . us?"

"Yes, she seemed . . . pleased. Here." Primavera held a small wooden box. "Your mother sent this for you to donate to the Cluny Abbey."

He removed the lid. "A relic?"

"Yes, it is the finger of Saint Stephen."

Pons sat down, absorbing it all.

Pons sent a letter by special courier to Rome informing his godfather Pope Paschall of his election to abbot. Although there was no reply for several months, Pons was in high spirits as he discreetly spent time with Primavera. He tried to avoid thinking of how he would miss her on the long journey to Rome for confirmation by the Pope. One morning, he was shocked when the messengers, who had left almost three months earlier, arrived notifying him that Pope Paschall would be in Cluny within several days to confirm his election to abbot. Pons heartily welcomed the Pope to the abbot's residence during his short visit. His godfather was on his way north to meet with Henry V, King of the Germans. The king had agreed to abide by Pope Paschall's decrees. In return Henry would be crowned Emperor of the Holy Roman Empire.

The confirmation of Pons as abbot was conducted in the new church. The church was not finished, but the barrel vaults that supported a ceiling a hundred pieds above the floor gave the spectator a feeling of grandeur and divinity. Ten years earlier, when the construction of the church had barely started, Pope Urban had consecrated both the high altar and matutinal altar. With this early blessing, the church received the designation as a basilica.

For the ceremony, in place of his black wool habit, Pons donned a linen tunic, over which he wore an outer tunic with wide sleeves, a dalmatic. He took off his shoes at the door of the church. After proceeding up the nave, he knelt and prayed on the topmost step at the altar where Pope Paschall waited. After blessing Pons's election by the monks, the Pope directed the officers to place a chasuble, a holy cloak with a cross emblazoned on the front, over Pons's tunic and dalmatic. Now layered with his formal abbatial vestments, the Pope crowned Pons with a mitre. He awarded Pons a signet ring and a crosier, a hooked staff, engraved with two silver keys forming a cross. The monks then filed by one by one, kneeled to kiss the Pope's ring, then gave the kiss of peace on the abbot's hand. Pons put on his shoes, retrieved by an assistant from the vestry, and stood with the thousands of clergy and secular visitors as the Pope gave a homily.

Afterwards, in the abbot's residence, his godfather directed Pons in his first task as abbot. He would travel to Leon and Castile to ensure the continuation of annual donations from King Alfonso.

CHAPTER XII GLENDALOUGH ABBEY, IRELAND

O'Broin gazed down the Gleann da' Loch, the Valley of the Two Lakes, nestled in the Whitlow Mountains of southeast Ireland. It had been almost a year since his arrival at Glendalough Monastery. From the top floor of the stone tower he could see both the upper and lower lakes, blue patches surrounded by slopes covered with dark green forests. He could barely make out the cliffs on the upper lake, where the original site of the monastery, Teampall na Skellig, had been founded by Saint Kevin in the fifth century. Now six hundred years later, O'Broin was atop a round tower, as tall as twenty men, like the stronghold at his former monastery in Kildare. A generation earlier the stone tower, topped with a conical roof, had provided warning and refuge from the Vikings. Their attacks on Ireland had ended, the monastery had thrived and expanded, and new edifices were built within the stone walls.

From his high vantage O'Broin could see the entire monastery, with a grid of streets and numerous stone buildings. There were several very old churches still intact, one fitted with a stone roof. The largest building was the cathedral, the first phase having been built two hundred years earlier in the tenth century. Another phase was under construction.

I wonder if that batch of ale is ready? It's about time to open the ale house anyway. O'Broin descended the five floors of the tower. The exit door was twenty feet off the ground and he climbed down a movable ladder. During the bygone era of Viking raids, the ladders had been pulled up when the tower was under attack. He made his way across the monastery to the main street paved with smooth round cobbles. *The size and shape reminds me of the crown of a monk's tonsure. I'm sure I can make up a joke about that similarity!* He laughed to himself, scratched his ten-day beard, unusual since the monks were usually clean-shaven. The monastery's barber had been sick and confined to bed.

A brass key hung from O'Broin's belt and sunlight flashed as it bounced with each of his steps. The monk had fashioned the unusual belt of braided flax cords. Although his brothers wore the traditional, thicker rope belts, they assumed he had woven his corded belt to carry the heavy key, not to show pride.

He had shown skill in making ale, working for the cellarer who was in charge of provisioning. O'Broin held the key to the alehouse, which was just outside the main gate where the monks served pilgrims and villagers from the nearby settlement. It was about an hour before the Nones service, and some of the farmers who had worked in their field since sunrise took their midday meal at the alehouse. The monks provided soup and bread at no cost, but a cup of ale was a penny and some visitors only partook of the *liquid bread*, as they called it. It was considered the best brew in the Kingdom of Laigin.

O'Broin passed through the stone arch under the gatehouse and left the monastery grounds. He looked up and waved to the gatekeeper sitting on the balcony above the archway. Not a monk, his residence was on the second floor of the gatehouse and he was obsessed with the idea he had the power to give permission for admittance to the monastery. "You may pass, Brother O'Broin. Have you any new jests?"

"Come have an ale and find out!"

The gatekeeper leaned over the balcony railing. "I see the barber has recovered from his illness; your pate looks newly shaven!"

"Ha! No! He is still sick . . . harrumph! I see . . . you jest of my receding crop." But O'Broin was rarely outwitted in a repartee. "I guess the good Lord made me this way and I was destined to be a monk, as you were destined to be the gatekeeper at Glendalough. Have you ever thought that when you die you may have to face Heaven's gatekeeper, Saint Peter?"

The gatekeeper's smile faded. "No."

"You are advised to keep free of sin. Saint Peter may take offense at what may seem like small infractions and may bar your entry to heaven. I had a dream last night that was sent by the Lord." The gatekeeper sobered.

O'Broin cleared his throat. "In the message from God, a man from the village had died and was at the gate to heaven. The gatekeeper tested him and asked if he had committed any sin for which he had not asked forgiveness. The man recalled a wrong he had done during a football game played between Saint Kevin's monastery and his village. So he repented. "Saint Peter, nobody noticed, but I touched the ball with my hand just before I scored the winning goal against Saint Kevin's. I am sorry, Your Holiness." The gatekeeper frowned. "I am not Saint Peter, I am Saint *Kevin*."

O'Broin turned and continued to the alehouse as the gatekeeper groaned. "One of these days I will get the best of you! Blasphemy—telling me you dreamed God told you this! No wonder they call you the Mad Monk!"

Waiting for O'Broin to open the alehouse, ahead down the path were several regular customers and a few pilgrims. *By the look of their clothes the strangers are probably from Dublin.* He greeted them with a nod, and used the heavy key, as big as his hand, to unlock the alehouse. His two assistants arrived from the monastery. Inside, one lit the fire to heat the soup prepared earlier and the other opened the shutters. O'Broin poured ale into fired clay cups and laid out loaves of hard bread. He sang a short song to enliven the quiet group.

"He who drinks . . . gets drunk.
He who gets drunk . . . goes to sleep.
He who goes to sleep . . . does no sin.
He who does no sin . . . goes to heaven.
So let's all drink . . . and go to heaven!"

The farmers, acquainted with his poem, raised their cups and chanted. "*Sláinte!* Health!"

The visitors were taken aback, but reluctantly held up their drinks. Then one said, "*Mein Skol, Dein Skol, Alle Vakkera Flikka*

Skol. My health, your health, all beautiful ladies' health." He tossed a coin onto the counter for O'Broin.

The monk examined the penny. It had been stamped: *Rex M.* "Where did you get this coin? It is not like the Saxon or Viking coins that come out of Dublin. That is where you are from, no? And your toast told me you are descendants of the Norse."

"We are from Dublin on pilgrimage to visit the holy places in Ireland. It must have been stamped in the county to the west, by the King of Munster. I think I got it in Killarney."

"That is the first coin I have ever seen made by the Irish."

"Aye, Brother. You are a monk—I am surprised of your . . . song about getting drunk." He swigged some ale. "This is good *coirm.*"

"Yes, so you recognize monk's barley ale."

"It is very good, but I taste something else—something other than barley."

O'Broin smiled. "Yes, we add gentian and sweet gale and a few other . . . uh, secret herbs."

The man took another swallow. "Good *coirm.* Tell me a riddle."

"Yes, this ale is proof God loves us! But here is a riddle that *you* can solve. How many Norsemen does it take to set fire to a lantern?"

The customer squinched his face and his two generous eyebrows became one.

O'Broin answered, "Why bother with a lantern—there's a monastery just over the hill!"

The visitor slammed his cup on the counter. "That's no longer true! We are now Christians! What kind of monk are you . . . one whose job is to piss off your customers?"

The farmers were laughing and one placed his hand gingerly on the man's shoulder. "The Mad Monk is funny, don't you think?"

"I am not entertained."

The farmer looked to O'Broin. "Show him the trick with your belt."

The man from Dublin looked at the monk's plaited belt, from which dangled a brass key. "I have not seen knots like that before. They are not seaman's knots."

"No, they are *knots of Solomon,* representing the union of man and the divine.

"Have a second round and I will start the show," said O'Broin. The stranger threw another coin on the table as they were poured ale.

O'Broin stepped into the center of the room, yanked off his belt which remained in a braided shape. A second snap of his wrist and the braids unraveled into a cord that shot out and stretched across the room. The key snapped with the full extension. He whipped the end back and began wrapping the cord around his neck, appearing to tie himself in a bundle by turning his body and rolling his head. Suddenly he whipped it free and the key shot out again as the cord stretched to its full length. He snapped the key back, this time the cord wrapped around and around his shoulders and arms. Incredibly, he unwound a second time and swung the cord, weighted at the end by the large key, around in wide arcs over the heads of the alehouse clients. As O'Broin continued the fantastic exhibition, he posed a riddle: "My life can be measured in hours . . . I serve by being devoured . . . Thin I am quick . . . Fat I am slow . . . Wind is my foe . . . What am I?

"A free ale to you that solves the riddle." He kicked from under his habit and the key shot across the room. At the other end of the counter was a lit candle. O'Broin snapped the cord back as the key reached the candle and snuffed out the flame without disturbing a drop of wax. O'Broin recoiled the rope in the air and caught his belt and key.

There was a loud chorus from the patrons, "*Sláinte! Skol*!" followed by cheering.

Day by day, O'Broin took pleasure entertaining the guests at the alehouse, but his antics eventually overflowed into his monk's life. One evening at Prime, although he kept the vow of silence as required during service, he signed jokes by hand to nearby monks. They responded with hand signals that represented laughter. He was reprimanded and O'Broin was excluded from the prayer services and meals for a full day.

O'Broin returned to normal routine of work, study, and prayer for several weeks. One night after Matins, as the monks were returning to their dormitories, each lighting their way with a candle,

O'Broin expertly flipped his candle in the air and caught it without putting out the flame. Another monk copied him, splattering hot wax on several brothers and creating an uproar. The prior did not appreciate the performance and confined O'Broin to the dormitory for three days. The prior then interviewed O'Broin and determined that the monk had not improved his attitude. He ordered O'Broin to report to the circuitor, the abbey officer in charge of discipline, for punishment.

O'Broin was escorted to the stables by two monks, who were present to witness. After removing his habit and undertunic, the circuitor lashed O'Broin three times on the back with a willow switch.

"Now are you ready to ask for forgiveness?" asked the flogger.

"But what must one do before they can obtain forgiveness of a sin?" said O'Broin.

The circuitor glanced at the monks with a blank look.

O'Broin answered, "Sin. One must sin first." He laughed at his own jest, but was silenced when the circuitor growled and in quick succession hit O'Broin four more times even harder.

"Well?" The circuitor said, breathing from exertion.

O'Broin recovered and said, "A bear chased a man in the forest, so he tried to climb a tree, but he slipped down into the bear's arms. He prayed, 'Lord let this be a Christian bear.' It was, for the bear said, 'Lord, thank you for this food.'"

The monks watching laughed and the circuitor whipped him again, paused, chuckled, hit him a second time, laughed, and finished with a third, harder lash, accompanied by a loud snigger, then said, "You are mad, monk! Such insolence. This is not the place for your humor."

O'Broin was in much pain, but was able to eke out a few more words. "Brother, how do you make holy water?

"Boil the hell out of it."

The circuitor threw the switch away and left. The prior put O'Broin in solitary confinement in the tower with only bread and water for a week, where he was to think about his misdeeds.

They treat me like this even after I make good profits for the monastery at the ale house. If it wasn't for my witticisms, the customers would only spend half as much. Oh well, I'll spend my time here in confinement making up new riddles.

O'Broin was released and back at the ale house entertaining guests. Unbeknownst to him the subprior was monitoring him from a table in a dark corner of the tavern. The subprior observed how O'Broin's talents profited the monastery. One of the regular customers shouted, "Mad Monk, tell us some jokes. We are bored!"

O'Broin walked out from behind the counter. "Have I told you about the oath of silence the monks must take?"

A random voice called out, "Maybe the other monks took an oath of silence, but certainly not you, O'Broin!"

Good! The audience is involved. But this mad monk would not let anyone have the last laugh on him. "Once I lived in a monastery where per their oath of silence, monks were only allowed to say two words every year. After my first year, I told the head abbot my two words: 'Better Food.' The head abbot hired a new cook.

"At the end of my second year, I used my next two words: 'Warmer Blankets.' The head abbot ordered new blankets.

"The next year, again I voiced my annual two words: 'I Quit.'

"The head abbot replied, 'Well good, all you've done since you got here is complain.'"

The subprior relished his ale as he sat in the back quietly enjoying the show. O'Broin did his trick again with his rope to snuff out the candle flame. The subprior applauded with patrons, and seeing no infractions, was about to leave. Then a heckler shouted, "We can see you don't follow the oath of silence, but what about your oath of celibacy, O'Broin?"

O'Broin was ready. "Here is a good riddle for you! What hangs at a man's thigh and wants to poke the hole it's often poked before?"

There was a smattering of obscene responses.

O'Broin smiled. "You are all wrong!" He looked down at his belt. "It's a key! You foul minded heathens!"

The subprior rushed out of the alehouse in plain view of O'Broin.

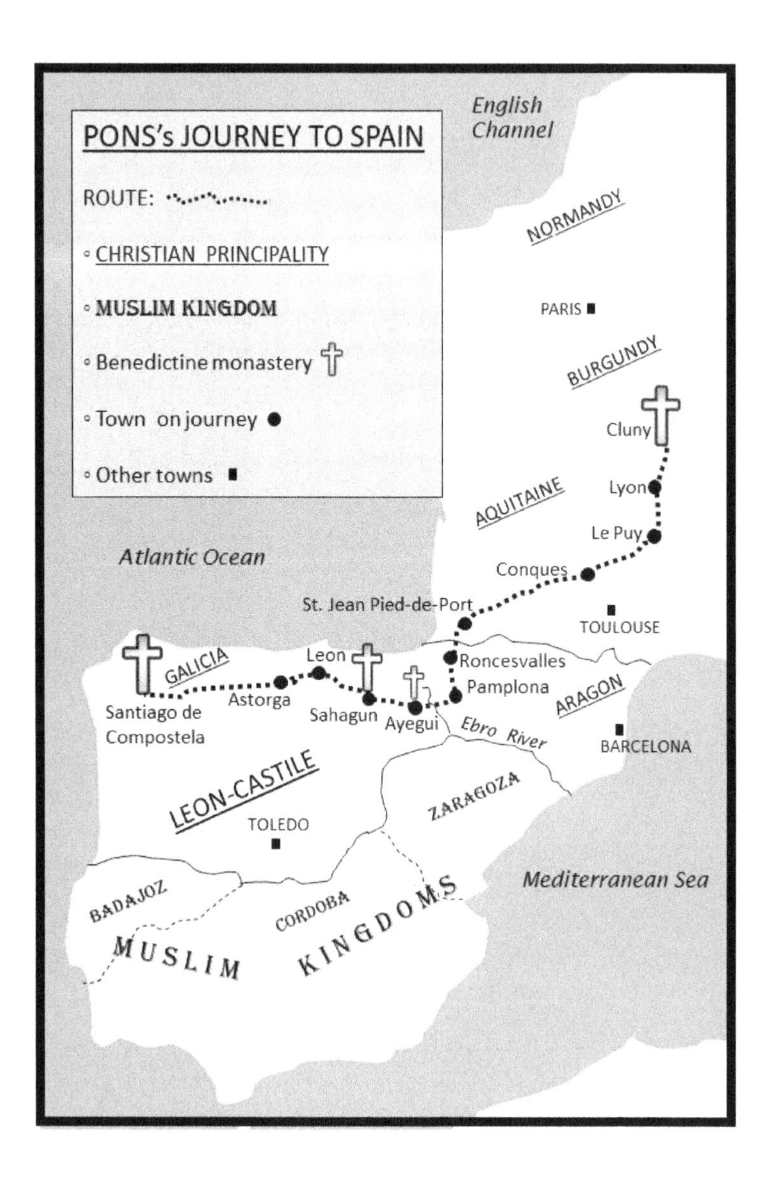

PONS's JOURNEY TO SPAIN
ROUTE:
CHRISTIAN PRINCIPALITY
MUSLIM KINGDOM
Benedictine monastery
Town on journey
Other towns
English Channel
NORMANDY
PARIS
BURGUNDY
Cluny
AQUITAINE
Lyon
Le Puy
Atlantic Ocean
Conques
St. Jean Pied-de-Port
TOULOUSE
Leon
Roncesvalles
GALICIA
Pamplona
ARAGON
Astorga
Santiago de Compostela
Sahagun
Ayegui
Ebro River
BARCELONA
LEON-CASTILE
ZARAGOZA
TOLEDO
Mediterranean Sea
BADAJOZ
CORDOBA
MUSLIM KINGDOMS

CHAPTER XIII VIA PODIENSIS

"No! Why should I hire eighty knights to escort me to Spain when I am appealing to the king to renew his annual contributions?" Abbot Pons shouted, "It will appear we are extravagant!"

Thomas, still prior and thus second to the abbot, said, "You must put on an elegant show, as a regal leader of the church—any pauper can ask for a donation. And for security as well. When Hugh traveled, he was always escorted by the Burgundian knights. Does your godfather the Pope journey without adequate bodyguard?"

Pons relented. He entered the black carriage, joining Guilen, plus two other young, robust monks to serve as personal guards. Chard, promoted to sacrist, would stay in Cluny. The coat of arms of Cluny, two gold keys crisscrossed over a sword on a red shield, was painted on the coach door. The forty horsemen behind and forty ahead, the vanguard flying the red banner of Cluny and the purple and yellow banner of Burgundy all made an impressive sight as they passed through the *Porte d'Honneur* leaving Cluny Monastery. The journey would take them south to Lyon, then to Le Puy, where they would follow *Via Podiensis*, one of the three primary roads used by pilgrims to cross France. Then at the foot of the pass through the Pyrenees Mountains, the three roads combined to form *Le Chemin de St. Jacques*, the Saint James Way, which crossed northern Spain to Santiago de Compostela.

The knights had been leased from the Duke of Burgundy and

had just cleared the front gate of Cluny. The crunch of wheels on the gravel road competed with the clops of a multitude of hooves. "Pons, you . . ." Guilen glanced at the abbot's guards, "um . . . Abbot Pons, you've come a long way since you first arrived at Cluny."

Pons nodded and recalled watching this same ensemble arrive on his first day at Cluny over three years earlier. *Yet here I am committing the same sin that I criticized then! In the Lord's eyes, this is not a good example of humility! I am wearing the formal vestments rather than the habit of a humble monk. And what a waste of resources, considering the financial status of the monastery.* He leaned out of the coach window. "Driver, stop the carriage! Return to Cluny."

The next morning, after arguing with Prior Thomas, the subprior, and other officers, Pons set out again but with a smaller party. The prior reminded Pons that the Duke of Burgundy would be offended, being denied the honor of escorting the abbot, and also losing the income from payment for his knights. Pons agreed to let half the knights escort him to Le Puy, where the *Via Podiensis* began and the pilgrim traffic increased, making it safer to travel. When they arrived at LePuy, Pons dismissed the knights who then returned to Burgundy.

Pons and five escorts now remained: Guilen, the two brothers from Cluny, and a pair of Burgundian knights. They all rode mules and the knights were disguised as postulants, dressed in habits but without tonsures. Under their habits the knights concealed hilted daggers, with blades one pied long.

Pons sensed zeal in Cominius's gait and he patted the mule's neck and whispered, "We are on a new adventure!" He donned his black habit for travel but had packed his formal vestments for the proper occasion. They left the city of Le Puy the next morning after praying at the Cathedral Notre-Dame-du-Puy, one of the oldest and most visited shrines.

Over the next week their ride was through the wild country of L'Aubrac, the high plateau, its treeless grasslands filled with grazing sheep and bursting with flowers, but with few people.

One of their stops was at the hospital of the Order of Aubrac where the kind monks fed and sheltered them with other pilgrims.

In addition, the knights of the Order of Aubrac patrolled the road to ensure safety for travelers.

From Aubrac, Pons's group descended into the valley of the River Lot, sometimes riding on the remnants of old Roman roads, sometimes on single track paths through hamlets.

Two weeks' journey from Le Puy, they reached the pilgrim resting stop at the town of Conques, where they paid their respects to the remains of a martyr, the young girl, Saint Foy. Afterwards, Guilen, Pons, and their party sat under a large tree and savored fresh bread soaked in olive oil purchased from a vendor outside the church. The vendor was rather talkative and as he served other customers, he recounted the story of the saint. "The ancient Romans tortured Saint Foy because she refused to make sacrifices to their pagan gods. She was martyred in a nearby town. And I will reveal a bit of history that the monks in the abbey won't tell you. Her relics were originally kept where she was martyred, but a monk stole them and brought them to the abbey here. Yes, stole them so the pilgrims' money would be spent here." Guilen and the other monks gave the vendor an annoying glance. He then added, "I am not complaining, that's how I make a living."

As Pons enjoyed the fare, he was fascinated by the impressive plane tree shading them, which had huge leaves and mottled bark. *My faith. I am supposed to be a pilgrim, but this arduous journey, so important to my godfather and the Church, is about money. One can be close to God without huge basilicas or cathedrals. But I am committed to the Church's ways and am so intertwined with it all.* He relaxed and smiled to himself. *Mm . . . someone nearby is baking—it's chestnut bread, Primavera's perfume. When all this is done, I have Primavera waiting for me when I return.*

Over a month after leaving Le Puy, the group entered the Basque village of *Saint Jean Pied-de-Port*, Saint Jean Foot of the Pass, located at the base of the Roncevalles Pass in the Pyrenees Mountains. The pass was near the junction of the three main pilgrim roads that came from all parts of France on the way to Santiago de Compostela, where pilgrims revered and prayed to the bones of Saint James. Saint Jean was teeming with pilgrims and traveling vendors preparing for the arduous mountain crossing. Mercifully, it was late spring, with a period of mild weather, and they had been told their hard climb through the pass would be rewarded with striking vistas of green hills, lush valleys, and granite-faced mountains.

They found a place to sleep outdoors at the edge of Saint Jean, among hundreds of pilgrims. The Basque village had few rooms, all of which were occupied. But the weather was pleasant, the moon was full, and the campfires and joyful resonance from people eager to continue their pilgrimage made a festive atmosphere. The two Burgundian knights had departed to find ale in the village and Pons's two Cluniac escorts took the mules to a nearby pasture, leaving Guilen and Pons to enjoy ballads sung by a man and woman. The pair chanted the Song of Roland. The story told of a knight who had fought a heroic battle for King Charlemagne against the Muslims at the Roncevalles Pass, where Pons would trek tomorrow. He was fascinated. *Their intonations are like the monks' chants when they sing liturgy, but these songs are also entertaining.*

The duo's next ballad was a love song which mesmerized Pons. When they finished, he joined a few others as he stood and clapped. The singers noticed his applause. As they drew close, Pons retrieved a few deniers for them.

The young woman dropped one knee and rose without touching the ground as she accepted the money. "Thank you, Father."

Guilen's look of irritation made her notice their habits. "Oh, I am sorry, you are not a priest, you are a monk. Thank you . . . um . . . Brother, er, Holy Brother."

Guilen was about to say something and Pons interjected as he laughed, "That is fine, young lady."

Guilen whispered, "He is an abbot."

She genuflected, placing one knee on the ground. "Please forgive me, Father Abbott."

Pons smiled warmly. "Please rise."

Her companion joined her.

"Your songs were magnificent!" said Pons. "There are women troubadours?"

"Um . . . forgive me, Father Abbot, in Occitan my vocation is known as a *jongleuress*." She looped her arm inside her companion's. "And my husband is a *jongleur*."

"Well now it is my turn . . . in learning correct terms. Where did you learn to chant so sweetly?" said Pons.

The young man bowed with a simple nod. "My wife Azalais and I were taught at Count William's court in Poitou. We learned from the count himself, so renowned that his sobriquet is 'The Troubadour.'"

"You use the term, sobriquet suggesting you are educated. Are you royalty who have left the . . . um . . . nest?"

"No, we are of low birth, but the duke was gracious to teach us. He said we were gifted, but would not allow us to continue if we married. We are now itinerant minstrels."

"And tell me about the love song you both so beautifully recited?"

Azalais was effervescent as she answered. "The song is called a *serena*, for lovers preparing to enjoy the evening together." Guilen glanced at Pons, which the young woman noted. "Oh, I have said something wrong! Of course, you have taken a vow of chastity."

Pons held up both hands. "No, no . . . it is fine. Those were very sweet lyrics: 'and a man who wins the joy of her love will live a hundred years. The joy of her can make the sick man well again, her wrath can make a well man die.'"

She calmed as Pons added, "Priests, monks, and abbots—must know of these things to better help the people, no?"

Azalais and Guy both kissed his hand and said their farewells. The young woman's eyes were moist. Pons noted that both were attired as pilgrims, carried a walking staff, and a gourd for their water hung from their belts. *They must have already traversed the Camino to Santiago de Compostela, as they both have the iconic seashell sewn onto their tunics.*

After they were gone, Guilen clapped Pons on the shoulder. "You handled that well! If only they knew! I know you are missing Primavera." Pons frowned.

Suddenly there was shouting as the nearby pilgrims fled so quickly that walking sticks, gourds, and other trappings were scattered across the ground. Azalais cried out as she ran toward Pons, Guy following. "They are here again! We already paid them the tax yesterday! Abbot Pons, help us!"

Moving among the crowd was a group of men whose garb suggested they were local Basques. They were seizing pilgrims and rifling through their clothes. The ruffians used sticks to beat those who resisted.

"Stop this at once!" Pons retrieved his staff and approached the melee, Guilen with him.

One of the aggressors addressed Pons. "Zer nahi duzu? Ordaindu al duzu?"

Azalais translated, "He says in Basque, 'What do you want and have you paid your tax?'"

"Ask him if any of them speak Occitan."

The man himself answered. "I do. Who are you, monk? And why do you interfere? I didn't see you last night when I collected the tax, so you must pay now." He voiced a command in Basque and his followers joined him. There were six rogues facing Pons. Most of the pilgrims retreated out of sight, but a few score remained.

Pons stared at the Basques and remained silent. The temper he thought he had mastered surfaced and beads of sweat formed on his crown despite the cool evening. After a long pause, the people murmured and jostled. The space was thick with tension as if the air would burst. *I feel paralyzed and at the same time ready to strike out and punish this barbarian! God knows.*

Guilen whispered, "Pons, say something, anything! Use your skills of negotiation and persuasion. Don't fight. It would be a bad example."

"Go find our guards," said Pons, without taking his eyes off his adversaries.

Guilen remained. "Leave you to vie on your own?"

"Go!"

Guilen hurried away.

Azalais shrunk behind her husband as she clung onto his arm, but her voice was strong as she continued to face the taxmen. "The rules allow you to collect taxes from vendors and performers, but you have been charging double, and you are not permitted to tax pilgrims."

The Basque leader sneered. "What does she know? You will listen to a woman?"

Pons ignored the question and answered, "Do you work for Lord Saint Jean?"

The Basque nodded.

"I will visit him in the morning and confirm the rules."

"A lowly monk can't tell me what to do!" The man appeared ready to spring. The closest pilgrims shied further away.

"Wait! God will punish you for violence!" He brandished his abbot's ring.

The man's posture contracted. "But . . . you probably stole it!" The Basque raised his club and lunged at Pons, his mates following closely behind. Pons pivoted to the right as he wielded his staff with both hands. He snapped the upper part of the staff from right to left and parried the club. Wooden bludgeons clacked loudly, followed by a grunt of pain from the attacker as Pons slid his staff down the opponent's weapon and smashed his foe's hand. Pons turned at once toward the man's followers as the leader glanced behind him but got no help from his comrades. The Burgundian knights had arrived and the threat of their long knives had convinced the Basques to drop their clubs.

The crowd surged forward and seized the taxmen. Other pilgrims grabbed clubs and looked to retaliate. Pons shouted, "Stop! Release them." They calmed and forced the tax collectors to sit in front of them.

The abbot addressed the crowd. "Don't you remember what most of you said this morning as you awoke and recited the Lord's Prayer? 'And forgive us our trespasses, as we forgive them that trespass against us.'" Pons pounded his staff into the ground. "We are all on this road to Compostela to fulfill our Christian duty. Let us then act like Christians!"

Guilen arrived with the other monks. He held Pons's vestments. The abbot nodded. Guilen wrapped the chasuble, a dark red cloak emblazoned with a white cross on the front, over Pons's habit, crowned him with the abbot's mitre and passed him the crosier. Murmurs and gasps stirred through the crowd.

Pons continued, "Words of truth from the sacred Bible. 'Repay no one evil for evil but give thought to do what is honorable in the sight of all. Always seek to do good to one another and to everyone. For if you forgive others their trespasses, your heavenly Father will also forgive you, but if you do not forgive others their trespasses, neither will your Father forgive your trespasses.'"

Pons asked vendors for wine and bread. Guilen paid them and the abbot led the people in communion. Later that night, his last thoughts as he covered himself with his blanket and fell to sleep were of appreciation for Guilen.

At dawn he woke to find his friend rekindling the campfire. "Brother Guilen, thank you for your wise guidance last night. You must have sensed I was ready to fight. You helped avoid a violent end. 'God himself helps those who dare.'"

"Is that from Scripture?" asked Guilen.

"Although many believe it is from the Bible," said Pons, "I am quoting Ovid, a Roman philosopher."

"Hmm," murmured Guilen. "Perhaps the Lord sent the Burgundians back just in time . . . and your advice to urge me to negotiate, as well as your idea of the vestments was . . . just enough time for God to notice."

They laughed together.

After Matins and breakfast, Pons and Guilen went to the village to call on the Lord of Saint Jean. As Pons explained the violent incident of the night before, he sensed the lord was not taking him seriously. When Pons reminded him of his influence and position in the Church and that those who bilked, assaulted, or robbed a pilgrim would be excommunicated, the lord changed his attitude. They agreed on what were fair commercial tax rates, and not to charge the religious pilgrims.

The lord called on a servant, who brought tapas and wine, and the men became more relaxed in each other's company. He redirected their conversation as he said, "When you reach Spain, be aware that King Alfonso, ruler of the Christian kingdoms of Leon and Castile, has recently died. The politics are in transition. The two kingdoms have been unified with Aragon, achieved by the marriage of the late King Alfonso's only living child, his daughter, Lady Urraca, to Alfonso the Battler, King of Aragon."

Pons pressed his lips together as he traded glances with Guilen. *The king is dead! Will the new king renew the donation?*

Pons and his escorts departed Saint Jean and for several days journeyed across the mountains. They arrived at the valley of Roncevalles, the Valley of Thornes, the site where the knight Roland had been immortalized in battle. They paid homage at the

Chapel of Sancti Spiritus, dedicated to Charlemagne. The church had been recently built next to a cemetery containing the bones of those who had died in the mountains on pilgrimage. Legend also said that the chapel had been erected over the ossuary containing the bones of Charlemagne's soldiers.

They stayed overnight at the Benedictine hostel next to the chapel. Pons did not reveal his identity, but as they did for all pilgrims, the host monks washed their feet and provided a warm meal and lodging. As they prepared for bed, Guilen sat on a pallet facing Pons. "It is reassuring that the monks here truly practice the Christian ideal of hospitality. And at the cemetery, I was told if a pilgrim died even miles away in the mountains, they were brought here and received Christian sepulcher."

Pons lay back on his pallet. "Yes, it is comforting, especially after the tax collectors' behavior."

"Is this journey solely to request funds?" asked Guilen.

"I hope we can make it to Santiago de Compostela. It is one of the three holiest Christian pilgrimages, besides Rome, and of course, Jerusalem."

"Pons, does making a pilgrimage to Santiago grant a plenary indulgence?"

"No, pilgrims only receive a full pardon of their sins if they die on the journey to Jerusalem. I did get a letter from Pope Paschall, a copy which was also sent to archbishops, asking my opinion on whether a pilgrimage to Rome or Compostela should remove or shorten the time the soul of the deceased was to go through Purgatory. I trust you not to reveal my thoughts to others . . . but the whole idea of us . . . mere humans, deciding this issue is . . . blasphemous."

"What was your answer to the Pope?"

"I answered that all three pilgrimages should be equal in rank and the rewards the same—full absolution of the pilgrims' sins."

CHAPTER XIV SPAIN

The next morning, they left Roncesvalles shrouded in fog. In the late afternoon they crossed the Arga River on the Magdalena Bridge and entered the city of Pamplona. After a night in the church, they traveled to the village of Ayegui and were welcomed by the abbot of the Benedictine monastery of Santa Maria la Real de Irache. For several days, they rested, pleased they could attend the monks' hourly services for a few daily cycles. They continued west to the town of Sahagun, the location of the largest Benedictine abbey in Spain, the Monastery de Santo Facundo and Primitivio. The monastery had been given the appellation "the Cluny of Spain." Pons hoped to find the whereabouts of the king and his wife Queen Urraca.

Due to their travel-worn and bedraggled appearance, to gain entrance they had to show the soldiers at the gate Pons's letter from Pope Paschall stating his rank as Abbot of Cluny. They were then warmly greeted and shown to the guest dormitory. Pons didn't know whether the local abbot decided to treat them modestly to fit their unpretentious arrival or if the monasteries of Spain were still faithful to Saint Benedict's rule of humility. But he was pleased they were to stay in modest quarters and not the abbot's residence.

After the last daytime service, the abbot showed Pons the tomb in the monastery church where King Alfonso VI had been recently buried. Then at the abbot's residence they talked of Pons's plans in Spain, conversing in Latin. Pons had learned only a few Castilian words. They sat in highbacked but unpadded chairs, each with a small table at his side with a plate of tapas and a cup of wine. Pons sampled another piece of bread, flavored with olive oil and topped by a sliver of meat. "This is rather tasty, Abbot. It must be some kind of fish?"

"Yes, anchovies and mackerel. We are near the sea. Perhaps you have not had these fish?"

Pons shook his head. "The wine is excellent, too. And your monastery. It well deserves being known as the 'Cluny of Spain.' I feel at home, and despite so many miles between us, we are joined together by our faith in the Lord, as well as close ties as brothers of the Benedictine Order."

"Yes, Abbot . . . Brother Pons."

"And at Cluny . . . my predecessor, the late Abbot Hugh the Great . . ."

"I was blessed to have met him years ago when he visited Sahagun."

"We were blessed to have had him as abbot. He began construction of Cluny's newest and most grand church, but it is still years from completion. The generous donations by the Leon-Castilian crown have funded its construction."

"We also have benefitted from the regal contributions. The Puente de Canto, a bridge you will cross when you leave Sahagun, was built by King Alfonso. Many of the Roman bridges still in use have been repaired by the crown and those destroyed by floods have been replaced by the king. Now, however, somehow we must find other sources of income, I'm afraid. Urraca can no longer afford to distribute the gold donations as her father did."

Pons's brow wrinkled. "As I have heard."

"Even before the marriage of the King of Aragon to our lady, Queen Urraca, the gold from the Muslim tribute had slowed. Shortly after they were married, the county of Galicia rebelled, bishops quarreled, and in our town the people are divided in opposition. So, with the Christian kingdoms distracted, the Muslims see our weakness and continue to deny the payments. In this recent civil strife, the peasants support me and the queen while the merchants threaten to attack the monastery."

Pons looked distressed.

"Abbot Pons, her father before her and now Queen Urraca herself has favored our abbey and ensured Sahagun and the monastery are well fortified and garrisoned. But I hope we can end this disagreement by negotiations and not violence.

"After Urraca's marriage united the four kingdoms, her husband designated himself Emperor and named her Empress of Leon, Castile, Galicia, and Aragon, but they have had a falling out. Urraca has accused her husband of physical abuse. I would not want her to be angry with me! To avoid the king, she has retreated to the fortress city of Astorga, sixty miles to the west. So far, he has ignored her. Much of his time is consumed battling Christians and Muslims alike. I must give him credit though, he maintains the bridges and the roads to Compostela and keeps them in good repair."

Pons leaned forward, "What can you tell me to better negotiate with her?"

"Before her father died, Urraca's first husband, Raymond of Burgundy, was killed in battle. Urraca's father designated her to inherit the kingdom as queen regnant, but the king's nobles and advisors pressured for her to be married. When her father, Alfonso VI, passed away, she did as she promised him and married the King of Aragon, Alfonso the Battler. He is a great warrior on the battlefield, but not a good husband. It is said that Alfonso is fanatical and sleeps in his armor. And Urraca is not a typical queen. She is strong and powerful, not at all suited for a subservient role. Urraca would have been satisfied and well capable in governing the Christian kingdoms herself. Her advisors, who initially recommended the marriage, now believe they made a mistake."

He finished his wine. His secretary arrived and poured them a second cup. They both plucked tapas from their dishes, nibbled in silence, and then sipped wine for a few quiet moments.

Pons gazed away as his bottom lip curled in thought. He looked back at the abbot. "It was her father who was Cluny's benefactor, but I must now ask one of them, Urraca or Alfonso—most likely her, to resume the endowment."

"I would approach both with the request," said the abbot. "Don't underestimate yourself. An alliance and influence with Cluny is valuable. May God guide you in your negotiations,

Abbot Pons. Be wary of Queen Urraca. No one says it to her face, but she is called *The Reckless One.* Perhaps she inherited her behavior from her mother, Constance of Burgundy, or her father, as they both were suspected to be adulterers.

"It will be possible to travel to Leon to see the king and then Astorga to see Queen Urraca. The unrest has so far only resulted in skirmishes between the rivals at the center of power. Pilgrims have not been harmed, and I am confident you can safely continue west toward Santiago Compostela. It is a desolate, mostly flat stretch and you will easily make it in two days to the great city of Leon, then one day further with a few climbs to Astorga."

Early the next morning, Pons and his men joined hundreds of other pilgrims as they crowded the streets of Sahagun, continuing their westward journey toward Compostela. The town was on the east side of the River Cea and as they approached a stone bridge, the Puente Cantor, Pons heard singing. The sun had risen behind them and the white stonework of the bridge dazzled in the sunlight. Beyond the arched bridge was a large grove of black poplar trees, the greens and whites of the illuminated leaves fluttering brightly against the azure sky. The crowd of pilgrims stopped to listen to the song. Sitting at the highest point of each arch along the bridge parapets and facing each other were the two minstrels Pons had met at Roncevalles, Azalais and Guy. Pons and his entourage dismounted. Guy accompanied his wife, playing a wooden gittern, a round-backed stringed instrument. She was not singing a love song, but chanted a *canso de la crozada*, a ballad of the crusade of Charlemagne, King of the Franks, undertaken hundreds of years earlier to open the pilgrims' road to Santiago de Compostela and free it from the Muslims.

The song was *The Legend of the Flowering Lances* and described the Battle of Sahagun between Charlemagne and the Muslim Aigoland, which had taken place just across the river, now occupied by a copse of poplar trees. The clash had raged for days and on the third night Charlemagne's knights thrust their lances into the ground. When they awoke in the morning, the soldiers found that the lances had grown bark and sprouted branches and leaves, a miracle attributed to God. Thousands of men were killed on both sides, and finally the Muslims retreated.

Years later, the meadow where the lances had sprouted became the grove of poplars just beyond the Puente de Cantor, named the *Field of Charlemagne's Lances.*

After the couple finished their ballad, the pilgrims crossed the bridge and a few gave the minstrels silver pennies. Pons asked Guilen to stay with him and for his companions to wait ahead across the bridge. He held Cominius's reins and greeted the pair, "Guy! Azalais! God provided us another chance to hear your blessed voices! What a surprise!" He passed Guy two deniers and laughed. "And you deserve these pennies! Your song was quite entertaining."

"Thank you, Father Abbot!" Azalais glanced at her husband. "We wrote the lyrics for the Legend of the Flowering Lances."

Azalais curtsied and kissed Pons's hand as Guy bowed slightly. Her face beamed as she said, "We won't be roving minstrels. Instead we will be staying in Sahagun." Azalais glanced at her husband and back to Pons. "We have been hired as teachers for the *Escuela de Juglares e Trovadores,* the first school of troubadours to be founded in Castile."

"Yes, yes, you would be very qualified. I remember you said you both studied under the master, Count William 'The Troubadour.'"

Guilen took a step, leading his mule. "Congratulations Guy and Azalais. Abbot Pons, I will be waiting with the others."

Pons embraced his minstrel friends and bid goodbye. "Perhaps we will meet again when we return from Compostela."

They rode their mules past the grove of the sacred poplars, then overtook the pilgrims they had been among in Sahagun. The road climbed gently upward into broad meadows. Pons and Guilen rode side by side for hours without needing conversation. The heat grew, and at midday they stopped at a shallow gully where low bushes and a stand of evergreen oaks grew. They dismounted and rested as they sat on the ground. A drove of wild black pigs that had been eating the fallen acorns fled with squeals into the underbrush. Guilen drank, then handed Pons a skin of water. Loud crunching made them turn to look. Guilen put his hand out for another drink of water. "Do you think the mules should be eating acorns?"

Pons smiled. "Cominius!" The mule paused and looked at

them. "Do you like those nuts?" The mule returned to eating.

"Pons, I noticed you enjoyed talking with pretty Azalais in Sahagun."

The abbot quickly looked around, but the others were out of hearing. "Guilen. What a bawdy jest! She is married, and for me, I am always thinking of Primavera."

"Azalais is fair, talkative, and bright faced, with her light hair, but you prefer the dark and quiet Primavera."

"Azalais is a performer," added Pons. "That is her calling from the Lord. We are monks. We should not be talking like this and should find a monastery to focus our minds on our faith." *Yes, the young girl is attractive, and she made me think of Primavera.*

After their rest, they continued across the *meseta*, the sun-drenched high plains of Castile. There were frequent low climbs and gentle inclines, which afforded sweeping views. The trail was straight for long stretches, following the course of an old Roman road. Only a few patches of trees near the streams or valleys provided shade. The intense sun beat down on open fields of grassy plains. They had packed their black habits in their saddlebags, and their light-colored under-tunics and wide-brimmed hats of leather made the ride more bearable. The straw-colored grasses waved in the balmy breeze as Cominius swayed under Pons in the hot sun, almost putting the abbot to sleep. *In several days we will reach Leon, then Astorga. I will need to talk to the king and queen in Latin. But no, now I recall, the abbot said Urraca's mother was Burgundian and her first husband was from Burgundy as well, the same county where Cluny is located. Perhaps she is fluent in the northern French spoken there?*

Hmm . . . Prior Thomas, the Bishop of Macon, Count William—my adversaries . . . all Burgundians. At that thought, Pons felt a sense of dread and glanced behind him. The Burgundian knights casually nodded. *Hmmm, it was the prior's idea to send them.*

In late afternoon rising above the *meseta* they saw a church belltower in the distance and beyond that the sharp-peaked Cantabrian Mountains. They entered a town through its main gate, the walls under construction. The place was busy with a livestock market and numerous mules. Processions of mules laden with wares for sale and barter crowded the streets. They came to the Church of Santa Maria to stay overnight with other pilgrims in the adjacent hostel. The building was new and much of the town was under construction. As they led their mules to the church courtyard, the priest greeted them. He was accompanied by a man who spoke in Leonese. The priest translated into Latin. "The man says you have fine mules, but they are not from Spain."

"No . . . they are from Poitou, in Aquitaine."

The man commented, and the priest interpreted, "He knows of Poitou and its high reputation for breeding mules. He breeds mules in Mano en Silla de las Mulas, but he is from the mountains west of Astorga, where his people, the Maragatos live. They are the best *arrieros*. Pons looked confused. "They are, as you say in French, the best *muletiers* and breed the finest mules in Spain."

Pons smiled and bowed. "Tell him thank you, and may God bless him."

The man smiled and nodded and went on his way. Pons turned to the priest. "He mentioned the name of your town, an unusual and long name, *Mano en Silla de las Mulas*. Something about mules?"

"It means, *hand on the saddle of the mules*."

"No wonder. The town is full of mules!"

The priest laughed and added, "The man you just met, all he talks about is mules. He wants me to pray for his mules. He insists mules are more sure-footed, more intelligent, more durable, and have more character than horses."

Pons patted Cominius on the nose. "You know that already, don't you!"

"The muleteer told me another important fact to remember," added the priest. "He says mules have a much greater sense of self-preservation and will balk at unfavorable conditions, although most people misinterpret this as being stubborn. They are always aware of their surroundings, so listen to them."

The following morning Pons led the way out the west gate of town to cross the Elsa River. Like much of the town, the bridge was still under construction, so a ferry served the people needing to cross the river. A raft had been poled from the far side after ferrying pilgrims and was tied up, loading the next dozen foot-travelers. As the ferryman cast off, he announced to the pilgrims gathered on the riverbank, "A dozen pilgrims on foot for each crossing or if there are mounts, two men and their mounts."

The boatman poled the raft to the far side and returned. As he approached the bank, Pons could see Cominius was skittish. Guilen must have felt the same. "Brother, that ferry isn't much more than a raft of logs. Nothing like the sturdy ferry that floated us across the Rhone River." Cominius refused to board. Then the other mules also became agitated.

"Come on board," said the boatman.

Pons stepped onto the raft holding Cominius's reins and leading the mule into the shallow water next to the raft. "You will be fine swimming beside the raft, my friend." Guilen followed onto the raft and led his mule into the water as he held his reins. The boatman waved for ten pilgrims on foot to get on the raft. As the ferryman poled across the river, the mules swam alongside. The pair of Cluniac monks in Pons's entourage did the same when they crossed, letting the mules swim, as did the two Burgundian knights. When all of the group and their mules had disembarked, the boatman collected the fares from the dozen walking pilgrims then insisted Pons pay four fares for each of the mules. Pons answered, "Your savior Christ said, 'For the love of money is a root of all kinds of evil.' Sir, you collected fares for full ferries for each crossing and I will only pay you for the men in my party that you ferried across, and one more fare for each of the mules."

They rewarded the mules, letting them graze the lush grass along the riverbank and watched as a pair of horsemen arrived on the far bank. The ferryman returned and loaded both the riders and horses on the raft. Halfway across, the raft capsized. Mercifully, riders and horses swam to shore. Pons mounted Cominius and looked to Guilen. "As the *muletier* said, 'Listen to your mule.'"

At noon the road climbed the foothills approaching Leon. The sturdy mules had never balked when they had crossed the dry *meseta*, but the creatures' pace was now more spirited passing through the well-watered valleys of the Esla and the Porma rivers, where there was plenty of grass to forage at their rest stops. The green valleys were in contrast with the dry straw-colored *meseta* they were departing.

They arrived in Leon and lodged at the hospital next to the Basílica de San Isidoro. The next day Pons would seek the king to appeal for the continuation of the Alfonsine donation.

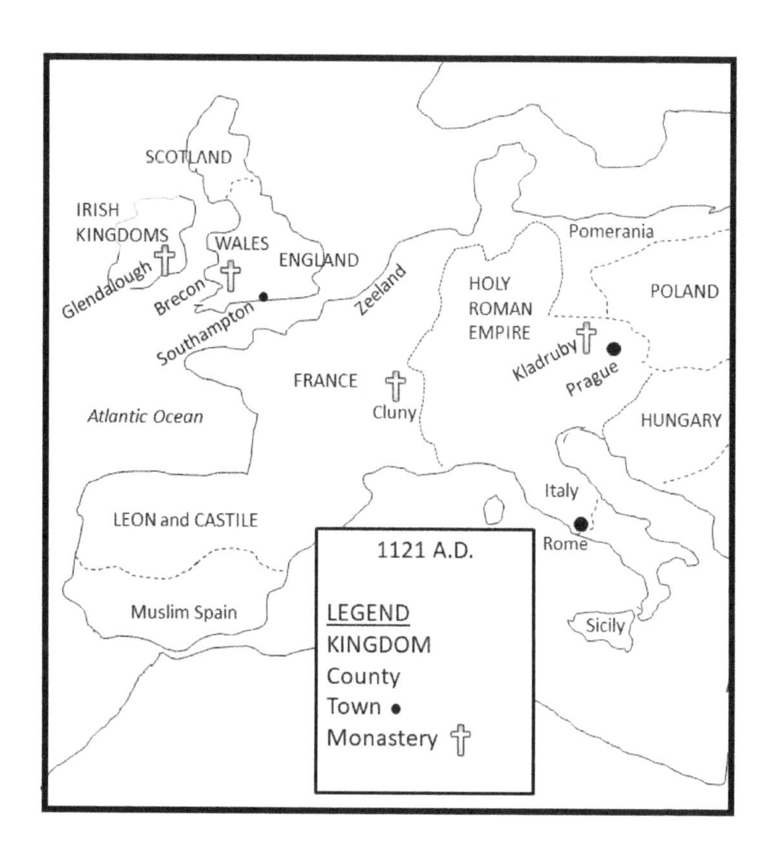
SCOTLAND
IRISH KINGDOMS
Glendalough
WALES
Brecon
ENGLAND
Southampton
Zeeland
Pomerania
HOLY ROMAN EMPIRE
POLAND
Kladruby
Prague
FRANCE
Cluny
Atlantic Ocean
HUNGARY
Italy
Rome
LEON and CASTILE
Muslim Spain
Sicily
1121 A.D.
LEGEND
KINGDOM
County
Town
Monastery

CHAPTER XV THE MISSIONARIES

O'Broin grabbed a loaf of bread from the tavern's counter, made sure he had his eating knife, picked up his walking stick, and turned to face Dublin. *As they have for a hundred years, Irish monks are yet traveling to the pagan lands of northern Europe. I am ready to follow them and leave Ireland.*

That night halfway to the city, he slept in a copse of trees, comfortable in his heavy woolen habit. He arrived the next afternoon at the Dublin wharves. There he found a group of monks at the waterfront and ran to join them. "I'm glad I caught up with you!" The monks turned in unison and peered at O'Broin.

The senior among them answered. "And Brother, who are you?"

"I am Thomas O'Broin, sent from Glendalough to accompany you."

"You must have been in a hurry! You still have a key on your belt."

O'Broin looked down and tapped the bald part of his tonsure. "I never use this key now. I've lost my locks!"

The monk chuckled. "We are from the Priory of the Holy Trinity of Dublin. It is in the same diocese as Glendalough. Yes that makes sense . . . although our prior did not tell us of you. But we are Benedictine brothers and the ship's passage is paid. There will be room, so I do not see a problem."

A helmsman rowed a leather hulled currach toward the dock. The craft was over thirty feet long, with a single mast, and fitted with oars. The hull was bull hides stretched over a willow frame then sealed with pine tar and topped by a wooden deck. O'Broin was not familiar with ships and wondered if this boat was seaworthy. He suspected the monks thought the same by the way they glanced back and forth between the currach and the nearby cogs, sturdy cargo ships. The senior monk spoke mostly to himself. "Those are *ships*! And this is our vessel? . . . Do boats like this sink very often?"

O'Broin rested a reassuring hand on the monk's shoulder. "Not too often. They usually only sink once."

"Don't be worried. We are only sailing to Wales," added the helmsman. "The winds are to the east, it's summer so the days are long. We will reach Caernarfon before dark. We can row as well, if needed. It's not the *Ark*, but my currach is very seaworthy."

O'Broin boarded last. "That makes me think of the flood in the Bible! Dear brothers, how many animals did Moses take on the ark?"

There was a pause, then murmurs, "He gathered two of each kind . . . um . . ." Finally one monk said, "It was Noah! Moses didn't build the ark!"

The others laughed with O'Broin. "You are very sharp! Here's another riddle. Now, being monks, this one may be difficult. Let's assume three men take this boat across the Irish Sea and it sinks. But not a single man got wet. How did they do it?"

The baffled monks looked at each other.

"They were all married!"

A lone monk snickered, then he whispered, "None was single." There was a pause, then the others laughed as well.

The helmsman gripped the steerboard. "Brothers, man your oars. We will unfurl the sail when we leave the harbor. Let us have more of the riddles while we row!"

They passed an anchored ship, the sailors aboard busy at work. O'Broin asked, "How do seamen say hello to each other?" He gave the monks a second to think, but no one answered. "They wave!"

There were groans. The helmsman added, "That's enough for now!"

The seas were not high, although a couple of monks fed the fish overboard. It was late afternoon when they arrived at Caernarfon in Wales, which was dominated by a Norman castle of the motte and bailey design. Ditches surrounded the wooden palisades which encompassed the bailey. High atop the earthen motte was a tower of stone.

O'Broin asked the helmsman, "That is a Norman castle? Merely wooden walls! I thought the *mighty* Normans would build stronger castles."

"You are headed to England?" said the helmsman.

O'Broin nodded.

The helmsman continued, "This Norman fortification is merely an outpost. When you reach England you'll see the great Norman stone castles. I am sure before long the Normans will be building them here. Then it will be Ireland's turn to be invaded."

The monks disembarked and O'Broin was the last off the currach. The helmsman whispered to O'Broin. "Those are good riddles for monks, but what kind of humor do you have for a sailor?"

"Are you married?"

The helmsman shook his head.

"When you visit the taverns, use these introductions to get the ladies."

He laughed. "Ladies?"

"I mean, to attract the prettiest, um . . . prostit, er . . . brasser."

He nodded.

"Say, 'Hey, Princess, you wouldn't happen to know where a lonely knight could scabbard his sword, would you?' or 'I may not be a priest, but I can get you to heaven, milady.'"

The helmsman laughed. "You are not like any monk I have ever met."

They trekked for two weeks from monastery to monastery, across Wales, where they were welcomed, joined in the services, and were fed and boarded. After dinner one evening at Brecon Monastery in southeast Wales, O'Broin headed for the priory cathedral to attend Prime. He patted his stomach as he walked along with his fellow Irish monks. "I enjoyed that vegetable dish served with the rye toast! What is it called?"

"We call it slake in Dublin. You've never had it?"

O'Broin shook his head.

"Oh, yes, you are from Glendalough in the mountains. The vegetable is seaweed."

A passing monk of Brecon overheard them. "The Welsh call it laver bread."

O'Broin raised his eyebrows. "Brother, I know Irish and Welsh are not exactly alike, but did I hear you say laver . . . bread? I understand laver is seaweed, but bread? I like the taste and prefer vegetables, but why call it a bread when what we ate was a cooked mash?"

The Brecon monk paused. "Perhaps it is because many Welsh prepare it by rolling the cooked laver in oatmeal and the dish then has the look of bread or cakes. That must explain it. Monks eat more simply . . . I suppose. You are all from Ireland? And where to next, England?"

"I am just following them," said O'Broin. "We are headed for a place called Bohemia. It would be helpful if I knew where we are going . . . that is to get oriented."

"We have maps in our library. I could show you later."

After Prime, O'Broin joined the Brecon monk in the library. The monk's attention was held across the spacious room on a couple of men poring over maps. "I am afraid we will have to wait, Brother, the maps I wanted to show you are being viewed by those two nobles at the table. Their family has made large donations to improve Brecon and they send their children here to be educated. They also pay well for copies of manuscripts and maps which they donate to other monasteries."

"Are they Normans?"

"No, those two are cousins, of the FitzPons family. Their fathers arrived with William of Normandy, but their family originated in Aquitaine."

One of the men noticed them, smiled, and gestured for them to come over. The cousins stood, bowed slightly, and looked at O'Broin. The FitzPons cousins and the monks completed introductions.

"I understand you are with the party on the way to Prague," said Alejandro. After a glance at O'Broin's belt, he added, "And your key, with it you will unlock the hearts of the Pomeranian and

Prussian pagans to the Faith?"

O'Broin laughed and bowed his head briefly.

"You were born in Ireland?"

He nodded.

"Which part?"

O'Broin answered with a straight face, "Sir, my whole body was born in Ireland!"

They shared a laugh.

The Irish monks departed Brecon the next morning to begin a six-day trek to the port city of Southampton. There they would seek passage across the English Channel. As they trooped along the road, one of the Dublin monks asked O'Broin, "I heard you have the task of delivering a manuscript in Winchester. What sort of document?"

"I went to the library to study a map to better understand our journey. There I met two nobles from the area, Simon and Alejandro, who showed me how to read a map of the lands where we will be missionaries. I am delivering a copy of that map to the monastery in Winchester." As they traveled on, O'Broin composed a riddle.

Several days later the group arrived at Winchester. O'Broin delivered the document, a rolled up parchment in a protective leather tube and held it before the monastery librarian. "Answer this question and this *map* is yours. I have seas without water, I have deserts without sand, I have cities with no people, and borders with no fences. What am I?"

It was prime sailing season and crossing the channel was uneventful. They had gained passage on a cog which sailed across the channel to the County of Zeeland, claimed by Holland and inhabited mostly by the Dutch, but governed by Flanders. They continued through Holland, traveling from one Benedictine monastery to another. By the end of the summer they reached Kladruby Abbey in Bohemia, eighty miles west of Prague.

CHAPTER XVI QUEEN URRACA *The Reckless One*

Pons and Guilen were admitted to Alfonso's palace in Leon and provided room and board, but the king was absent. He had just finished a military campaign putting down a rebellion by the Galicians, then had moved on to take the city of Zaragoza from the Muslims, and was now leading his army further south. He was proving that he had earned the name of *The Battler* as he led the northern Christian kingdoms in the *Reconquista*.

The group left Leon and came to an old Roman milestone engraved with the original name of the city, Asturica Augusta, which had evolved over the years to be Astorga. The town was surrounded by fortifications built a thousand years earlier by the Romans. Pons had to show the guards his letter from the Pope to be allowed through the main gate, the Puerta del Sol, open but well-guarded. Once inside the walls, Pons and his men walked their mules through streets crowded with soldiers. They halted at the Church of San Bartolome, next to a lodging for pilgrims. The hostel, one of numerous in the city, was part of a cluster of buildings that included the home of the attending monks, a priory subordinate to the monastery in Liebana northeast in the Cantabrian Mountains. The prior, headmaster of the monks, notified Pons to bring their mules inside the courtyard for boarding and safekeeping. He was delighted Pons would stay as well as join them for the Vespers and Compline that evening. At the prior's request, after the scripture readings at supper, Pons described Cluny Monastery to the brothers of the priory.

Afterwards the prior and Pons met with Bishop Pelayo, the patriarch of the Diocese of Astorga, at the prior's residence. The bishop was housed there temporarily because his new palace was under construction. After a short while the prior dismissed himself. The bishop and Pons discussed the Crown's donation to the Cluniac Order and the status of the diocese, talking late into the night. Pelayo revealed that most of the clergy and bishops, including the powerful Bishop of Compostela, Diego Gelmírez, were allied with Alfonso against his wife Urraca. Pelayo was one of the few who supported her.

Pons attended Prime the next morning as Psalms 21-26 was recited. Soon after, the bishop escorted Pons to Queen Urraca's residence a half mile away. The night before Pelayo had sent a message announcing Pons's arrival, and the queen had returned the messenger with a note that she would be pleased to receive him. The sun was just rising above the hills and the warmth at their backs replaced the coolness of the dawn, making a pleasant walk to the middle of the city.

At the central plaza, workmen were busy atop scaffolding. The foundation and walls of the Bishop's Palace were completed on one side of the open area. Shops fronted with colonnades were located on two sides of the flagstone square. The bishop held his arm out toward the activity. "Queen Urraca donated the land for the palace. The Church sold part of the property to merchants for their shops and residences in order to pay for the labor and materials."

The final side of the plaza was occupied by the queen's fortified residence. Archers with crossbows were stationed on a crenelated parapet above the entryway. One of the two guards armed with halberds at the entrance to Urraca's villa bowed to Bishop Pelayo. "Your Excellency! The queen is expecting Abbot Pons." He opened the massive oak door reinforced by bands of iron, the metal hinges groaning from its weight, and they entered an atrium.

A steward appeared as the bishop departed. He escorted Pons to a long receiving hall lined with columns. At the far end was the queen, bearing a rather severe countenance, seated alone on a regal throne elevated above the floor. Although Pons had brought his vestments anticipating a meeting such as this, he had decided to wear his black habit. The steward left and Pons did his best to move with confidence down the empty corridor, feeling small and insignificant.

As he drew near Queen Urraca, she deftly slid off her seat of power, keeping her eyes on Pons, and stepped down to welcome him. She was only a bit shorter than Pons, but her dark hair was gathered on top and crowned with an amethyst studded diadem. Her posture alone, however, made her look taller . . . and regal. Now that she was standing, Pons appreciated her gown with trumpet-sleeves that widened from the elbow and draped nearly to the floor. Her voluminous skirts contrasted with the pleating that formed a snug fit under her breasts. This last vision of her purple regalia stirred Pons under his heavy woolen habit. He reminded himself. *You will be with Primavera soon. Do not be distracted.*

Pons stopped within a few paces of the queen. As he bowed, the air held the scent of a flower garden. "Queen Urraca, thank you for receiving me."

She spoke perfect Burgundian French. "I should be thanking you, Abbot Pons, for your presence. My husband and most of the clergy have abandoned me."

"Cluny is devoted to your late father and your family. Please, let me mend the problems with your husband. The Pope has asked me to negotiate."

"Ah! The Pope! Pope Paschall, your godfather. Have you heard? He terminated my marriage with Alfonso of Aragon, because we have the same great-grandfather. It seems the marriage is annulled on the grounds of consanguinity!"

"I am sorry, Lady Urraca."

Her dark eyes were unwavering. "No, do not be. I am pleasantly satisfied. Alfonso wants to battle the rebels, the Muslims, and me! He does not want to govern . . . or be a husband . . . that is . . . he is not a lover and not a man of affection. He complains I counter every decision he makes!"

"Surely, you exaggerate!"

Urraca laughed and reached out, the scent of roses enveloping Pons as she touched his shoulder fleetingly. He flinched and gasped from the overpowering fragrance, recovered, then laughed with her.

"The rosewater is very fragrant, no? First brought by crusaders returning from the Levante, or should I say Outremer, the crusader states."

Pons nodded. "The quarrel with your husband . . . your former husband . . . can it be as serious as war? Astorga is full of soldiers. Will you be safe?"

"Alfonso has a highly trained corps of Aragonese knights, the *Militia Christi*, and has just organized another order, the *Confraternity of Belchite*, whose motto is: *'Never to live at peace with the pagans but to devote all their days to molesting and fighting them.'* But I have the armies of Leon and Castile loyal to me. We have superiority in numbers and though I do not lead in battle as does Alfonso, I am as clever, and I am involved in the strategy of my generals."

Urraca called out in Leonese toward the columns where curtains hung. They were parted by a female servant to reveal a pair of high-backed chairs and a small round table upon which were glasses of wine and a plate with food. "Please let's enjoy tapas." They relaxed in the chairs and sipped wine.

Urraca smiled. "You seem to relish the sardines on toast. Most visitors from the north grimace as they take their first bite."

"I had them earlier on the journey and they are delicious. These chickpeas—they are roasted, no? Very good with the olive oil, and seasoning . . ."

"It is rosemary."

"These . . . um, nibbles, these, *canapes*—I did not see these until I crossed the Pyrenees."

She laughed. "For some reason, my father could only drink and eat small amounts at one sitting. He also found that having food while drinking—drinking wine, that is—lessened inebriation. To reduce the drunken behavior of his subjects, he decreed that canapes be served with wine. The tradition started of placing the bread on the top of a cup of wine, covering the drink. So they are called tapas.

"Your journey has been long? Did footpads steal your wardrobe? I see you are dressed informally."

He glanced down at his habit. "It is not a faux display, Queen Urraca. I believe in following the stoic life dictated by Saint Benedict and I encourage my monks to do the same."

She flashed a polite yet genuine smile. "I am the same . . . in a way. I have my place—I must look and act as royalty . . . as I have ever since I was a child. Do you know I was married when I was only eight?"

"No . . ."

"Not to Alfonso, but to Raymond of Burgundy. He died in battle, never to see our two children reach maturity. I love them, and wish I could spend more time with them, but I am, in a way, just as much a slave as is a peasant—I must assume the responsibilities left to me after my father passed away.

"But forgive my chatter, please, tell me of your journey and of course of the magnificent Cluny Abbey."

Pons leaned back, sipping wine. "We have much in common, Your Majesty . . ."

"You will call me Urraca. May I address you as Pons?"

"Yes, certainly. I was given to the Church, given to be educated and live at a monastery, when I was four. I was expected to become the Abbot of Cluny, so my life was planned, as yours."

"We only have freedom . . . to pursue our own interests, when we are hidden from the world . . . as we are now." She reached across the table and touched his hand. *She is in control, her scent, her clothes, her aggressiveness . . . if this has to happen, I must gain something for Cluny.*

Urraca stood. He could not ignore her upright posture, an example of someone who commands. "I know why you are here. We will talk of your issues later." She removed her diadem and placed it on the table. From behind the curtains the stringed music of a chorus of gitterns began, joined by the sweet voice of a trobairitz. Pons was astounded when Urraca twirled, her feet light with the music, removed her outer gown, the trumpet-sleeves spinning to the floor. *This must be the fabled silk cloth. Its fluidity and gentle rustle exude sensuality. And that delightful song reminds me of Azalais. The rose scent . . .* Pons, dreamy eyed, finished the rest of his wine.

An hour later, Pons lay comfortably in the dark. *This bed is much too comfortable, and this pillow is too soft. Where am I? Oh yes . . . in Urraca's quarters. It must be night, for there is no light. Have I been here that long?* He was naked and felt his groin. *We had sex! But I am clean as if I had just taken a bath.* The scent of rosewater puffed from under the cover. Then he remembered.

Urraca had entranced him. *I remember drinking more, then more wine, as she removed layer after layer of silk. The glass never emptied. Then I was here in this bed, in the dark and Urraca was on top of me. I felt her, smelled her rose scent, but I could not see her. With Primavera I always saw her face and her body, but here I was deprived of that. Urraca lowered herself onto me and pounded me with such intensity and for so long I wondered how I could stay aroused, but I remember enjoying it. And her servants must be used to her loud screams, for no one came until we awoke. They bathed us in the wooden tub scented with rose water. Oh, Lord, forgive me! I should be contemplating your glory instead of entertaining these thoughts.*

Where is she now? Suddenly light pierced the room as curtains were pulled back. It wasn't a servant, it was Urraca. She wore her sparkling crown, but nothing else, reached over, and yanked the cover off Pons.

"A monk with scars and muscles! You look more like a warrior than a holy brother! Oh, yes . . . you follow the ethic of work . . . never mind your other vows." She buried her face in Pons's groin, as he caressed her breasts hidden among her long dark tresses. Pons quickly finished.

He fell asleep and an hour later, Pons again lay comfortably in the dark. *This same bed, the same pillow. I am still in Urraca's quarters. Again, the scent of rosewater. I remember a warm cloth. He felt the bed sag as if someone joined him. It must be Urraca. Just that thought along with the strong fragrance of her rosewater has aroused me again.* The curtains were opened to light the chamber. Urraca reclined on her back and gazed at the ceiling, her alluring breasts and shapely thighs bright in the sunlight as she lay in her naked glory. Pons didn't need any encouragement.

Again he slept, and awoke comfortably in the dark. *I am still in Urraca's quarters. The bedclothes are, of course, the scent of roses.* The nap refreshed him and the clean bouquet of rosewater followed him as he rolled out of bed. Pons found a scrap of parchment, drew the curtains and read the message written on it.

Return tomorrow and we will discuss the donation to Cluny.

She had added her unique signature,

Pons left the queen's palace feeling guilty, but also very hungry. He found a tavern across the plaza that served cocido maragato, a stew made of chickpeas and pork. He stood at the bar and as he began to eat, a patron with gregarious nature told him something in Castilian which he didn't understand. The man, through pantomime, gave Pons the understanding that he should eat the meat first, then the chickpeas, and lastly the soup. Pons complied and assumed it must be a local custom. They leaned on the counter and ate quietly side by side for a few moments, then the man laughed as he wafted air toward his nose, sniffed, pointed at Pons, and he said, "Flores! Muy bien!"

Pons finished his meal and returned to San Bartolome Priory. When he attended Compline, he realized the monks nearby took special notice of him, and he knew it had to be the scent of rosewater. Later when they were out of the hearing of others, Guilen quietly jested with him about his unusual bouquet. He stopped the teasing abruptly when he saw Pons was sullen and withdrawn.

Pons slept well that night. After breakfast he returned to Urraca's palace alone. He was escorted to her library where the queen sat behind a writing desk which had ornately carved flanks and legs. She remained seated as she placed a document to the side on a stack of parchments. Pons bowed. "*Bon dia* . . . Queen Urraca."

"*Bon dia*, Abbot Pons." She tilted her head toward the chair across the desk. As he sat, Pons understood this meeting would be business and thus the proper time to make his request. After they enjoyed spiced wine, he phrased his words carefully, humbly asking if she would donate funds to Cluny so he could resume construction of what he described would be the faith's largest church.

Urraca had a sultry look. "Your performance yesterday deserves for me to say yes . . ." Quickly her visage stiffened, "But my treasury must be preserved to keep Leon and Castile free of

Alfonso. To be true to my late father's wish, I married Alfonso and for a short time, we had a Christian empire that was capable of driving the Muslims from Spain. But I have failed . . . rather the marriage has failed, and now my duty is to at least preserve what Father has left me."

She pushed a small wooden box across the desk.

He opened it. "Thank you. A relic?"

"Yes, it is a tooth of Saint John the Baptist. Very rare. It will attract pilgrims and donations for Cluny."

"You are generous. And I will pray that your differences with Alfonso can be resolved without bloodshed. Are you sure you do not want me to mediate?"

A darkness shrouded her as the queen looked down and shook her head.

I have betrayed Primavera and done all this for nothing. Why did I succumb to this woman? Stop! Pons, think like the negotiator Abbott Frotard trained you to be! He had me practice at Saint Pons as he played the role of both religious and secular adversaries. Watch their posture. I must not give up. Will I be too bold if I resume our intimacy? She is now acting the formal queen. I believe she is implying our romantic liaison is over. Pons took up his chair and placed it on the same side of the desk as Urraca, facing her, but not too close. The shadow passed from her. She appeared curious rather than offended.

Pons settled into his chair. "We have a common objective."

Urraca raised her eyebrows.

"I will be continuing my journey west," continued Pons, "to meet the Bishop of Santiago de Compostela."

The queen looked irritated. "The bishop . . . Diego Gelmírez, is allied with Alfonso, as are most of the other bishops."

"Yes, Bishop Pelayo told me. I have been sent to make peace in Spain. If I could convince Diego to withdraw his support from Alfonso—or at least be neutral, would that help?"

Her tilt forward, barely perceptible, encouraged Pons. "If I receive Diego's cooperation, I have been authorized by the Pope to inform him that the Diocese of Santiago de Compostela would be raised to metropolitan status, to an archdiocese, and thus Diego Gelmírez would become an archbishop, overseeing all the dioceses in Spain."

Urraca smiled. "I am impressed. Your proposal has convinced me . . ."

She retrieved a parchment from the pile on the desk and signed it with her unique icon at the bottom, then signed the other documents. He glanced at the top page and recognized her signature from the note she had left him the day before.

The queen inserted the documents into a leather case, stood, and handed it to Pons. "Last night I considered signing over to Cluny several of my properties in Burgundy, but now I am certain. I inherited them from my first husband. There are five deeds here, one for each of the next five years. If I still rule after that, I will continue to make annual donations of property."

"Thank you." Pons accepted the case, her eyes told him it was goodbye, and he kissed her hand. He turned on his heel and crossed the room. Her royal posture slumped and her eyes teared as she watched the abbot's parting.

Pons left the palace and trudged toward the priory. *In another life, what could we have become? No, I am merely feeling lustful. I am no different from the scheming nobles and clergy that I detest. Did she trade sex for her properties? No! . . . I should think so highly of myself? God help me! I recall what my mother said, "Where is your maturity, where is your worldly sense? You assume the Church is kind and fair to everyone, as Jesus taught."*

Pons attended the rest of the services in a blur that day. He sensed Guilen wanted to say something, but his friend knew better and would wait. After dinner Pons went to the priory stables to see how his mule was faring after the long journey. Pons moved Cominius to an empty enclosure and groomed him. He appreciated their time together and imagined Cominius shared the feeling.

Guilen joined them. "Pons, you remain downcast! Do you wish me to pray with you?"

Pons refused to look at Guilen and continued to brush Cominius. "I will mend."

"Perhaps you'd rather have the company of an animal? I admit my mule is a trusty mount, but I don't have such camaraderie with it." Guilen was about to leave.

"No, wait, Guilen. Forgive me. With the Lord's help and the love of a brother such as you, I will recover."

Guilen placed his hands upon Pons's shoulders. His eyes cast down to the shorter man. "I assume the queen did not resume the crown's annual donation to Cluny?"

"No, she will not . . ." He was interrupted as the Burgundian guards passed, after feeding their mounts, and then departed. "No, she will not resume the donation." Pons's eyes widened. When the knights were out of hearing he said, "I didn't know they were in the stables. I wonder if they heard me?"

Guilen seemed puzzled. "Why does it matter?"

"I believe they are a threat to me . . . to us. We need to keep aware of them. Tomorrow we head toward Compostela to complete our pilgrimage."

Guilen clasped Pons's shoulders. "Don't be so morose. That's something to look forward to." He stepped away and sniffed his hands. "The same rosewater scent you were covered with yesterday," he whispered. "That's why you are gloomy! I know you are more concerned with honor than with money. That's what depresses you! You regret now that you were with her!"

Pons's eyes were fixed with Guilen's, but he did not answer.

"You are the abbot, but you were my brother long before that. And you are only a man. You will go to Santiago de Compostela and do penance. God will know your sincerity. Trust God and he will give you direction."

Slowly, the corners of Pons's mouth turned up. "I am blessed that God has given me such a wise friend!"

The next morning when Pons was alone with his two escorts from Cluny, he warned them of his fear that the knights could be spies for the Count of Burgundy and might pose a danger. Pons had handpicked the Cluniac monks because he regarded them as very loyal, but he did not mention his suspicion that Prior Thomas was involved. The abbot's party left Astorga and the road climbed most of the day into the Leon Mountains. As Cominius plodded uphill, Pons was pulled down by the guilt of his insincerity to Primavera. *When we reach Santiago, I will pray as long as it takes to feel in my bones that the Lord has forgiven me.*

It was sunny and hot and they stopped to quench their thirst amid one of the frequent stands of trees. A Burgundian knight found a tumbling stream and replenished his water gourd as he also led his mule to drink. The knight yelled as the mule resisted when it neared some fallen timber. "I thought these creatures were supposed to be smart. They haven't had water all day!" he pulled harder on the reins. The mule refused to move further. Suddenly, she kicked backward and brayed with fright. The knight shouted, "A den of vipers!" The mule bucked, stomped the ground, and kicked again, throwing snakes into the air. A viper latched onto the knight, then fell off. The knight dropped to his knees, his forearm beginning to swell from a snakebite. In the ruckus a monk was kicked by a mule and leaned over, holding his ribs. Guilen and the other monk beat the bushes with their staves and drove away the snakes.

Pons remained frozen, still in depression. Guilen laid out a blanket for the knight who was already in shock, and took him to the shade of a tree. He cleaned the wound with wine.

The other knight retrieved the mule, which limped back. "The viper bit his mule as well."

Pons broke out of his stupor. "Guilen, despite all the times we worked in the herb garden, I can't remember if there were plants to treat snakebite!"

Guilen pressed a wet cloth on the man's forehead. "Saint John's wort. The infirmarian said if poisoned, crush the leaves in wine and drink it. Snake venom is a poison, is it not?" Guilen looked up at the monks. "Do any of you remember what Saint John's wort looks like?" They shook their heads.

"Pons, the meadow is full of flowers. Let's examine them and perhaps the sight of them will stir our memory!" The two men rushed about the meadow examining the wildflowers. In a short time, they both returned, each with a handful of leaves and flowers. As they discussed what they were going to do, a passing mule train led by a pair of local *Maragatos* stopped. As a muletier hurried over, Pons asked, "Do you know how to treat snakebites?" Although the Maragato did not understand Pons, he noticed the wounds. He snatched the plants they had gathered, selected the dandelion leaves, stuffed them in his mouth, and began chewing.

"What? Give those back . . ."

"Guilen wait . . ." said Pons.

The muletier handed dandelions to Guilen and motioned for him to chew the leaves. He then extracted the pulpy mass from his mouth, formed a poultice, and pressed it on the mule's snakebite. He gestured for Guilen to do the same for the knight. The muletier tore a strip of cloth from his tunic and strapped the poultice to the mule's leg. With a combination of hand signals and the few words Pons knew in Castilian, they understood they were to change the poultice. The muletier told the injured monk to spit. There was no sign of blood and he smiled. Then he put his hands together as in prayer, slightly bowed, and joined his fellow *Maragato* to continue their journey. Pons shouted after them, "God bless you!"

"Don't worry about finding Saint John's wort," Pons directed. "Find more dandelions and continue the *Maragato's* remedy. Since we have two injured men, we will spend the night here and try to nurse them back to health."

They made their camp under a large oak tree and took turns making fresh poultices for the knight and warmed around a small fire as the air cooled in the evening. His fellow Burgundian camped in the meadow to guard the mules and to change the poultice on the mule.

Guilen glanced at the injured knight as he slept, then looked back at Pons. "The poultice may be working. He still has a fever, but now he is sleeping. I hope God will answer our prayers and save him."

Pons nodded, then he chuckled.

"What is funny?"

"Did you notice the muletier who helped us? He treated the *mule* first, then only afterwards he said to treat the knight."

"Yes." He laughed.

The monk who had been mule kicked in the ribs, stifled a laugh which turned to a groan of pain. Guilen looked at the sleeping knight, then across the meadow, and lowered his voice. "Pons, do you still think the knights are a threat?"

"Because of my despondent behavior they probably assume I was not successful in my request for the crown's donation. And, . . . they might also have heard us in the stable when I told you the bad news."

"So Thomas wanted you to regain the funds for Cluny, then afterwards would have you assassinated before your return. Then he would have the chance to become abbot," said Guilen. "But now that you have not recovered the donation, he doesn't need you at all."

Neither man commented for a few moments, then Guilen continued, "But perhaps God sent the vipers to lessen the chance. Now there is one less knight that can harm you. We are three. We can defend ourselves."

"But he is a trained soldier. We will take turns staying awake tonight—to care for one knight and keep watch on the other."

Hours later, although the campfire had burned low, there was enough light to care for the feverish knight. Against his own wishes, but because Pons had demanded it, Guilen woke the abbot to take his turn to watch the knight. Guilen quickly fell to sleep. A hundred paces away, the Burgundian knight who was guarding the herd secured his own mule and scattered the rest into the night. Cominius at first refused to leave but fled when the knight hit him with a switch. The knight moved quietly toward the campfire.

Pons chewed more dandelion leaves into a paste. He removed the old poultice from the knight's arm and replaced it with the newly masticated pulp. He noticed that the knight's scabbard was empty.

Far off, Cominius brayed as in fear, diverting Pons's attention toward the meadow. Suddenly a figure brandishing two long knives appeared out of the dark into the circle of campfire light. The man ran through the coals and they exploded into a spray of embers and ashes, snuffing out the light.

Pons rolled away from the oncoming attacker. Then he heard grunts and clashing attended by a horrifying gurgling sound. He heard the same sound a second time. *Where is my staff? I need light!* He felt about, found it, and guessing where the fire had been, smashed the coals, creating a light emitting shower of embers. In the flash of light he saw the ground covered with bodies, and standing above them a Burgundian knight, his eyes filled with murder, holding two blood-soaked knives.

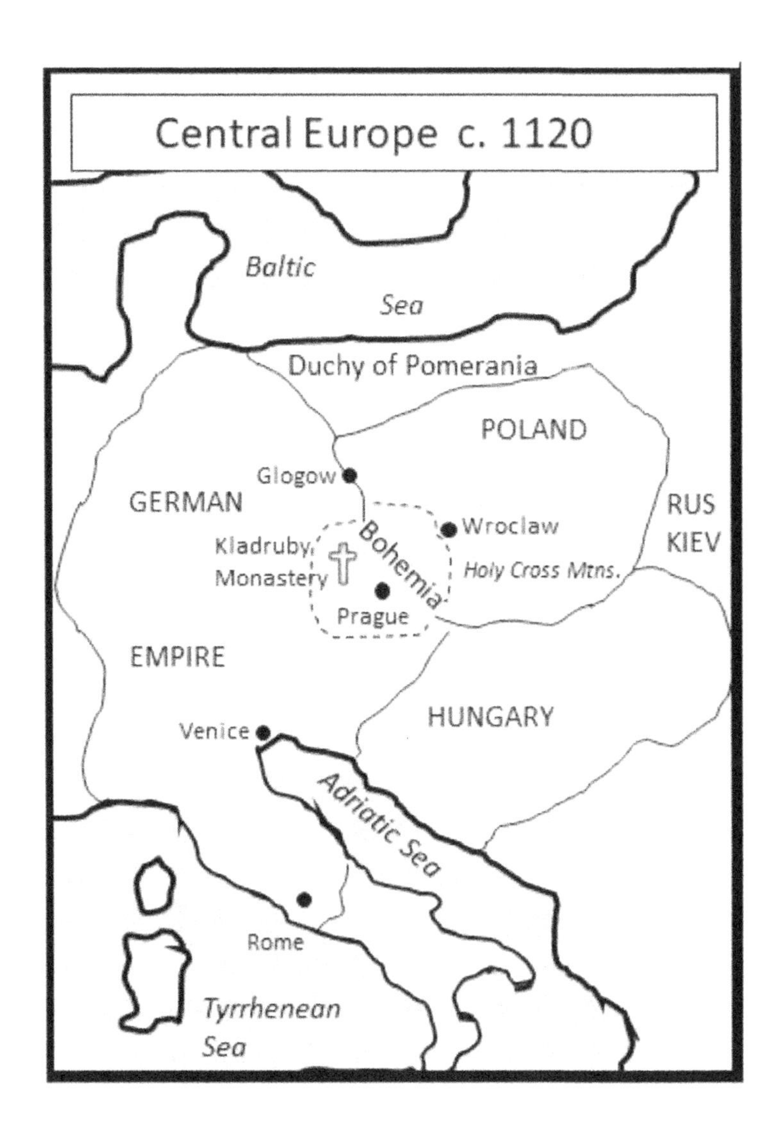
Central Europe c. 1120
Baltic
Sea
Duchy of Pomerania
POLAND
Glogow
GERMAN
RUS
KIEV
Wroclaw
Kladruby
Monastery
Bohemia
Holy Cross Mtns.
Prague
EMPIRE
HUNGARY
Venice
Adriatic Sea
Rome
Tyrrhenean
Sea

CHAPTER XVII THE POLISH KNIGHT

Markiz Janusz Kozubowski, military commander, rode ahead of the column of knights as they departed the city of Wroclaw. His long dark hair extended from under a pointed helmet, which had been made in Persia and obtained through trade with the Rus. The surface was handsomely decorated with copper leaf and being without a face plate, the knight's bushy mustache was noticeable. The helmet was topped with a tuft of horsehair dyed a bright red. An aventail, a flexible curtain of mail, was attached to the lower edge of the helmet and extended to cover his throat, neck, and shoulders.

The markiz's knights wore conical helmets fitted with nose plates, like those of the Normans. Under their red cloaks each knight had on a chainmail tunic which reached to their knees. They were armed with one-handed, double-edged swords, sheathed in leather scabbards reinforced at the tip by metal chapes. The scabbards bounced from the knights' belts, the steel chapes glinting in time with the warhorses' gaits. The knights were also armed with throwing axes on their belts and spears, couched into pockets in their saddles.

Several weeks earlier, Kozubowski's liege lord, the ruler of Poland, Duke Boleslaw III, had invaded Pomerania to conquer the pagan lands. After the duke had secured the territory, he had planned to send word to Kozubowski to lead his knights and escort Christian missionaries to the conquered lands. A message had arrived from the duke, but instead of the expected orders to bring missionaries, Boleslaw had commanded Kozubowski to bring his knights and join his army at Glogow. The town was under siege by a combined army of German knights, Saxon foot soldiers, and a contingent of Bohemian cavalry led by their Duke Svatopluk. The joint forces were led by Henry V, the German king and emperor. After two weeks of siege, the town was on the verge of surrender.

Sixty miles south of the besieged city, Kozubowski's troop crossed a fortified bridge as they departed Wroclaw, a city built on an island in the Odra River. The entrance to the bridge was defended by a barbican, a double tower above a drawbridge, and was known as the Dragon Gate. Kozubowski glanced at the sculpture of the mythical creature as he passed through the gate. Guarding the Dragon Gate had been his first duty as a commander. *Those were good days! The intense training regimen I developed for my troop. Over time my men became an elite corps of knights, known as the Dragons. Our duke's conquest of Pomerania to convert the pagans was a holy undertaking, yes . . . it was a crusade. But I am inspired to join the greater campaigns in the east, to protect Jerusalem and to keep it in Christian hands.*

The troop of thirty knights made a forced ride, covering the sixty miles to Glogow in less than two days. The markiz and his knights stayed secluded in the forest across the Odra River, east of the besieged city. He sent lookouts north to reconnoiter and find the location of Boleslaw's army. Kozubowski's scouts encountered Polish messengers from Glogow. They reported that King Henry had granted the citizens a five-day respite so their town leaders could ask for Duke Boleslaw's permission to surrender. King Henry had made the townsmen send their children as hostages to enforce the truce, but had promised to return them alive no matter how Boleslaw answered. Kozubowski's scouts discovered Henry's army had camped west of Glogow. The bulk of his army surrounded the city, with lesser ranks across the river on the east side. The next day Boleslaw arrived from Pomerania with his Polish forces and swept away the meager German forces east of the river, establishing his army's camp there. He ordered Kozubowski to his headquarters.

Kozubowski found the large tent where Duke Boleslaw

Krzywousty, The Wrymouthed, sat in conversation with several of his officers. He had an enormous mustache that concealed his disfigurement, which he had acquired as a youth. He had once smashed his head into a wall, enraged because his father had lost the important Polish city of Krakow without a fight. When Boleslaw had become duke, he had recovered Krakow and had developed an alliance with Kiev by marrying a Rus princess. His military success in Bohemia in transforming the duchy into his vassal had threatened the king and had prompted his invasion of Poland. Kozubowski had the utmost respect for Boleslaw's zealotry, because it resulted in triumph.

As he entered the tent, the duke rose to meet him. "Markiz Kozubowski! I have destroyed the opposition in Pomerania! Your missionary campaign escorting Otto and his clergymen to convert the pagans will be delayed. First, we must stop Henry's invasion."

The markiz bowed. "Yes, Your Grace." Kozubowski briefed the duke on the status of the siege, including the hostages. The German army was twice the size of Boleslaw's combined force of 500 knights and 3,500 infantrymen.

Boleslaw cleared his throat. "I will not surrender Glogow. If the townspeople surrender, when I get Glogow back, I will crucify them all! As of now, I will begin with sorties and follow with an attack . . ."

The markiz recognized his lord's temper and saw the dark cloud growing. *I have seen this behavior before, he will attack without a plan.* "As you commanded," said Kozubowski. "I have readied defensive positions at the river crossings to prevent a counterattack."

Diverted, Boleslaw's expression relaxed. "I ordered . . .? Yes, yes, it would be foolish to cross the river and fight the larger army. In addition, many of our men are exhausted and wounded after the battles in the north.

"We will keep the river between us and Henry's forces. Slip into the city with a handful of your Dragons and rally the citizens to continue the fight. If Henry keeps his word, he will return the children. We will bog his army down and prevent his invasion of Poland."

The five-day armistice expired and with the arrival of the Polish army, Henry knew the city was not planning to surrender.

Leaders of the city brandished a white flag from the battlements and appealed for the emperor to return their children. The Germans brought the hostages forward, not to be freed, but as human shields. They were tied to catapults and the siege engines were rolled forward to assault the city.

Kozubowski beheld the grim spectacle from Glogow's walls as the garrison's archers attempted to shoot the enemy troops without harming their progeny. It was a horrifying sight as many of the young hostages were wounded or killed by arrows or crushed by siege engines during the battle. The defenders repulsed the attack and the German forces retreated. The townspeople were in mourning and the streets resounded with the wails of mothers.

As the day ended, the Germans lit bonfires near their catapults and began launching flaming pitch-filled logs. Most of the citizens were frantically controlling the resulting fires. Only a few soldiers manning the fortifications saw a figure in dark clothes appearing in and out of the light of bonfires near the catapults. Within a short time, several children were heard crying at the base of the city wall bordering the river. The lone stranger wearing the black habit of a monk emerged again near the catapults. With the skill of an acrobat, he scaled the frame of a catapult and slashed the ropes pinning a young prisoner, but two German artillerymen blocked their escape. The monk grabbed the severed ropes from the ground, whipped them around and entangled the soldiers and their weapons. In the moments they took to unravel themselves, the monk had vanished into the dark with the freed children.

Several more times the stranger went back and retrieved hostages. Cheers erupted from the Polish soldiers on the wall. "The monk is saving our children! God has sent an angel!" Kozubowski learned that some children were now safely inside the town. He climbed to the wall and observed the row of catapults lit by the bonfires. *Now that the Germans have been alerted, they will be waiting. Whoever he is, he is crazy to try this by himself. Truly God is protecting him in his insane quest. He is mad, this monk!*

Kozubowski rushed to collect a few of his knights. In a short time, and without orders, Kozubowski led a score of the Dragons, raided the enemy camp, routed the German guards at several of the catapults, and set the siege engines on fire. With the diversion, the men rescued a handful of children. In the encounter the black-robed monk joined them as they returned to the city.

When Boleslaw learned of the raid the following morning, he ordered the markiz to his tent. With the duke was a tonsured monk wearing a black habit of the Benedictine order. Boleslaw was red-faced as he raked Kozubowski. "Act without my permission again and I will have you executed!"

Kozubowski was motionless, straight as a rod, without making eye contact with the duke. "Yes, Your Grace."

"Your duty is to win this battle and not take such risks. The people of Glogow and the army depend on you. And jeopardize your men's lives? Because of your success destroying siege engines, I will not punish you . . . this time."

"Yes, Your Grace."

"Your reputation as a warrior . . . a warrior who gives no quarter was shown when we invaded Prussia, when your Dragons took no prisoners."

"And you have always been focused on driving your enemy ahead, crushing them with no mercy and ignoring distractions, even from the women sobbing for their fallen men."

"Yes, Your Grace."

"Tonight, you will conduct more raids, but no more rescuing hostages. And take this crazy monk with you. I cannot get information from him . . . I can read Latin but I cannot speak it well. In fact, his Latin is accented, making it hard to understand him. He may have valuable information and he is your prisoner to interrogate."

The markiz nodded, bowed, and as he left, O'Broin followed him. Kozubowski headed toward his tent as O'Broin walked beside him. "I assume I was to leave with you?"

The markiz glanced at the shorter man. "Yes, I forgot you don't know Polish, so I'll speak Latin."

"He is angry about the rescue attempts?"

"Yes. He prohibits any more rescues, but other than the few children we recovered last night, I fear the rest have perished."

"We did our best," added O'Broin. "War brings out the evil in men. Even Christian men."

"Where have you come from?"

"I was living at the Kladruby monastery north of Prague, when the Bohemian calvary recruited me to perform last rites for those who perished in battle. You saw what they did to those poor children! But I would not pray for those cruel, alleged Christians, or stand by and watch, so I acted."

"I respect your determination . . . and of course what you did to save them."

Kozubowski halted in front of his tent. A broth thick with meat bubbled in an iron pot above the hot coals of a fire. He skewered a morsel of pork. "The Germans attacked Poland, then killed the children. And our battles against the pagans was for their own good. After we conquer Pomerania, we will build churches for them. But I would rather crusade in the Outremer and fight infidels." He offered the piece of meat to O'Broin.

"No, I do not eat the flesh of dead animals."

"So you *are* a madman—you eat live animals!" The markiz laughed. "But a warrior must eat meat, bread, and beer to develop a strong body!"

O'Broin laughed.

"All right," Kozubowski smiled. "I respect the martial abilities you showed last night. Perhaps *you* do not need meat."

The deaths of the townspeople's children had been devastating, but the tragedy bolstered their will to fight. They repulsed several more German assaults over the next few days. Further clandestine attacks each night by Kozubowski's Dragons caused more enemy casualties, destroyed catapults, and weakened their army, which eventually convinced Henry to abandon the siege of Glogow.

Polish scouts reported a contingent of the German knights had remained in the camp near Glogow. The rest of the knights, the German foot soldiers, and Bohemian calvary marched south and looted Polish villages. Duke Boleslaw reinforced the garrison of Glogow with infantry, and with most of the German siege engines destroyed, he was confident the city could withstand further assault. He then led his smaller force on the other side of the Odra River parallel to the German army. The Polish knights, led by the Dragons, conducted hit-and-run attacks. After several days the German army arrived a few miles west of Wroclaw. Henry camped and prepared his forces to attack the city.

Duke Boleslaw relied on Wroclaw as a base to govern western Poland. The fortified city was at the crossroads of two important trading routes, the *Via Regia*, which led west to the Rhine River, and the Amber Road, named for the orbs of the lustrous, hardened resin. The prized amber was gathered along the beaches of the Baltic Sea, transported along the road to the Adriatic seaport of Venice, then traded across the Mediterranean.

From his vantage point in a copse of trees, Kozubowski observed the German army making camp west of Wroclaw. He glanced behind him to the east and studied the walled city, located on an island in the river. The keep of the duke's castle soared above the city walls. Built of large cut stones, the tower had been erected at the summit of a manmade hill. Nearby, Benedictine monks had constructed Saint Martin's Cathedral, the only other structure visible above the walls. *Wroclaw's fortifications are well-made, but the land is flat. There are no hills or rocky terrain, so unlike my homeland at Ogrodzieniec Castle. One day I will return to my birth land in the Holy Cross Mountains. As a youth I remember climbing Lysa Mountain, the highest peak. I made my way through the pine forest and across vast fields of loose rocks, proud of my accomplishment, until at the top I found a Benedictine monastery. I respected those monks, doing back breaking labor and surviving on top of a mountain.*

The markiz returned to Wroclaw to report to the duke. Boleslaw decided to engage Henry's army in the fields just west of the Dragon Gate and to fall back to the fortified city if a retreat was necessary. A year earlier Kozubowski had defeated many of these same Bohemian knights led then by the Czech cavalry commander, Duke Svatopluk. Since then, however, Svatopluk had ousted the ruler of Bohemia allied with Poland and had pledged his loyalty to Henry. Kozubowski looked forward to a rematch with his great rival.

At sunrise, the Dragons led the Polish army out of Wroclaw to form battle lines. Boleslaw placed his infantry at the center and the mounted knights comprised both wings. The Germans hastily set up their own formations. Duke Boleslaw ordered his army to advance with the morning sun in the Germans' eyes. Kozubowski noticed there were only a few score cavalry in the enemy lines and shouted to Boleslaw, near the center, mounted among a troop of knights. "I don't see the Bohemian knights. It could be a trap!"

Boleslaw called a halt to the advancing Polish lines. Suddenly a Dragon scout approached from the south, lashing his mount at a gallop. The knight pulled up, and breathing hard, reported to Kozubowski. The markiz looked to Boleslaw and relayed the scout's message, "The Bohemian knights have returned to Prague!"

Boleslaw signaled for a charge. The infantry ran forward, the Dragons enveloped the enemy flanks, and King Henry's army was crushed. The king, however, escaped with his knights and retreated to Germany.

The war had ended, and the Pope demanded both rulers do penance for the sin of Christians fighting against Christians. King Henry would not go to the Outremer, the collective term for the crusader states of Antioch, Tripoli, and Jerusalem. He did instead contribute one hundred knights for the crusade to the Holy Land.

Duke Boleslaw refused to leave Poland, fearing Henry would invade, and he did not have the extra resources to send knights. But he designated Kozubowski to recruit volunteers to join the crusade planned by the Venetians.

Kozubowski and O'Broin rode out of the Dragon Gate across the Odra River. They made a wide detour around the field where the Battle of Wroclaw had been fought two months earlier. Wild dogs still frequented the battlefield, devouring so many German corpses with such a frenzied intensity that no one dared venture there. The site became known as *Psie Pole*, the Dogs' Field.

O'Broin, riding Kozubowski's spare horse, said, "It is only you and me."

"And a few Bohemian knights," said Kozubowski, "Duke Svatopluk is no longer supporting King Henry. I think some of his knights will join us. We go to Prague to recruit, then take the Amber Road to Venice."

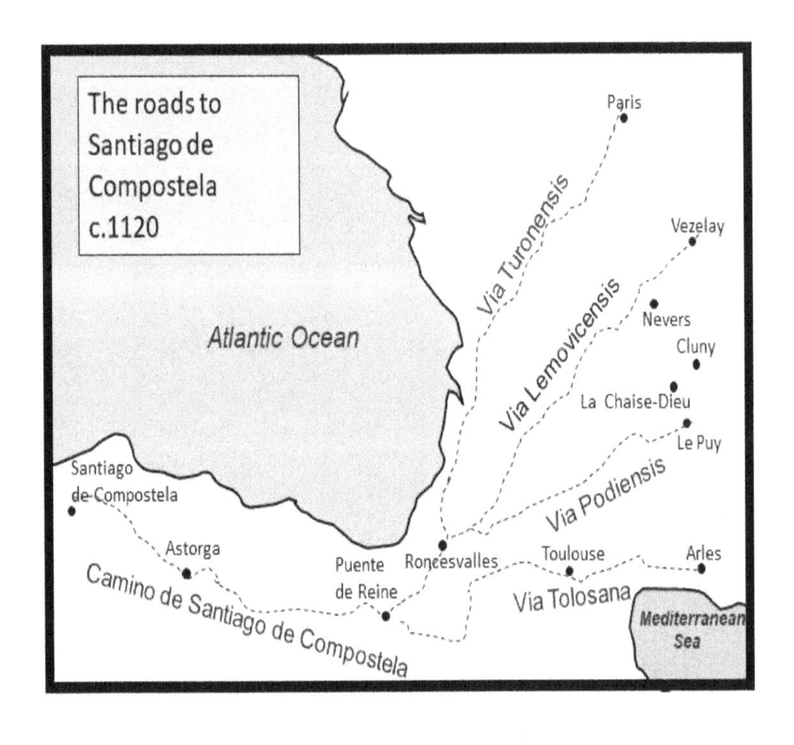
The roads to Santiago de Compostela c.1120
Atlantic Ocean
Paris
Vezelay
Nevers
Cluny
La Chaise-Dieu
Le Puy
Via Turonensis
Via Lemovicensis
Via Podiensis
Santiago de-Compostela
Astorga
Puente de Reine
Roncesvalles
Toulouse
Arles
Via Tolosana
Camino de Santiago de Compostela
Mediterranean Sea

CHAPTER XVIII EXILE of the POPE

Pons had joined a group of Benedictine monks returning from Santiago de Compostela to LePuy, France. Their journey across Spain took a month. Pons believed the Lord had sent the brothers so he could travel in the safety of company. The monks were friendly, a few even talked to their mules, like Pons, but more importantly their presence heartened him after the tragedy. Now thirty days east of Compostela, the monks rode silently in meditation. *How did I survive that assault? Oh, my God, I killed a man! I killed that murdering Burgundian! He slaughtered my brothers. I shudder every time I remember their bloody and lifeless bodies. Somehow I buried Guilen, I buried all of them. I prayed over their graves. Even the villain.*

Then I finally reached Compostela, where I learned that Pope Paschall had died in Rome. My remorse over the death of Guilen was compounded by the loss of my godfather, who had guided me most of my life, the man who had taken the role of my father. The Lord provided the Bishop of Compostela, Diego Gelmirez, who spent hours counseling me. He helped me work through the pain after the deaths of my friend and godfather. He acknowledged my penance for manslaughter. We became friends and he helped me accomplish my mission. Pope Paschall had promoted Gelmirez to archbishop and he agreed not to oppose Urraca in her quest to keep Castile and Leon independent from her former husband. Perhaps this will be enough to promote peace in Spain. I should put all that behind me. As I near France, the thought of Primavera gives me hope.

The party of monks arrived at Roncesvalles and the priest at the Chapel of Sancti Spiritus welcomed them to spend the night at the hostel. In the morning, after attending Mass in the chapel with other pilgrims readying to climb into the Pyrenees Mountains, Pons thanked the priest and said farewell. The cleric said, "God bless you and have a safe voyage, Abbot Pons. Before you leave, I just learned that the allies of the German king, Henry, have forced the new pope, Gelasius, out of Rome."

"But Pope Gelasius was elected only a few months ago!"

"Yes, and Henry reacted immediately when the new pope enforced the Church's rights of investiture of bishops."

Pons's lips tightened. *Those were concessions that Paschall gained even though King Henry threatened his life!*

"Gelasius is now in exile at Cluny," added the priest.

Footpads, mounted thieves, and even robbers disguised as pilgrims worked the pilgrimage routes and Pons knew it would be dangerous to leave the party of monks on the Via Podiensis to travel alone. The party was mounted, however, and when Pons explained his need to return to Cluny, they increased their pace. They reached Le Puy and turned north to La Chaise-Dieu, where Pons spent the night.

The next morning, Pons attended Prime and ate breakfast in the refectory as the lector read scripture. Afterwards he met a small group of pilgrims traveling north to Cluny and arranged to travel with them. As they readied to leave the stables, the Abbot of La Chaise arrived. "Wait, Abbot Pons! I just received word that Pope Gelasius has died! The Lord has provided a way to get to Cluny before his funeral. A trio of papal messengers who were on their way to Cluny will escort you."

He excused himself and joined the messengers, whom Pons considered another godsend. They pushed their steeds and arrived in Cluny on the afternoon of the fourth day. As they neared his abbey, Pons wished he could have seen Primavera first. But with the messengers in escort and the death of Gelasius it was not possible. He entered the Porte d'Honneur, thanked the escorts, and paused to study the abbey grounds as the others went on ahead to the stables. He continued up the lane, lined by sharp-tipped cypress trees and surrounded by a wide meadow. The midafternoon service Nones, recited at the ninth hour, had just finished and Pons saw monks filing out of the basilica. He planned to leave his mule at the stable then inform Prior Thomas of his return. A figure in a black habit dropped out of the line of monks and hurried across the grassy sward. *It's Chard!* Pons broke into a wide grin, but as Chard neared, he noticed his friend held a grim face. *Of course! Chard is concerned, wondering why I am returning alone! I am overjoyed to see him, but I must respect his emotion from my sad news. I have had months to grieve the loss of our friend Guilen.*

Pons dismounted, embracing Chard. Pons's voice broke as he looked over his friend's shoulder, "I am sorry, but our brother Guilen is with the Lord." The abbot released Chard and held him at arm's length. "He loved both of us and I will miss him and his wisdom.

"And what of Pope Gelasius?"

"His funeral was yesterday and they buried him in a crypt in the basilica. The bishops and abbots who attended Gelasius's funeral have left, but the cardinals who traveled from Italy to accompany Gelasius in exile and the Archbishop of Vienne remain in the guest residence."

Pons paused. *Well, I hurried, but missed the funeral.* He glanced in all directions although they were alone in the large meadow. "I must warn you before I get preoccupied. The Burgundian knights that Thomas sent to escort me to Spain tried to kill me and I suspect the Count of Burgundy was involved. We must be more careful than ever."

Chard's eyes were moist. "And what of the other Cluniac brothers on the pilgrimage?"

"They are dead as well." Pons squeezed his shoulder. "Later we will pray together. Guilen followed Christ's way and showed great care for others even to the day he died.

"I must go see Thomas and then ask the clergy what I can do to help in choosing a new Pope. Will you take Cominius to the stables?" He offered the reins to Chard and turned to leave.

"No! Wait! I must tell you . . . oh, God's bones! But it is better I tell you, rather than you hear from Thomas."

"Tell me what?"

"Primavera is gone."

Pons froze in step.

"Burgundian soldiers took her away. It was over a month ago, after Thomas announced that an encyclical had arrived from Pope Gelasius committing monks and clergy to strict adherence to Pope Urban's decree on celibacy."

"Mary Mother, no!" Pons's face was scarlet. "When Urban published that decree, he commanded religious and secular rulers to sell the concubines, wives, and children of the clergy into slavery!"

Pons turned with hurried steps as Chard grabbed his sleeve, but the abbot yanked it free. Pons stumbled, Chard ran past him and blocked his path. The abbot's eyes were filled with rage. "No! Pons, you must calm yourself! Remember you once quoted from Ephesians—'In your anger do not sin . . . and do not give the Devil a foothold.' Stop! I pray. I know you are about to do violence to Thomas."

Pons shoved him out of the way and surged ahead. "More than violence. I will kill him!" Chard ran after his friend and caught Pons, threw both arms around his neck and they tumbled forward, falling together to the ground, and disappearing among the long grass. They wrestled, Pons tried to break free from Chard's grip. Pons cried out as they lay in a heap, "Did you know I killed a man in Spain? I killed a human being! And now I killed my Primavera! She would have still been safe in Saint Pons had I not brought her here!" He ceased struggling and tears rolled down his face.

They both lay on the ground without speaking. Cominius had joined them and his calm presence was welcoming as he pulled grass and chomped the stalks. Pons stroked the mule on the nose. "It took my two best friends to steer me from *'giving the Devil a foothold.'*"

Chard added, "And from the book of James, 'For man's anger does not bring about the righteous life that God desires.'"

"You are right, Chard."

Despite his anxiety, Pons reminisced with Chard, telling stories of Guilen as they walked to the stables with Cominius. On their way many monks greeted the abbot and welcomed him back, so by the time Pons left his mule at the stables it was the hour of Nones. As they entered for the service, Chard whispered to Pons,

"Avoid Thomas. Don't even look his way."

Afterward, Chard continued to escort Pons as he sought the circuitor. Pons asked him, "Has Prior Thomas been occupying my residence?" At the expected nod, Pons said, "Please inform Thomas to vacate the abbot's premises before Compline today."

In the late afternoon, Pons reclaimed the abbot's house and Chard stayed to monitor his friend. The archbishop's secretary delivered a message welcoming Pons home and notifying him that Guy of Burgundy desired to meet with Pons after he rested from his journey.

The next morning after Prime, Pons scheduled a meeting with the archbishop at his residence. He waited to meet him in the atrium. *My mind is a blur. Everything is happening too fast. I don't have time to grieve Primavera. Perhaps that is better. He is the Archbishop of Vienne, Guy of Burgundy, the son of Burgundian nobles. But just because he is Burgundian doesn't mean he sent the assassins or had anything to do with Primavera. I must remember that Archbishop Guy was loyal to Godfather Paschall and helped in the investiture fight against Henry.*

There was a knock on the abbot's office door, which Pons acknowledged. Chard opened the door and Archbishop Guy and Thomas entered. Pons sat behind his desk across from two highbacked chairs for the archbishop and Thomas to sit. Chard stood behind Thomas. Pons locked eyes with Chard and read: *Stay calm, friend.*

Pons retrieved cups from the shelves behind him and poured wine and added tepid water. He forced himself to look at Thomas as he handed him a cup, but only fleetingly, and looked right through him as if he were an object not really there.

"Thank you for receiving me, Abbot Pons," said Guy, "after your long journey. I hope your excursion was fruitful."

"Yes, thank you, Your Excellency! And it's my pleasure to see you."

Guy sipped on the diluted wine. "We should use our familiar names here, no? I will call you Pons?"

"Of course . . . Guy . . . or is it . . . Guido?"

The archbishop laughed. "You overheard the Italian cardinals. They call me Guido. It started on my first trip to Rome. Here in Burgundy, it is Guy.

"Alas, poor Gelasius. He worked so hard and had planned to conduct a synod in Lyon. After the abuse he sustained in Rome, the arduous trip here, he, with his advanced age, became ill in Macon and was brought to Cluny. Even the excellent care he received did not save him. It was the Lord's decision to take him."

Pons's eyebrows raised. "Gelasius was abused?"

"He was assaulted by the Frangipani, a Roman family who supports Henry. He was then arrested, imprisoned, and an antipope was placed in the Vatican. With the help of the faithful people of Rome, Gelasius escaped, traveled by ship to Pisa, on to Genoa, and then to Melgueil."

"Melgueil?"

"Yes, he stayed at your brother's castle. Your mother donated funds for the Pope and the attending cardinals to travel across France.

"I know you will be very busy with your return to Cluny and I will not take up more time but I must tell you the primary reason I came to see you. Before Pope Gelasius died he recommended that either you or I should succeed him as pontiff."

"Well, I am very . . ." Pons was at a loss for words.

"There are seven cardinals now at Cluny that followed the late Pope into exile," continued Guy. "Cardinal Von Urach has just arrived from Picardy, and Cardinal Da Crema from Lombardy, late for the funeral, will be here in a few days. We will have the necessary nine to elect the new Pope. Cardinal Scannabecchi will conduct the election."

Guy stood. "May the cardinals pick the best man! Whoever it is, he will need the Lord's help in ousting Henry's antipope from Rome."

Guy paused as he turned. "The Lord's help *and* the courage of a warrior monk! I heard about your trip to Spain, rejecting the military escort. It's a wonder you survived the journey!"

Pons, stunned, hesitated, then rose to his feet and embraced the archbishop. "Yes . . . thank you, Your Excellency."

Thomas and Guy left. Pons looked at Chard.

"You did very well, Pons," said Chard. "You didn't let Thomas's presence bother you."

Pons was silent and looked preoccupied. "Thank you, Brother, for staying.

"As for the archbishop's comment about the next Pope, I am stunned!"

Pons recovered. *I am not going to let Thomas or this election or . . . anything bother me now.* "I have been away too long, I need to get busy—operating the monastery, and resuming construction of the basilica. "Chard, please schedule the monastery officers to meet here after Sext."

The divine services of the sixth hour were completed and the officers were seated around the table in the abbot's dining hall. Pons asked why Estienne, the subprior was absent. The monks glanced at each other in silence, then stared unabashedly at Thomas. Without hesitation he answered, "We will never see that traitor again!"

None of the officers reacted, obvious to Pons they had already known. Thomas looked at Pons, "He has gone over to the Cistercians at the monastery in Citeaux."

All the officers were mute, including Chard, who had taken over as sacrist when Pons had left for Spain. *Guilen is gone, now Estienne is gone . . .*

He listened without comments or questions as each officer updated him on the status of the abbey. Construction on the new phase of the basilica was at a standstill for lack of funds. Then Pons showed them the relic of John the Baptist donated to Cluny by Urraca, which drew a few murmurs of thanks. When he reported the queen's donation of the properties and unrolled the five deeds of land in Burgundy, the officers raised their voices in praise to God.

The monks became somber again when the circuitor reported the Pope's decree of celibacy and its subsequent enforcement. Pons glanced around the meeting table. "Did you read this document?" The officers nodded and murmured *ayes*, followed by Pons glaring at Thomas. "Do you have a copy of the encyclical?"

Thomas seemed unruffled. "The copy is in the library." Pons detected a slight nod from the librarian. The meeting ended and Pons directed Thomas to stay.

They entered the abbot's office. Thomas frowned at Chard as he poured wine for them. Pons noticed. *Lord, help me stay calm!*

"With Estienne gone," said Pons, "Chard will now be my aide."

Pons briefed Thomas on the political and ecclesiastical issues during his Spanish pilgrimage, the negotiation to obtain the Burgundian properties, the potential for war that could suspend the funds again, and the Diocese of Compostela being raised to metropolitan status. As Pons sat behind his desk, he discussed renewing the abbey construction, how to rehire the skilled labor, and the funding for both. Thomas was self-assured and collected and Pons did not sense any unease from him. *I will find out the truth soon enough. I need to keep him close and watch him. He knows well the political situation in Burgundy and he will give me his cooperation because even if he eliminates me, he will want to rule over wealthy and thriving Cluny. But he will not succeed. I* will *find what happened to Primavera. I hope to God she is alive!*

Pons rolled open the parchments with the land deeds. "I want to sell a few of the properties at once so we can restart the construction. Which ones will bring us the best price?"

Thomas shuffled through the documents as Pons and Chard looked on. He paused at one deed. "This property at Vezelay. The land has special value because it has orchards that produce salable crops. Also, it is well placed at the start of a major pilgrimage route to Compostela. The Benedictine monks at Vezelay claim to have the relics of Mary Magdalene and want a larger church for pilgrims to revere Mary's relics, and they will pay well for the property."

"Good. And any others?"

Thomas studied the deeds.

"Here, this property in Nevers. It is at a strategic location. The French king intends to expand his domain eastward into Burgundy, but the Duke of Burgundy resists such efforts. The tract would bring a good price because both the king and the duke covet it. Have them bid on it."

Pons ended the meeting, "I will consider your advice. Thank you, Prior." Thomas left without further comment.

"You are quite the man of control, Brother," said Chard. "Years ago you would have been sweating and lost your temper."

Pons swallowed his wine. "His advice is valuable—I think of him as a tool, as an object, not a person."

"Very good, but I will be staying close by—just in case."

Pons added, "He thinks we will continue to spar and counter

as we did before I left for Spain. Let him *think* that. I remember once reading a passage by Livius, 'All things will be clear to the man who does not hurry.'"

During the next week, the cardinals held discussions on who to elect as the next Pope. With the dignitaries occupied, Pons strolled about the monastery alone, appearing to renew his connection with the holy place and stopping to chat with the community, in particular the Cluny guards. Through casual banter, without arousing suspicion, he learned from the guards that the purge that included Primavera was conducted by Burgundian soldiers from Lyon. He believed the local guards had no knowledge of her fate. As he returned to his office, the image of a Tornier interrogating the Rouge captive flashed through his mind and was replaced by Pons himself beating Thomas to reveal the truth.

Pons went to see the librarian, other than Chard his most trusted friend at the abbey. They were surrounded by thousands of books, greatly loved by both men, who together had expanded the Cluny library during years of collaboration. *I trust him to keep this secret, but this is risky. If I am found out, I will be excommunicated.*

It was painful for Pons to talk of his loss. Pons uttered, "My, uh . . . friend . . . Primavera, who lived in Cluny village. I lost her when . . ."

"I know of the purge by Thomas," said the librarian.
"I am very sorry, Abbott Pons."

"Do you know anything about . . . what happened to any of the women?" asked Pons.

"They were likely sold as slaves and sent off to the Muslim lands," said the librarian. "Slaves are taken to the Levante or North Africa by sea through Genoa or Venice. The third main slave route is by land, by itinerant traders who move slaves from eastern Europe through Lyon and then across the Pyrenees to be sold in Muslim Spain."

Pons hung his head. His friend placed a hand on the abbot's shoulder.

"She was a Christian, yes?"

Pons nodded without looking up.

"It is sad," continued the librarian. "Of course, the Church forbids Christians to enslave Christians, but we have some very disgusting men in our Order. Her captors would have lied and sold her as a pagan. But being a Christian, she has the Lord, no? Let's pray for her."

They recited the Lord's Prayer together and asked for God to protect Primavera. After a quiet interval, the librarian said, "Father Abbot, most likely she was taken to nearby Lyon, then through Toulouse and then to Spain." The librarian paused in thought. "Years ago we sent letters to other monasteries to request new books. Can we initiate some communication through our fellow monks and librarians to inquire of her fate?"

Pons looked up, his eyes were bright as they met the librarian's. "No, no . . . not the other libraries, but your remark gave me an idea . . . and hope I might find Primavera.

"Please bring me two sheets of parchment and a quill."

The next day, Pons sent two letters carried by Benedictine monks traveling on Cluniac business. One letter was to his first cousin, Alfonso Jordan, the Count of Toulouse, and the other to his mother in Melgueil.

Within a week, six of the nine cardinals present in Cluny had elected Archbishop Guy as Pope. As was tradition, the Pope took a new name and chose Callistus II.

Pons was suspicious of the papal election. Guy was the son of the Count of Burgundy, and the election was not conducted in Rome as usual but in Burgundy. Pons requested that the election be approved by the full College of Cardinals in Italy and by the people of Rome.

Several weeks later, Pope Callistus II and his entourage departed Cluny and went to Toulouse where he held a synod to update the rules against investiture, simony, and married or concubinary clergy. Pons attended the conference, and while there met his cousin, Alfonso Jordan, who had inherited the title of Count of Toulouse from his father, the late Ramon of Saint Gilles. He had received Pons's letter. Although they had not found Primavera yet, Alfonso assured his cousin that the guards at the city gates were questioning any women whose description matched Primavera, who accompanied traders or travelers passing through Toulouse. They were still hopeful they might find her.

Pons left the Pope's entourage in Toulouse and returned to Cluny. Before meeting with his monastery officers to inform them of the proceedings, he looked over the council minutes which established the history behind the Church's position against married clergy.

> *Pope Damasus declared that priests could continue to marry, but that they were not allowed to express their love sexually with their wives. Pope Siricius abandoned his wife and children to gain his papal position. Then he decreed that all priests could no longer be married. Pope Gregory VII decreed that anyone to be ordained must first pledge celibacy and that the Church cannot escape from the clutches of the laity unless priests first escape the clutches of their wives. Nicolas, a deacon appointed by the twelve disciples of Christ, had refrained from intercourse as though in imitation of those whom he saw to be devoted to God. He endured this for a while but in the end could not bear to control his self-gratification, but because he was ashamed of his defeat and suspected that he had been found out, he ventured to say, "Unless one copulates every day, he cannot have eternal life."*

Pons slapped the document on the table. *This is absurd! I am supposed to read this nonsense to my officers?*

From Toulouse, the Pope traveled to Reims near the German-Burgundian border to meet with King Henry to again discuss investiture. Pons remained in Cluny to oversee the building efforts. He had sold the properties Thomas recommended and was eager to continue work on the new abbey church.

During one of Pons's daily inspections of the new church construction, he paced the length of the new basilica's nave, finishing at the east end in the semicircular apse. There he waited for the architect, Hezelon de Liege, a monk and a mathematician, to arrive to discuss the columns for the ambulatory. *I counted 300 steps from the altars to the apse. Let's see, my foot is about one pied du roi, one royal foot, and each step is over two pieds. So the basilica is 600 pieds long! I believe this basilica is longer and has wider naves than both the cathedrals of Saint Sernin in Toulouse and of Santiago de Compostela. Yes, Hezelon told me Cluny's basilica was larger than any church in Europe.* Above him he could hear the clinking of fired-clay pieces jarring against one another as the workers set the Roman tiles in place to complete the roof. The ceiling was one hundred pieds high, formed by the pointed barrel vaults. *I sense God most profoundly when I stroll in a cloister—much more so than in the enclosed space of a church. It must be the quiet walk along the colonnades encompassing the peacefulness of the garden.*

Hezelon arrived with several men and bowed. "Abbot Pons, construction is unimpeded again!" He studied the location where they would erect new columns. "And thank the Lord the rain has held off to enable the work in the quarry."

"Will you use the same granite as for the walls, Brother Hezelon?"

"Yes . . . well . . . Father Abbot, yes, the pinkish-grey stone we used for the walls does look like granite, but it is hard sandstone."

"Does this sandstone come from Cluny's quarry?" asked Pons.

"Yes, Father Abbot. But the columns are ornamental and will not be under a heavy load, so instead we will use limestone. That is, *fine* limestone, from which the craftsmen can sculpt beautiful capitals. The stone is from the quarry at Lye, near Macon. And this same stone is being used for the intricate decorative carvings throughout the basilica."

"Lye . . . do the craftsmen also make Roman tiles for the roof there?" added Pons.

"Yes, those clay pits and drying huts have been used for centuries . . . well . . . even during Roman times." Hezelon laughed. "Of course—that's why we call them Roman tiles."

"Where did you study to be an architect?"

"I learned mathematics at the cathedral school in Paris. Then I visited and studied at Saint Sernin and other cathedrals. And the Lord has guided me in all my work!"

During the following months, Pons devoted long hours working with the architect Hezelon. Unforeseen changes in the construction were necessary and Pons remained accessible to give his approval. The work kept the skilled craftsmen busy creating the intricate and ornate sculptures and reliefs which now lined the nave and chapels. Above the ambulatories, laborers draped woven tapestries imported from Flanders, which depicted stories of the Bible. The beautiful carvings and tapestries illustrated the Biblical scripture, providing meaning to the illiterate pilgrims.

Thomas, who had attended the council at Reims in Pons's place, returned after traveling with Pope Callistus's entourage throughout France. He met with Pons that afternoon to report on the activities at the conference.

"Abbot Pons, the Pope is arriving in Cluny tomorrow."

"His Holiness and his cardinals are always welcome. Notify the officers to prepare the monastery. What will be the Pope's agenda?"

"During the council in Reims, the clergy voted to canonize Abbot Hugh here at Cluny. The Pope will oversee the ceremony. Also, I suggest you should, to quote the Bible, *gird your loins*. I rode ahead to give you warning—the Pope was disturbed by the widespread and harsh criticism of you at the synod in Reims. Have you seen these circulars?" Thomas handed him copies of two documents that publicly denounced Pons as extravagant and wasteful of Cluny's resources. They were written by Berard, Bishop of Macon, and Humbaud, the Archbishop of Lyon, both Burgundians. Pons knew they were jealous and threatened by Cluny's status. Thomas gave a smug look. "Pope Callistus may recommend a new abbot for Cluny."

Pons's jaw muscles clenched and his pate tingled with the onset of perspiration, but the tone of his voice remained controlled. *What lies did he circulate in Reims? Stay calm. Don't react to your emotion. Wait to see what the Pope does.* "Thomas, return here after Compline. We will meet with the officers to prepare for the Pope's arrival."

After Thomas left, Chard, always close, entered Pons's office. "Brother, you are strong! I heard that weasel's comment about a new abbot for Cluny."

The next day after Prime, with the monks of Cluny attending, the Pope led Mass, then continued with the ceremony to raise the late Abbot Hugh to sainthood. His escorting cardinals, as concelebrants, honored the abbot as they gathered around his tomb next to the matutinal, the morning altar of the basilica. To close the ceremony the cantor led the monks in song, their chanting voices resonating with a holiness that matched the enormous capacity of the basilica.

That morning Pope Callistus had told Pons that he wanted to address the brothers of Cluny after the canonization but did not hint at the topic. Pons stood with his Cluniac brothers waiting as the Pope, flanked by the cardinals, faced the congregation. *Thomas can't be right. The Pope would not chastise me in public regarding the complaints at Reims, but the bishop and archbishop also criticized my governance of Cluny . . . and I am sure Thomas added salt to my wounds! So am I finished?*

Pope Callistus spoke. "I will address the rumors surrounding Abbot Pons at the synod in Reims. You may have heard that you could lose your abbot. Abbot Pons, come forward."

No! Did I underestimate Thomas and his allies?

Pons walked to the pontiff, kneeled and kissed his ring. When he rose the Pope held a miter, the pointed headpiece of high level clergy. For formal occasions Pons wore an abbot's linen miter, but the miter the Pope held was white damask silk, the same fabric as those of the attending cardinal-bishops. The Pope lowered his eyelids and Pons understood he was to kneel again. As the Pope placed the cardinal's miter on Pons's head his voice echoed across the basilica. "Abbot Pons remains as abbot of Cluny, but to show my utmost respect for him, I raise him to cardinal-deacon as well."

The Pope did not stay long in Cluny. His contacts in Italy reported there was now enough support for him in Rome to remove the antipope who had been seated by King Henry. The next morning he departed with his entourage for the long journey to the Vatican.

Pons, relieved, returned his focus to completing the Maior Ecclesia. Several months later, news came from Italy that the Roman citizens had filled the streets to welcome Callistus's return and had expelled the German troops of King Henry. The people and the Italian cardinals approved of Pope Callistus's election. Utilizing Norman mercenaries, the Pope then had the antipope arrested and imprisoned.

Pons continued to work long hours with the intent of completing the project during his tenure as abbot. It had been almost three years since he had asked Count Alfonso in Toulouse for help to find Primavera. The messages his cousin sent over the years reported no success in finding her. Pons had given up hope for help from his cousin, but still had faith in his mother. When he hadn't received a response from the first letter to her, he sent another. The hours of participation in the eight divine services per day, along with the busy construction schedule, barely suppressed his worried thoughts of Primavera's welfare. At other times he prayed alone to stifle his agony of self-torment.

In early September 1122, he received a letter from the Pope. The envelope was addressed to: *His Eminence, Cardinal Pons, Abbot of Cluny.* Pope Callistus, aware of Pons's ability to negotiate, asked him to attend the Concordat of Worms. The Pope believed it was the chance to finally abolish the claim by King Henry of his right to select bishops. The Pope had excommunicated Henry for his invasion of Rome and appointment of an antipope. And in protest to Henry's actions, many of his barons in Germany had rebelled. Pons traveled for two weeks to reach Worms, Germany. The synod was conducted over several weeks, with Pons leading the negotiations to strengthen the Church's rights to investiture of bishops. Rules banning simony and concubinage were also revised. By the end of October 1122, Pons was back in Cluny.

He was ready to return to his routines at the abbey and move the construction of the newest phase forward. The Pope, however, did not want to delay the final confirmation of the Concordat of Worms. He called for Pons to attend the First Lateran Council in Rome, set to begin the following March.

It had been three years since Primavera had disappeared. Pons readied for his trip to Rome and fleetingly thought about stopping in Melgueil to ask his mother personally for help, still confident of her network of contacts in southern France and Spain. *There will not be time on the way to the council, but I will stop on my trip back to Cluny.* Pons sent a third letter to his mother asking for help and notifying her of his visit. The plan gave him new hope as he prepared for the long, tiring journey to Italy.

Over six hundred abbots and three hundred bishops from across Europe attended the conference in Rome. By the end of March, the meeting had ended. The council confirmed decrees against simony and concubinage among the clergy. During the council the King of Jerusalem had appealed to Pope Callistus for military reinforcements, who in turn distributed an encyclical to all "*bishops, kings, counts, princes, and other faithful to God*" across Europe to provide crusaders. The Pope specifically asked the Doge of Venice, Domenico Michiel, to lead the crusade, knowing the Republic had the largest fleet in Europe. To encourage volunteers, the Pope granted remission of the crusaders' sins "*for those who go to Jerusalem and offer powerful aid to the defense of the Christian people and to vanquishing the infidels.*" The Pope also made it widely known that the Church would safeguard the families and property of the crusaders who traveled to the Holy Land.

Before Pons left Rome to return to Cluny, Pope Callistus called him to the Vatican. The Pope received Pons at his residence, the Lateran Palace. Pons genuflected and stood before Callistus, who was seated on the Pope's throne, the Chair of Saint Peter. They were alone except for two Norman mercenaries guarding the entrance to the receiving hall.

"Cardinal-Abbot Pons, I have received several letters from the monks of Cluny protesting your unfavorable behavior . . ." Pons glanced back at the guards, favoring privacy. The Pope smirked. "They don't understand Burgundian . . . as I was saying, among these accusations was the wasting of funds by hiring one hundred Burgundian knights to escort you to Spain. Also, buying expensive, nonreligious books for the library. Thirdly, providing travel expenses for monks to convey your concubine to Cluny . . . then paying her living expenses with church money."

Pons remained silent. *In addition to these lies, Pope Callistus sits here occupying an expensive and ornately carved chair, embellished with ivory and gold. The monetary value of his clothes alone could feed ten families for a year.*

The Pope waited, and when Pons did not comment, he continued. "Another complaint is that you reduced the costs to feed your monks by insisting on a strictly vegetarian diet, especially significant, because you insist that they do rigorous physical work."

Pons was incredulous. *I am disciplining them to follow the rules of Saint Benedict and return to austerity!*

"Also, the Duke of Burgundy states in a letter that you lost your temper and injured his soldiers when they participated in a training session at Cluny."

Pons prayed he was not showing his irritation. *Another accuser who is the guilty party.*

"In addition," the Pope continued in monotone, "you have been having sexual relations with a woman for years, violating the oath you took of celibacy."

It was not the first time Pons had contemplated that subject. *St. Peter, the first Pope, and most of the apostles were married. Clergy had stable married lives for the first thousand years of the faith. What about the elder monk who abused me as a child? If the Church enforces celibacy, the clergy will commit far worse sins.*

"Abbot Pons, sexual relations interfere with a monk's duty to be pure and holy and commune with God."

Pons still did not respond. *Greed, greed, greed! The Church kept the money they gained when they sold the concubines and their children into slavery. Greed is their primary motivation to impose celibacy. They want to stop the clergy who are nobles from having progeny, so the Church can then assume their inheritance. The monks who charge me are guilty of exactly the actions for which they accuse me. They project their sins onto me. I have cut back on expenses at the abbey and they accuse me of being wasteful. I have tried to restore Saint Benedict's rules on diet and hard work yet they want meat and are lazy. Yes, I had relations with Primavera, but many of them did likewise, as they continue to do.*

"Do you have any defense of these allegations?" asked Callistus. "One letter is from Thomas, your own prior. Over fifty Cluniac monks also signed it."

Thomas has already replaced his concubine in Cluny village after the purge which took Primavera, and he accuses me! Many accusatory sinners project their sins on others. But knowing that does not make me feel righteous. Callistus is from the Burgundian family that I suspect tried to assassinate me in Spain. Not only am I disgusted with the Church, but I have no hope of continuing as abbot.

"I resign as Abbot of Cluny."

The Pope's impassive gaze flashed to one of surprise. "Abbot Pons, you have shown yourself to be a master negotiator, I expected more of a fight . . ."

"Pardon me, Your Holiness," Pons bowed and headed toward the hall's exit.

"I accept your resignation," said Callistus at Pons's back, "but do not return to Cluny!"

Pope Callistus raised a hand. From behind, a guard joined him from his place of concealment.

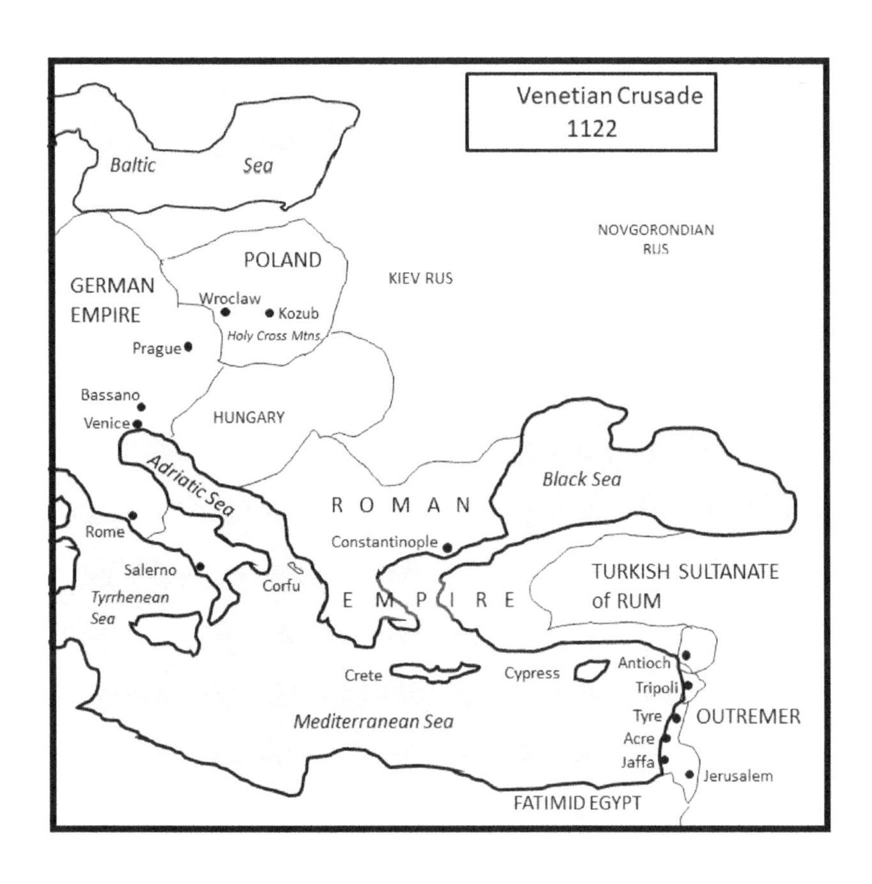

Venetian Crusade
1122
Baltic Sea
NOVGORONDIAN RUS
POLAND
KIEV RUS
GERMAN EMPIRE
Wroclaw
Kozub
Holy Cross Mtns.
Prague
Bassano
Venice
HUNGARY
Adriatic Sea
Black Sea
ROMAN EMPIRE
Rome
Constantinople
Salerno
Corfu
TURKISH SULTANATE of RUM
Tyrrhenean Sea
Antioch
Crete
Cypress
Tripoli
Tyre
OUTREMER
Mediterranean Sea
Acre
Jaffa
Jerusalem
FATIMID EGYPT

CHAPTER XIX THE VENETIAN CRUSADE

Pons stormed out of the Lateran Palace. As he crossed the Tiber River, several people had to step out of his way, his anger was so encompassing. He finally calmed as he entered to pray at Saint Peter's Basilica. During his meditations, it came to him that he would undertake a pilgrimage to the Holy Land. He wasted no time. By way of the Vatican guards, he met several Papal knights and joined them to enlist in the Venetian crusade. A week later the group arrived in a valley north of Venice and camped among thousands of volunteers waiting to embark on the Venetian fleet.

Within a few days of their arrival, Pons rode Cominius beside Zeph, one of the Papal knights he had traveled with from Rome. The knight straddled a destrier, a large, specially trained warhorse. Zeph was an Italo-Norman, whose mother was of Norman descent and his father a Neapolitan noble. The knight was descended from Robert Guiscard, the Norman count who had conquered southern Italy. The pair followed the *Amber Road,* formerly designated by the ancient Romans as the *Via Claudia Augusta,* north to the town of Bassano. The priest at the duomo gave Pons directions to the farm on Mount Grappa where he would leave Cominius.

When the fleet was ready to sail, the crusaders would break camp and follow the *Amber Road* south to Venice. There were horse transports in the fleet for each knight to bring two destriers, but there was not enough space for other mounts.

Pons patted Cominius one more time before he left him at the farm. He trusted the farmer to take good care of his mule, though he would greatly miss the pleasant creature. In a way, he was relieved that there was space only for the destriers. He had found a good home for Cominius and now his mule would be free of the rigors of the sea voyage and the hazards of the war in the east.

Returning to the crusader camp, Pons rode Zeph's spare horse. Their mounts picked their way over the rough ground and descended the trail along the western slope of Mount Grappa. Pons's senses absorbed the dramatic landscape high above Bassano, a mile below. The town was located at the mouth of the *Valsugana,* a valley which led north through the Alps, its rocky peaks enveloped by clouds. To the south under a clear blue sky, a plain stretched fifty miles to the Adriatic Sea. *That's where the island city of Venice is located. When will the Doge announce our departure for the Outremer?* Looking ahead, Pons could make out the covered bridge that crossed the river bisecting Bassano. South of the town, curls of smoke rose from the valley floor where cookfires blazed amid the crusaders' encampment.

As they passed through Bassano again, the men stopped at a shop to buy supplies. Pons dismounted and studied the Roman milestone next to the curb and read the Latin engraving on the stone. "'Via Claudia Augusta. Built by Tiberius Claudius Caesar Augustus Germanicus in the year Hosidius G. and Volasenna Severus were consuls. Fifty-six thousand paces.' Um, that is fifty-six miles, north to Trento. Forty miles south to Altino."

Zeph held the reins of the horses. "Your Latin is excellent, Father Abbot!"

Pons crossed his arms, turned to Zeph, and locked eyes with the knight. Zeph's disheveled blonde hair was in contrast with the tonsures of the Norman knights of two generations earlier. The abbot had learned on their ride from Rome that Zeph had attended the medical school in Salerno, then the University of Bologna. After his academic life, he had become a knight and joined the Papal Guard. *If anyone could critique my Latin, it would be this scholar.* "Just because you have spent a decade at the universities, doesn't mean . . ." They laughed.

Zeph looped the horses' reins through an iron ring that had been attached to the milestone for securing horses.

"At the farm your horses obeyed when you told them to stay,

instead of tying them," said Pons. "I was impressed they did not wander."

"They *were* tied."

"What?"

Zeph kept a straight face as he said, "*Ground tied.* That's what it's called to train a horse not to wander."

As they entered the apothecary shop, the owner, standing behind a counter, smiled and greeted them. "*Bon di!*"

Pons responded, "*Buon giorno*, er . . . *bon di*!"

"The greeting is not *buon giorno*, like in Rome?" said Pons as he glanced at Zeph. "In fact, it is similar to Catalan: *Bon dia*."

"Father Pons, at times we have difficulties understanding one another because you speak Occitan and I speak Norman French. Similarly, the people of Bassano speak Venetian and have the same problem with my Neapolitan dialect. But we will see."

Zeph turned to face the shopkeeper. "*Prego signore, due caraffe aquavite di vinaccia.*"

The merchant retrieved two terracotta jugs of spirits and placed them on the counter. He laughed. "*Buono*! *Si, si, grappolo d'uva . . .grappa.*"

"It must be the local name for aquavite," said Zeph, laughing. "*Grappolo d'uva* means 'a bunch of grapes.' And they use the shortened name: grappa. It is easier to say than *aquavite di vinaccia.*"

Zeph then ordered herbs, trading Neapolitan and Latin names until the shopkeeper understood. He ordered *Achilles millefolium*, yarrow, *Hypericum perforatum*, Saint John's Wort, and *Mandragora officinarum,* mandrake.

He finished and paid two deniers, using silver pfennigs. The shopkeeper hesitated, peered at the coins stamped with the patron saint of Bohemia, but then held them up, smiled, and said, "*Grazie*!" Travelers from central Europe frequented Bassano using the Amber Road to Venice and foreign coins were not rare.

Pons glanced at the jugs on the counter. "And I assume you will not let your comrades back at camp drink all this grappa?"

Zeph laughed. "That's why we bought two jugs. One for sterilization, the aquavite, the grappa, is more effective than vinegar or wine to clean wounds."

Zeph and Pons continued their conversation as they left the

shop. The storeowner shouted, "*S-ciao!*"

Zeph looked back through the doorway and shrugged his shoulders as he scrunched his forehead. "S*ignore?*"

The man repeated, *"S-ciao vostro . . . schiavo vostro."*

Zeph smiled and said, "*Si, signore—S-ciao!*"

They stepped onto the street and Zeph said, "He said to me: 'I am your slave.' It must be Venetian, I have never heard it before."

"Even with all your education at Salerno, there is more to learn, no?" said Pons.

"Yes, always. In Salerno I had excellent teachers. A husband and wife, Trota and Giovanni Plateario, and their son, Mateo, are experts in medicine. They have learned from the texts and practices of the ancient Greek, Roman, and Arab physicians. Salerno is the leading medical school. The German Emperor Frederick decreed several years ago that his court physicians had to be trained in Salerno."

Pons and Zeph purchased fresh vegetables, bread, and wine before they left the town, then returned to the crusader camp and rejoined their troop. Weeks before, Pons had arrived in Bassano with a handful of Norman knights from Rome, and they had formed the troop with knights from Poland and Bohemia. The Bohemians, the Polish knight, Dzierzko of Plock, and a few men from Mainz, Germany, had been recruited by Kozubowski, the Polish markiz, military commander, of Wroclaw. Two monks, O'Broin, the Irishman, and Gallus, had accompanied them from Poland. Gallus was a monk and historian from an island monastery in the Venetian archipelago and had been doing missionary work in the north. The rest of the troop was made up of the knights' squires and peasants. Zeph and Pons were heartily welcomed by their troop, who were gathered around a small cookfire preparing their meals.

There were 2,000 crusaders in the camp—knights, squires, and peasants from all parts of Europe. Domenico Michiel, the Doge of Venice, and the elected leader of the Republic, had marshalled 15,000 Venetian infantry, marines, and sailors from the city for the crusade.

Venice had been extremely prosperous from sea trade, and its fleet rivaled the navy of the Eastern Roman Empire. The *Greek fire* used by the Romans, a blazing gelatinous oil spewed onto enemy ships, the formula kept secret, had made them the most powerful fleet in the Mediterranean. But the Venetians had their own military secret: their shipbuilding innovations. In the quarter of the city known as the Arsenal, shipbuilding was conducted behind high walls and hidden from the populace. Only authorized workers were allowed to enter and were forbidden to reveal the manufacturing methods. In the Arsenal, craftsmen prefabricated standardized parts, which were then assembled into a ship. Canals, like those that traversed the entire city, were used to convey ships under construction from one assembly area to the next. Over 120 major ships had been built for the crusade at the Venetian shipyard in less than four months.

Several days after Pons returned from Bassano, he gathered with his fellow monks outside their tent along with the most pious knights in their troop for Vespers. The monks chanted as Gallus administered Holy Communion to Kozubowski, Dzierzko, and a few Bohemians. Pons began the Nicene Creed and the others recited the credo with him.

When they finished, O'Broin asked Pons, "I have heard that the Christians of the East worship differently."

Kozubowski seemed to become taller as he glared at the Irish monk and uttered in Latin, "Be more respectful! Address him as Father Abbot."

The knights did not comprehend Kozubowski's Latin, but their eyes grew wide and their bodies stiffened. Pons smiled and interposed. "Thank you, Markiz Kozubowski, but I am . . . on leave from that responsibility now. This crusade is my pilgrimage. We can address each other with respect without using titles. We are all brothers here, no?" The Bohemian knights departed and the three monks and Kozubowski remained.

Zeph arrived holding a terracotta cup. "Is service finished? Would you like to share grappa?"

O'Broin made a cursory bow. "I did not mean any disrespect, Father Abbot . . . or Markiz Kozubowski."

Pons shrugged.

"I'm happy you joined us, Zeph!" said Pons. "I imagine with your education you can contribute to what I expect will be an enlivening conversation . . . or a . . . debate."

The men sat and passed the cup. O'Broin sipped. "Wheh! You

said this elixir is made from grape pomace?" He coughed. "How do they make it so strong?"

Zeph answered, "There is a legend that a Roman soldier smuggled a copper vessel from Egypt, a still, used to produce aquavite. He stole it from Cleopatra's palace, and when he returned to Bassano, he made the first grappa."

Only Gallus laughed. The men appeared bewildered, including Kozubowski who asked, "Who is Cleopatra?"

Zeph cleared his throat. "Um . . . I guess I am not very good at jesting. A shopkeeper in town told me the story. I know that the Benedictine monks in Salerno are experts at making grappa. And they taught us at the medical school that spirits will clean wounds better than vinegar or wine." He laughed, "When you drink it, you can tell it is stronger."

"Back to my question," said O'Broin. "A generation ago the Roman church and the eastern church declared they were no longer one. What happened?"

"I heard they conduct their Mass in Greek," Kozubowski snorted, "not Latin, as they should. And the Greeks allow their priests to marry."

"True, but during your grandfather's day and before, most Roman Catholic priests had wives."

"No!" Kozubowski snapped, "I don't believe it."

"Yes, it is true," said Gallus, "and although Roman Catholics deem the Pope as unerring, the Greek Orthodox Christians instead follow the Archbishop of Constantinople, but only as their holy superior. Also, Roman Catholic leaders have changed some doctrines, but the Greek Orthodox resist such changes."

"When I lived in Prague, curious about the eastern Christians, I began a journey to Hungary," said O'Broin, "to visit the closest Greek Orthodox churches. But it was too dangerous to travel alone and after barely escaping a few encounters with footpads, I returned to Bohemia. Then I joined this crusade to go to Constantinople. Gallus, those last comments you made have justified my wish to make the journey. You said the Greek Orthodox church opposes change in its doctrine, so the church of Constantinople must have preserved Christ's message with less adulteration."

The men turned their attention from the Irish monk to Pons,

who added, "I have read that a generation ago, the East and West had a controversy over icons. The Christians of the West accused the Greeks of heresy, worshipping paintings of Christ, although the West reveres the statues of baby Jesus and Mary in its churches. It disturbs me that such a minor squabble should divide the church. Gallus, what can you tell us?"

"I agree it seems trivial, and the final provocation that split the churches also seems insignificant to the layman, but it is enormously important for the clerical leaders and biblical scholars. The Roman church added three words, just three words, to the original Nicene Creed. In our service this afternoon, we recited the creed of the church of Rome, 'We believe in the Holy Spirit, the Lord, the giver of life, *who proceeds from the Father and the Son.'* When the faithful recite the creed in the Eastern churches, they declare: 'We believe in the Holy Spirit, the Lord, the Giver of Life, w*ho proceeds from the Father.'* The Western church leaders believed the Holy Spirit must proceed from both the Father *and the Son* to verify the Holy Trinity."

All were silent for a few moments. "Is this the only difference in the two creeds?" asked Pons.

Gallus paused. "When I placed the two documents side by side and studied them, except for what I just mentioned, they were identical, with two inconsequential exceptions. The word *seen* is substituted for *visible* and *unseen* is replaced with *invisible*."

"Gallus, your knowledge is extensive. Where did you learn so much?" asked Pons.

"I read every book I could find. By traveling, however, I learn first-hand and meet people and better understand their beliefs and culture. In fact, I am writing a book on my experience in the north, *Gesta Principum Polonorum,* Deeds of the Princes of the Poles. It includes the siege of Glogow and the Battle of Wroclaw in which O'Broin and the markiz fought."

"I look forward to reading your work someday," said Pons. "And when you compared the two creeds, was the part 'for our sake He was crucified under *Pontius Pilatus'* included in both copies?"

Gallus nodded. Pons recalled that as a youth, when he had first learned to write his own name, *Pontius* and had then recited the Nicene Creed, he had felt guilty. Over the years, this feeling had recurred each time he repeated the creed.

Zeph handed Pons the cup of grappa. "Cheer up! Love the Lord with all your heart, and all that . . . that's what is important!"

Pons sipped and passed the cup to O'Broin, who hesitated, didn't imbibe, and passed it on.

"You better enjoy it now," said Gallus, "the Muslim religion prohibits their followers to drink spirits. I'll wager that most of the wine will be hoarded by the priests to give Communion, so it may be hard to find wine in the Outremer!"

O'Broin asked, "You know the *real* difference between the religions?"

He paused for effect, not expecting them to answer:

"Jewish people do not recognize Jesus Christ as the Messiah. The Greek Orthodox do not recognize the Pope as the leader of the Christian faith. And, the Muslims do not recognize each other in a tavern."

Before the men's laughter ended, Kozubowski added, "Leave the Trinity for the scholars to argue over. Stand up, we are being lazy! Retrieve your walking staffs. We must train hard, because *all* of us will have to fight when we reach the Holy Land. I will show you how to use your staffs as an infantryman would fight with a spear."

Kozubowski and his knights recruited the non-combatants, including the monks and peasant laborers in their company of crusaders. They brought walking sticks and lined up with the knights' squires, who would partner and tutor them.

The Polish markiz shouted, "Fight!"

Most of the untrained peasants brandished the weapon with a *third-staff* guard, where the positions of their hands divided the staff into three equal sections. The squires and one of the monks, however, were alternating from this basic hold to extending their staffs, gripping with both hands near one end of their weapon. They were frequently more successful in reaching their opponent.

After a time, Kozubowski yelled, "Stop! Assemble over here."

The exhausted men, particularly those with bruises and a few that were bleeding, appeared relieved the session had ended. Zeph retrieved vinegar and strips of cloth from his tent and bandaged the men's wounds. As Kozubowski began to speak, Zeph guided a peasant toward his tent as he pressed a cloth to a bloody wound on the man's head. Zeph whispered to himself, "I'm glad I brought the silk thread, but I thought sutures wouldn't be needed until we fought the Muslims."

The markiz ordered the men to sit and for a squire to come to the front. Kozubowski said something to the squire in Polish, and the man adopted the third-staff guard. He then continued in Latin, "Most of you used this hold, which is useful in dealing with enemies that have closed in on you, but you can strike them or keep them farther away starting with the *quarter-staff* guard." The squire changed to hold the staff near one end, a quarter length of the staff beneath his lower hand and the longer end at head-level of his imagined opponent. "This is the preferred starting position. Then you can extend strikes more rapidly and switch to third-staff easily, if necessary."

The markiz directed a pair of squires to demonstrate a few entries and parries, including how to change from the quarter-staff guard to a position named the *rudder guard*, because it pointed down at an angle like a boat's steering oar. This guard could be used to parry low attacks. He had them show how to use feints, multiple ways to thrust using one or two hands, and when holding a spear, how to use the blade to slice when pulling the weapon back from an extension.

He ran the men through several more sparring sessions. When they finished, more of the men required Zeph's medical attention.

"A decent start! Tomorrow we form lines and simulate battlefield combat against sword attacks."

The knights and the monks explained details of the markiz's lecture by translating his remarks from Latin into the peasants' vernacular. The men staggered back to their tents to rest.

Kozubowski approached Pons and slapped him on the shoulder. Pons sensed the markiz was relishing the training. *This is his world. He looks very pleased.* "Pons, where did you learn to wield the staff? You used the *third-staff* and *quarter-staff* grips with great skill!"

Pons answered as he rubbed a knot on the side of his head. "From bargemen, when I traveled on the Rhone River."

"Good techniques, but when are you going to learn how to *fight*!"

The markiz turned to leave. Pons, bewildered, asked, "What?"

"You need to follow up and not pull back when you have your opponent on the defensive. This is not a game!"

The markiz left camp the next morning to seek out the forge in nearby Padua to order daggers and spearheads for his infantry. His men tramped through the nearby forest to cut new longer staves to make spear shafts.

O'Broin called out as they hiked through the soggy river bottoms, "Are we looking for oak saplings for our staves? They are surely the hardest wood. Most of these trees aren't oaks. They have egg-shaped leaves and stringy things hanging down."

Nearby, Gallus answered, "Those trees are alders. They may not be as good for spear shafts as oak."

They found a copse of small oaks growing around an older tree among the alders. As they hacked down several small oak trees and trimmed the branches, Gallus added, "I now remember how important the alder trees are to Venice. God surely blessed the city by providing such a tree!"

"What do you mean by that?" asked O'Broin.

"I watched the laying of foundations of some buildings in Venice. They drove alder trunks, at least fifty pieds long, into the bottom of the shallow lagoon. Then they poured rocks among the pilings to make the building foundations. The architect told me the Venetians have been doing this since the founding of the city for centuries and that even the oldest alder pilings have never rotted, as long as they remain submerged under the seawater."

For several more weeks, the crusaders at the camp in the *Valsugnana* trained as they waited and trained and waited some more. Kozubowski was merciless in his regimen for the men, but he seemed to know just how far to push each man. He would get the knights to work harder by criticizing their honor, the squires to improve by hitting them with a switch, would scream at O'Broin and Pons, but use much more gentle persuasions with the peasants and Gallus. The foot soldiers became a disciplined infantry unit, trained to support the mounted knights on the battlefield. The training had its injuries and Zeph was kept busy providing medical aid. Two months after Pons had said farewell to Cominius, the crusaders were notified the fleet was ready to sail.

But as it was, Pons would not set foot in Venice and would only see the grand city from his ship as the fleet sailed out of the lagoon. The doge had not wanted thousands of foreign troops in the city, even for the few hours needed to embark on the ships.

At sunrise on August 8, 1122, thousands of native Venetian soldiers and marines embarked from Saint Mark's plaza onto their transports. The crusader troops from France and other parts of Europe had marched from Bassano to Altino, a former Roman port, the waterfront still suitable to load men and horses onto ships. Altino, some 500 years earlier, had been devastated by Attila the Hun and abandoned. The surviving residents, along with those fleeing the Huns' destruction of nearby Verona, Padua, and other Roman cities, had sought refuge on the islands of the Venetian lagoon. From there had arisen Venice, known as *La Serenissima*, "The Most Serene Republic of Venice."

Venetian sailors, free citizens of the Republic, rowed a score of war galleys, the vanguard of the fleet, out of the lagoon. Each galley was also equipped with lateen sails and flew the flag of Venice, a red banner with the golden image of a winged lion. The doge's flagship, a large war galley with a tall sterncastle and forecastle, followed. The gonfalon of Saint Peter, the papal banner awarded by Pope Callistus, snapped in the wind atop the highest mast.

Next to depart were the tall Venetian cargo ships, which were sailing ships with three decks loaded with supplies and men. As the ships cast off from Saint Mark's square, thousands of citizens filled the plaza shouting farewells to their sons, brothers, husbands, and fathers. Adding to the din were the bells clanging at scores of churches throughout the island communities of the lagoon, including those of Saint Mark's Basilica, announcing the exodus.

The third group of ships, the double-decked horse transports, sailed from Altino. A thousand knights with their squires had guided 2,000 warhorses into the holds of the transports. Pons and his Italo-Norman, Bohemian, and Polish crusaders were on one of these large ships, the *Saint Peter*. After the knights and squires checked the straps and canvas slings to brace the horses in the hold, the knights joined Pons and the monks on the top deck of their ship. The cityscape of Venice was marked by the campaniles, the bell towers of the churches, the doge palace, and the domes of Saint Mark's Basilica along the waterfront. As they sailed further away and the city receded, Pons regretted he had not been allowed to visit the city. *La Serenissima! The buildings appear to float on water. Rome had also once been great. There I saw many abandoned buildings; many were in ruin or were being dismantled for reuse in new structures. But this city is more vibrant and growing. The campanile under construction in the plaza is already hundreds of pieds high and still rising. Gallus told me the Venetians are the direct descendants of the ancient Romans. Will this city someday be the center of an empire?*

Another squadron of war galleys was the last of the fleet to leave, following the flotilla of horse transports. They sailed across a narrow part of the Adriatic to arrive at the city of Pula in the early evening, with a few hours of daylight to spare. In the best conditions, a trade ship could sail to the Outremer in one to two weeks, but the war galleys were crowded with men and weapons, and there was not enough space for the sailors and marines to sleep. With this limitation, the fleet only could sail about 50 miles each day and only during daylight hours, making a stopover each night. The time to sail to the east coast of the Mediterranean usually took two months.

The fleet sailed along the Dalmatian coast, stopping overnight at major Venetian ports, Zara, Spalato, and Ragusa, until after two weeks they arrived off the east coast of the island of Corfu, a possession of the Eastern Roman Empire. The citizens of the empire spoke Greek, and as descendants of the former western empire whose capital had been Rome, they also called themselves Romans, *Romaioi* in their language.

All fifty of Kozubowski's company were on the top deck, leaning on the side wale of their transport ship, anchored a half-mile off the island's main port of Corfu Town. "Why aren't we going to shore?" asked a Bohemian knight.

Kozubowski shrugged as he said, "I don't know." The phrase was similar in Czech and Polish, but his shoulders conveyed the most convincing answer.

Hundreds of pieds across the water, they watched a small Roman boat leave the island fortress and meet with a Venetian galley. Kozubowski looked around and asked, "Are the Venetians and Romans enemies?"

Zeph answered, "My Norman grandfather fought against the Romans on this very island. At that time the Venetians and Romans were allied against the Normans."

Gallus had overheard. "That was 40 years ago. Corfu, a province of the Roman empire, was under attack by the Normans. The Venetians sent a fleet that broke the siege. As a reward for their help, the Roman Emperor, Alexios Komnenos, granted the Venetians exemption from taxes in all the trade ports of the empire. His son John, however, who succeeded Alexios, retracted those commercial rights."

One of the ship's mousers jumped up on the top of the side wale and Zeph scratched the grey tabby behind the ears. As he watched the encounter of the two distant boats, he spoke to the cat. "Zula, where's your mate Stein?"

Pons noticed. "You are petting Stein. Here comes Zula." She gracefully joined the male cat with an effortless vault from the deck to the rail. Pons stroked her back. The feline had eyes as turquoise as the sea.

"The male is called Pietro by the Venetian sailors," said Pons, "because the ship is the *Saint Peter*, but the German knights have been calling him Stein."

"These cats are small," added Kozubowski, "but have my respect—they catch many rats. The other day below deck, Zula had caught a rat so big, it dragged on the floor as she carried it. Meanwhile another mouser that I named Caesar was lazily sleeping on my horse's back."

"Why do you call that huge white cat Caesar?" asked Zeph.

"Because he rides a great leader's warhorse. I am the great leader of this company, no?"

They laughed as O'Broin added, "This long voyage has made us desperate for amusement. Our conversations have deteriorated from deep religious debates to naming cats."

Suddenly there was shouting from the men along the rail and from sailors on nearby ships. Pons looked across the strait and the smaller boat from Corfu was rowing away from the galley, as Venetian crossbowmen fired upon them. The galley plunged oars and began to pursue the fleeing Roman vessel. A stream of flames shot in an arc from the smaller boat and lit the galley on fire.

"They are using the Greek fire! I have heard that water cannot put out its flames."

Signal flags unfurled on the doge's ship and the fleet began to sail to the shoreline north of the city. Bells rang within the walled town as people fled to the safety of the fortifications. The war galleys sped ahead of the fleet and marines quickly jumped ashore, but they were not fast enough to reach the city walls before the gates closed. The Venetians exchanged several flights of crossbolts with the defenders before they retreated. For the rest of the day, the Venetian army disembarked unopposed.

That evening among the cookfires, news spread that the doge planned to capture the city and pressure the emperor to restore the tax-free commercial privileges that Alexios had promised Venice.

Over the next week, attacks from the sea were coordinated with assaults from the land but were repelled. Another Venetian galley was set aflame by the defenders' Greek fire. In the first encounter, the Romans had used a pump to spray the fiery chemical onto a Venetian galley. This time they ignited terracotta pots filled with the flammable liquid and catapulted the conflagration onto the deck of the Venetian warship. The pots shattered on impact and the fire spread rapidly. The crew had no choice but to abandon ship. Determining that further assaults would be too costly, Admiral Domenico Michiel decided to maintain the siege in an attempt to starve out the inhabitants.

Kozubowski's company had not been included in the assaults. Despite their differences in nationality and language, the men bonded as they continued to train as well as socialize in camp. O'Broin carefully watched the batch of Irish ale he had been preparing from foodstuffs they had foraged from abandoned farms. Day by day, he was looking less like a monk. As had the other monks, he had traded his woolen habit for linen shirt and tunic, and he also quit shaving and grew a beard. Gallus and Pons, however, shaved each other's face and tonsure. Some men had looted a farm and slaughtered a few sheep. O'Broin did not eat meat, but he removed the ankle bones of the sheep, cleaned and dried them, and made five pieces for the game of knucklebones.

Kozubowski's daily training sessions had made the men so fatigued that the simple hand game was about the only activity they had energy for at the end of each day. Kozubowski, Pons,

Zeph, and a few squires joined O'Broin and sat with him cross-legged in a circle. O'Broin practiced as the others watched. He placed five bones on the ground in front of him and threw a pebble in the air with his right hand. While the stone was in the air, he grabbed a knucklebone with his right hand, and caught the stone back in the same hand. He placed the bone back on the ground with the others, then repeated the sequence, but snatched two of the knuckles this time. The cycle was repeated as he picked up three, then four, and finally all five bones before he caught the stone once again.

The men played several times, their skills increasing with each game. Kozubowski sat, took a gulp of water from a skin, then wiped his mouth on his sleeve. "Monk! You are very quick with your hands and have won the last few games. Let's see how good you are with the variation of the game played in Kozub."

Instead of the stone, the markiz lobbed one of the knucklebones up in the air and caught it on the back of his other hand. "You see the knobs on the bone and how the sides are distinct? There are four ways the knucklebone can land. Each position will give you certain points. This one I just snared is only one point." He rolled the bone over. "This is a difficult side to balance the bone. It is four points."

"Is there more to this game?" asked Zeph.

"Yes, yes. You can take the points for the throw of a single bone or toss up another. But you must keep the first one balanced or you will lose all the points. Up to four bones can be thrown." He glanced around. "And of course, there is betting."

The game started, and O'Broin took the challenge, tossing the knucklebones and catching them on the back of his hand to accumulate points. Bets were placed on each toss. As they watched O'Broin show his dexterity, Pons asked Kozubowski, "You said you played bones in . . . Kozub. Is it a place in your homeland?"

"Yes, it is a village in Poland. I lived there as a young man, but I was born at Ogrodzieniec Castle. It is in the southern mountains of Poland, one of the *Eagle's Nests*, the name for the strongholds protecting our lands from the Hungarians. My father, Kozub, was a captain of the guards, and when he retired, he bought land north of the mountains where the land was fertile. He farmed and built a manor. The village that grew around the estate was named after him. And in our language, Kozubowski can mean 'from Kozub' or 'son of Kozub."

"And you?"

Pons chuckled. "Hmm, you are Kozubowski and grew up in Kozub. I am Pons and grew up in Saint Pons, founded by my ancestor, Ramon Pons."

"Was your father Pons?"

"No, I am related to Pons through my mother. My father was the Count of Melgueil and left me at the monastery when I was four. I never knew him—he is now deceased. And your father, he was a warrior?"

"Yes, then later a baron, a noble farmer, but he and my mother made great success producing baskets."

"Baskets?"

"Yes, *kozub* means basket . . . but the Bohemians tell me that in the Czech language, *kozub* is their word for fireplace. My mother was very skilled at weaving the strong baskets used to carry food . . . or anything. But my parents then made larger baskets out of strips of oak and mounted them on two-wheeled carts. Lighter, but just as strong as wooden carts."

The men next to them were shouting about bets and points in a knucklebones game, but an even louder uproar and the rush of sudden activity drew their attention. Approaching was a squadron of war galleys, too far away to tell from the gonfalons what navy they belonged to. The Venetians rushed to their warships and hundreds of sailors pushed and pulled war galleys off the beach. A handful of galleys offshore weighed anchors and dipped oars to intercept the approaching fleet. Sailors climbed the masts to get a better view. As the ships sailed closer, Pons saw flashes of red among the gonfalons whipping above the ships bearing down on the island. He looked at the red gonfalon flapping above the Roman fortress and feared they had sent reinforcements. Then he heard cries of "Genoese! They are Genoese galleys." As the ships neared, Pons could see the Genoese pennants clearly, a white field with a bright red cross.

The Venetians sent ahead a galley and learned the squadron from Genoa was joining their crusade. There would be no battle—the Genoese were not there to lift the siege and help the Romans.

Kozubowski and other officers were called to a meeting that evening. When he returned it was late and most of his men had retired to their tents. The markiz joined Pons, O'Broin, and Zeph as they chatted around a small fire.

"I'll tell you what I learned at the officers' meeting. First of all, we break camp tomorrow and sail for the Holy Land. The Genoese report that King Baldwin has been captured and the Christians of the Outremer need our help as soon as possible."

The men glanced at each other, and in the campfire light Pons could see the relief in their faces.

Yes. Finally. I was becoming very disillusioned with the Church. Venetian Christians fighting Greek Christians because of greed. We all joined this crusade to help the Christians in the Holy Land, not to fight battles for Venice.

Kozubowski continued, "The doge was initially concerned when the Genoese arrived. Whereas Venice has alternated between being an ally or being a hostile to the Roman Empire, Genoa has remained close allies with Constantinople, ever since the first crusade to the Holy Land when the Genoese navy transported and then fought alongside the crusaders.

"The Doge knew the Genoese could not break the siege with only five galleys, so when the Genoese admiral, Guglielmo Embriaco, pledged that he is joining us to support the Pope's crusade, he was believed."

"But they did get the Venetians to lift the siege," said Gallus.

The men looked puzzled.

"By reporting that King Baldwin was captured by the Turks," added Gallus. "Do you think it was a ploy?"

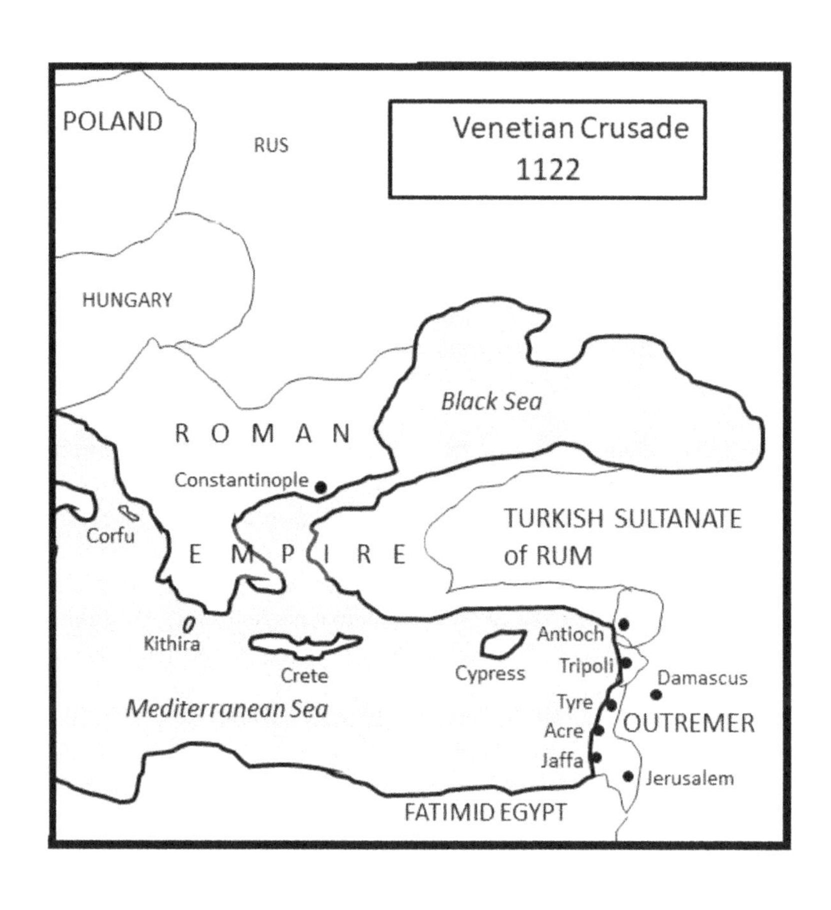

Venetian Crusade
1122
POLAND
RUS
HUNGARY
Black Sea
ROMAN
Constantinople
Corfu
EMPIRE
TURKISH SULTANATE
of RUM
Kithira
Crete
Cypress
Antioch
Tripoli
Damascus
Mediterranean Sea
Tyre
Acre
OUTREMER
Jaffa
Jerusalem
FATIMID EGYPT

CHAPTER XX THE BATTLE OF JAFFA

The fleet left the island of Corfu and sailed along the west coast of Greece, stopping each night for the galley sailors to sleep ashore. Both human and equine passengers on the horse transports went ashore only every three or four days, and otherwise slept on the anchored ships. The squires were kept busy mucking out the horse stalls, a putrid job that left them covered in odorous filth. To clean off the muck, the young men would dive off the ships. As they knifed into the water, starbursts of dark smudges exploded amidst the clear turquoise waters of the Aegean Sea.

The doge was determined to reach the Outremer without delay and had not allowed raids on the coastal towns until reaching the island of Kithira. It was an important stopping point for the Roman navy to resupply and rest, but had only a small garrison. The Genoese galleys, acting as scout ships, had sailed ahead of the fleet and reported that there were no Roman warships anchored at the island.

The doge began a raid on the island's port town. Venetian galleys beached on the shore and marines disembarked, then spread out down the streets. From their transport ship anchored not far offshore, O'Broin, Pons, and Kozubowski watched as townspeople fled to a fortified hill. They joined a few hundred soldiers of the garrison on the acropolis, an immense rocky outcropping over three hundred pieds above the sea level.

The first mate of the ship joined Pons and his comrades as they leaned on the ship railing. Zeph appeared with Zula in his arms, and placed her on the rail at a convenient height to scratch her head. "It's due time we made a raid," said the first mate. "The Romans owe us. My grandfather was killed defending their empire and now they reject our trading rights."

Zeph translated the mate's Venetian to Latin for his comrades.

Kozubowski moved over to allow space for the first mate along the side wale. The Venetian nodded as he watched the activity on the shore, where there was screaming and shouting. The markiz spoke to the mate as Zeph translated. "Venice and Genoa are great trading rivals, but the Genoese squadron has been given the prestigious duty of scouting ahead of the fleet?"

The first mate did not answer, and Zeph said, "Capisci?"

"Si," answered the first mate.

"The doge trusts them?" Kozubowski added. "Genoa and the Romans are allies. After the attack on Corfu, what if the Genoese are setting a trap for the fleet?"

"Basta! Enough!" burst the first mate, but he quickly calmed. "Our doge is a brilliant admiral. The Genoese have faster galleys. They are lighter and narrower in the beam. So the doge, in his genius, assigned them to sail ahead and scout for the fleet. But I have heard the Genoese ships are more easily damaged upon impact. So in everything else, Venice is superior to Genoa."

After Zeph repeated the first mate's comment in Latin, O'Broin laughed. "And I thought it was because the Genoese were more manly than the Venetians and could row faster!"

Zeph hesitated, then translated.

The first mate was red-faced.

Zeph said, "Many are feeling cramped and bored on these ships, but it does not justify attacking a Christian town again."

"I agree, we are on crusade to fight Muslims, not Christians," added Pons. *God would not want Christians fighting Christians! Both the Latin and Greek churches have failed to stop this internecine warfare.*

The first mate raised his eyebrows and Zeph told him what they had said. The mate grew angrier. "Are you fools? No, perhaps it is merely your ignorance in the way of the world!"

"The history of the world is just one war after the other,"

admitted Kozubowski. "We fought the Germans and they are Christians. O'Broin, you remember how they tortured the children?"

O'Broin answered, "Nothing of what men do surprises me. It is disgusting."

Still enraged, and with no warning, the first mate took his anger out on the cat. "The bishop said that cats are the Devil and they are sneaky and evil!" He pushed Zula, distracted by her pampering, off the railing. She disappeared from view.

O'Broin quickly leaned over and looked downwards. "Why did he do that? She's clinging to the side!"

"He said the cat was a devil!" said Zeph.

Kozubowski picked up the first mate like a sack of grain and rolled him on top of the side wale, balancing him precariously on the edge. "If that cat doesn't make it back on deck, you are going for a swim!"

O'Broin said, "We might lose her. Then we must keep the first mate. Is the mate good at catching rats?"

The commotion attracted the captain, who intervened with several Venetian sailors. They pulled the first mate onto the deck. "I can expel you from my ship, you fools!" said the captain. "Or at the least I will give you lashes. A captain is God on his own ship!" He barely calmed enough to continue speaking. "One of you will take the punishment for the others and . . . yes, by fighting for my entertainment." He gestured to the largest Venetian sailor nearby. "One of you will fight him."

Kozubowski took a step forward, but the first mate pointed at O'Broin and said, "No, I want the loud-mouth monk to fight!"

The men made space on the deck, the sailors gathering behind their man. To O'Broin's benefit he had earlier abandoned his burdensome wool habit and now wore a belted tunic made of linen. Also, the ship was anchored in calm water, eliminating an advantage the mariner's sea legs might have given him. The monk circled to his right and the sailor cut him off. O'Broin circled the opposite way, and he was cut off again. The sailor feinted a few attacks. The encounters became more aggressive and he made contact, but O'Broin spun, twisted, and broke free. Shouts from the sailors goaded their man. He became angrier and frustrated the more he tried and failed to tackle the monk. The sailor pulled a knife from his belt then slashed back and forth, but O'Broin avoided the blade. Pons reached under his tunic for his eating knife and yelled, "Where's your knife?" O'Broin did not respond. The sailor made a few more feints. O'Broin parried one slash that was close to his face by blocking his adversary's wrist with the back of his hand, then spun away.

Pons held out his own knife to O'Broin and shouted, "Here!" Everyone glanced at Pons, and no one noticed that the Irish monk had removed his belt made of braided cord. Their attention was quickly diverted to Zula as she leaped off the rail and darted across the space between the fighting men. O'Broin's antagonist glanced at Zula as the cat ran between O'Broin's legs. The Irishman snapped the rope toward his adversary. Weighted by the large key, the rope uncoiled and shot through the air. It wound around the sailor's neck several times. O'Broin yanked on the cord and the sailor gasped for air, pulled on the rope to loosen it, and lunged at O'Broin thrusting with his knife. The Irish monk sidestepped, looped the rope around the sailor's weapon hand, then slipped behind his opponent. He pinned the knife to the sailor's chest and wound the rope around the sailor's neck one more turn. As the sailor choked, O'Broin held out his hand to Pons, who passed him a knife. O'Broin held it up to his opponent's face, "This is not to cut you free, sailor. Now, I ask you, are we done?"

The Venetians looted the town and the fleet spent the night anchored off Kithira. It was the middle of September and most sea travel was curtailed from October to spring because of the notorious winter storms of the Mediterranean. The galleys were vulnerable to the rough seas due to their low freeboard and the doge set sail knowing they needed to reach the safety of the Outremer coast.

A week later, the fleet stopped overnight at the Roman island of Cypress. There, the doge learned that the Muslim Fatimids had launched a fleet from Egypt to attack Christian cities. They reached the Outremer coast north of the city of Jaffa and sailed south to intercept the Muslim flotilla. The doge sent the five Genoese galleys ahead to scout and followed with the rest of the fleet.

A day later a Genoese galley returned, its sails furled, with all oars rowing steadfast, since the winds were unfavorable. Soon after the galley came alongside the admiral's ship, his flagship raised signals for the warships to follow. Skiffs were launched from the flagship and other galleys to deliver orders to the captains of the transport vessels.

Following the admiral's orders, the ships' captains piloted the two deck and three deck horse transports into two parallel lines sailing from west to east. The galleys, the fighting ships, were located behind the larger transport ships, out of sight from the approaching Fatimid fleet. The plan was to trick the Muslims into believing that the Venetian fleet was an unarmed pilgrimage convoy.

On the southern horizon Pons could see the white gonfalons flying on several approaching galleys. The white field of the pennants mingled with flashes of red as the wind lashed. Although he could not distinguish the symbol at this distance, he knew the colors were of the bright red cross of Saint George, the patron saint of Genoa. *The red cross! The Genoese were to lure the enemy to us. The Fatimid fleet must be right behind them! Certainly there will be much, much blood today.*

Lined along the ship's rail were the fifty men of Kozubowski's company, armed and ready to repel boarders. On the forecastle and sterncastle were Venetian marines with cross bows. Sailors were ready to maneuver the ship. Over fifty cargo ships were sailing east in two lines, similarly armed and ready to receive the onslaught of the Fatimid galleys. The Genoese squadron had to lure the Fatimids as close as possible to the transports and not reveal the hidden Venetian galleys. The doge maneuvered his war galleys so his ships would be under sail running down wind *and* rowing all oars. The Genoese could then easily outpace the enemy and surround the Egyptian fleet.

Pons saw that the Fatimid galleys were now only a few hundred paces away. *As we readied for the battle, the Venetian sailors told us when the enemy archers loose their arrows we must take cover behind the side wale. This cargo ship has only a score of marine archers, so we can't prevent the Fatimids from boarding and we will have to fight them hand to hand.* To Pons's right was a Bohemian knight, and beyond him he caught O'Broin's eye. "Oh, Irish Brother, what have we gotten ourselves into? Aren't we monks supposed to just work, pray, and study!"

O'Broin's eyes were wide as he laughed like a mad man. "I hope the ship doesn't sink!"

Pons looked alarmed. "Why, can't you swim?"

"No, but I can walk on water . . . and I stagger on ale."

Ahead, the Genoese galleys turned to fight. Several Fatimid ships engaged them, but the rest kept coming, spreading out to attack the transport ships. Among the Muslim ranks were Sudanese archers armed with traditional bows. They could release three arrows for each arrow shot by the Venetian crossbowmen.

Pons waited with his troop crouched on the deck, their backs against the side wale, protected from the arrows. Missiles zipping over their heads, arrowheads thunking into wood, errant bolts clattering across the deck, and men shouting magnified the cacophony.

It is just as the sailor warned us. There are hundreds of arrows. If any of us look above the side wale, we will be dead.

Pons was banged sideways and heard a deafening thud as the hull groaned and shuddered. The rain of arrows slowed to a drizzle. Kozubowski bellowed, "Stand and fight! Fight! Fight!"

After many hours training under the markiz, the troop reacted instantly to his command. Pons stood with the troop and raised his spear to ready position over the side wale. To his surprise, the point ended a hand's width from the chest of a Fatimid sailor. The monk hesitated and the man hacked the spear with his sword, breaking off the spearhead, then raised his weapon and slashed down. Pons grabbed the man's wrist to redirect the blade, and with his other hand used the broken shaft as support to keep balance. The Muslim fighter fell on the jagged end and was run through. Another Fatimid appeared above, Pons drew his dagger, and the enemy sailor delivered a sword cut that was certain to decapitate him. He ducked under the whistling blade, grabbed the sword of the fallen Fatimid and before his attacker could deliver a second cut, he slashed deep gashes in the Muslim's thighs. As the Fatimid collapsed forward, Pons plunged his dagger into the man's heart but slipped on the bloodied deck, landing on his back. He was trapped under the body of the Fatimid sailor he had slain.

Another enemy assailant boarded the ship and stood above Pons, as the monk frantically tried to free himself. Zeph, on his left, locked eyes with Pons. Instead of helping, Zeph watched as the Fatimid raised his sword to finish Pons.

To his right O'Broin was relentlessly sliding his spear to full extension, piercing the Fatimid sailors, and pulling back. Repeating and repeating, his weapon flicked like a viper's tongue. The Irish monk redirected his attention to the Fatimid threatening Pons. O'Broin plunged his spearpoint into the ribs of the Fatimid who fell back. Pons freed himself from the bodies. Zeph was gone.

The Venetian galleys sailed from their hidden locations behind the transports and surrounded the Fatimid fleet. The enemy ceased boarding the transports to defend against the Venetian counterattack. The Fatimid galley and Pons's vessel were still tied together and Kozubowski yelled a war cry in Polish, as he and his knights boarded the enemy ship.

During the last hours of the battle, the fighting shifted away from the transport ships. The battle continued between the galleys as the Fatimid vessels were trapped between the cargo ships and the Venetian warships. The crusaders destroyed most of the Egyptian ships and captured scores of others. Thousands of Fatimid sailors were killed, and in a single battle control of the eastern Mediterranean, the Levantine Sea, shifted to the Christians.

While their comrades and the crew disposed of the enemy dead into the sea and rinsed the deck with buckets of seawater, O'Broin and Gallus helped Zeph treat the wounded on their ship. Pons attended the most injured who were on the brink of death. To those he gave Final Communion. Next, for a handful of wounded men, he performed the *Sacrament of Anointing the Sick,* appealing to the Holy Spirit for healing. He did not have o*leum infirmorum*, oil of the sick, but O'Broin, who had originally joined as the cleric for last rites, provided him with a vial of oil that had been blessed by Bishop Menhart of Prague.

A flotsam of ship timbers and bodies were jammed between the ships. The seawater was tinted red for a thousand paces in all directions. Beaches nearby became littered with corpses and the air soon held the odor of death.

After hours regrouping, the fleet got underway and cleared the watery necropolis. Pons held a memorial funeral for several of the deceased men slain while defending the ship and two who had been lost at sea. Pons prayed: "Merciful God, we entrust our brothers to you. Give them happiness and peace forever. Welcome them now into Paradise, where there will be no more sorrow, no more weeping or pain, but only peace and joy with Jesus, your son. Amen."

The deceased were buried at sea, as the fleet sailed northeast toward the port of Acre. Pons gazed toward the horizon, seeking peace, but his near-fatal encounters during the battle flashed through his mind. O'Broin joined him and leaned on the side wale. Pons slapped him affectionately on the back. "Thanks, Brother, you saved my life."

"What?"

"When I was trapped. You speared the Fatimid who would certainly have killed me."

"I should have let you get what you deserved for making such a bloody mess!" said O'Broin.

"I like that. You jest about everything. But I want to ask you a serious question. Did you see Zeph during the battle?"

"No. The battle was furious! The Bohemian fighting next to me had just fallen and I saw the gap in our defense, so it was chance I even looked in your direction. Then I glanced again and saw you on your back. I only had time to spear the Fatimid above you and had to return to fighting the enemy in front of me."

"O'Broin, do you think God was on our side today?"

"Why do you ask that?"

"It was a miracle, time after time when I should have been killed, I survived."

"Fortune, luck, quick reactions. That's what saved you."

"And what of God's help?"

"Didn't I hear you thank me, not God, for saving your life? I didn't see God today."

"Yes, um . . . well, He *is* invisible."

"Ha, Pons made a jest!" said O'Broin. "It seems to me that wars of religion are squabbles about who has the strongest imaginary friend."

The fleet arrived at the port of Acre, a city on a peninsula with a good harbor. Two decades earlier, King Baldwin's forces had captured Acre after a siege and the city had prospered as the main port for Jerusalem. South of the harbor was a sandy shoreline where the galleys beached. The crews went ashore and established the crusader camps, just north of the Belus River. Without enough light in the day to finish unloading, the horse transports remained anchored until the next morning to disembark at the quays.

In the morning, the transports were docked. Ramps, sturdy gangplanks, were lowered from the ship hulls onto the wharves. After the warhorses disembarked, the knights rode the destriers out of the city through Saint Anthony's gate, the squires following on the spare mounts. Both men and beasts were glad to be free of the confines of the ship holds. A half mile south of Acre, they joined the crusader camps near the mouth of the Belus River, a pleasant watercourse lined by poplar and sycamore trees, where the horses foraged on lush grass. The river's source was a spring just six miles inland that provided plenty of fresh water.

The three monks, Zeph, and the markiz sat together after the evening meal in their camp. O'Broin made irreverent comments about every subject. Kozubowski was recounting the Fatimid soldiers he had dispatched in the sea battle, and Gallus voiced his concern about a pilgrimage to Jerusalem. "I heard that the doge is going to Jerusalem tomorrow. There he will negotiate terms to reward the Venetians for aiding the King of Jerusalem. I wish we were going with him. He'll have made his pilgrimage to the Holy City, but will we ever get there?"

"He's only going to make sure he is paid. It doesn't sound like a crusade to save the Holy Land," said Pons. "How greed drives men!"

"I am here to fight for the Faith and expect nothing except food for my horse and myself," added Kozubowski. "But the Venetians have committed a huge fleet. It is fair to ask for compensation." His gaze swept over the three monks. "So, why are you here?"

"It's closer to Constantinople," answered O'Broin.

Gallus shrugged, "You already know—to pray at the Church of the Holy Sepulcher in Jerusalem. They built it on the place where Emperor Constantine's mother Helena discovered the three crosses and Christ's tomb."

Pons was still wondering about Zeph's behavior during the battle. He watched the Norman and when he made eye contact, he tried to detect anything unordinary. *Why did he just stand there when I was helpless? Or did I imagine it?*

"Pons . . . Abbot Pons! What brought you here, the same as Gallus?"

I am not sure. "Yes . . like Gallus—to do pilgrimage."

The men began turning in for the night, and Zeph left for his own tent. Pons asked O'Broin, "I know Zeph is a knight from Naples, educated at Salerno and Bologna. Do you know anything else about his background?"

"He was born in Naples, is part Neapolitan and part Norman, and became a knight employed by the Vatican. Oh, yes . . . he said he was a bodyguard for Pope Callistus."

A wave of anxiety passed through Pons. My break with the Pope was not amicable. A Pope's bodyguard? Is that why he turned his back on me in the battle? I must watch him closely.

A week passed and the crusaders spent the days training, then playing knucklebones in the evenings. Doge Michiel eventually returned from his negotiations in the Holy City. Because King Baldwin was still held hostage by the Turks, the doge made a pact with the king's regent, William, the Prince of Galilee. They agreed to join forces to capture Tyre, the remaining coastal city in Muslim hands. Michiel and William drew up a contract, the *Pactum Warmundi*, that would reward the Venetians one-third of Tyre plus a street, bakery, bathhouse, and church in every city in the kingdom of Jerusalem.

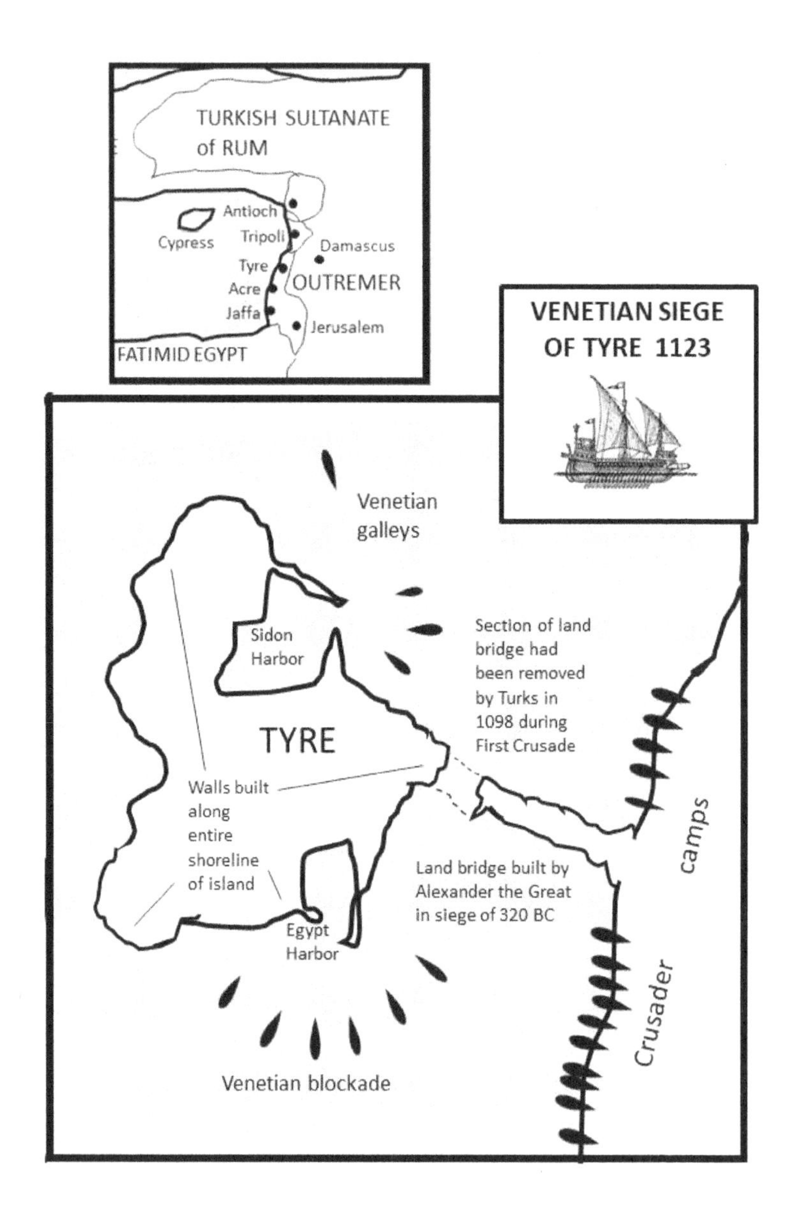
TURKISH SULTANATE
of RUM
Antioch
Cypress
Tripoli
Damascus
Tyre
Acre
OUTREMER
Jaffa
Jerusalem
FATIMID EGYPT
VENETIAN SIEGE
OF TYRE 1123
Venetian
galleys
Sidon
Harbor
Section of land
bridge had
been removed
by Turks in
1098 during
First Crusade
TYRE
Walls built
along
entire
shoreline
of island
Egypt
Harbor
Land bridge built by
Alexander the Great
in siege of 320 BC
camps
Crusader
Venetian blockade

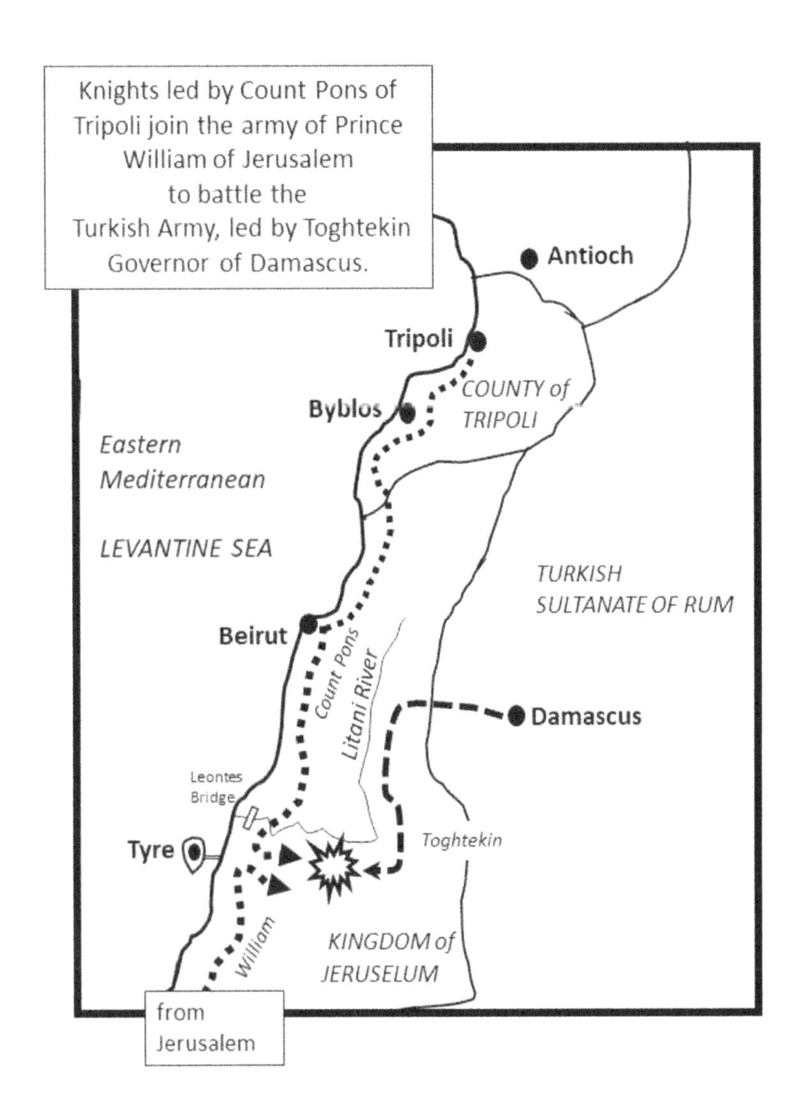
Knights led by Count Pons of Tripoli join the army of Prince William of Jerusalem to battle the Turkish Army, led by Toghtekin Governor of Damascus.
Antioch
Tripoli
COUNTY of TRIPOLI
Byblos
Eastern Mediterranean
LEVANTINE SEA
TURKISH SULTANATE OF RUM
Beirut
Count Pons
Litani River
Damascus
Leontes Bridge
Toghtekin
Tyre
William
KINGDOM of JERUSELUM
from Jerusalem

CHAPTER XXI THE SIEGE OF TYRE

The Venetians waited two weeks in Acre for Prince William, who arrived from Jerusalem with 100 knights and 1,000 foot soldiers. After a few days' rest, the prince marched north with his forces on the coastal road as the Venetian fleet sailed along the coast to meet them at Tyre. The island city was a half mile off the seacoast, heavily walled and connected by a man-made land bridge to the mainland. Tyre had been founded by the ancient Phoenicians thousands of years earlier and had been a thriving island port when Alexander the Great had ordered a land bridge built from the mainland to the island, enabling him to conquer the city. The causeway was two hundred pieds wide, constructed of stones from the ruins of the former city of Tyre on the mainland, as well as cedar logs from forests that had been on the nearby hills. Tyre was now occupied by the forces of Toghtekin, governor of Damascus, a vassal of the Turkish Sultanate of Rum, a large empire that rivaled the Holy Land and the Roman Empire.

The Venetian fleet arrived off of Tyre in midafternoon. The city had two harbors on opposite sides of the island. The doge established a sea blockade by positioning squadrons of galleys outside of the harbors. Other galleys patrolled off shore to intercept Fatimid reinforcements by sea. The camps of the Venetian sailors and marines were near the mainland beaches, which gave them rapid access to reinforce the sea blockade. To hamper the crusaders' approach to the city, the Turkish defenders had removed a section of the land bridge that led to the island.

Crusader soldiers and horses disembarked and camped at the

mainland end of the land bridge, with forces from Jerusalem blocking access and egress to the city by land. Combined with the sea blockade, the city was now surrounded. The crusader knights, including Kozubowski's company, were camped on the outer perimeter to defend and repel the expected Turkish reinforcements. Of the fifty men in Kozubowski's troop who had started the crusade, forty-five were still effective, after three fatalities in the sea battle and two recovering in camp. Fifteen mounted knights from Poland and Bohemia plus their squires made up the fighting group, together with peasant laborers and a few monks.

A week after the Venetians' arrival, with his perimeters secure, Doge Michiel attacked Tyre by sea. The galley decks were not tall enough to scale the high walls of the city. Instead, the doge used the galleys to tow a few of the double deck and triple deck transports to the walls. Marines on the galleys supported the assault with crossbow fire.

The offensive began simultaneously on all sides of the island. A few of the large ships became caught on rocks in shallow waters and the Venetian crews were exposed to deadly fire from the Turkish archers. The defenders catapulted boulders over the walls, firing from hidden positions. Their bombardment smashed ships' hulls, masts, and superstructures, and crushed Venetian sailors as the vessels approached the seaside walls of the city. As a result, only a handful of the ships reached the walls, and the assault was terminated. The Venetian fleet returned to the beaches for repairs and to treat the wounded.

On the following morning, the doge ordered the construction of siege engines to breach the city walls. The once extensive cedar forests that had covered the nearby Lebanon Mountains had been exploited for thousands of years. Now, stands of cedar trees which could provide enough timber for the siege engines were several days' ride into the mountains. The Venetians instead planned to disassemble several of the captured Fatimid vessels to build two siege towers as well as trebuchets, catapults that worked as massive slings.

A few days after the failed sea assault, the squires, peasants, and monks of Pons's company gathered with a thousand Venetian sailors on the sandy beach. It was a sunny fall day with a gentle breeze and the surf was calm. Most of the men were shirtless and wearing only their *braies*, linen underwear closed with a drawstring at the waist. They waited as four of the Fatimid galleys that had been seized in the sea battle south of Acre were rowed to the shore and beached. A ladder was placed against one of the ship's bows, and a handful of Venetian officers climbed onto the deck and examined the vessel.

O'Broin said, to no one in particular, "I never thought I'd end up on a beach standing around under the hot sun in my underwear! Hey, Gallus, you have two holes in your *braies*!"

The Venetian monk examined his shorts, "Where?"

"You put your legs through them when you pulled them on!" said O'Broin. Standing behind the Irish monk, Pons laughed. O'Broin said, "Oh! I didn't see you because of the glare. The shine from your tonsure blinded me."

O'Broin talked on. "And this sun will darken me. They will never recognize me if I return to Ireland."

A peasant laborer said, "Yesterday, I bought a head cloth from a camp merchant. With today's hot sun, I shouldn't have left it in my tent. He showed me how to wrap the cloth around my head to protect against the sun and you can use it to cover your mouth if the sand is blowing."

"Which merchant sells these . . . coverings?" asked Pons.

"Most of the traders sell them—the Egyptians call the head cloth a *shemagh*."

Another laborer added, "I guess that's why those archers in the sea battle were so dark, living under this Outremer sun?"

"No, good man," answered Gallus. "The Lord made them that way, dark skinned."

The peasant's eyebrows knitted together. "I have never seen men so dark."

"You have never heard of the Ethiopians?"

He shook his head.

"Those archers were from Sudan, a land south of Egypt near Ethiopia, another place where people are born dark skinned."

The man's face was blank.

"It is a holy land," Gallus added. "The Christian church of the Ethiopians is older than that of Rome or Constantinople."

The peasant placed his fingertips on his forehead and blinked. "There is so much to learn! Black men from Sudan, Ethiopia, the oldest churches. . . how do you know this? "

"I read books about wonderful lands, which compelled me to travel and see them myself," said Gallus.

Pons had been distracted by activity at a beached vessel. He pointed. "Who were those men who climbed on that ship deck?" asked Pons. "Architects?"

A Venetian sailor overheard him. "They are the engineers who build and direct the operation of the siege engines. The one wearing the straw hat is the chief engineer, Donatello Siano, and the other four are *gynours*."

"*Gynours*?"

"Trebuchet engineers."

They could hear a voice on the ship giving directions. "Remove the deck planks, cut the mast down, and pass them to the men on the beach." Siano descended the ladder and addressed the *gynours*. "Use the decking planks to build a wooden ramp to pull the ship out of the water." With his sword he drew two parallel lines in the sand, the width of the ship's keel. "Place the longest planks like this."

He drew lines at right angles across the two parallel lines, "Cut planks five pieds long and nail them across, like this."

The engineers inspected the other beached ships. The *gynours* organized the men into four groups to make a wooden track for each galley. After the ramps were completed, hundreds of men pulled on ropes in unison to slide the galleys out of the water and along the wooden tracks. Others used long stout poles as levers and rocks as fulcrums to pull up on the ship's hull. The shouts of the *gynours* encouraged the men to pull in unison: "*Uno, due, tres. Tirate*! Pull! *Uno, due, tres. Tirate*! . . . "

After the vessels were pulled onto the beach, the men took a water break. As the engineer walked among the workers and shouted thanks to the men, one asked him, "Sir, I was pulling hard on a pole, but I didn't think we raised the ship."

"Oh, you may have not noticed," said Siano, "but you lightened the load just a little, which helped the others pull the ship out of the water, believe me. The famous Syracusan engineer Archimedes once said, 'Give me a lever long enough and a fulcrum on which to place it, and I shall move the world.'"

After the break, men swarmed over the vessels and disassembled the ships.

The next morning the workers returned to the beach and lugged the recovered beams, planks, and masts from the beach to the land bridge where they would build the siege engines. Most of them took a quick swim to wash off the sweat and sand. Pons and his comrades were assigned to a group to assemble one of three trebuchets. Siano gave instructions to the *gynour* leading their team, then left to direct other workers.

They built a wooden frame, a rectangular platform, ten pieds wide and thirty long of thick beams. The squires then handed out bread, wine, and fish.

Siano returned and sketched an image of a pyramidal tower, truncated near the top. "Next you will build the tower. The height of the pyramid will be about five times that of a man, twenty-eight pieds, yes?" The *gynour* nodded. "And you know how to attach the tower, and make the counterweight and swing arm?"

"Yes, sir."

Siano hurried away to the next trebuchet being constructed, as the gynour supervised. A handful of workers arrived hefting a ship's mast, forty pieds long, that had been removed from a captured galley, and placed it on the ground. They assembled a hopper, an open-top wooden box, five pieds on each side, and attached it to the end of the mast. A carpenter drilled a hole through the mast eight pieds from one end and inserted the fulcrum pin, made of a thick iron rod. Men hoisted the mast with the hopper affixed to the top of the pyramidal frame, slid it in place with ropes, and attached the assembly to the fulcrum pin.

Carts arrived loaded with cobblestones. The mast was pivoted on the fulcrum and the stones were moved to the hopper. As the workers rested, drenched from the exertion, they watched as a carpenter attached a rope thirty-two pieds long to the longer end of the mast. A wide leather band, large enough to hold a stone half the weight of a man, was fixed at the end of the line.

O'Broin took a drink of water as they passed a skin, then wiped his brow. "That was hard work lifting those stones. But it was worth it because I thought that box was for us to sit in as they flung us over the city walls!"

"Perhaps that is the only way you could get to Heaven," said Kozubowski.

O'Broin laughed with the men, was handed the water skin again and drank. His comrades leaned in, eyeing him. Pons stood, hands on his hips and said, "Well?"

"What?" said O'Broin. "Maybe I don't want to go to Heaven. That's where all the virtuous women go!"

Construction of the siege engines was completed. Following tradition, the trebuchets were given names. Mules pulled and men pushed three trebuchets, rolling *No Wall's Friend, The Fist of God,* and *Saint Mark's Hammer* over masts from the dismantled ships to within 300 pieds of the city walls, the maximum range the catapults could launch heavy stones.

They began lobbing the boulders at the city walls across the opening in the land bridge. After a few trials, they found the range, and the heavy stones began reducing the walls. But catapults hidden behind the city walls returned fire.

Mules and crusaders pushed and pulled the siege towers further along the land bridge. With great efforts by men and beasts, the siege towers were hauled to the water's edge at the break in the land bridge. The towers were higher than the Turkish walls and the Venetian crossbowmen loosed hails of bolts upon the defenders. Meanwhile, the Venetian trebuchets had created a breach in the city fortifications.

The Venetians floated a pair of captured ships into the canal the Turks had excavated through the land bridge and scuttled them in the shallow water. Several thousand Venetian marines and foot soldiers from Jerusalem moved along the land bridge and began crossing the ships to storm the city wall.

The first of the crusader infantrymen began crossing and boulders hurled from the Turkish catapults hit one siege tower, then the other. Shouting and screaming of men reached a crescendo as the top of one tower shattered and the other tower collapsed, flinging crossbowmen through the air and crushing Venetian foot soldiers. The water in the opening of the land bridge became a tangle of broken timbers, rubble, and bodies. Without siege towers, the doge ordered his soldiers to retreat and called off the attack.

Kozubowski's men did not see action during the unsuccessful Venetian assault on Tyre. On the following day, the troop was sent north for scout duty. They rode on the coastal road, the armored knights on their warhorses; the squires and monks, armed with spears and oval shields, followed on mules. The crusaders had adopted wearing *shemagh*s, the Egyptian head covering, useful protection against the sun and sand in the arid regions. They also each wore a white cross sewn on the front of his tunic. Pons glanced at O'Broin and Gallus, riding the mules purchased locally by the army, like himself. *I wonder how Cominius is doing on Mount Grappa? It seems long ago in another world.*

An hour north of Tyre, the company arrived at a Roman bridge spanning the Litani River. A troop of French crusaders were camped there, who, now relieved of their duty, returned to Tyre. The commanders had told the markiz they expected a Seljuk Turk relief force from Damascus to travel along the Litani valley through the hills to reach Tyre.

Kozubowski sent Zeph, O'Broin, and Pons east to scout along the valley. Moving inland, they passed between low hills and turned north with the river. The land was sparse of vegetation, with scattered cedar trees. The lower reaches of the mountains had been denuded by the ancient Phoenicians two thousand years earlier to build their trading fleets. Far to the north on the mountains, however, the higher elevations were still dark with cedars.

The three rode inland up the Litani River valley for about five miles, then turned around and began to retrace their path to the bridge before dark. Pons and O'Broin took up the rear. In a short time, Pons sensed rapid hoof beats from behind. O'Broin turned his mount to face the threat. Pons shouted, "Zeph! Riders are approaching!" Pons urged his mule ahead with his shield and spear ready. Beside him, the Irish monk did the same. The trail curved with the river between the hills. They moved slowly forward, neared a bend in the trail, and suddenly out of a cloud of dust a pair of riders dashed into view. Pons glanced over his shoulder, expecting to see Zeph backing them, but he was not in sight. The oncoming horsemen pulled their reins hard to a stop. A large gold cross was sewn on the rider's tunics and Pons noted the same gold cross was emblazoned on the men's red shields. *It is similar to the coat of arms of Toulouse, the gold cross on a red field.*

"Brother, who are you?" asked Pons.

One soldier answered in Occitan, Pons's native language, "We are scouts for Count Pons of Tripoli. He should be at the Leontes Bridge now with his knights. Toghtekin is less than ten miles up the valley and is approaching with an army!"

Both O'Broin and Pons looked at each other with blank faces. One of the riders skirted them, paused, and said, "Tisserand, take them with you and monitor the Turks!" He galloped on. The hoof beats receded and Pons twisted in his saddle, the leather creaking. "I guess Toghtekin is the Turkish leader?"

The scout nodded.

Pons looked at O'Broin. "Zeph is gone!" He forced himself to ignore the desertion of the knight and focused on their scouting duty as Tisserand gestured to follow him east for several miles. They dismounted and led their mules off the trail behind one of the rare copses of cedar trees amid the barren landscape. They stayed hidden as Tisserand proceeded on foot to survey the area. A mounted patrol of Turks passed during his absence. Near sunset he rejoined Pons and O'Broin. "Toghtekin's army is camped a few miles away. We must inform Count Pons. Do either of you know this trail well enough to reach the Leontes bridge in the dark?" The sky was clear with only a crescent moon. They both shook their heads.

"Then I am going. I do not think the Turks will send troops along the trail at night, but they could send Hashashins. You must stop them. If you think they slipped through, you must warn the crusader camp at the bridge."

"I am not familiar with the term, Hashashins," said Pons.

"They are cutthroats specially trained for stealth and deception to murder the leaders of their enemies. It is said that the Hashashins are invulnerable in single combat when they are energized with hashish, made from a flower grown in these valleys."

He departed on foot, leading his mount.

Pons looked at O'Broin, as he copied the other monk and removed his *shemagh,* with the sun down and the air cooling.

"You want to sleep or take first watch?" The Irish monk lay down and bunched up his *shemagh* to use as a pillow.

The next hour Pons became tired of gazing at the stars and dark silhouettes of the nearby hills. He recalled his time with Primavera in the watery cave. *It seems like a lifetime ago . . . it was sensuous, so wet there . . . and so dry here . . .* His reverie was interrupted by the shifting of loose rock below. *What?* He stole towards the trail, scarcely able to see in the low moonlight, taking his mule, knowing the animal had excellent night vision and a keen sense of self preservation. *Was it a wild animal, a lone man, or were the Turks stealing by to make a night attack at the bridge?* As he clutched his steed's mane with one hand, and his spear in the other, the mule suddenly moved to the left, pushing Pons with him. He felt a swish of air past his face and on impulse jabbed his spear forward and then pulled it back. The point had found something. A man grunted and a body thumped on the ground, followed by the clatter of metal on stone. He could barely make out a dark mass thrashing on the ground for a short time, then silence. More rocks on the trail scattered. Pons didn't move. The mule was quiet and motionless. *God's bones, why didn't I wake O'Broin?*

Suddenly acute pains burned across the side of his neck as a gurgling sound pierced the dark in front of him. Pons saw a shadowy form where the sound had come as it fell away. The mule shied away from the disquieting forms on the ground, and Pons stumbled. O'Broin's whisper came from behind, "Keep moving backwards."

They found their way to the copse of cedars. Pons's neck was painful but not bleeding. They waited in silence until the ragged breathing of the second victim ceased, then waited longer. Pons whispered, "That must have been your spear shaft on my neck."

"I guess so. Are you bleeding?"

"No, just wood burns. That was close. The Lord must have guided your spear. It was a miracle the blade was turned flat against my neck."

O'Broin snickered. "No, it was your fat head! I barely saw your tonsure in the moonlight, so I speared past it at the black silhouette."

“Hail there, monk. The one with the haircut with a hole in it! Wake up!” O’Broin sat on his mule. The sun was rising. The monks had alternated sleeping and keeping watch through the night. Pons rolled out of his blanket and looked up. O’Broin handed Pons the reins of his mule. “Your cousin is here with an army!”

The marching of feet, creaking of leather, snorting of horses, and clinking of metal drew Pons’s attention. Visible above the thickets along the trail were Christian knights riding high on their warhorses, spears pointing to the Heaven the Pope had promised them if they perished in the crusade.

Count Pons had arrived from Tripoli with almost one hundred knights. At the bridge over the Litani the count had been joined by William who had brought five score of knights and one thousand foot soldiers. By mid-morning the crusader forces had marched inland and assembled on a plain opposite the Turkish army, with the river on their left. The Muslim commander, Toghtekin, governor of Damascus, had chosen to fight in an area where mounted archers could maneuver. Count Pons had a history fighting the mounted archers of the Turks and Fatimid Arabs. William acknowledged the count’s order that the knights must resist the feigned retreats of the Turkish horse archers. The tactic was their primary strategy in breaking up an enemy formation.

Among the Christian infantry drawn up in the center, two lines deep, were Pons and his comrade monks armed with shields and spears. A score of knights led by Kozubowski held the right wing, and a score of French knights were at the left wing near the river. The majority of the knights were massed behind the foot soldiers. There had been no time to bring the Venetian marines, all effective crossbowmen, thus the crusaders had only a few score archers. Most of the Turkish forces, numbering about one thousand, were mounted archers. Their foot soldiers were in reserve to ready the spare mounts and protect the camp.

The battle began as Count Pons expected. The enemy horse archers skirmished with the crusader center and wings in small groups, riding within bow range, loosing arrows, and retreating. The Christians raised shields and returned arrow fire. For an hour, again and again, groups of ten to twenty horse archers badgered and harassed the knights at the wings, goading them into a chase. Suddenly Kozubowski appeared to take the enemy's bait as he led a score of knights after a group of withdrawing horse archers. Toghtekin had patiently waited for the Christians to break formation and sent a mass of horse archers forward on all fronts to envelop the small band. But Kozubowski cut sharply to the left, breaking off the chase and led his knights parallel to the line of crusader infantry. Many of the pursuing Turks were caught between the crusader infantry and the company of knights, but the most serious threat emerged when two hundred Christian knights in reserve followed Kozubowski's path and crashed into the flank of the mass of the horse archers. Most of the Turkish cavalry was now hemmed in by the river and their own reserve troops and could not retreat in order.

Count Pons had taken point in leading the iron wedge, the tactic applied by armored knights of heavy calvary in a mass attack. But the tactic would be vulnerable if the Turkish horse archers could maneuver, regroup, and surround the crusaders. The Count of Tripoli was gambling he could pin the enemy against the river, so the crusader knights had to close the distance rapidly.

Enemy horsemen fleeing the count's iron wedge crashed into the lines of infantry, resulting in a melee of riderless steeds and hand to hand combat. Kozubowski's knights were in the middle of the fighting as they turned on the horse archers. Pons, alongside O'Broin and Gallus, used spears to unseat enemy riders caught in the press of horses and men. Turks who had become unhorsed were spinning and slashing with their swords. The monks defended by keeping chins down, closing the gap between their helmet and shield, and exploiting the reach of their spears.

The three monks became separated from the other infantry and were fighting in all directions. A pair of knights rushed to help. Kozubowski and his mount, both wild-eyed with rampage, trampled a pair of enemy soldiers on Pons's left, the warhorse biting and kicking the enemy as rider and steed blasted through. Zeph followed, galloping straight for Pons. The knight held his sword high. Pons's eyes locked with the Italo-Norman bent on slaughter. *He left me to die in the sea battle without success, so now he will kill me himself. Zeph is the Pope's Hashashin!* Zeph abruptly reined his destrier to a stop, and the knight finished a powerful cut with his sword. *Primavera!*

Consciousness remained a few moments as the severed head fell. Blood spurted with the final heartbeats and splattered on Pons's shoulders. Then the headless body fell to the earth.

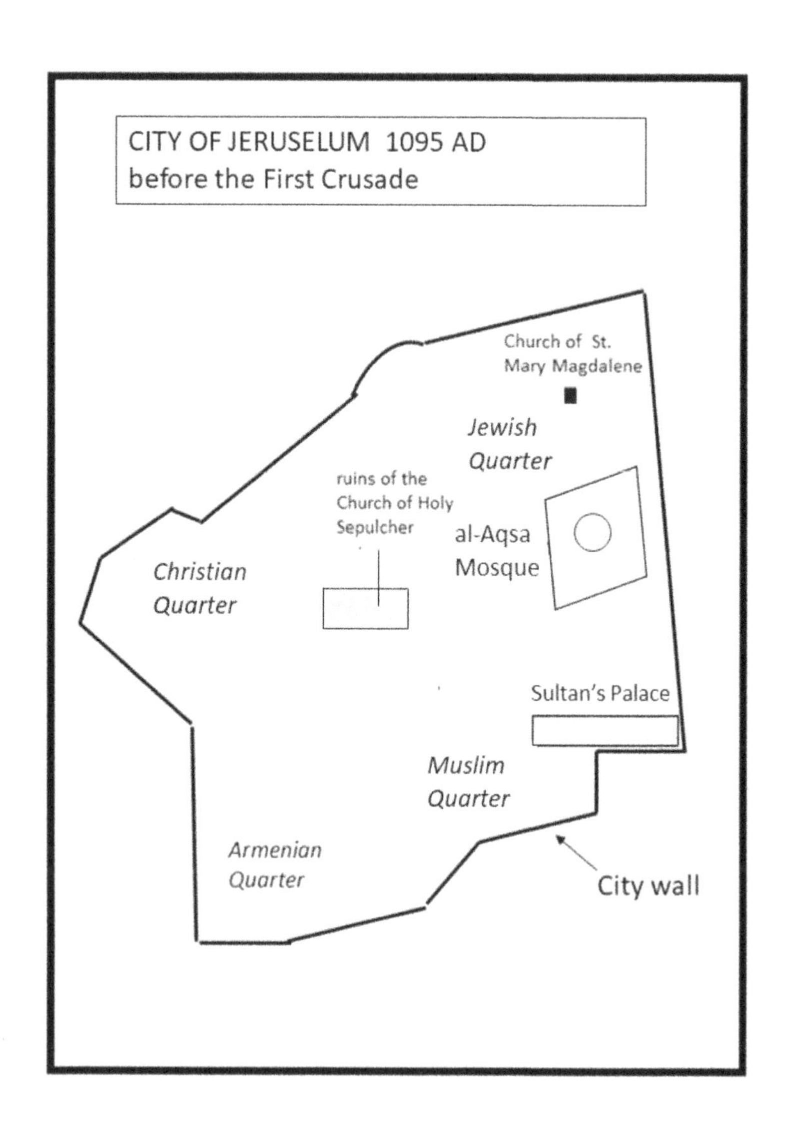
CITY OF JERUSELUM 1095 AD
before the First Crusade
Church of St.
Mary Magdalene
Jewish
Quarter
ruins of the
Church of Holy
Sepulcher
al-Aqsa
Mosque
Christian
Quarter
Sultan's Palace
Muslim
Quarter
Armenian
Quarter
City wall

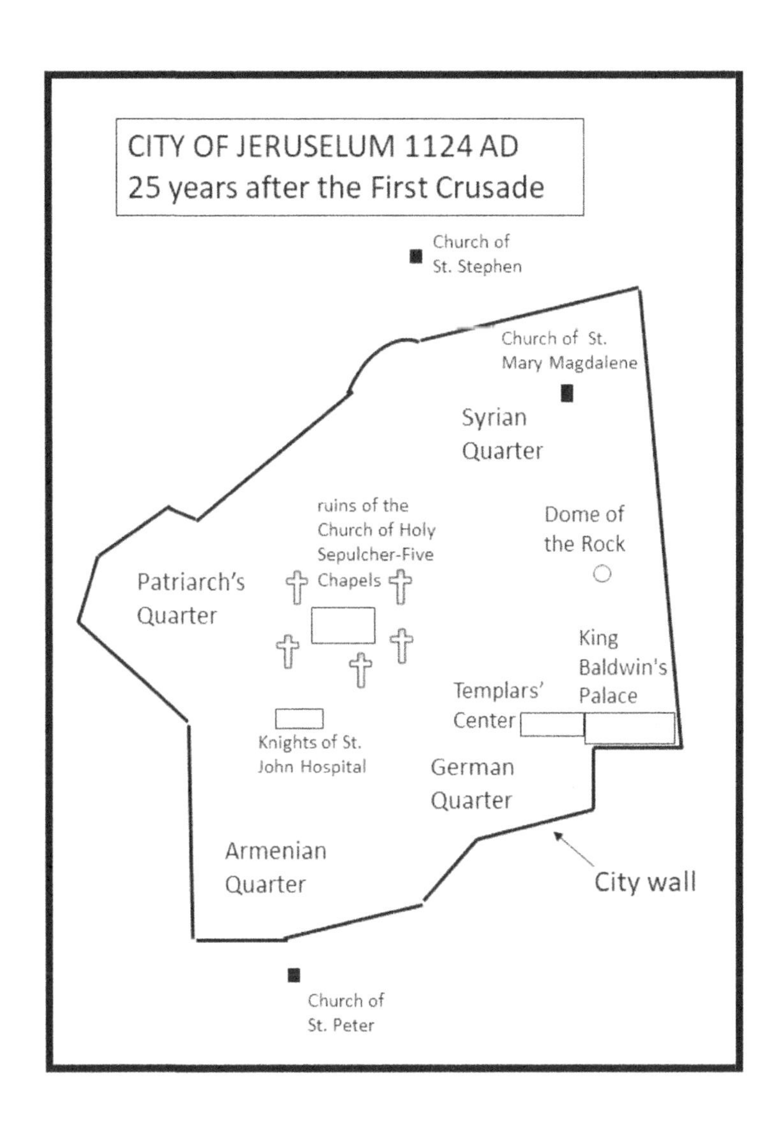
CITY OF JERUSELUM 1124 AD
25 years after the First Crusade
Church of
St. Stephen
Church of St.
Mary Magdalene
Syrian
Quarter
ruins of the
Church of Holy
Sepulcher-Five
Chapels
Dome of
the Rock
Patriarch's
Quarter
King
Baldwin's
Palace
Templars'
Center
Knights of St.
John Hospital
German
Quarter
Armenian
Quarter
City wall
Church of
St. Peter

CHAPTER XXII   JERUSELUM 1124 AD

Following his defeat at the Litani River by the Christian army, Toghtekin led his Turkish forces back to Damascus. Count Pons did not pursue the Turks, knowing he would be subject to ambush in the mountain gorges. He stationed a company of knights at the Leontes Bridge and with Prince William of Jerusalem led the crusader army to Tyre.

After the battle, Pons had been busy praying for the wounded men, conducting the *Sacrament of Anointing the Sick*, and giving final communion for the mortally wounded, as well as praying over the dead. The crusaders were emotionally and physically exhausted as the army traveled the last few miles to the besieged city, and most of the men rode without conversation. Pons reined his mule beside Zeph, hoping to make sense of the knight's behavior. The knight refused to look at him. Pons hesitated. *How do I get him to be forthcoming? He could still be plotting.* "Zeph, I thank God for your aid. When you charged at me in the battle, it appeared you were going to remove *my* head!" Pons forced a laugh.

Zeph turned with stern gaze.

Is he angry? Tired? I can't tell.

The knight answered. "Abbot Pons, I am loyal to those to whom I swear allegiance."

"Yes . . . yes . . . that is a sign . . . of a man of honor. Do you mean as to following Kozubowski's commands? As a warrior obeys the knight's code?"

Zeph raised his voice, "No, I mean I have decided to follow the

Lord's will and not the Pope's!"

"And?"

"I was *never* going to murder you . . . I am sorry that I hesitated in coming to your defense at the sea battle. "

Pons breathed out. "Thank you, Zeph."

"You knew, didn't you?" asked Zeph.

"I was suspicious, but when you swung your sword, it was too late and I thought I was done. It seems we are both disillusioned with the Pope. But we *can* depend on the Lord. I believe He guided O'Broin to save my life at the sea battle and as you just said, guided you to *not* kill me."

Zeph sighed, "Yes, we have the Lord, and each other."

The triumphant crusader forces returned to Tyre and set up their camps alongside those of the besieging troops. News of the victory raised morale throughout the crusaders' ranks. The joint commanders, Doge Domenico Michiel, Count Pons of Tripoli, and William of Jerusalem, agreed to continue the siege. They had control of the sea and now the surrounding lands, having repelled the Turks.

A few days after his return to the crusader camp, Pons strode among the tents of the knights of the Outremer, searching for his cousin, the Count of Tripoli. Whipping in the breeze above the rows of tents was a gonfalon festooned with a gold cross on a red field, where he located the count's headquarters. Pons identified himself to the guard who returned in a short time, holding the tent flap open. The count emerged and peered at the abbot, eyebrows furrowed and head tilted to the side. The count was half a head taller than Pons, had a dark beard and moustache, and was some twenty years younger. He smiled, "Yes, even a generation removed, I see the resemblance!" He embraced the older Pons. "Come in, Cousin!"

The count gestured for Pons to take one of the stools in the large tent. They sat in silence as a squire brought a pitcher of wine and a pair of terracotta cups. "First—the business of war," began the young count. "I heard that Hashashins attacked you while on scout duty . . . and you killed them both! Unheard of!"

"A bit of luck, and my comrade's and God's help, Cousin."

"Oh, yes, yes. The Lord is on our side, of course. But the

Hashashins are very dangerous. Two of them entered my tent that same night in camp at the Leontes Bridge."

The older man's eyebrows shot up.

"The murderers killed my second in command, who was sleeping in my place. God rest his soul, I am indebted to him for his sacrifice. Unfortunately, the Hashashins escaped."

The count's bearing abruptly lightened as he raised his cup, "Sante! To our ancient name, Pontius!"

The abbot hesitated, then toasted, "Sante!"

The younger man continued, "Yes, we are, um . . . second cousins, your Uncle Ramon de Saint Gilles was my grandfather. We are both Pons and my great-grandfather—your grandfather — was Pons." The count sipped wine. "You know we carry on the ancient surname of our clan, yes? It was originally Pontius."

"I was not told. My family gave me to the Benedictines when I was four. I have read of the martyrdom of Saint Pontius and of another ancient Roman—Pontius Cominius, but thought it was just a coincidence that I had the same name."

"No matter, you and I are here now and we are both descendants of Saint Pontius de Cimiez. My mother told me of my ancestor when I was a lad," said the count.

"You are a very confident young man," said the abbot. "How old are you?"

"I am 25, and have been count since I was 12, leading knights into battle since I was 15."

"I am a forty year old monk, a um . . . let me say, retired abbot, and in the last month I have seen only now my first battles. On our way to the Outremer, the hostilities of Christians against Christians have disturbed me. What other horrors might I see during this siege?"

The count gave a tired sigh. "Both Christians and Muslims have committed many atrocities. Alexios, the former Roman emperor, was a friend and ally of Grandfather Ramon and told him the history of the first Muslim invasions of the Roman Empire—the jihad or holy wars. Grandfather related the accounts of the wars to my father. At the time of the jihadi wars, Jerusalem was almost entirely Christian and after a long siege, the city fell to the Muslims who killed tens of thousands of the inhabitants, and as many were enslaved.

"When the Christians recovered Jerusalem in 1098, the year I was born, Ramon was one of the crusader leaders that led the assault on the city. He captured the southern gate and let the Muslim defenders live. Godfrey de Boulillon, however, who entered the northern gate, ordered his men to slaughter everyone they encountered, soldiers and citizens alike. Ramon's misdeed was that he lost control of his own men who joined in the massacre. According to Grandfather's tale, the crusaders killed most of the Muslims. And they indiscriminately killed native Christians and Jews, yes, both groups had helped defend the city, but the carnage even included women and children. There were native Christians and Jews who took refuge at the Dome of the Rock and survived. They were forced to clean up the dead in the city. The Jews were then sold as slaves."

A pang of guilt shot through Pons. *Slaves. Enslaved Europeans are sold to Muslims. Even if Primavera survived, she could be here, in the east, suffering!*

He recovered. "Um . . . I believe that Ramon would have tried to avoid the carnage," said the abbot. "I met him the year he left Toulouse for the Outremer. He was an honorable man. And Cousin, will you avoid such atrocities at Tyre?"

The count gazed across the tent past his cousin. "Let's pray to God we can."

"I wish I had known my grandfather," said the count. "I was five or six, living in Toulouse, when he died in the siege of Tripoli. Then my father brought me to the Outremer and captured the city." His eyes returned to the abbot. "And as for Tyre, it will be difficult, with greed and revenge driving the crusaders. Plus there are not only Muslims and Jews living in Tyre, but also Christians." The count leaned back and drank. "Have you done pilgrimage yet to the Holy City?"

The abbot shook his head.

His younger cousin smiled. "I will be granting leave for soldiers to pilgrimage to Jerusalem. Your company will be among the first."

As Pons departed he was encouraged, not only that he had met his cousin, but that the count appeared to have good moral standards and might avoid needless atrocities. But the last thoughts filled Pons once again with remorse, knowing that he was responsible for Primavera's plight. He dragged himself back to camp, head down.

During the lulls in fighting, the camp followers provided distractions for the crusaders, such as gambling, wine, and prostitutes. The men, however, were losing patience with the siege and were calling for the commanders to again assault the city. Prince William led expeditions to capture several inland towns to expand his domain, but the booty was trivial compared to what they expected from Tyre, a wealthy city of 40,000. Crusaders also took leave for pilgrimage to Jerusalem. To assure Count Pons and Prince William that the Venetians would stay until they conquered Tyre, Doge Michiel had his helmsmen bring the fleet's sails and rudders ashore, except for the vessels blockading the harbor.

Kozubowski's company, down to forty men, left Tyre in the vanguard of a small army. The force was comprised of fifty-odd knights from Germany and two hundred Genoese sailors and marines. They reached the port of Jaffa in two days, where many non-combatant pilgrims disembarked to travel overland to the Holy City. The pilgrims usually made the journey in large groups of a hundred or more for safety. Still, bandits and footpads preyed on them, sometimes more than just to rob, but to murder, or capture and sell as slaves in the Muslim countries.

The crusaders from Tyre camped east of town along with a group of pilgrims which included women. In the morning, Pons, O'Broin, and Gallus sat in front of their tent and shared from a skin of diluted wine. They munched on hard bread. "I'm glad I got rid of that black habit!" announced O'Broin. "In this sun, this pale linen tunic is much more comfortable."

"I agree," said Pons.

Gallus watched a group of Cistercian monks readying for Jerusalem. "I regret casting away my habit. It represents our Benedictine Order. But wearing the tunic may have saved my life. A habit would have hampered me in the battles."

"At least the Cistercians' habits are gray, not so hot in the sun," added O'Broin.

"Last night," said Gallus, "a Cistercian told me after the Christians captured Jerusalem, they found the True Cross when restoring the Church of the Holy Sepulcher. I am eager to see it."

"How could that be, Brother Gallus? You are a learned

historian," said Pons. "I read that Emperor Constantine's mother Helena visited Jerusalem hundreds of years ago, and *that* was when they found the True Cross. She had the cross taken to Constantinople and sent a fragment to Rome. But my uncle sent back a sliver after the capture of the city and I have seen fragments throughout France and Spain. Now they claim the cross is in Jerusalem?"

"Hmm," O'Broin scratched his chin. "How can there be so many pieces? I guess that's why all the cedar trees in the Outremer have been cut down."

Pons was used to the Irish monk's blasphemous jests, but held his laughter as Gallus exclaimed, "Good monk!"

Before he could say more, a knight approached. Stitched on his tunic was a red cross overlaying a black and white field. "*Bon jour.*" He continued in Burgundian French, "I am Andre de Montbard, please, I wish to talk with your company's officer."

Gallus and O'Broin looked to Pons, who spoke French. Pons said, "Gallus, will you inform the markiz?"

As the Venetian monk left, Pons asked the knight, "Sir, I am not familiar with the crest on your tunic."

"I am from Jerusalem, but I am a Templar Knight. We protect pilgrims traveling between Jaffa and Jerusalem." He pointed to a group of pilgrims departing for the Holy City. Mounted knights escorted them; white crosses on a red field were emblazoned on their uniforms. "That is another order devoted to protecting pilgrims, the Order of Knights of the Hospital of Saint John, more commonly known as the Knights Hospitaller."

"A very good cause, sir," said Pons.

Kozubowski arrived and stepped away with the templar, both conversing in Latin.

Shortly, the markiz ordered the troops to prepare for Jerusalem. Several hundred pilgrims traveled with them, among them Cistercian monks. The templars were a small order and needed assistance due to the large volume of pilgrims and at the templar's request Kozubowski had agreed to protect the group during their pilgrimage to the Holy City.

When they arrived in Jerusalem, they found that the basilica— the Church of the Holy Sepulcher— originally built above the cave where the Christians believed Jesus had been entombed, was in ruins. The basilica, constructed by the Romans in 320 AD, had stood for three centuries until Muslims destroyed it. After the Christians recovered Jerusalem in 1099, King Baldwin had erected five chapels around a courtyard where the basilica ruins remained. Each chapel was decorated with a scene from Christ's passion. During Pons's pilgrimage, the restoration of the basilica was currently underway.

During their week in the Holy City, Gallus and Kozubowski returned each day to pray at the shrines of the five chapels. Pons accompanied them and experienced a spiritual enlivening at the site. O'Broin visited the shrines the first day with them, then spent the rest of the days exploring the city. He found taverns and entertained for free food and drink. At other times, the crusaders escorted the pilgrims around Jerusalem and protected them in their camps. There was a thriving souvenir industry in the city. Pilgrims pilfered stones and dust from the ruins. They also had tattoos of the cross inked into their skin and purchased slivers of wood claimed by the vendors to be remnants of the *True Cross*. When Pons inquired about the location of the cross, he was met with blank stares.

After their stay in Jerusalem, Kozubowski's troop of crusaders escorted the flock of pilgrims they had pledged to protect to Jaffa, then headed north on the coastal road. Pons rode on his mule next to Kozubowski, recalling what he had seen in the city. Kozubowski had been quiet as they rode north. Pons glanced at him. "Markiz, were you satisfied with your pilgrimage?"

The markiz tilted his head back and looked up as he answered. "Yes, the presence of the Holy Spirit was close to overpowering! It was as I had imagined it would be . . . I sensed the spirit of Christ . . . of God . . . more profoundly than any time in my life."

Kozubowski turned his attention to Pons. "But why is there no Jewish quarter in the city? There are Jewish quarters in Prague and Wroclaw, even after the Rhineland massacres during the First Crusade. It doesn't seem right there is not a Jewish quarter in the ancient capital of King David."

"Massacres?" said Pons. "I remember years ago hearing about a few Jewish merchants murdered in Germany by crusaders plundering on their way to the East."

Kozubowski glared at Pons and raised his voice. "A few

merchants murdered? Thousands . . . tens of thousands of Jews were killed by crusaders on their way to the Holy Land, because they regarded them as infidels, no better than the Muslims. The Duke of Poland, however, graciously welcomed Jews to our lands and gave them protection. "

"I was only repeating what I had heard," said Pons.

Pons recalled his conversation with his cousin a few weeks earlier. *Dear God, don't let there also be a massacre at Tyre.*

Pons said, "I know why there is no Jewish quarter in Jerusalem any longer. The crusaders killed or enslaved the Jews in the Holy City. The former Jewish quarter is now inhabited by Christian Syrians."

"War, war! Christ's nails! It's all the same!" barked Kozubowski. "I want to finish the siege and get back to my homeland!"

"Markiz, you are a tough and capable leader. You are also a pious Catholic and your concern for people of another religion makes me think you can't hide that you have a good heart."

"Hmph!"

Pons sensed his comrade's response was a feeble display of anger to hide his sensitivity. So when he glanced at the markiz, he expected a smirk, but the knight's thoughts had moved elsewhere, and he had a wistful expression. They rode in silence for a while, then unexpectedly, Kozubowski declared, "I am going to marry her when I get back!"

"Marry? Who?" asked Pons.

"Rachel. Her name is Rachel. She is strong *and* beautiful. When I was recruiting knights in Wroclaw, I saw her for the first time, fighting off a gang of street thugs who had been terrorizing her neighborhood. Surrounded by ruffians, she whirled about, her walking stick hitting out like lightning. Before I could reach her, they had fled, tending broken hands and knotted skulls. I asked her if she needed help and she smiled, but shook her head."

"And what happened after that?" asked Pons.

"She left. When I asked about her at the nearby tavern, the men said, 'Oh, she must like you! She moves about with a stern face and doesn't smile at men anymore, because they got the idea they should court her.' She runs the family's silk weaving business, since the crusaders killed the men in her family during the

Rhineland massacres."

The markiz let out a lengthy breath. "I have never talked to her, but I know she is the one I want to marry. It's been almost a year since I left Poland. Perhaps she is married already."

"I understand your feelings. I also would be passionate to return home," added Pons.

Kozubowski said, "What an odd remark coming from a monk. I assume, a *celibate* monk?"

"Have you spoken with O'Broin about celibacy?" said Pons.

"Well, yes, he told me he has known women, but he is not a typical monk and . . . you are . . . or *were* an abbot." He peered at Pons. "Oh, I see. You broke your vows. Perhaps that is why you left the abbatial rank?"

"No, but I was in love, once. Like you, I knew it the first time I saw her. But she was . . . it's hard for me to say . . . " Pons felt his throat constrict, "She was abducted and likely sold as a slave."

"Lord! I am sorry, Pons!"

Pons suddenly felt out of breath. *Dear Lord, wherever she is, please give her strength and don't let her suffer. And let her remember how much I loved her!*

"So, yes, let's finish this siege," answered Pons, "so you can get back to her."

On the third day after departing Jaffa, Kozubowski's troop arrived in Tyre and rejoined the crusader camps. As the monks pitched their tents and cared for their mounts, they learned that envoys from the Turkish governor had arrived from Damascus to negotiate peace. The crusader leaders and the Muslim emissaries had been holding deliberations for two days to decide the conditions of surrender. In the afternoon the commanders ordered the officers to meet with their superiors. Rumors spread that the parley had concluded. Within an hour, the officers returned to brief their men. Shouts of anger as well as relief echoed across the large encampment as Kozubowski addressed his men, "The city has surrendered."

Pons joined in as the men called out, "Thank the Lord!"

"Before I tell you the terms, remember why we came here, good soldiers of Christ. Decades ago the first crusaders won

Jerusalem. The capture of Tyre will strengthen the Christian control of the Holy Land."

The men waited in silence. Pons held his breath. *Please God don't let the atrocities be repeated! The slaughter of the Rhineland Jews, the massacre of the Christians in Antioch and Jerusalem, and yes, the killing of the innocent Jews and Muslims. Lord, be merciful!*

"The entry into the city will be controlled, orderly, and disciplined. The commanders will not tolerate violence or pillaging." Kozubowski continued, "Our blockade has intercepted and seized ten Fatimid cargo ships heading for Tyre. A bonus from the value of the shipment as determined by Count Pons, Prince William, and Doge Michiel will be awarded to every crusader.

"Our leaders accepted the Turkish governor's condition of surrender to allow the citizens who want to leave the city to take their families and property with them to Damascus. And the people who want to stay will keep their houses and possessions."

Several of the men grumbled their disappointment. Kozubowski slapped Pons on the back in exhilaration as the abbot exhaled with relief. *Men may have corrupted the Church, but I still trust our Lord. Dear God, thank you.*

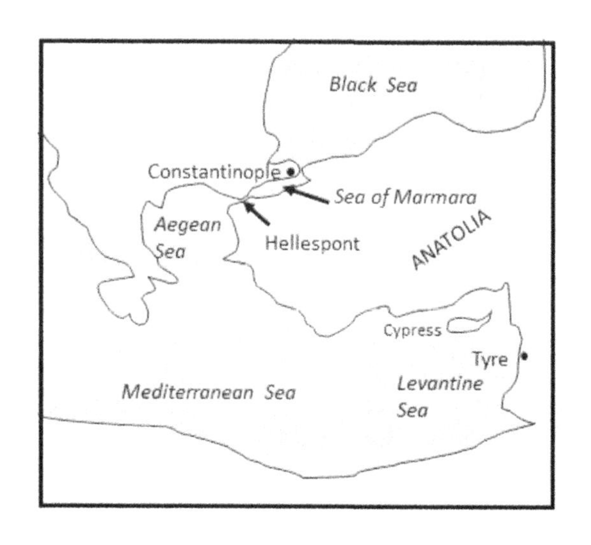

CONSTANTINOPLE 1124 AD

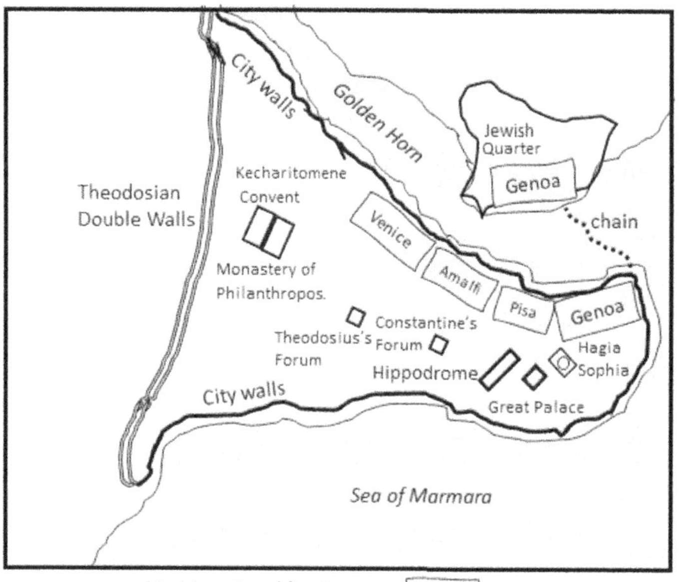

Maritime Republic Quarters Amalfi

CHAPTER XXIII CONSTANTINOPLE

The Levantine Sea was calm as the crews of the Genoese squadron rowed their galleys out of the northern harbor of Tyre. Pons and Kozubowski watched from the wharf as O'Broin and Gallus departed. The markiz was still laughing at the Irish monk's comment about the farewell between Pons and Gallus. The monks had continued grooming their tonsures and had bald crowns. Kozubowski repeated what O'Broin had said when Pons and Gallus embraced, "Two bald guys put their heads together and they just made an ass out of themselves!" Tears streamed down the markiz's cheeks.

"Yes, I'll miss the Irishman, too!" said Pons.

The galley crews spent the first nights onshore at the ports of Sidon and Beirut. They beached a few days in Byblos, a seaport in County Tripoli inhabited by colonists from Genoa. The Genoese had a close relationship with the Romans of Constantinople, and Admiral Embracio, certain the Venetians would raid Roman islands on the return to Venice, split off from the crusader fleet. Over the next month, the squadron sailed to Cypress along the south coast of Anatolia and across the Aegean Sea to Constantinople.

Nearing the end of the sea voyage, the sails of Admiral Embracio's flagship were kept furled as the crew had strained against the cold wind blowing from the northeast. They had passed through the Hellespont earlier in the day, the narrows connecting the Aegean Sea to the Sea of Marmara, and now sailed along the shore of Constantinople. The waters were busy with commercial vessels passing in and out of two fortified harbors. Chasing the fishing boats, colonies of seagulls dipped and squawked.

Gallus pointed to a white edifice, a quarter mile long and over forty pieds high, dominating the skyline of the city. "That is the Hippodrome where I saw the chariot races."

"And that imposing dome," added O'Broin, "must be the Hagia Sophia you told me about."

"Yes, the largest cathedral of the Greek Orthodox faith. You must pray at the church."

The squadron reached the east side of the peninsular city and turned north, passing over a submerged chain that in time of war the Romans raised to block enemy vessels. They entered an estuary that provided a large sheltered harbor. Along the waterfront were four separate fortified dockyards. The galleys entered the first yard. Gallus motioned with his hand as he said, "We are docking at the Genoese wharves; the next yard north is owned by the Pisans, then the Republic of Amalfi, and finally the Venetians. Italian merchants own the warehouses and buildings behind each dockyard and occupy the quarters granted to them by the empire. Did you see the submerged chain when we entered the harbor?'

O'Broin nodded.

"As Embracio mentioned, the Genoese are favored merchants and were granted an additional quarter across the harbor, adjacent to the Jewish quarter. In fact, they are so trusted that they control both ends of the chain, across the harbor and here at the Genoese quarter." He pointed to a cluster of buildings and fortifications, overlooked by a tower. "There are mechanisms in the tower that raise the chain and block off the harbor if there is a threat to the city."

The Genoese spent the rest of the day securing their ships, and Gallus showed O'Broin around the city. They purchased wool cloaks to keep warm. That evening Admiral Embracio invited them to dine with him on the second story veranda of a merchants' guest house, overlooking the harbor.

The servants brought dishes of shellfish, sausages, and fish, as well as fresh vegetables, some covered with spiced sauces.

Embracio used a fork to stuff more sausage in his mouth and packed in some bread, and speaking as he chewed, "O'Broin, I see you are not eating any meat. The fish is fresh, caught just this morning in the Sea of Marmara.

"The small fish, *psaria gumus*, only live in the surface waters of the Marmara, are fried whole, and the slabs without the heads are meat from the *kilits*, swordfish, but the other kind is from the *ble psari,* the blue fish, that I believe are the tastiest."

O'Broin forked some green beans. "These vegetables are very good, admiral. This . . . tool is useful. I have never seen such a utensil."

The admiral chased his food with more wine, swallowed, then said, "The vegetables are from the gardens within the city walls, so they are very fresh. And the Romans call the utensil you are using a *piroúni.*"

The men looked puzzled and the admiral repeated the word in Latin, "*furca*."

O'Broin laughed. "Pitchfork? Yes, of course, that's what it looks like. A miniature pitchfork!"

"Your Latin is so uncontaminated, O'Broin," said Embracio.

The men finished their food and sipped on wine.

"Brother Gallus, you told me you have once before visited the city. But there is always something new to discover. Will you include your experiences of the Outremer and Holy Land in your books?"

"Yes, and I would also like to visit the city archives to learn more of Constantinople's illustrious history."

"With the Lord's grace, you have asked the right man!" He raised his cup, "Salute!"

The monks appeared puzzled, but toasted as Embracio continued. "I am a comrade-in-arms with the emperor's brother-in-law, Nikephoros Bryennios. My fleet reinforced his army with crossbowmen in his glorious victory over the Turkish sultan at the Battle of Philomelion. He is not only a masterful general of the imperial army, but a historian, like you. He is writing a history of Constantinople together with his wife, Anna Komnenos, the emperor's sister, who is perhaps an even greater scholar than he.

Today I learned he has departed for the Danube on a military expedition against the Hungarians. But, I will send a message to Anna, asking for your admittance to the archives. I am certain she will give permission to a scholar such as you and with my endorsement."

They relaxed with the wine spiced with anise and observed the sunset. O'Broin commented, "The sun sets, the rich golden light unfolds beauty upon the harbor's waters."

"Brother O'Broin," asked Embracio, "are you a monk *and* a poet?"

"He is closer to a monk and a *warrior*," Gallus laughed, "but, most of the time a monk and a jester!"

"No," answered O'Broin, "I heard a sailor say the harbor is named the *Golden Horn*. Is it because of such gilded sunsets?"

"Hmm . . . good observation," said Embracio, "but perhaps it refers to the wealth brought into Constantinople because of the busy harbor on its shores."

The next morning, Embracio handed Gallus a parchment signed by Anna Komnenos to admit him to the imperial archives. On the way, they passed numerous shops which sold food. Sitting on the threshold of almost every shop was a slumbering cat, confident no one would step on them as they napped. O'Broin bought two slices of boukalleton bread sweetened with figs, cut from a round loaf with a hole in the center.

Finishing the bread, they approached the steps leading to the archives in the Imperial Library next to the emperor's Great Palace. O'Broin was brushing the crumbs off his beard and tunic, and fiddling with his hair. "Why are you worried how you look?" asked Gallus as they climbed the steps.

At the top of the stairs was a portico supported by a row of Corinthian columns. At the entrance, between the pair of center columns, stood two women. They were unlike the women O'Broin had seen across the city. There he had observed working women with bonnets covering their hair or affluent women who had draped scarves to cover their hair and neck. These women wore identical maroon turbans. Peeking from the bottom of their head covers were coils of braided hair. Their faces and necks were uncovered. They didn't wear the stylish pointed leather shoes common among the citizens, and instead of long tunicas hiding their feet, the hems of their maroon dresses were several hands above the ground revealing sturdy ankle boots. The women were also devoid of the abundant jewelry the nobles displayed and each had a scabbard containing a dagger attached to her belt.

One guard blocked Gallus as he entered the building. He gave her his letter of admittance from Anna Komnenos. She nodded at her comrade and waved Gallus to enter. As her companion escorted the Venetian monk to the door, O'Broin started to follow. She raised her arm in front of him and said in Greek, "*Stamato*!" repeating in Latin, "Stop!"

"I am with him," said O'Broin.

"The message from Princess Anna only gave permission for Gallus to enter."

"But . . . oh, you speak Latin!" added the monk.

"Indeed! I am the princess's guardian. She receives emissaries from across the world. And, I . . . we . . the Minervan Guards, protect her. We must anticipate any threat. You don't speak Greek?"

O'Broin shook his head.

"But your Latin is . . . how would I say . . . very precise."

"Artema, so close in name and beauty to Artemis, the Huntress herself, only lacking a bow and quiver to match her magnificence, how are you eligible to make such a statement?" was O'Broin's retort.

Her jaw dropped ever so slightly, then she appeared angry and briefly rose on her toes. "I began my schooling at the Judaic Academy on the Pontic shore of the Black Sea. Then I continued my education with the princess's tutors as her aide and as a *Romaioi*, a citizen of the empire. Romans speak the most proper Greek *and* Latin," said the turbaned guard. "I thought you were a Greek monk, shaggy and bearded, escorting your companion from Venice, the western monk . . . I mean . . . your Brother Gallus, clean-shaven and with tonsure."

"I am not a monk of the Orthodox church. I am . . . Brother Gallus's . . . um, guardian, just as you watch over the princess."

"I understand such loyalty," said the guard, " so you may enter . . . although you may . . . perhaps . . . wait here for him. Gallus will be quite safe."

"Ah . . . yes . . . I'll stay. How do you know about Gallus?"

"As I said, the princess's guardians know all."

Ha! She knew all that from the princess's letter to Gallus, which I also read. Gallus neglected to ask for the guards by name, which were listed in the letter: Artema and Romana.

"And I am prescient as well. Your name is Artema, am I right?" said O'Broin.

The snapping of hobnailed boots on the stone road below distracted them before she could answer. A squad of imperial guards in red and gold tunics and armed with double bladed axes marched to the base of the stairs leading to the library. The troop stopped as the officer in charge ordered, "Halt!"

The officer, longhaired, dark, and fierce in appearance, ran up the staircase, red cape flying behind him, taking three steps at a time. When he arrived, his expression suddenly turned to a smile as he addressed the female guard in Greek. "Lady Artema, where is my lovely Romana?"

"Fist! Your patrols of the imperial grounds always conveniently intersect with Princess Komnenos's appointments," said Artema. "And don't call me lady."

O'Broin mumbled to himself in Latin, "His name is Fist?"

The officer peered at O'Broin. "Latin? Who are you? Are you Genoese or Pisan?"

"Originally I am from Ireland," said O'Broin. "And you and your men? Those axes recall tales of the Vikings who used to raid my homeland."

His chest swelled, "I am Rus! Hroorberht the Fist, Captain of the Varangian Guards." He glanced at his men. "Most of my men are Saxons, but a few are Norsemen. My grandfather told me the Vikings founded Kiev Rus."

"Did you say you were Hroorberht the Fist?" asked O'Broin. "Are you good at combat with your hands?" added the Irishman.

"Yes, and elbows, and feet, and knees, and . . ."

"And he has used his head, too . . ." added Romana. She had left Gallus inside the archives and returned. "Hroorberht is an expert in Pankration."

"Pankration?" questioned O'Broin.

"It is a fighting style of the ancient Greeks." said Romana. "These Varangian guards, who protect the emperor, and the

Minervans, who guard the female members of the imperial family, are trained in the art."

"I'd like to learn this martial art," said O'Broin.

The Rus captain laughed and said, "Not just anyone is privileged to train in the ancient combat."

Artema said, with a bit too much enthusiasm to hide her interest, "Fist, let him prove he is worthy."

The captain looked at her with disbelief.

"Perhaps he can teach us . . . something of Irish combat," added Artema.

At this, Hroorberht shouted in the Rus tongue to a Varangian guard and the man tossed an axe up from the street. All eyes were on the pirouetting axe. Suddenly, a rope coiled around the handle, stopped the weapon in flight, and the axe crashed on the steps with a loud clatter. O'Broin yanked hard on the rope and caught the axe by the handle.

"We have a trade, Irishman!" shouted Hroorberht the Fist.

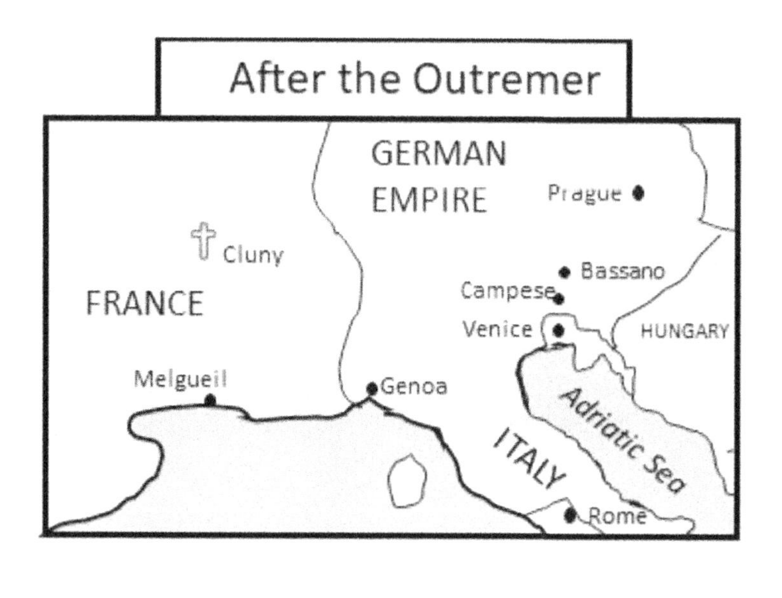
After the Outremer
GERMAN EMPIRE
Prague
Cluny
Bassano
Campese
FRANCE
Venice
HUNGARY
Melgueil
Genoa
Adriatic Sea
ITALY
Rome

CHAPTER XXIV RETURN FROM THE OUTREMER

The Venetian fleet wintered at Tyre, and in the spring sailed back to Venice, on the way attacking and pillaging one Roman island after another. The people of Venice welcomed Doge Domenico Michiel as a hero. He added much wealth to the city and his raids forced the Romans to restore the promised commercial privileges to Venice.

Kozubowski's troop parted ways and the men headed for their respective homelands. Two days north of Venice, Pons rode on the Amber Road with Kozubowski and Zeph. Mount Grappa dominated the landscape. Pons rode a mule he had bought after they disembarked and planned to trade the animal to recover Cominius. *I hope my friend is in good health.*

They stopped in the town of Bassano in the *Valsugana* and had a last cup of wine together, reminiscing of their experiences in the Outremer. Pons raised his drink, "*Salute! Salutem*! and *Zdrowie!* Markiz Kozubowski, may you find Rachel. And Zeph, may you learn Polish!"

Zeph toasted, "You are right. I can converse in Latin only with the few Poles who are educated."

The markiz punched him in the shoulder, showing mock anger and spilling Zeph's wine. "Are you insinuating that Poles are not civilized?"

"No, no . . ." said Zeph. "Pons is right—I need to learn Polish to woo the barmaids! The educated women, few as they are, will be out of my reach."

"What are you going to do next, my little friend?" Kozubowski asked Pons.

"The Pope banned me from Cluny. But I will still work, pray, and study . . . right here in this beautiful valley," answered Pons.

"Alone?" asked Zeph.

"No, Cominius will be with me."

Pons held the reins of his mule as he watched the two knights leave for Poland. *Little by little, my crusader life falls away. I miss O'Broin and his wit. Also gone are the academic and stimulating discussions with Gallus. And now this unhappy parting. The markiz was a demanding leader, but he knew how far to push his men, strengthening them without breaking them. And Zeph refused to carry out the Pope's order to kill me. He now flees to Poland because he has jeopardized his own safety.*

Leaving the lower town straddling the Brenta River, he urged his mule to climb the hill to the castle above the town. In the distance was Mount Grappa. He passed through the castle gate and arrived at the Cathedral of Santa Maria, which was surrounded by the residences and towers of the rulers of the commune, the Ezzelini family. Inside the cathedral Pons kneeled and prayed. *I will rejoin Cominius and we will find a glen or high meadow on Mount Grappa. In the solitude of nature, God will tell me what to do.*

As he stood to leave, the church priest waiting nearby greeted him. "I remember you, Brother Pons. You lived in the crusader camps and visited Bassano a few times. I am pleased to see you have returned safely from your pilgrimage!"

"Thank you, Father."

"Will you be rejoining the brotherhood?" asked the priest.

He does not know my past as an abbot, only as a Benedictine monk. "No, Father, I plan to lead an eremitic monk's life . . . in nature . . . in the forests of Mount Grappa."

"You have seen the horrors of war in the Outremer, Brother Pons. Perhaps you need to pray with your brothers? Could it be that deep sadness compels you to become a hermit?"

"It disturbed me to see men killing each other, whether they are Christian or Muslim," said Pons. "And the Venetians raided the empire's islands on the way east and again on our return, where Christians killed Christians. But I have seen men rise above the hate. The Turkish governor negotiated to protect the citizens, both Christian and Muslim, when he surrendered Tyre. And thank God, the Christian conquerors kept their word and did not do violence or pillaging."

"Thank the Lord that the conditions of war may have improved in the Outremer," said the priest. "Decades ago, the first returning crusaders reported that when Jerusalem fell, there was widespread slaughter." The priest gently clasped Pons's shoulders and studied him. "Well then, you seem to have weathered the conflict," said the priest.

"Father?"

"I believe you have the strength to live alone, praying for your own salvation. When you become restored, pray and help the nearest of those in need." The priest released his gentle hold and folded his hands together at his waist. "People come from miles around to hear Mass. Many of them are destitute and need help, which I cannot give."

"Go on . . . yes?"

"Two hours upriver is the village of Campese—what is left of it. A fire killed several in the town and destroyed homes and their chapel. Perhaps you will meditate in the hills above the beautiful valley, then when the time is right, go and help them?"

Pons thanked the priest and departed. He climbed Mount Grappa to reach the farm where he had left Cominius and found his friend in good health. He was delighted when the mule seemed to recognize him and nuzzled his face. Pons imagined that Cominius's frisky gait on their trek to Campese was his welcome home.

When he reached the village, Pons surveyed the devastation. Many of the townspeople were still living in tents and lean-tos. He canvassed nearby towns and petitioned for help. The Ezzelini family of Bassano and the nobles of the communes of Camposampiero and Crespignaga responded with donations of food and money for reconstruction.

Over the next few months, Pons thrived from the hard work rebuilding the homes and church, and he nurtured friendships with the people of Campese. The hamlet was without a priest and he performed communion for the villagers and read scripture to them.

Three months later Gallus arrived unexpectedly. The Venetian monk found Pons tending a raised garden in front of the cave where he had been sleeping. Gallus jumped off his mule and embraced his friend. Pons clasped Gallus's shoulders. "Brother, how did you find me?"

"I returned to the monastery in Venice, and after a few months I felt confined. I became a friar so I could satisfy my urge to travel and be among the people. In Crespignaga I heard that you founded a monastery in Campese."

Pons's eyes widened. "A monastery? Maybe a monastery of one!" He laughed as he patted Gallus on the shoulder.

"Knowing your work ethic, you are enough!" said Gallus. "Is there work for me?"

"Yes, and I am pleased you are here, Brother."

"The monastery now has two monks!" laughed Gallus. "*Friar* monks, living and working amongst the villagers." He glanced at the cave entrance. "How very austere! But appropriate for Benedictine monks. I see you are wearing the black habit of the Order."

"I believe in Saint Benedict's rules, but I am disappointed in how the Order has deviated from the saint's intentions. But, come, it's time for Vespers. It is good to share the service." He looked over the rows of plants. "And we'll pick a few vegetables for our meal."

After the service the men ate in silence. Then Pons retrieved a skin of wine from his grotto. "Dinner is finished!" he declared.

"What happened to O'Broin? Tell me about Constantinople!"

"O'Broin is now a royal aide and is part of Anna Komnenos's staff. He had accompanied me to the imperial library, where I met the princess and had her permission to study at the archives. O'Broin as usual, full of wit, convinced Anna's personal guards, both females, to let him join them and the emperor's special troops—the Varangians— to practice martial skills. Then he fell in love with one of the women."

The monks hooted until their eyes watered. "That fast?"

"Yes, she had complained that when training for hand-to-hand combat, the Varangians would not spar with the females, so O'Broin volunteered to practice with the women. Before I left, the captain of the Varangian guard also joined in the training, to supervise, so he said . . . but O'Broin told me the man had feelings for another of the female guards."

"After his wanderings, O'Broin has found his place," said Pons.

The men talked of their experiences into the night, so engaged they entirely forgot Compline, the sunset service.

For the next few weeks, Pons and Gallus worked in the village and were close to finishing the new church. Campese was on the Amber Road between Venice and the pass through the Alps and travelers were common. One afternoon several knights stopped nearby to rest.

One approached and Pons glanced, then quickly glanced again. *It's Zeph!* He put down his tools and went to greet the knight as he shouted, "Gallus! Look who's here!"

"I remember you said you'd be somewhere in this valley, but it is vast and I never thought I'd see you again."

The men embraced, full of smiles and backslaps. "The Pope has died," said Zeph.

"Hmm. You were in Poland, and you found out before us? Well . . . now you can return to Rome."

"I learned that the election of the new Pope was a chaotic fight between two powerful families in Rome. The Italian cardinals elected the consul of the Pierleoni family, but he was attacked during the enthronement ceremony." Pons and Gallus looked astonished.

"Yes," continued Zeph, "physically harmed! Wounded, the new Pope resigned and the Frangipani family proclaimed Cardinal Lamberto as the Pope. There were skirmishes in the streets until the Frangipani bribed the opposition and a second election formally chose Lamberto. He has adopted the name of Honorius."

"Mary Mother!" said Pons. He nodded toward the other knights. "Are you traveling with them?"

"Yes, one will continue with me to Salerno, where I will join my family and practice medicine. The other knights are making a pilgrimage to Compostela."

Gallus and Pons invited the travelers to their cave, where the monks served them vegetable stew. Gallus had added red wine to enhance the flavor.

"Delicious stew! Do you make your own wine?"

"We planted cuttings, but it will be a few years before they fruit," said Gallus. "Then we will be a real monastery."

"A winery *and* a library, *then* we will be a real monastery," added Pons. "Salute!"

Pons eyed Zeph. "And tell us about Kozubowski."

"He was heralded and praised in Prague, in Wroclaw, and in Krakow," said Zeph. "The duke declared him a national hero and held dinners and celebrations in his honor."

"I can see Kozubowski relishing the triumphal return," said Pons. "I recall he was passionate about a woman in Wroclaw. Do you know if he found her?"

Zeph's eyes brightened. "Yes! She was engaged to someone, but the markiz would not let that interfere with his courting. He told me that it was God's will he had returned just in time. Kozubowski was persistent and they were soon married."

Pons stared at the campfire. *Zeph is returning to his family, O'Broin and Kozubowski have found their kindred spirits. I have lost my Primavera. And I am responsible. Dear Lord, I hope Primavera is yet alive and is not suffering—but why do I torture myself still? I must accept she is dead.*

A breaking dawn found Zeph journeying to the south and Pons setting out west with the knights on their way to Compostela. Pons knew their route would pass through Melgueil and he wished to see his mother, praying she was alive. Gallus intended to invite a few monks from Venice to join him in Campese and told Pons once he got back, they would have a genuine monastery.

Two weeks' journey west of Campese, Pons said farewell to his traveling companions. They continued west and he turned south. He sensed he was nearing Melgueil when he swatted a few mosquitoes, but recalled they were not as bad here as the swarms at the marshy etangs west of the town. In the center of town, dominating the flat terrain, was a lone hillock rising above the houses and church spires. The grassy knoll was topped by a castle, his brother's chateau. Fortifications encircled the bottom of the hill. When Pons arrived at the gate and identified himself, the guard hesitated, unconvinced. Pons displayed his abbot's ring and the sentry whispered to a second guard who escorted Pons up the stairs to the chateau.

Near the top of the long stone stairway, a youthful man in his teens sparred with a small boy of about five. The clacks of their wooden swords echoed off the stone wall of the chateau. The competition was highlighted by a mixture of painful yelps and nervous laughter as they fought. *The older youth must be my nephew I met here about six or seven years ago. And the younger one . . . I have another nephew!* The boys were engrossed and neither paid attention to Pons as he passed into the chateau.

He followed the guard into an enormous hall, where the vivid colors of the large tapestries caught his attention. When Pons became accustomed to the diminished light, he saw Almodis standing next to the massive oaken table that dominated the room. Her smile was genuine as she held out her arms. *Mother looks well. How different from my last visit.* He kissed her cheek and they shared an embrace.

She sat at the table and gestured, "Please, my son, rest." A servant placed glasses of wine on the table.

"You look well, Mother." Pons sipped the wine, savoring the quality.

"And you. Since I saw you last you have had enough experiences to last a lifetime, no?"

"You heard of my election to abbot?"

She nodded.

"And my . . . resignation?"

She smiled. "I have followed the events of your life . . . the construction of the great basilica, your abbacy, your pilgrimage to the Outremer."

"I am gratified you have so much interest in my affairs, Mother, and it relieves me, in part, from reciting the worst of my encounters in the crusade—many are gruesome. When I have collected my thoughts, I will tell you about my pilgrimage to Jerusalem . . . and I met Uncle Ramon's youngest son, Pons of Tripoli."

"Where is Raimundus?"

"He is away . . . spending money. Sometimes for excellent reasons, to help his people, but many times wasting it on destructive habits." She took a sip of wine. "He has not changed.

But, you—you appear . . . my intuition is you have learned much in these last several years."

"And Raimundus has another son!" said Pons. "You must be pleased."

She blinked. "We . . . we will talk more. The servants have stabled your mule and will deliver your saddlebag. You must be tired from your journey. Go, rest. You have the same room as your last visit. At dinner you can tell the family of all your travels."

Pons stood and tenderly clasped her hands. "Thank you. I remember the room had a wonderful view . . . and the breeze kept away the mosquitoes."

Pons started up the first flight of stairs full of energy. *I am not tired, but I welcome the rest before socializing with my brother. Mother was following my life's progress these past years. Why was she watching me so closely? It's almost as if she has two personalities. One she keeps more hidden, her maternal nature, and the other a scheming, political power-hungry character. I don't really know her. Should I trust her?* Halfway up the second flight, his feet grew heavy. *In Campese, I worked all day in the garden and trekked around the hills. Why am I so tired now?* With weary legs, he made it to the top and paused. He opened the door to the room and froze in mid-stride.

CHAPTER XXV PARIS

Bernard Gros, prior of Cluny Abbey, waited with Chard in the cloister garden, their ecclesiastical business at the Abbey of Saint-Germain of Paris now completed. The Benedictine monastery was one of a thousand daughter abbeys with allegiance to Cluny. With such prestigious credentials, no one would interfere with a prior's rendezvous in the garden. Bernard sat and meditated amid the songbirds, quince trees, and the babbling water fountain. Estienne joined them in the peaceful setting, escorted by a pair of King Louis's elite guards. The guards remained out of hearing as the former subprior of Cluny sat on a stone bench opposite the pair.

Estienne spoke barely above a whisper, blending in with the tranquility of the peaceful setting. "Tell me why you want Peter replaced as abbot of Cluny."

Bernard was expressionless. "He has had the Qur'an translated into Latin. Why did he do this? He must want to contaminate Christians by the Devil's words!"

"Do you have a replacement in mind?"

Bernard glanced back and forth from Chard to Estienne. "Yes, Pons should return. He was dismissed for false claims and most of the Cluniac monks still support him." He stared at Chard.

"It is true. Most of the Cluniac monks will welcome Pons back," said Chard. "But how would this be possible?"

Bernard glanced at the guards. "We have the king's support now. The Pope himself was installed through a violent act. Why shouldn't we do the same at Cluny?"

"No!" Chard snapped. The guards paid notice, but calmed when his voice returned to its conspiratorial level. "Pons will not cooperate if there is violence or force, and what's more, abbots are elected for life."

"Chapter 64, Election of an Abbot," said Estienne. "The rules of Saint Benedict justify replacement."

The monks leaned forward. The steady murmur of the fountain was interrupted as birds splashed.

Estienne recited Parts 3 through 6:

> "May God forbid that a whole community should conspire to elect a man who goes along with its own evil ways. But if it does, and if the bishop of the diocese or the abbots or Christians in the area come to know of these evil ways to any extent, they must block the success of this wicked conspiracy, and set a worthy steward in charge of God's house. They may be sure that they will receive a generous reward for this, if they do it with pure motives and zeal for God's honor. Conversely, they may be equally sure that to neglect to do so is sinful."

The natural sounds of the garden took over as the men contemplated.

Then Chard said, "But is Peter's translation of the Qur'an a great enough transgression to justify his removal?"

"There is another contentious matter that irks the traditional faction in the order," said Estienne. "The philosopher Pierre Abelard travels across the land and visits monasteries, but he insists on carrying on his dialectic arguments with the monks, using Greek style logic to debate parts of the Bible. He irritates the brothers and has been accused of heresy. Abbot Peter has given Pierre Abelard sanctuary in one Benedictine abbey after another, against the wishes of many priors and brothers."

"Chard, I suggest," said Estienne as he glanced at Bernard, "as Sacrist of Cluny, you prepare a contract regarding Chapter 64 and include these two evils as examples for Peter's dismissal. I'm certain Prior Bernard will approve the document."

Bernard nodded.

"When the contract is ready," said Estienne, "Bernard must find an excuse to send Chard to visit the Benedictine abbeys in Provence. I will be here in Paris. Notify me and I will meet Chard in Melgueil. With the contract and our support we will convince Pons to return to Cluny."

CHAPTER XXVI MELGUEIL

The Burgundians had at last caught Pons. They wrapped the long sleeves of his habit around him, knotted them, and tied him to a wooden post. A few feet away Primavera was bound to another stake. Men stacked firewood around their feet. Thomas, his old nemesis, grinned as he lit the pile, and Pons felt the heat growing. The burning wood crackled and popped . . . and flames roared.

The next rumble of thunder woke Pons from a fitful sleep. He was shaking. *Where am I?* He rolled over in the soft bed glancing out the window. Lightning flashed across the angry sky. *It's night-time.* Then memory flooded his wakening mind—he sat up and cried, "Primavera!"

Her voice was full of sleep. "Hmm? Yes? What is it, my love?"

"I was having a nightmare. But you are here and our lovemaking tonight was not a dream! I do love you, Primavera," he whispered.

"I love you too, as well. How do you feel? You're hot."

He flung off the blanket. Their naked bodies were visible in a flash of lightning. *She is not as thin as I remember, and is perhaps healthier.* The sudden illumination had revealed signs of his arousal. Primavera yanked the blanket to cover them, and laughed. "I am chilly, come closer and warm me." Pons eagerly complied.

An hour later they were exhausted, but lay awake, listening to the thunder. Pons said, "What you told me earlier . . . that Estienne helped you flee . . . flee the Burgundian soldiers years ago—when

Thomas purged Cluny of concubines and wives. Thank God he was loyal to me, but he gave up his life as a monk! Where is Estienne now?"

Primavera kissed him. "Can we please talk tomorrow?"

"And Ponsel, little Pons, he is our son? I am overcome with joy!"

"Go to sleep, tomorrow you will . . . um, you will meet him." She dozed. Pons draped an arm over her and tried to sleep, but his mind raced.

They slept late and did not have breakfast with the family. Pons woke as Primavera was dressing. He rolled out of bed. "I want to see my little Pons, right away!"

Primavera did not appear to share his enthusiasm.

"What's wrong, love?" said Pons.

"Before you meet Ponsel, we must talk with your mother."

They met in the study on the second floor, part of his mother's suite. Primavera and Pons sat on a cushioned divan opposite Almodis in a high-backed padded chair. The servants set small plates of bread, cheese, *espices de chamber,* and glasses of wine on a low parlor table, the three legs made of ornately carved dark wood. Almodis nodded and the servants left.

"I had these sweets brought, since you missed breakfast," said Almodis. With an earnest smile, she added, "Absence sharpens love and nothing else is important."

Pons hesitated to eat or drink.

"Please enjoy."

He tasted a wafer.

"Do you like the flavor? They are made with anise.

"You are wondering why I wanted to talk. I do love you, both of you, and want you to maintain a relationship. Remember, I helped send Primavera to join you in Cluny. And then I gave her safe haven here before I even knew she was pregnant, which had to be kept secret from the Church and from Thomas."

"Mother, you never answered my letters! Primavera was here the whole time!" blurted Pons.

"And she was safe. Had you found out, the Church would have also and we all would have been punished," said Almodis. Her voice grew firmer, "And she would had been arrested and taken away for good!"

Pons's face was red.

"And you would have never seen Ponsel!" added Almodis.

The abbot looked down and calmed. *I could have been with them years ago. Why hadn't I returned here after I left Rome, as I intended, instead of going to Venice? Yes, I remember . . . I had given up hope.*

Pons returned to his questioning. "Where is Estienne? "Did Thomas become abbot?"

"Thomas was transferred to Lyon. Estienne is about," answered his mother. She finished her wine and placed the glass on the table. "He is my confidant."

"Your spy?" said Pons.

"Don't be so naive. He protected you and if not for him . . ." she looked at Primavera.

"Yes, Mother . . . thank you," said Pons. "I shouldn't be surprised. This is part of your plan. The plan to hold power. But I failed you . . . the family, when I resigned."

She blinked and shifted in her chair. "The official word was that the Pope dismissed you."

"And he attempted to have me murdered on the crusade," said Pons. "Just as the Burgundians tried in Spain."

Almodis's eyes grew wide.

"The Burgundians remain envious of Cluny's power and influence within their own realms," said Almodis. "And the Vatican is resentful that for thousands of Cluniac monks their first loyalty is to Cluny instead of to Rome. When Callistus, a Burgundian, became Pope, the noose tightened. When the Burgundian cardinals elected his replacement, Honorius, it tightened again. With the Abbot of Cluny, Peter of Montboissier, as a supporter of the Pope, we are being strangled out of influence and power."

"We . . . you mean the House of Toulouse?" said Pons.

She nodded. "But we have Estienne."

"Yes?"

"He is working on a pact with Bernard Gros, the prior who replaced Thomas."

"How is it possible that Estienne can return to Cluny?" asked Pons.

"He is in the north among those nobles who oppose the Burgundians. Our ally, Bernard, informed Estienne that most of the Cluniac monks dislike Peter and wish you to return."

"That's impossible!" barked Pons as he threw back his head. Then he glanced at Primavera and calmed. "In addition, I am ready to leave the Brotherhood and live with my son and . . . Primavera will be . . . my wife."

Primavera wrung her hands and broke eye contact with Pons. He stared back at his mother. "What have you done!"

"You had a satisfactory relationship at Cluny and can so again. Five years ago, I rescued Primavera from certain slavery and invited her to live here. When Ponsel was born, she agreed to raise your son here." The women regarded each other. "For Ponsel's good, she has made the right decision."

Primavera was impassive, hands relaxed on her lap.

"We have a most important virtue in common," said Almodis, her voice gentle, "mothers doing the best for our sons. Thank God he guided your paths to cross."

Almodis's voice hardened. "The monks will re-elect you as abbot. Primavera may either live in Cluny village as before or stay here, if you agree to cooperate. But Ponsel stays in Melgueil."

Pons looked back and forth between the women.

"Ponsel knows I am his mother," said Primavera. Her eyes were moist. "I have told him you were away on pilgrimage. His father's return will fill him with joy." She looked at Almodis, who nodded.

Pons held Primavera's hand and lowered his chin, then glared at his mother.

"When is this overthrow to take place?" asked Pons.

"Estienne's negotiations with Bernard are encouraging. We are waiting for him to return and give us word."

Over the next few weeks Pons relished the time with Primavera and his son. He relinquished wearing a habit. He played with Ponsel on the grassy slopes of the chateau, and accompanied the family to the chapel and the shops in town. He observed study sessions as Almodis tutored both Ponsel and Primavera, both eager to learn. Pons told his son of his pilgrimages, depicting the cultures and geography, but left out descriptions of the violence.

He learned that Primavera's older sons were doing well as monks in Saint Pons. Almodis had made frequent donations to the abbey, and ensured the abbot was aware the gifts were from the young men's "grandmother."

As they waited for Estienne's return, weeks became months and Pons hoped that the scheme to replace the abbot had been dismissed. Ponsel joined him in grooming Cominius and Pons reveled in showing his son how to ride, and encouraged him to show kindness to animals. He watched his nephew play with Ponsel with wooden swords and taught them both how to use the quarter-staff in defense against the sword.

Six months after Pons reunited with Primavera, Estienne, the former subprior of Cluny, arrived in Melgueil with Chard.

CHAPTER XXVII THE PLAN

After his reunion with Chard and Estienne, they gathered with the family for dinner in the great hall of Chateau Melgueil. Pons's brother, Count Raimundus, sat at the head of the long table, Almodis at the other end. At the count's right was his fifteen year old son and at his left was his wife. Next to her was Pons, his son Ponsel, then Primavera. Pons was determined to remain cheerful as he gazed at Estienne and Chard across the table. *For now, I must suppress my concern why they're here and simply enjoy their company.*

Between bites of peppered eel cooked in olive oil, Chard spoke of pleasant memories of the hosts' generosity during his earlier visits to Melgueil. He recalled the first time when he had passed through with Pons on the way to Cluny and again when he and Guilen had escorted Primavera from Saint Pons to Cluny village. He then toasted the dowager, count and countess, for having him again as a welcomed visitor.

The guests were eager to hear of Pons's travels to the Outremer and he related the sea voyage and his pilgrimage to Jerusalem. He mentioned the battles to add excitement to his story; he spoke of enormous castles, the great fleets of ships, and siege engines that hurled boulders, but sensitive to his young son's age, avoided violent details. When he recounted the Templars' work safeguarding the pilgrims, Ponsel's eyes widened and he scooted forward in his chair.

"Once again, very fascinating, Brother!" said Raimundus. "Did you know the Pope has given approval of the Templars as a military order?"

Pons shook his head.

"And Chard, how was your journey from Cluny?" asked the count.

"Most of the way we floated down the Rhone River on a pirogue guided by a waterman, stopping each night at a monastery or church. It was an effortless trip. When we go north, it will be upstream and much slower . . . Pons well remembers the hard work poling against the current."

Ponsel had listened attentively the entire dinner, remaining quiet, but suddenly glanced at Pons and blurted, "My father said he had to fight thieves on the river. Were you in the fight?"

"Ponsel! You have done well this far," said Primavera. "I told you only the adults may speak."

"For a young boy he has shown much discipline," said Almodis.

Raimundus laughed as he said, "Chard, you were with Pons in that river battle, no? We have heard my brother's rendition, I want to hear your version!"

Chard leaned toward Ponsel and said, "Son, your father is first a man of peace. He negotiated with the rivermen, a gang called the *Rouge*, and they left without a fight. But wicked men paid them to return and fight us. Then we had to fight. Your father is a monk first, then a warrior, but when battle was necessary, your father was a warrior *and* a monk."

"That's all?" said Raimundus. "Wasn't there more to the river skirmish?"

Chard appeared irritated by the count's words and glanced at Pons, who shifted in his seat. "And your father is humble. Perhaps he didn't tell you he taught the monks at Cluny to defend themselves. Yes, he is an expert in the quarter-staff."

"He taught me the staff!" said Ponsel.

"And, your father has a sense of humor, too," said Chard as he cast an impish look at Pons.

Pons slapped his hands on the table. "Fine, I will say it, Chard. At the end of the fight, I fell into the river."

Raimundus laughed the loudest. Ponsel looked confused at first, but then joined them.

After the meal, Almodis invited Chard, Estienne, and Pons to her study. She handed her son a rolled parchment. He gazed downward, hesitating to open the document, fearing its contents. As servants placed glasses of wine on the table, he noticed the table legs. *It's odd the carvings depict lions' heads, an animal I know only through the Bible. Am I being thrown into the lions' den, like Daniel? God help me make the right decision.* He had an almost irresistible urge to abruptly stand and fling the table and its contents into the air. He let out a lengthy breath, however, unrolled the parchment, and read the declaration.

After he finished, Pons leaned back and sipped the cinnamon spiced wine. "I see you have cleverly justified dismissing Peter from the abbacy by quoting Saint Benedict's rules. And you have listed the prior, sacrist, librarian, and monks of Cluny as supporters of this document. But none of them have signed it."

"This document is meaningless without Bernard's signature," said Estienne. "He will sign it, and Chard and the other officers listed will sign it when we return with you to Cluny. We are confident most of the Cluniac monks wish you to return. Their respect and love for you have not diminished since you left."

"I noticed the circuitor was not listed. Won't the guards be loyal to him?" asked Pons.

"We have the townspeople and local nobles of Cluny village siding with us," said Chard. "The nobles' soldiers will be in our support. They outnumber the Cluny guards and I believe just their show of force will avoid violence."

"I trust both of you, but why should we trust Bernard?" said Pons. "Wait, is he Bernard Gros . . . from Murles?"

Almodis nodded. "He is of the House of Montpelier, County Melgueil, vassals of your brother and ultimately the House of Toulouse."

"I remember him now," said Pons. "It is interesting he was born only a day's ride from here. He entered the monastery of Cluny during my abbacy. And now he is prior. Why does he want Peter replaced? I have heard the abbot is capable."

"Bernard deems the monasteries must stay independent of secular and non-monastic control," said Estienne. "In his opinion, Peter is giving up power to Pope Honorius. The Pope is suspicious of our order and has shown favor to the Augustinians and the

Cistercians instead. The Pope has taken control at Monte Cassino Abbey, the first monastery founded by Saint Benedict. This breaks with centuries of tradition and conflicts with the charter authored by the Saint. With Peter now at Cluny, the Pope is making the same moves for more power."

"Chard, you and I have shared much. Estienne, you risked your life to save Primavera. Let me think it over tonight. Can we discuss this further tomorrow?"

"Certainly, Brother," said Chard. He handed Pons a booklet. "You will find this interesting to read."

The title was *De Contemptu Mundi, On Contempt for the World*, by Bernard Gros.

Later that evening as Primavera slept nearby, Pons read by candlelight. He was tired from their lovemaking, but was eager to read Bernard's essays. The prior had written a satire of the flaws of humankind, religious and secular, revealing corruption in society and in the Church. Pons had to suppress his laughter several times, so as not to wake his paramour.

Pons's mind raced and he did not sleep well. He woke early. Primavera slumbered peacefully beside him as the sun rose and the light entered the window. He glanced at her serene face. *She is strong! When she was raising two boys in poverty, she never complained. Now she walks a narrow path between my mother and me, but she sacrifices for Ponsel.*

As he lay in bed, Pons considered the positive and negative outcomes of the dangerous venture. *Saint Benedict himself wrote that if an abbot's behavior runs afoul of his responsibilities, he should be replaced by the community. Peter has committed two sinful actions, translating the Qur'an and giving sanctuary to the philosopher Abelard accused of heresy. If the brothers of Cluny vote him out, that is proper, according to Saint Benedict's rules. The Frangipani family violently removed the elected Pope and replaced him with Honorius, their own candidate. That was much worse than simply removing an abbot and re-electing his replacement. Yet I must not be too naive nor should I assume the secular powers will not interfere. We have the backing of the prior, the officers, the vast majority of the monks and the local townspeople and nobles of Cluny village. How will the Count of Burgundy and the Bishop of Lyon react? The original charter of*

Cluny by William of Aquitaine asserted that Cluny was independent of secular control, and that autonomy has been preserved for centuries. Rome has never directly interfered with abbatial elections at Cluny. Instead, the Vatican had elevated Abbot of Cluny to Archabbot, the abbey being the mother of a thousand monasteries. It makes sense! Pons was energized. He vaulted out of bed to reclaim the abbacy.

At breakfast Pons's appetite was good and his disposition was bright. Almodis called a final meeting with Pons, Estienne, and Chard to discuss details of the plan. Pons announced he would return to Cluny and they agreed to leave in three days.

Pons spent the next few days with Primavera and their son. One of the sunny afternoons Ponsel and his parents chased each other in the grass surrounding the chateau. Finally out of breath, they collapsed together on the ground, hidden in the tall grass. "I wish we could lay here in the warm grass, hidden forever!" said Ponsel.

Primavera pointed up as she rested on her back, "Look, Ponsel, the blue, blue, blue . . . of the sky. What do you see in the clouds?"

"Oh!" shouted the boy, the timber of his voice showing excitement.

"What?" asked Pons.

"The clouds are ships taking me far away. I am flying high above looking down on you now and can see you in the high grass!"

Pons laughed. "You have a good imagination, Ponsel. So, my son, do you want to travel and see new lands?"

"Yes!"

"Good, you will be the wiser for it."

He glanced at Primavera. *I savor these moments and will remember them forever. What if this is the only time I will be with my son? What is an important lesson I can leave with him?*

"Ponsel, your mother has taught you God's Ten Commandments. Which one is the most important?"

"Um. I can't remember any."

"Do you love your mother and father?" said Pons.

Ponsel nodded. "That's the most important commandment!"

"Are you sure? Can you recall any others?"

"Now I remember, God says don't lie . . . and don't steal and don't kill."

"When Jesus's disciples asked him that same question: 'Which one is the most important commandment,'" said Pons, "Jesus answered, 'Love the Lord God with all your heart, all your soul, and all your mind, and love your neighbor as yourself.'"

"Like the Templar Knights?" said Ponsel.

"What? . . . Oh, yes . . . you remember the Templars . . . the knights I told you about who protected the pilgrims? Yes, son, their works certainly obey that commandment."

Two days later, the monks were preparing to return to Cluny. The family had said their farewells at the chateau door and Pons, Chard, and Estienne readied their mounts at the bottom of the castle hill. Primavera and Ponsel stood by as Pons tied his saddle bag to his mount.

"Why aren't you taking Cominius with you?" asked Ponsel.

"I am leaving him for you, son. Do you remember how he got his name?"

"Um . . ."

Primavera whispered, "The Roman soldier."

"Oh, yes . . . you named him after the Roman soldier. The man's name is the same as mine, Ponsel, um . . . really Pons like you. . . Pontius. The first word I learned to write."

"Very good, son. I will make a copy of his story at Cluny and send it to you. It will help you as you learn to read."

Pons kneeled in front of his son. "Cominius has been with me everywhere, even to Spain!"

"Did he go with you to Jerusalem?" said Ponsel.

Pons shook his head. "I wanted to have him along, but it was more important for him to remain safe, so I left him in Italy where he received the best care."

"And you came back!" said Ponsel.

Pons hugged his son and kissed Primavera as tears covered her cheeks.

CHAPTER XXVIII RETURN TO CLUNY

On a clear spring afternoon in Burgundy, three monks in black habits rode through the *Porte d'Honneur* into the Cluny Monastery. The guards waved for them to pass. "I hope you had a pleasant journey, Brother Chard!" said a sentry.

Pons held the reins steady to prevent his mule from veering off the entrance road. *Cominius also would have wanted to browse in this lush meadow, but he would have obeyed and stopped pulling. I didn't recognize either guard. They must have been recruited since I left. There is a cool breeze and the sun is mild, but my scalp is tingling. I hope the first brothers we see are my supporters and not my antagonists!*

The monks crossed the wide meadow and reached the monastery grounds. The bell tower sounded. It was the end of the ninth hour, Nones had just finished, and hundreds of the brothers filed out of the basilica. *It's been years since I left. I am excited to see the progress on the basilica.*

"I thought they had rid us of you!" The voices came from a knot of monks that rushed to block the road. "And look! Estienne is here! Call the guards! Where is the prior? Inform him!" Pons recognized the speakers as some of the brothers who had supported Thomas.

The throng grabbed the mules' bridles and tried to dismount the monks. Chard broke free and spurred his mule into a gallop across the field, exiting through the front gate. A score of hostile brothers surrounded Pons and Estienne and pulled them from their saddles.

Other monks arrived and moved to intervene. "Thank God Pons has returned! Let him go!"

The two groups jostling each other sandwiched Pons. The sentries from the front gate arrived as one yelled, "What is happening here?"

The antagonists shoved Pons and Estienne toward the guards. "Remove these traitors!"

The circuitor arrived with several more guards and formed a circle around the pair. Clusters of opposing monks began shoving each other and a few came to blows. The guards began marching their two detainees toward the gate and a fresh crowd of monks surged past and blocked their way. The circuitor signaled for the guards to train their spears on the monks to keep them at a distance.

"No! No!" yelled Pons. "There was to be an election, not violence! The community of monks always *elect* an abbot."

"His words fixed the monks' attention. Queries echoed among the crowd. "New election? What election?"

Then Prior Bernard's voice boomed above the muttering, "Stop! Stop this hostility! Guards lower your weapons!"

The sentry captain paused and glanced at the circuitor who nodded. The guards complied.

Bernard cast his voice across the crowd of monks, "Brothers, return to the monastery."

Clusters of monks drifted away, but many remained. Questions for the prior arose from the crowd. "What election? Is Peter being dismissed? Is Pons coming back as abbot?"

"Brothers," said Bernard, "please let me escort Pons and Estienne to the abbot's residence where we will meet with the officers. There will be an announcement soon to clarify the situation."

As the crowd dissipated, the circuitor glared at Pons, drew close to him and whispered, "These actions are treasonous! The Pope and the abbot both ordered that you could not set foot in Cluny again!" He held a dagger against Pons's back. "Yes, we will go to the office, but not to plan an election. To plan your arrest."

He raised his chin to the guards who seized Bernard and Estienne. The group moved toward the abbot's residence.

As the circuitor prodded Pons forward, the dagger pressed into his back. *My sleeves will protect my hands and I know where the dagger is and can deflect it. But then what? I can't run in this habit and the guards have spears. Will our plan fail?*

Hooves pounded the gravel behind them. "Stop!" yelled Chard, accompanied by the Baron of Cluny and a troop of mounted soldiers. Bernard gasped as he turned and saw the circuitor had Pons at knifepoint.

"Are we to have bloodshed—*here* in the monastery?" said the circuitor.

The baron glanced at the circuitor's guards. "No, I will not fight my kinfolk," said the baron. "And I don't think they will fight their relatives either."

The guards pointed their weapons at the ground and gathered with the baron and his men. Bernard held out his hand and the circuitor handed him the dagger. "Are you going to side with Pons? He can't return as abbot!"

"You will understand when I show you Chapter 64 of Saint Benedict's rules. We arranged our arrival to coincide with Peter's absence," said Bernard. "By the time he returns, we will have Cluny under complete control."

The guards returned to their posts and the baron rode back to the village with his men. The prior patted Pons on the shoulder. "Indeed, we have accomplished our plan without violence."

Bernard escorted Pons and Estienne to the abbot's residence. To avoid renewed conflict, he urged them to remain there and not attend the divine services. Anticipating tempers would quiet by the next morning, he planned to call the monastery officers together for them to sign the protestation dismissing Peter, and to discuss the new election.

That night Pons had trouble sleeping. *Why did I agree to something so controversial? At Campese, I convinced myself that I was living as Jesus wishes, simply, honestly, helping others. Everything changed so fast after my return to Melgueil. I have become a hypocrite! I told myself that the Church, not God, is the making of Man, including his evils, yet now I have become part of that organization again. What have I done? But . . . after I reclaim the abbacy, Primavera can rejoin me. Yes, it will be as before when she lived in the village.*

The next morning at Prime, the sun cast its early rays through the east windows of the basilica as the lector read Psalms I through III. The chanting that followed by the assembly of 250 monks was both powerful and meditative, resonating across the voluminous space. When they completed the hymns, Bernard stood before the brothers and signaled to Pons, who joined him. "Prime is finished and our vow of silence during service is lifted. Pons is back in Cluny after spending years completing the three holiest pilgrimages, Santiago de Compostela, Rome, and finally Jerusalem. He has returned to share with his brethren the blessings and wisdom he gained at these holy sites. Do any of the ordained brothers here object to Pons returning to his abbacy?"

The monks were silent. Pons examined the assembly. *The monks' approval is overwhelming but not unanimous. According to Bernard, a few score out of 300 refused to attend Prime this morning in protest of my return, but it seems this change in abbots might succeed.*

After Prime, Prior Bernard called for a meeting of the officers at the abbot's residence. The officers were seated when Pons and Bernard entered. The figure standing at the head of the table made both men gasp. It was the Abbot of Cluny, Peter of Montboissier.

Peter gestured at the chair and said, "Please sit, Brother Pons."

Pons tried to control the heat rising within as he crossed the room. Chard made eye contact. *I wonder if I appear as nervous as he*? He scanned the other seated monks. *There is Thomas! And next to him is Humbaud, the Archbishop of Lyon.* Pons faltered, then reached the chair. *I am finished.*

"What in Heaven were you thinking?" said Peter. "Cluny is in turmoil, thanks to you!" Peter looked at the archbishop.

"It is in my power, and in my opinion after hearing the facts," said Humbaud, "that Brother Pons, you have committed transgressions that require me to excommunicate you, as recorded in this document." He held a parchment. "Due to the severity of the offense, only the Pope can absolve you, if he accepts your declaration of repentance. Until that time Brother Pons, you still are a Christian because you have been baptized, but you are considered a *non-existent* to the Church. You may not take part in public worship nor receive any of the sacraments, including

Communion. You will be placed under arrest by the Count of Burgundy, removed to Lyon, and then to Rome."

The archbishop's tired eyes scanned the monks at the table. "For the rest of those here that aided Brother Pons in his contravention, I have the authority to absolve each of you, but only if you vow never to speak of this event to anyone."

The monks nodded. Pons noted Estienne was absent. *Just as he rescued Primavera years ago and delivered her to safety, perhaps he will deliver the truth to my mother.*

The archbishop ended the meeting as he said, "The Count of Burgundy will garrison his troops at the monastery and keep order as long as required to ensure peace among the brotherhood."

After weeks in isolated confinement in Lyon, Pons was taken to Rome where he was imprisoned in the Castle Sant'Angelo on the right bank of the Tiber River. He was less than a mile from Saint Peter's Basilica, built by Roman Emperor Constantine 800 years earlier on the site where Saint Peter had been martyred and buried. The castle, basilica, housing for clergymen, and former papal residence, all of which made up the Vatican, were enclosed within fortifications near the mosquito infested, marshy Tiber lowlands. Two Popes had died of Roman fever, believed to be caused by the *mal aria*, the bad air, rising from the swamps. Because of this, the current papal residence at the Lateran Palace was across the river on higher ground.

Pons woke in a sweat and now had the chills. He scratched the numerous mosquito bites that constantly tormented him since arriving at the prison. He struggled merely to stand and look out his cell window. Pons's line of vision followed the Sant'Angelo bridge as it crossed the Tiber River. Rome's landscape was dominated by church towers. *How long have I been here? Every week the Pope's aide has come, and he has been here three times now, carrying a message from Honorius asking me if I am ready to repent. Me, repent? What about the Pope himself? He continues the violence, bribery, and deceit that placed him on his throne. His supporters wounded the justly elected pope, who died from those same wounds! Honorius took part in a murder!* Pons shouted out the window, "Honorius, you want *me* to repent? The only Pope who can judge me is *Saint Peter*!"

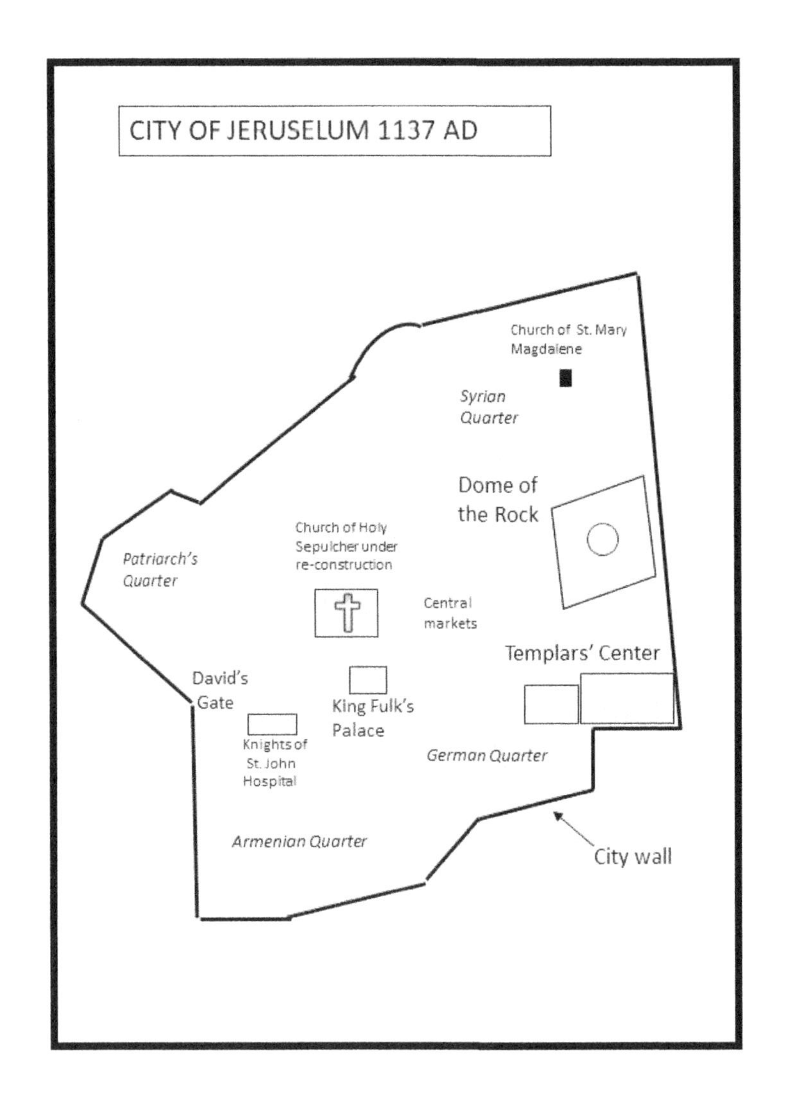
CITY OF JERUSELUM 1137 AD
Church of St. Mary
Magdalene
Syrian
Quarter
Dome of
the Rock
Church of Holy
Sepulcher under
re-construction
Patriarch's
Quarter
Central
markets
Templars' Center
David's
Gate
King Fulk's
Palace
Knights of
St. John
Hospital
German Quarter
Armenian Quarter
City wall

CHAPTER XXIX JERUSELUM 1137 AD

After escorting another group of pilgrims from the coast, Pons rode through David's Gate, the western entrance to Jerusalem. Ahead was the king's new palace, a stone citadel rising above dwellings built of mud bricks. Riding behind Pons was his mentor, Godfrey de Saint Omer, one of the original founders of the Templar Order. The narrow streets were crowded and Pons dismounted. Most of the pedestrians were Christian pilgrims, with a minority of Jews. Muslim pilgrims, allowed in the city during the daylight hours, had become more common since King Fulk of Jerusalem had made an alliance with the Islamic leader of Damascus. As Godfrey got off his pedigreed warhorse, Pons noted the seal of the Templars displayed on Godfrey's shield—two men riding a single horse. As a Templar knight, Pons had three war horses for his use, plus the services of a squire. *The Order has made significant advances in the decade since its founding. Godfrey told me at the time he and the late Master Hugues began the Templar Order, they were so poor they had just one horse between them.*

They led their mounts through the central market to the southeast corner of the city to the Templar Headquarters, next to the former al-Aqsa Mosque. Squires took the reins and ushered the animals to the underground stables. *It is exhilarating to ride these magnificent destriers, but I miss my friend Cominius. I remember him grazing the lush grass at Melgueil when I left him. But Cominius is not trained as a warhorse and would not have fared well during the skirmish we fought last week against the desert raiders.*

Godfrey and Pons shared bread and wine, then attended Nones. Afterwards they sat outside to warm in the afternoon sun. An enormous courtyard lay between the Templar center and the Dome of the Rock. Muslim pilgrims were not allowed inside the former mosque, but the templars had built a *pergula*, a roofed, open-air oratory, to provide shade for them. A man kneeled in the oratory while a Christian townsperson stood over him, gesturing and shouting. Godfrey started toward them and said, "I know the man praying, he is a Muslim. It appears we must defend pilgrims even inside the city."

Pons followed his mentor. As they neared, they overheard, "You should pray facing the east, not the south!"

"It is our tradition to pray towards Mecca, which is south," answered the kneeling man.

"But the church doors face east, the direction Christians pray."

The man stood. "This site is holy to Muslims as well!"

"Mahmud!" Godfrey said, as he patted the Muslim on the back. "I have not seen you in Jerusalem in a while."

Godfrey turned to the antagonist, "Good man, how long have you been in Jerusalem?'

The man studied the Templar's white tunic, emblazoned with the large red Templar cross. "A few months, sir."

"This place is holy to three religions," said Godfrey, "Christianity, Islam, and Judaism. Pilgrims of these creeds are free to worship here without harm or molestation."

The stranger moved on. They left Mahmud in peace to pray.

Godfrey has been a brilliant mentor and like a father to me. A painful memory grabbed Pons. *I never saw my father again after that time in Melgueil—poor soul died from the mal aria emitted by the swamps in Rome. My father would have approved of the tolerance shown by Godfrey. Father once told me, "Love God and your neighbor." And I hope he would approve of his son, a Templar, who has outgrown his childhood name, Ponsel.*

AFTERWARD

Warriors and Monks: Pons, Abbot of Cluny is a novel of historical fiction, but the story is based on real events. After researching hundreds of books and on-line sources, I summarize here some of the historical facts of Pons, Abbot of Cluny.

Like all of the principal characters in *Ancestry Novels*, Pons of Melgueil, aka, Pons of Cluny, was an actual person. Born in 1075 in the town of Melgueil near the south coast of France (modern day Mauguio), Pons was only four years old when his father sent him to the Benedictine monastery at Saint Pons de Thomieres. Years later, he was transferred to the headquarters of the Benedictine Order at Cluny Abbey, in Burgundy France. In 1109, he was elected as Abbot of Cluny by the 300 monks who lived at the monastery. As leader of the Order, he administered over one thousand satellite abbeys located throughout Europe.

During his tenure he carried on the construction of the *Maior Ecclesia*, The Great Church. When completed in 1130, this basilica was the largest Christian church in the world until Saint Peter's Basilica[1] was constructed centuries later. Pons increased the output of the scriptorium, copying and producing valuable books.

When Cluny's annual endowment from the King of Leon was discontinued, Pons traveled to Spain[2], but failed (as did his predecessor) to persuade the king to resume the annual cash donation. His negotiations were not without success, however, as records show that Queen Urraca gave valuable properties to Cluny after his visit and continued the gifts in later years.

Pons acquired three sacred relics for Cluny, which attracted more pilgrims and their donations for the abbey. Relics obtained during Pons's term included a fragment of the Cross, a finger of Saint Stephen, and a tooth of Saint John the Baptist.

Historians describe him as a shrewd negotiator[3], mediating differences among the Church leaders at synods and councils. He was also known to have a quick temper. When Pons required the Cluniac monks to once again follow the austere rules of Saint Benedict after years of neglect, many of the Cluniac monks rebelled. Using what a modern psychologist would term *projection*, the rebellious monks accused Pons of wasteful use of resources.

Pope Callistus called Pons to Rome to answer to the allegations. Historical sources conflict as to whether Pons resigned or was dismissed, but after meeting with the Pope, instead of returning to Cluny, he joined the Venetian Crusade and traveled to the Levante. While in the Outremer[4], Pons made a pilgrimage to Jerusalem. When he returned from the crusade, he founded a monastery north of Venice at Campese.

Although forbidden by the Church to return to Cluny, a few years later he visited his former Cluniac brothers at the abbey. At the insistence of monks, local citizens and nobles[5], he was forced to resume his place as abbot. Arrested, ex-communicated, and imprisoned in Rome, he refused to repent to the Pope. In December 1126, he died of Romanus ille pestifer morbus, Roman malignant disease or Roman fever, most likely malaria[5].

He was buried as a pauper, but later, at the request of Abbot Peter the Venerable, his remains were transferred to Cluny.[5] There is no mention of what happened to his tomb. Protestants sacked Cluny in 1562 during the Reformation, and then the insurgents of the French Revolution destroyed most of the monastery in the 1790s. The library was burned and the abbey buildings were quarried for stone. The original structures that remain are two Gothic churches, the abbot's guest residence, and a few towers and fortifications.

1. Old St. Peter's Basilica was built by Emperor Constantine in the 4th century and was replaced by the new St. Peter's Basilica, which then became the largest church, completed in 1606.
2. Library of Iberian Resources Online, *Spanish and Portuguese Monastic History,600-1300,*Charles Julian Bishko.
3. Agnès Gerhards, the Abbey of Cluny, Complexe, Brussels, 1992.
4. A name applied to the medieval French crusader states, including Armenia, Antioch, Tripoli, and Jerusalem, from French outremer (adverb) 'overseas', from outre 'beyond' + mer 'sea'.
5. The Cardinals of the Holy Roman Church, Biographical Dictionary, Pope Callistus II (1119-1124), Consistory of January 1120 (II), Celebrated in Cluny.

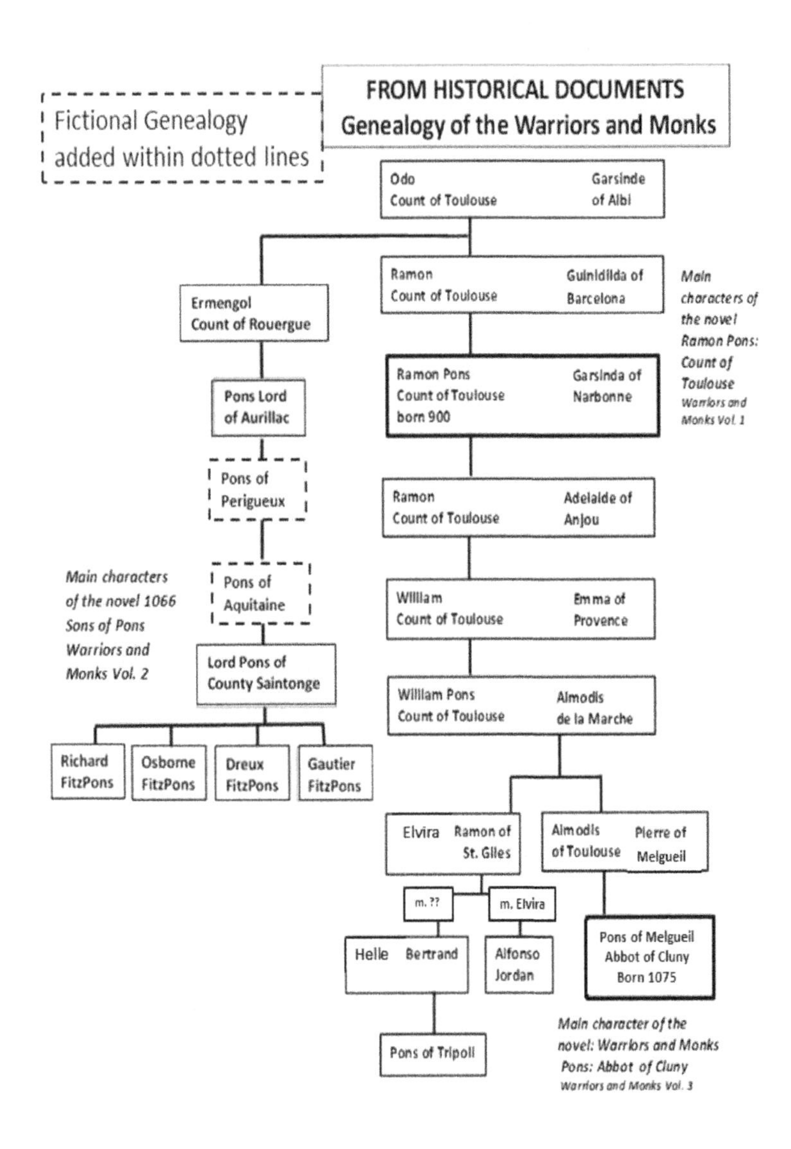

Fictional Genealogy added within dotted lines
FROM HISTORICAL DOCUMENTS
Genealogy of the Warriors and Monks
Odo Count of Toulouse
Garsinde of Albi
Ramon Count of Toulouse
Guinidilda of Barcelona
Main characters of the novel Ramon Pons: Count of Toulouse Warriors and Monks Vol. 1
Ermengol Count of Rouergue
Pons Lord of Aurillac
Ramon Pons Count of Toulouse born 900
Garsinda of Narbonne
Pons of Perigueux
Ramon Count of Toulouse
Adelaide of Anjou
Main characters of the novel 1066 Sons of Pons Warriors and Monks Vol. 2
Pons of Aquitaine
William Count of Toulouse
Emma of Provence
Lord Pons of County Saintonge
William Pons Count of Toulouse
Almodis de la Marche
Richard FitzPons
Osborne FitzPons
Dreux FitzPons
Gautier FitzPons
Elvira
Ramon of St. Giles
Almodis of Toulouse
Pierre of Melgueil
m. ??
m. Elvira
Helle
Bertrand
Alfonso Jordan
Pons of Melgueil Abbot of Cluny Born 1075
Pons of Tripoli
Main character of the novel: Warriors and Monks Pons: Abbot of Cluny Warriors and Monks Vol. 3

WHAT DO YOU THINK OF WARRIORS AND MONKS?

Thank you for purchasing this book. I know you could have picked any number of books to read, but you picked this book and for that I am extremely grateful.

I hope that it added interest, knowledge, and entertainment to your everyday life. If so, it would be appreciated if you could share this book with your friends and family and post comments on Facebook and Twitter.

If you enjoyed this book and found some benefit in reading it, I'd like to hear from you and also hope that you could take some time to post a review on Amazon. Your feedback and support will help this author to improve.

I want you, the reader, to know that your review is very important and if you'd like to **leave a review**, all you have to do is use the following link. At the link, click on the book, then find reviews, and follow the instructions.

Thank you, Michael Ponzio

https://www.amazon.com/Michael-A.-Ponzio

Michael A Ponzio Author Facebook:
https://www.facebook.com/AncestryNovels/?ref=bookmarks

Amazon's Michael A. Ponzio Author Page
https://www.amazon.com/Michael-A.-Ponzio

Author's Ancestry Novels website:
History & Historical Fiction: Pontius, Ponzio, Pons, and Ponce
https://mikemarianoponzio.wixsite.com/pontius-ponzio-pons

ABOUT THE AUTHOR

Have you ever wanted to live in another time and place in history? Have you imagined what it would be like to take the place of an ancestor? Michael A. Ponzio's lifelong experience reading books on history combined with his love for family and travel has inspired him to bring these visions alive, by writing a series of "Ancestry Novels."

Since childhood, Mike Ponzio has read books about ancient history. He traded books and stories with his father, Joseph E. Ponzio, and they discussed the origins of the family surname. Mike traveled around the Mediterranean to Europe, Asia, and Africa, visiting many of the locations he would later write about. He continues to travel and write *Ancestry Novels* which he imagines may have taken place during the lives of ancient ancestors.

Mike met his wife, Anne Davis, in 1975 at a University of Florida karate class. Since that time both have taught Cuong Nhu Martial Arts. With John Burns, they wrote and published six instructional books on martial arts weapons. Mike retired in 2015, after working as an environmental engineer for thirty-seven years. Anne and Mike have raised four sons. They are all engineer graduates, following in the footsteps of their Davis and Ponzio grandfathers.

Ancestry Novels by Michael A. Ponzio.
The title characters are historical.

The Ancient Rome Series (Lover of the Sea):
Pontius Aquila: Eagle of the Republic
Pontius Pilatus: Dark Passage to Heaven
Saint Pontianus: Bishop of Rome

Warriors and Monks Series:
Ramon Pons: Count of Toulouse
1066 Sons of Pons: In the Wake of the Conqueror
Warriors and Monks: Pons, Abbot of Cluny

Made in the USA
Columbia, SC
13 November 2020

24441739R00173